THE HUSSAR'S DUTY

Book 3 in The Winged Warrior Series

by Griffin Brady

ISBN 979-8-9853283-6-3

Cover design by Jenny Quinlan, Historical Editorial
Maps by Cathy Helms, Avalon Graphics LLC
Edited by Jenny Quinlan, Historical Editorial
Proofread by WordServings
Trefoil Publishing

DEDICATION

To those dedicated to investigating and chronicling history as it truly happened.

CONTENTS

Battle of Cecora 1620

Moscow

Polish-Lithuanian Commonweath

Juszyn
Maksimkovo
Vratov

Legend

1. Silnyrod
2. Matejko Manor
3. Mohylów
4. Kamieniec
★ Major city

Warszawa

Muscovy

Lublin

Biaska Castle

Vistula R.

Rzeszow   Żółkiew

Podolia

Wild Plains

Kraków

Austria

Halicz

1. 2.
4
Chocim

Khanate
of Crimea

Azov
Sea

Prut R.

Dniester R.

Crimea

Iassy   Cecora

Moldavia

Black Sea

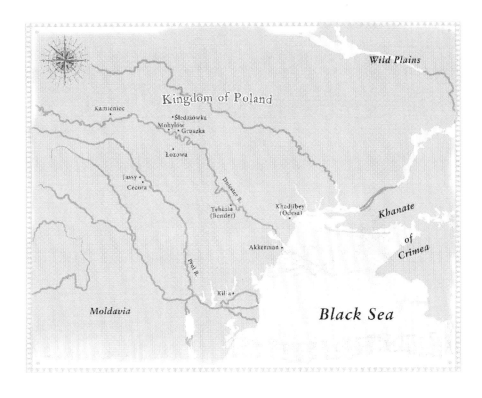

CHAPTER 1

Looming Shadows

Halicz, Podolia, 1620

Lord Commander Jacek Dąbrowski was not a patient man under the best of circumstances. The current circumstances were draining his limited reserves faster than a soldier could drain his wodka ration.

"What do you mean, you have only twelve? The agreement was for eighteen. Where are the other six?" he barked at the stooped man before him, who, despite his considerable girth, seemed to shiver uncontrollably.

Jacek had dismounted yet still towered over the proprietor. A full head taller than most men of his acquaintance, with a look that called up the fearsome and cursed Vikings of old, Jacek was used to intimidating folk. And he availed himself of his size whenever it suited him ... especially when he was vexed. Right now, he was spectacularly vexed. He had a higher power to answer to, and her name was Oliwia. *She* had sent him to collect eighteen warhorses, and his mind was already whirring through various scenarios where he would present this shortage to her without incurring her disappointment. The outlook was grim. Her anger he could withstand. In fact, he would welcome it. But disappoint her? He would rather charge into a line of pikemen.

His eyes swept once more over the man's orderly outbuildings and came to rest on the corrals, as if his will alone could conjure the beasts he sought. Alas, it merely confirmed the breeder was telling the truth.

Nevertheless, he jerked his head toward his best friend and second, Captain Henryk Kalinowski, who sat astride his mount. "Take one of the men-at-arms and search the stables, the sheds, anywhere a grown horse could be hidden away." At least Jacek could tell his wife that they had searched dutifully for her stock.

Henryk nodded his understanding and beckoned a guard from their party to follow him, and the two set off. Jacek's peach-fuzz-faced brother-in-law, Filip Armstrong, fell in behind them.

Jacek's irritation mushroomed. "Filip, with me."

Filip paused long enough to stare down at Jacek from his saddle. The countenance beneath Filip's fur-cuffed *kolpak* might have been proof of his youth, yet he possessed a full-grown hussar's swagger … one he had yet to earn.

At sixteen, Filip was mostly lean limbs, with hair the color of walnuts and eyes of storm-cloud gray. Currently, a tempest was brewing in those storm clouds, which were pinned on Jacek. What emotions lurked there? Scorn? Defiance? Anger? Likely all three.

Jacek returned the glare with a glower of his own. Handling the lad was becoming more challenging with each passing hour, yet Jacek could remember himself at the same age, even though his years had since doubled. He understood. Filip was straining to break the bonds of childhood and declare himself a man. But Jacek could not, would not, allow this pup to buck his authority. There was an order to be followed, and Jacek had a duty to see that it was obeyed.

The breeder interrupted their silent impasse, his eyes bouncing between Jacek and Filip. "Begging your pardon, m'lord. Your men are welcome to look all they please, but your horses were appropriated along with my other stock three days ago by the grand hetman of the Crown." The man offered a hand, palm up. "As God is my witness, I wish I had more to offer you."

Jacek refrained from gaping. "Żółkiewski took them?"

2

The breeder nodded. "The man himself. He needed them for his troops. There is trouble at the border with the Ottomans."

"There is always trouble at the border with the Ottomans," Jacek grumbled. *And their damned minions, the Tatars.*

"It may help you to know he paid for them in full, so you only owe for the three, and he left behind one of my most exceptional mares, a sable with exquisite lines." The breeder's tentative smile did little to assuage Jacek's exasperation.

Henryk and the other soldier trotted from between two outbuildings. Henryk shook his head.

Jacek rolled his eyes to the expanse above and released a protracted exhale. The vault overhead was the color of a bluethroat's feathers and unmarred by a single cloud. A docile breeze ruffled newly sprung crocuses clumped about the farmhouse's dooryard. A perfect spring day in Halicz … under different circumstances.

The sun was high and hot for mid-March, melting the vestiges of winter into a muddy mess, which only added to Jacek's foul mood. Negotiating the boggy roads with their caravan of wagons, eight men, and extra horses made the going slow, and he was anxious to return to Biaska Castle and his own soft bed.

Jacek dropped his gaze to the quaking breeder. "My men will fetch the horses while you and I conclude our dealings." He flicked his gloved hand. "Lead on."

Bowing and scraping and scurrying, the breeder led him across the dooryard toward the farmhouse. Had Jacek been in a better temper, he would have found the sight amusing.

Jacek lifted his chin to Filip. "Fetch the coin from Marcin to pay the man."

Filip's eyes widened. "Why me? Hussars do not handle money! That is for merchants, retainers, and townsfolk. The riffraff!" He spat the last word with added disdain.

Jacek gritted his teeth to keep from expressing his urge to throttle the youth. "Let me remind you that you have yet to rise from retainer to hussar.

Besides, you must understand how to deal with matters of commerce. There is more to being a knight than swordplay."

Filip looked around at the other men, a hopeful expression on his face. If he was expecting one to come to his defense, their smirks were sure to disappoint. They were likely as weary as Jacek of the boy's superior attitude.

Jacek had been balancing on a drainpipe, trying not to single out his wife's brother for favorable treatment while ever aware she might object. If Oliwia had her way, Filip would remain out of harm's way for the rest of his life … unrealistic, especially for a lad who had dreamed of nothing but being a warrior since age six.

The would-be warrior dismounted with an irritated huff.

Lord, give me the tolerance I need to preserve his scrawny neck.

Hours later, the tension had been drowned in several jugs of *piwo* and *wodka*. Henryk signaled to a harried tavern maid for more, thanking her with a wink when she acknowledged the request.

The men might have rejoiced in completing the mission successfully, but Jacek was left to ponder the measure of that success. He had been excited for the assignment at the outset, for it had given him purpose, a reason to lead men once more. The undertaking, however, had proved a failure. And while he feigned celebration with his companions, relief that they were done and headed home at dawn was the emotion that prevailed. They had been gone three long weeks, and he missed his wife and children. How much had the baby grown during his time away? Would he find Oliwia with child again when he returned? The possibility caused unexpected warmth to bloom in his chest.

He took pride in the fact that he was a father three times over. His wife had blessed him with a daughter and a son of his own, and he had adopted Oliwia's six-year-old boy by her late husband. The love Jacek felt for the lad was as strong as what he felt for his own offspring. Adam knew only one pater, and that would ever be Jacek.

If he pushed—and the weather and mud relented— in two weeks' time they would pass into the Jura Highlands of lesser Poland, where Biaska lay among the sprawling Eagle's Nests fortifications. He resolved to push—shove, if he had to.

Clustered about a rectangular table in a corner of the bustling tavern, the men exchanged stories that grew bawdier with each pitcher of drink consumed. Jacek observed with muted amusement and made sure his men didn't wind up brawling.

Their attention soon turned to the tavern maids, and bravado spurred them to place bets on which ones would be willing to do what with whom. Filip was eager to jump into the fray, though his inexperience showed each time a maid looked his way and a red blaze ignited his cheeks. Giving him no quarter, the men mocked him mercilessly, which only caused the lad to flush hotter.

Henryk leaned to Jacek's ear. "Filip's been asking me to take him to one of the stews."

Jacek masked his surprise and let his tongue wag with imprudence. "He'd be better off with one of the tavern maids. A few appear willing enough."

"Like that one over there who favors you?" Henryk dipped his head toward a maid who had bestowed Jacek with several blinding smiles since their arrival. "I daresay *she's* more than willing to let you take her for a tumble." He paused to scratch his chin. "Why do the maids always favor the monks? It's the challenge, I suppose." He tossed back the remaining wodka in his cup.

Seated beside Jacek, Marcin, his *pacholik*—his retainer—scoffed and quickly averted his eyes when Jacek slid him a sidelong glance. A minor lord and a hussar himself now, Marcin had served Jacek longer than either man could remember—which was probably why Marcin dared show his impertinence.

Ignoring the pacholik, Jacek turned to Henryk. "Are you calling *me* a monk?"

"When you're on the road, most definitely."

"Because I take my marriage vows seriously?"

5

"So do other men … when they are in their own homes and not trekking about the countryside." Henryk tapped his chin. "Of course, that explains why you've been so mordant of late."

Jacek's unwillingness to betray his wife's trust went far beyond staking himself to his vows. Truth was, in the five years they had been wed—and earlier besides—he found no other woman as alluring as she. Yes, many were nice to look at, but beyond that his interest not only flagged, it buried itself in the dirt. Oliwia had always stirred wants and needs in him he could not understand and he had given up trying. In short, she was the only one for him and ever would be.

"I am neither mordant nor monkish. Now about Filip—"

"He says a whore will teach him what to do in a maid's bed." Henryk shrugged. "There's a certain logic in that, yes?"

"Did you explain that a whore's also more likely to give him the pox?" Jacek said dryly. "And why didn't he come to me with this … this request?"

Marcin snorted—in his cup this time—and Henryk guffawed. A moment later, Henryk caught his breath. "That would be akin to asking a blind man the color of a piece of cloth. Besides, he probably doesn't wish to hear your sermon on the sins of the flesh." Henryk's voice took on gravity with the last words, and he spread his hands and looked to the ceiling as though he were praying over a congregation.

Jacek had no such sermon, and he opened his mouth to deliver the rejoinder scrabbling up his throat. It died there when a familiar name pricked his ears: Żółkiewski.

He swiveled his head in unison with Marcin, searching for the voice's source. Seated at a nearby table was another group of men, locals by the look of them, and they were buzzing with animated conversation.

When Jacek picked up the word "pasha," he swiped a jug from his own men, ignored their protests as he sauntered to the other table, and placed the vessel square in the center. "If you have news of the trouble at the border, I would like to hear it."

One man, a stocky fellow with an impressive brown mustache streaked with gray, glanced up at him. Dressed in the finer attire of a merchant, he took Jacek in with eyes like polished pebbles, then broke out in a grin. "If you are offering your drink, I would like to tell it. Sit, my friend."

Jacek squeezed between him and another man. He reached for the jug and topped off every man's drink. There were five, and all but the big merchant were dressed in farmers' rough cloth.

The merchant held up his drink. "I am Mantas Butkus of Halicz, a grain trader, and on behalf of my companions, I thank you." After a tip of his pottery cup, he introduced the others, and Jacek gave each a nod in turn.

Jacek debated what to tell the man of his own profession. Did he even have one he could name? Was he still a commander of soldiers? Not lately; in fact, he wouldn't even call himself a soldier. Lord of an estate? No, that title belonged to his wife. Wrangler of horses didn't fit either, so he pushed the frustrating exercise deep into his belly to fester along with his other qualms about what his role had become. Best to stick with what he knew about himself.

"I am Jacek Dąbrowski of Biaska."

A man seated in a corner at a far table, his back to the wall, whipped his head toward Jacek and lowered it just as quickly. Jacek's new companions held their cups high and saluted him with a *"Na zdrowie!"* He joined them, tipping a small measure to his lips as he slid his gaze back to the corner, where the man stood abruptly and headed for the exit with several companions. The mystery man was broad of stature, but Jacek could not make out his features for the kolpak pulled low over his brow.

Mantas dragged the back of his hand across his mouth, yanking Jacek's attention back to him. "Now. What would you like to know, Pan Dąbrowski?"

"Tell me everything about the unrest at the border."

Mantas nodded. "Do you know what happened to the Crown's envoy to the Ottoman Empire?"

"The man Żółkiewski uses as a translator?"

"The same. He was sent to Istanbul late last year. But he has shortly returned after being met with hostility and threats of war from the new grand vizier, Ali Pasha. It is rumored the king believes the threat is real and has tasked the hetman to recruit an army. As we speak, the quartz troops are being put under the command of Crown Field Hetman Stanisław Koniecpolski."

Jacek didn't mask his surprise. "Where?"

"Right here in Halicz. I tell you, Pan Dąbrowski, war with the Porta is coming. I can smell it."

No wonder Biaska's horses had been appropriated! Jacek's blood pulsed with anger—or was it excitement at the thought of clashing with the enemy? Relations at the border had always been a seesaw of confusion, what with magnates scrapping for more power and Ottomans installing whichever ruler suited their ambitions in Moldavia and her neighbors.

He had little time to contemplate border politics, for a boy burst into the tavern, looking about frantically. Jacek recognized him as the ostler's son.

"Who belongs to the warhorses?" the boy cried.

Jacek shot to his feet. "What is it?"

The boy jabbed his forefinger over his shoulder. "They're trying to steal them!"

CHAPTER 2

Rodzina

Lady Oliwia Dąbrowska watched the ferret-faced steward with keen interest. Similar conversations took place several times weekly here in Biaska Castle's solar—sometimes daily, depending upon the urgency.

A late March sun cast watery beams through panes of wavy glass, throwing golden light upon the oaken desk that divided them.

Today, Tomasz was relaying his concern for Biaska's affairs, not with words but with his mannerisms: twitchy hands and sweat-beaded brow. And no wonder. Biaska's finances verged on collapse.

The man had navigated Biaska over many years through the choppy waters of commerce. Highly skilled and honest to a fault, he was her most trusted adviser, his worth to the estate incalculable. Beyond esteeming his management abilities and his fluency in eight languages, she appreciated that he never treated her like many other men did: as a dim-witted woman incapable of more than warming a man's bed and bearing his babies. Although if she did say so herself, she performed those duties splendidly as well. And from what he had told her over the years, her husband agreed. Then again, Jacek was a most compelling reason to fulfill those obligations in the first place. Other than childbirth, she found them to be no hardship whatsoever, and in this moment she yearned to fulfill part of them. Jacek had been gone too many weeks, and she missed him as she missed the sun in the sky during a long spell of overcast days.

Shaking herself from her daydreams, she sharpened her focus on her estate manager.

"So you see, my lady, with our unusually cold weather shortening our growing season by several weeks, our yields have lessened. And who knows when the cold will relent? Only God controls the weather."

"And God does not favor us lately," she grumbled.

He straightened, pulling his nose from his ledgers. "God favors no one in the Commonwealth of late, and it is far worse up north. The Baltic, along with many rivers and lakes, is frozen. These severe winters cause people to suffer greatly."

Oliwia scoffed. "I have no sympathy for them. Every man and woman for themselves." Tomasz winced, and she instantly regretted her thoughtlessness. Jacek's voice floated through her head. *"While I admire your candor, Liwi, it can be difficult for many to hear."*

"I apologize, Tomasz. I was speaking of Swedes and Muscovites, not the good people of Gdynia, where you hail from." She cleared her throat. "How does your family fare?"

"As well as can be expected." Tomasz pushed his spectacles onto the bridge of his nose. "What concerns me most at Biaska is its tenant farmers. With fewer crops, they will fall short of what they owe you from the demesnes."

Oliwia blew out a great breath. "Which means our own stores will dwindle more rapidly."

"Surely you will preserve the castle's supply for yourself, my lady."

"I cannot let our families starve, Tomasz."

"No, my lady. Of course not. Well, that being the case, it is a blessing your husband will soon return with eighteen head to replenish your stock of warhorses. While the investment has depleted our treasury, I have no doubt it will prove a profitable gamble. The deposits you amass from your buyers will tide the estate over for a time."

Another reason she longed for Jacek's return. He was bringing her warhorses, for which she had paid dearly, to supplement those she was raising on their estate. Naturally, they would require more refinement to become full-fledged combat horses that would fetch a high price, but Biaska's remarkable horse trainer would address that.

Yes, she had much to look forward to with Jacek's return.

"But will that be enough, Tomasz?"

His mouth opened and closed.

She laced her fingers together. "I see. Well, let us explore another idea. Lately, I have been contemplating Silnyród."

"Your estate in the borderlands?"

"The very one. What if I sold it?"

He blinked rapidly. "To whom, my lady?"

"I have not yet worked out that detail."

A rap sounded on the oaken door.

"Come," she commanded.

A guard poked his head in. "Messages for you, my lady." In his rough paw, he held a small collection of folded parchments, which he handed her. Her heartbeat took off like geese taking to the sky. Perhaps one would be from Jacek. Thanking the guard, she dismissed him and quickly shuffled three missives, searching for her husband's familiar handwriting. Her heart decelerated when she saw none. One letter in particular, though, caught her eye, and she flipped it over and inspected the seal. Her brows knitted together in a frown.

"Are we done, Tomasz?" she asked absently.

"Ah, Silnyród?"

"It will keep."

"Yes, my lady."

She raised her head. "Until later, then."

Tomasz gathered up his papers, executed a quick bow, and pivoted on his heel. She ripped open the letter, barely noticing the quiet thud of the closing door as he quit the solar. Her gaze swept over the words, and an errant gasp escaped her. She read once more to be sure she had not mistaken the message.

Muttering to herself, she rose and paced to and fro. How long she marched, her thoughts unwinding and rewinding, she had no idea.

"M'lady?" The small squeak at the solar's entrance had Oliwia pivoting to face her maid.

"Yes, Nadia. What is it?"

"Anka sent me, with her most profound apology, to tell you that she is at a loss. She has tried for well over an hour, but Piotr is inconsolable." The mousy girl fairly shrank back into herself for reasons Oliwia could not understand. She had never beaten the maid, nor would she. Jacek thought the girl so adored Oliwia that she hated to disappoint her with bad news of any sort, but that didn't make sense either. Whatever the reason, Oliwia had vowed long ago to safeguard the girl.

"No need for apologies, Nadia. I have brought this on myself." Though Piotr was already six months, Oliwia continued to nurse him, which directed all manner of questioning stares her way. To nurse him at all was unheard of among noble women; it was the reason wet nurses existed. But Oliwia wasn't quite ready to let go, and she had other reasons—good reasons—besides.

In addition to feeding Piotr, she had resorted to bringing Jacek's miniature replica to sleep with her at night, for she missed her husband's reassuring presence in her bed. His strength blanketed her in security, warmth, love. He was the half she needed to make her whole.

Her reasoning didn't matter, though, because the babe had grown so attached that he often cried for her throughout the day. What would the child's father say when he returned home and discovered this invasion beneath the bedcovers? She could picture his raised eyebrow now, accompanied by the paternal scowl that cleverly disguised a heart as soft and malleable as bread dough.

A smile touched her lips at the thought. "I am on my way." Realizing she still clutched the letter, she folded and pocketed it. "Nadia, it seems visitors will soon descend upon us. Would you see to it that the guest quarters are prepared? Better arrange for a valet as well."

Nadia curtsied. "Of course, m'lady."

Picking up her skirts, Oliwia flew down a short flight of steps to the great hall, where she spied her other children, Adam and Margaret, playing with one of the greyhounds under the watchful eye of Jacek's widowed sister,

Tamara. Satisfied, she turned left and raced up a long, winding staircase. Her heels clattered, echoing off the stone walls as she went. Before she had reached the floor that housed the nursery, her child's piercing cries reached her, and she increased her pace.

As she opened the door to the antechamber, she spied her crimson-faced, watery-eyed child fussing in his poor nurse's arms.

Oliwia spread her arms wide. "Come, come now. What is all this caterwauling about, my little lord? Surely you can't be hungry. I just fed you."

The child stilled, turned toward her voice, and hiccupped, his little fists opening and closing to the beat of a moth's wings. Anka, a moon-faced blond with dark blue eyes, relinquished him into Oliwia's grasp, and relief eased the woman's beleaguered features. "I am so sorry, m'lady, but nothing I have tried will soothe him."

"And he has no fever?" His fits never stemmed from a fever, for which Oliwia was immensely grateful.

"No, m'lady. Perhaps it is his teeth bothering him."

"It's all right, my little darling," Oliwia cooed to him. Piotr settled against her shoulder, his entire body relaxing on a sigh. To Anka, she said, "Have you had your midday meal yet?"

"No, m'lady."

"Go, then, and get something to eat. You must be famished."

The girl lit out of the door, and Oliwia ambled into the nursery proper and sank into an armchair near the hearth, where embers glowed red. Piotr fell asleep against her shoulder, no doubt exhausted from his tantrum.

She stroked his finely fuzzed head. "Whatever am I to do with you, little one? You've presented me with a thorny problem I must resolve before your papa returns. And, dear Mary, I pray that will be soon." For not the first time, fear clawed at her like bile in her throat. What if Jacek wasn't all right? What if he never came home?

"Stop it!" she admonished herself aloud.

"Stop what?" Oliwia startled at the sound of Tamara's voice and looked up to see the young woman grinning at her from the doorway between the nursery and the antechamber. A half foot taller and a year younger than

Oliwia, Tamara wore her light brown hair in braids. Her pale green eyes were set in an oval face and brought to mind those of a curious cat.

Oliwia adored her, for she had become the sister Oliwia never had. Apparently, Tamara found Biaska pleasing as well, for her visit had lasted nearly two years. Was it Biaska, though, or a certain dashing captain named Henryk who had captured her attention? What a pity for her the man was a rogue who loved women too well to settle on just one—and that Jacek would string him up if he suspected Henryk fancied his little sister.

Tamara possessed a quiet beauty and sweet nature that drew many suitors to her, but she deftly fended them off with the excuse she still mourned her late husband—who had died in battle three years prior. The well-worn reason, she had once confided in Oliwia, offered a diplomatic advantage both ways: it shielded her from unwanted courtship and preserved an admirer's pride.

The diplomat advanced into the room. "Are you scolding my nephew or speaking to yourself again? Should I worry for you, sister?"

Oliwia let go a sigh. "No need. I was merely fretting over your brother and mine. They have been gone so long, and I am anxious for their return."

Tamara pulled a chair close and sank into it. She caressed Piotr's plump cheek with her forefinger. "My brother is too stubborn and wily to find himself in trouble, and your brother is under his protection. They are fine."

The memory of a time six years prior, when Oliwia had believed Jacek lost forever, reared up and shook her hard. The anguish was almost as raw now as it had been then. "Your brother is not infallible," she mumbled.

"No," Tamara countered lightly, "but fairly near it." She elbowed Oliwia. "Come now. Do not dwell in the past. Look around you and recognize what I see." She held her hands up, palms out, and turned in her seat. "You have built a wonderful life and beautiful children together. Surely if God had intended otherwise, Jacek would not have returned. And truly, I'm not sure how much God had to do with it. I believe my brother *willed* himself back." She shook her head, her smile broadening. "As I said, stubborn."

Despite her maudlin memories, Oliwia chuckled. "I must admit it quiets my mind to know Filip is with him."

"But you were hesitant to let him go, were you not? Your brother, I mean."

"So much can go wrong on the open road: illness, injury, attacks from men and beasts. I was hesitant to let *either* of them go, even though they did so at my bidding."

"Had you asked it of them, would they have sent other men in their stead?"

Oliwia shook her head. "No. My wishes rarely control their actions. Think on it—my brother has spent this past decade emulating Jacek. He wants the life Jacek had before we married."

"That is natural. He has nearly attained manhood."

Oliwia laughed. "He would argue he *is* a man. But you are right." She looked into the embers, where another distant memory shimmered. "I have spent his entire life doing exactly what our dying mother asked of me— protecting him—and it has become such a part of me that stopping would be akin to pulling out my own beating heart."

Tamara patted Oliwia's unoccupied shoulder. "You have fulfilled your promise admirably. Look how strong and vital he is. As for my brother, I think your wishes direct his actions more than you know. I find it rather amusing how eagerly he steps on his toes to see you content."

The thought pleased Oliwia. Jacek did work so very hard to oblige her every whim, not that she had many that needed accommodation. But he put a high value on her happiness and never fell down on his promises. Tamara was right. The life they had created together at Biaska was one Oliwia cherished with her whole being, and she clung to its fragile thread in a way she could not cling to him. Doing so would merely push him to seek adventure away from her and their home.

"That may be, but I do worry this idle life is not enough to appease him. I suppose I have hoped for the impossible. Under that stubborn hide beats the heart of a warrior. Lately, I sense a restiveness in him." Which was precisely why she had asked him to collect the horses. She had hoped time on the road would quench some of his longing for a military mission.

Her eyes had been wide open when she had married Jacek; the warrior was ingrained in him as much as protecting her loved ones was in her, and that very nature was one among many traits she admired about him. But the Commonwealth offered numerous conflicts a soldier could embroil himself in, and any hetman worth his salt coveted a commander like Jacek. She fretted her husband's lust for adventure would soon take him from her.

How would she cope if he were gone on campaign for six months? A year? Longer? He had only departed three weeks ago, and already she ached to hear the confident timbre of his voice, to feel his gentle—ofttimes impassioned—touch, to bask in the smile he gave only her. She missed his teasing, the way he cajoled her to laugh.

She turned toward Tamara. "After all this time, do you still miss your husband?"

A smile quirked a corner of Tamara's mouth. "I miss what I believed him to be." Oliwia's confused frown must have shown, for she rushed on. "What I mean is, I was young and impressionable. He swaggered about, and I was naught but a starry-eyed girl. Consequently, everything he did was without flaw. But looking back with the eyes of a woman, I realize he was bold, yes, but he was also brash and rather enamored of himself. Were he still alive, I'm not sure my affection would have endured." She feathered her fingers across Piotr's crown. "I do miss having children."

"You are young yet. There is still time."

Tamara nodded, though her expression said she didn't believe as Oliwia did.

Oliwia dropped her voice to a conspiratorial whisper. "Your late husband reminds me of Pan Henryk. Are you drawn to similar men?"

Tamara's eyes went wide. "Do you believe I am interested in Henryk?"

"Are you not?"

Tamara let loose a laugh that startled Piotr, but he quickly settled. "I'm sorry," she whispered, covering her mouth to hold in bubbling giggles. "No, I am not attracted to Henryk, though I appreciate why most women are." She wiggled her eyebrows, and Oliwia's thoughts leaped to whether Tamara knew of her own history with Henryk. "I have known him a long time," Tamara continued. "He is like a brother to me, nothing more. Besides, why would I want to be tied to another scoundrel?"

Oliwia blinked. "Your husband was a scoundrel?"

Tamara's gaze swung somewhere beyond the nursery window. "Having a husband die in battle is not the only way to lose him."

Oliwia suddenly remembered the letter in her pocket, and dread welled in her chest.

CHAPTER 3
The Trick of Straddling Fine Lines

Jacek woke the men before the morning sun had crested the horizon, letting their grumbles slide past his deaf ears. *Let them grouse.* After last night's near horse pilfering, he had assigned his men to rotating sentry shifts and ordered those not on guard duty to bed—their *own* beds at the inn, which they shared amongst themselves and not with any of the "ladies of Halicz," as they had anticipated.

He had taken his own turn at guarding the stock and was as weary as they, but he sought distance between his herd of warhorses and the long shadow of Halicz. The breeder had not exaggerated about the sable mare, and Jacek planned to claim her for his own the moment he laid eyes on her. He would not allow the beauty to be stolen.

They had stopped the bandits from their thieving, but to his aggravation, they had not apprehended them despite a spirited chase. The brigands had melted into the night and dissipated as if made of smoke. They must have been locals, availing themselves of the town's every nook and cranny. Another reason to leave Halicz behind them.

Today, he pushed his men to a city twenty-three miles northwest. As they rode, his uneasy gaze continually strafed the countryside but noted nothing unusual. Why hadn't he brought more men? Because he had meant to leave Biaska's garrison intact, and because eight men—counting Filip, eight and a half—was usually an ample enough squad to escort a herd of horses across Podolia.

His men advanced in a column formation under a low-bellied sky, with two at the front as a vanguard and two on either side of the horses and wagons. Bringing up the rear were Filip, a guard, and himself. The sounds of hooves thudding on soft ground, the creak of wagon wheels, and the swishing of grasses as man and beast passed were the only noises filling the air. He remained on high alert but let the cadence lull him into imagining scenes that sprang from what he had learned last night. Those visions were filled with foment at the border, clashes with the enemy, and the battles that might come. Podolia seemed to be in the grip of a mushrooming tumult that rose like a lengthening shadow.

What if … what if war was imminent? He had fulfilled his obligation to the Crown, yet deep in his soul he had not discharged his debt to his country. What if he were called upon to lead men into battle against the Turks? What if Żółkiewski himself asked Jacek to join his forces? Given his history with the hetman, and the fact that Biaska had holdings at the border, the possibility was gathering moss as it tumbled through his head. Meanwhile, the thrum in his bloodstream grew more raucous, and while anger was part of the current inside him, excitement was the more prevalent emotion.

He was more fortunate than most in his wife, his family, and a domestic life as idyllic as any man could hope for. With that sublime existence came duties beyond himself: to Oliwia, to their children, to the many folk who depended upon the estate. It should have been enough, and yet …

Lately, he had felt the itch to join a campaign, to ride out and cut down the enemy with his underused *szabla husaria*—his hussar's sabre—to experience the thrill of victory coursing through him. But then obligation and Oliwia's fear of losing him tugged him back. While being thusly valued filled him with something warm and immeasurable, at times he envisioned a velvet collar encircling his neck, cinching down, choking him. Had she put it there, or had he trussed it about himself?

He was driven to do everything within his power to not disappoint her, but if the call came, he had no choice. He would go. It was his duty, was it not?

The wagons grinded along at a pace that set Filip's teeth on edge. His thoughts wandered from a full platter before a warm hearth to laying his head on a fluffy pillow to casting off the invisible yoke his brother-in-law had fastened about his collar.

He tried to catch Jacek's eye, but his brother-in-law darted his gaze to and fro, swiveling his head side to side in a motion that caused the pheasant feathers fastened to his kolpak to wobble.

"Why do you continually look about?" Filip did not check the sharpness that edged his voice.

Jacek turned a scowl on him. "To stay alert to brigands."

"Brigands?" Filip scoffed. "We are within Commonwealth borders. Surely you do not believe highwaymen would dare attack us or that Ottomans would venture so far from their own lands."

"Tatars would."

"What's the difference?"

Jacek's forehead furrowed. "Surely you jest. You have been at Biaska these last ten years and still do not know what separates the two?"

Of course Filip knew the answer, but a mischief-maker inside him could not resist the opportunity to goad his staid brother-in-law. "Perhaps you should enlighten me again so I have it right when someone asks the question of me."

Jacek's glower deepened. "The Ottomans, or Turks, hail from the Ottoman Empire, while the Tatars hail from regions north of the Empire—Crimea, Budjak, and so on—and they act as vassals to the Ottomans. That should suffice for any explanations you need make."

Now Jacek's head swung side to side again, his body seeming to stiffen. "Filip, I want you to exchange positions with Henryk."

The motion lifted the hairs on Filip's nape. Though Jacek was at most times exasperating, he had an undeniable ability to sniff out trouble. Filip himself scanned their surroundings—mostly open ground, save a forest on their right flank—but when he detected nothing, he loosened his grip on his reins and blew out an annoyed breath. "First, there is something I would speak with you about." His gaze shifted to the guard beside them. "Privately."

Incredulity overtook Jacek's features. "Now?"

"Yes, before we reach the city."

"Your timing is lacking," Jacek groused. Nonetheless, he ordered the guard to fall behind and steered Jarosława, his prized warhorse, toward Filip. The mare needed little coaxing because she always seemed to sense what Jacek wanted of her, unlike Filip's gelding, Carlisle. The beast was far more interested in his feed than in heeding Filip, and though Filip had begged for a proper combat horse, his sister and brother-in-law had denied him at every turn. "We need them for the profit they will bring," Oliwia insisted. As for Jacek, he maintained Filip didn't work hard enough to overcome Carlisle's stubborn ways. "Two of a mane," he had said more than once. "When you have shown you can master this simple animal, then we will discuss the merits of you having a warhorse."

This disagreement was but one of many thorns pricking at Filip when it came to his infallible brother-in-law.

Jacek drew alongside Filip. "What is it you wished to speak with me about?"

Filip opened and closed his mouth, but the words stuck in his throat. He removed his kolpak, only to reset it on his head. The confidence that had brimmed in him only moments before had abandoned him.

"What is it?" Jacek prodded.

"Tonight, when all the men go to the … the …"

Jacek's eyebrow dipped. "If you can't articulate it, then you're certainly not ready to experience it."

How was it his brother-in-law reached into his mind and read the most private thoughts there?

Filip squirmed. "The place where the ladies are."

21

"Which place would that be? There are ladies everywhere." Jacek flung his hand in the air, as if summoning women to emerge from the trees.

Damnation! His brother-in-law knew exactly what it was Filip was trying to express. Why couldn't he relent?

"The, um, sporting house." Filip fairly coughed out the answer, and Jacek seemed to suppress a chortle. His brother-in-law had a way of reducing Filip to a mere child of twelve, which was likely how Jacek perceived him.

Filip steeled his spine. "Henryk says there are several where we are going." His voice had taken on a hopeful tone, and he loathed that he sounded so feeble, so inexperienced.

Jacek removed his own kolpak and raked his fingers through his trimmed hair, scratching his scalp. "And so there likely are, though there is no certainty the men are headed to any of them tonight."

Disappointment flooded Filip's veins. "Why not?"

Jacek flicked a finger toward the slow-moving procession ahead of them. "We are crawling toward our destination, and if we continue at this pace, we will arrive long after the ... sporting houses have closed."

Filip's brows drew together in confusion. "Henryk says they never close."

"I do believe you have been spending too much time in Henryk's company."

Filip cast his eyes to the side and inched his chin upward. "Well, if the other men are going, then I wish to go too."

Jacek looked up, as if gauging the shifting weather. "'Other men,' you say. So you consider yourself a man as well."

Ever-simmering anger began to bubble up. "Yes, despite what you or my sister believe."

"Let's leave the matter of you having achieved manhood for the moment. Would you agree Dawid and I are both men?"

Bewilderment had Filip giving a slow nod.

"Yet, if we in fact reach town tonight *and* if the men possess enough stamina to *visit ladies*, Dawid and I will not. So you see, brother, your reasoning does not hold. Not *all* the men are going."

"No one takes me seriously as a hussar, least of all you," Filip retorted. "How else am I to prove I'm a man?"

Amusement shone in Jacek's eyes. "There are many other ways of proving yourself a man besides bedding a woman."

Filip lifted his chin several inches, mustering pride. "Such as?"

"Such as taking a shift at sentry tonight and every night for the rest of our journey home."

What? "Why?"

"To safeguard the stock. There is trouble afoot, and warhorses are more valuable than a saddlebag full of gold right now."

"That is what the guards are for!" Filip hissed in indignation.

Jacek arched an eyebrow. "Every man among our number *is* a guard, myself included."

"So you, our commander, intend sleeping with the horses?"

"Sleeping? No. There shall be no sleeping. In order to guard them, one must remain vigilant—which means staying awake. And so will you when your turn arrives."

Filip fixed a fierce glare on Jacek.

Jacek's lips twitched. "Our party started out as eight men and one boy. You want to prove you're a man? Behave as the other men do—I'm speaking of camp and duty, not a whorehouse—and we shall return as a party of nine men. Think on that."

Filip chuffed. "I would prefer to prove my manhood in battle." An idea brightened. "If we *should* encounter a Tatar raiding party, I can do just that." Though Filip still doubted one would venture this far into Commonwealth lands.

Jacek humphed. "You are not yet battle-tested, nor will you be until your training is complete. Besides, if your sister should learn you were in a scuffle on my watch, she would banish me from my own home."

Filip tightened his grip on his reins. "How am I to become battle-tested if I am not allowed to join a fight? I am in an endless circle!"

"Never mind that there have been very few fights to join. When the day comes that you can defeat a Tatar or best any of the hussars at Biaska Castle, then you *might* be ready."

"Which will be never," Filip grumbled.

"Don't be so quick to get your head lopped off, lad."

"I can hold my own with any Tatar." Filip's chest puffed out an inch or more.

Jacek cleared his throat as if to stifle yet another laugh—at Filip's expense. "That may be, but your sister does not agree, and if I allow one single hair on your head to be stirred, she will have mine on a pike." His brother-in-law had a habit of running his fingers over a jagged scar that decorated the left side of his face, and he did so now. Filip could have sworn he shuddered. Was he uneasy?

"Besides," Jacek continued, "one must never assume a Tatar will be dissuaded by distance or weather, nor that he will be easily vanquished. Not when there is a chance of profit to be wrung from the carcass of a human or animal, no matter how meager." He settled his kolpak back on his head.

A rustle of leaves, followed by a bird call, and Jacek held up his hand. "Listen," he hissed.

Another bird sang out, though the pitch was unfamiliar. Off.

Jacek looked toward the dark wall of trees as though trying to pierce them; he slid Filip a sidelong glance. "Have you spoken your piece? If not, then we must save it for another day. It's past time you changed places with Henryk."

The herd of horses came to a grinding halt, and Jacek stood in his stirrups. "Christ and all the saints! What devilry is this now?"

A prickle of unease slid up Filip's neck.

CHAPTER 4

The Archangel

"Jacek!" Henryk's bark snapped Jacek's head toward him. Henryk waved his arm in a beckoning motion. "We have guests!"

Jacek slid each wheel-lock from its leather holster at the front of his saddle and re-seated it—from habit—then unsheathed the sabre hanging on his left and gripped it in his right hand.

Filip checked his own blade. "Do you want me to come with you?"

"No. Stay with the guard, and stay alert." Filip would be safer back here, Jacek reasoned to himself. When the boy opened his mouth, presumably to protest, Jacek quickly added, "We are too few, and I need you to bolster the rear guard," before he cantered off to join Henryk. Hopefully, that would satisfy the lad for now and make him feel important.

Henryk had left his post and now flanked Marcin at the front of the herd, so Jacek headed for them just as Henryk barked an order at the other half of the vanguard. That man turned and sped back to the position Henryk had just abandoned beside the herd.

What the devil?

As Jacek reached Henryk and Marcin, the answer to his question revealed itself. The two men fairly bristled at a stranger who, with three other men, stood broadside in the rutted path, blocking their way.

A chill chattered up Jacek's spine, and it occurred to him that these men might be the reason he had felt eyes on him throughout the day's journey. Had these strangers been tracking them? He tightened his grip on his sabre but held it low beside his leg, out of sight. He didn't fool the lead man, however, whose eyes flicked down to Jacek's right hand before leveling on Jacek.

Assessing, calculating, Jacek took the man in quickly. Fit and broad of stature, he appeared to be of an age with Jacek, and also like Jacek, his weathered countenance spoke of many days in the saddle. Where Jacek was clean-shaven, this man wore a luxuriant horseshoe mustache that matched the chestnut color of his eyebrows. His rich dress signified he was *szlachta*—of the nobility—from his cardinal *żupan* to his butter-yellow boots.

The dress and demeanor of his men, however, suggested soldiers, though the term was generous—ruffians might have been a more apt description. Certainly not servants to the lord, but more men-at-arms with unpolished edges. Right now, their attention was riveted on the nobleman, as though awaiting a signal. A szabla husaria, similar to Jacek's own, hung sheathed on the man's left. His saddle was of finely tooled leather, with twin holsters straddling its front. In each one rested the butt of a pistol. The tip of a koncerz—or small lance—was visible on his right. A fine powder horn and pouch crossed his trim front. The man was Jacek's mirror image.

He returned Jacek's scrutiny, his mouth hard with a touch of menace. And then he smiled, transforming his features into what women might deem handsome. Jacek might have been looking at two entirely different people.

"What brings you to these parts, friend?" the stranger said smoothly.

Jacek eyed him warily. "We are on an errand. And you, friend?"

The man held up an open palm, and Jacek observed that his companions were better armed than he had first estimated. "We are simply out enjoying a day of hunting." The man was lying. Neither he nor his men carried any game or pouches, and the weaponry was all wrong for hunting: none of the men displayed bows and quivers or the proper muskets. Besides, if any of them was hunting, it would have solely been the well-dressed man; the others would have been his lackeys, there to skin and carry what he killed, not hunting as his equals.

Jacek caught the nobleman scanning the herd before he snapped his gaze back to meet Jacek's. The smile broadened. "Fine stock you are shepherding. Might they be for sale?"

The air beside Jacek stirred, and the soft thud of hooves told him Filip now flanked him. Quelling his irritation, he kept his gaze steady on the man and gave him a nonchalant shrug. "This stock is adequate for everyday use, but they are not for sale."

The man raised a russet eyebrow and quickly lowered it.

Jacek stood slightly in his stirrups, adding height to his Norse-sized frame. "Might I have your name, *friend?*"

The man pressed a palm to his chest and bowed his head. "Of course. I apologize for my lack of manners. I am Gabriel Wronski. Named, of course, for the archangel." Wronski gave a sly wink.

Not an archangel, thought Jacek, *but Wronski suits.* The word meant "crow," and the uneasiness surrounding this stranger reminded Jacek of the wily carrion bird.

"And your name, sir, if you would be so generous as to share it?" Wronski added.

Wronski had not preceded his name with "Lord," nor did he offer where he hailed from. And neither did Jacek. "I am Jacek Dąbrowski."

Something passed behind Wronski's eyes. He quickly hooded them and tapped his forefinger against his chin. "Hmm. Dąbrowski. Alas, the name does not have a familiar ring to it."

Liar. It was an old name, a proud name, and many families had spawned from that name—including a minor magnate to whom Jacek bore no relation. "I am aggrieved, sir, that neither do I recognize yours." Two could play this overly polite chess game. "Do you hail from nearby? Halicz, perhaps?"

Wronski flipped a casual hand. "Here and there. I am but a vagabond with no home to anchor my soul. And you, my lord?" The man's eyes narrowed.

27

"I hail from the west, in the countryside not far from Kraków. My men and I are charged with delivering this lot there."

Wronski seemed to take stock of Jacek's paltry entourage, and his lips curved in a devious smile. "Might you be interested in a friendly game of cards, then?"

The question was a bold and somewhat surprising counter. "I am not a gambling man." Jacek dabbled in the occasional card or dice game as a way to pass the time, betting less than he could afford. A dozen warhorses were not a prize he could—or would—offer up on his luckiest of days, and he was certain they were the prize Wronski wished him to wager. "However, if you and your men care to join us, we will soon be stopping for our midday meal. You are welcome to partake, such as it is." He felt the weight of Filip's surprised gaze upon him. And there was another lesson to teach the youth: how to play at cards without revealing one's hand.

Wronski wagged his head and grinned. "I thank you, Lord Dąbrowski, but my men and I are expected in Buczacz tonight and must not delay."

One of Wronski's companion's coughed, and Wronski slid him a glower.

Jacek took mental stock of every contradiction out of Wronski's mouth. "We are ten miles out of Halicz," Jacek pointed out, "which means you have more than fifty miles to cover, yes? That is quite a distance. A shame it will prevent you from continuing your hunt, for surely you must hasten in order to reach Buczacz before the gates close for the night."

Wronski seemed to hesitate, then beamed another smile, seeming to pour every ounce of charm he possessed into it. "Yes, you are correct. We were so carried away chasing game—"

Henryk flicked a finger toward Wronski and his men. "With little luck, it would appear," he said dryly.

"Ah, well. Game is scarce these days, especially for those who are less skilled." Snickering, Wronski lifted his chin toward the man who had coughed, eliciting a puzzled look. Then Wronski turned back to Jacek and saluted. "We must make haste. Godspeed, my friend."

"And to you," Jacek replied.

Jacek and his group remained motionless as the backs of the four men were swallowed up in the woods beyond.

When they were out of earshot, Filip blurted, "Those men were clearly up to something. And why did you invite them to share our midday meal? It's meager enough as it is."

"You have excellent instincts, Filip. That 'hunting party' was shiftier than the sands of Egypt. As for offering to share a meal, I'm not surprised they refused. And here is a rule to live by: keep your friends close and your enemies closer."

"That makes no sense. What does it have to do with—" Realization seemed to grab hold of him. "You wanted to keep them close to see what they were about."

Henryk pulled Filip's kolpak over his eyes. "The young pup may be learning after all, Jacek." Henryk grinned at Filip's flailing protestations.

Ignoring their antics, Marcin kept his gaze riveted on the dark woods where Wronski and his men had disappeared. "I do not trust them, my lord. What do you make of them?"

Henryk and Filip, now with his kolpak cocked on his head, both stilled and turned toward Jacek.

"You do not trust them because they're not trustworthy. Their story was riddled with more holes than a beggar's tunic. First, Wronski claims they are hunting, yet they are not equipped for it, nor have they bagged any game. He is clearly a nobleman who does not introduce himself thusly—and who only acknowledged me as such in a slip of the tongue—and he obviously knows what a warhorse looks like, if his keen attention toward this lot is any indication. He then asked if the stock was for sale, followed by a sudden invitation to a game of cards. As soon as he understood I would neither sell nor gamble the beasts away, he was pressed to ride over fifty miles in the late afternoon to reach Buczacz, which is nigh on impossible to do before nightfall. There was most assuredly more lurking behind that genial facade, and we would be wise to take precautions."

He called the men to him and made one of the most lamentable announcements of the voyage. "No diversions tonight. We will guard the horses in pairs, and we will sleep in shifts so we can relieve one another." Still addressing the men, he turned to Filip. "And Filip will be part of our rotation."

Filip's mouth swung open. All manner of words streamed behind his eyes, though he seemed unable to utter a single one.

Jacek lowered his voice for Filip only. "Here is your chance."

For the rest of their trek that day, Jacek turned a deaf ear to the men's groaning about being deprived of their entertainments. As night fell, they struck camp within a mile of the city.

"I wouldn't have needed long in the city," Marcin muttered.

"According to Biaska's wenches, you never do," Henryk chided.

The group—save Marcin—erupted in laughter, then returned to their griping. Jacek perched on a rock, elbows on his thighs, and registered every man's words, every expression. Had he been so soft on this journey that even a simple sentry command caused the men to grumble aloud? They were Biaska's own men-at-arms and should have accepted so obvious a job as guard duty—nay, suggested it themselves, even—without the murmured complaints passing among them now. Then again, maybe he didn't deserve their respect at this moment. Had he been sharper, he would have known they were being tracked before Wronski and his men could get ahead and cut them off.

At least Henryk and Dawid refrained from joining in the criticisms—or kept their carping to different failings, such as the quality of the victuals or the mission's slow plod, with which Jacek wholly agreed. Another bright side, he thought wryly, was that for now, the men accepted Filip; sharing their woes seemed to give them permission to voice them ever more loudly.

It occurred to Jacek he wasn't merely *growing* soft—he had *grown* soft. Not so long ago, he could have slumbered on the hard ground surrounded by a cacophony of men and horses, like any hardened soldier trained to sleep when sleep was available. But now? The undeniable comforts of Biaska Castle lured him. There, his children's laughter filled him with joy during the day. Nights spent in his own large feather bed, its curtains drawn against the chill, and his wife's soft body in his arms made sleep a warm, drowsy affair that lulled him into unconsciousness like a babe being rocked in its mother's arms. The contentment he found at home made living in camp rougher and much less appealing.

As if heaven's mischief-makers had listened in on his thoughts, an acorn which had apparently been clinging to an oak for the better part of two seasons chose that moment to drop, and it landed squarely on his crown and bounced off. He rubbed the tender spot, plopped his kolpak back on his head, and returned to his mind's meanderings.

Had the temptations of home so thoroughly invaded his tough hide and rendered it so pliable that he treated Filip less harshly than the others? In assigning tonight's sentry duties, he had allowed the lad to take only one shift, and the last at that, thus allowing him to sleep first. Though they said nothing, the men had noticed. He could see in their eyes that they believed he coddled the boy. Were they right? Were his desires to please his wife overriding his instincts as a soldier?

His fingers found the sore spot on his head once more and rubbed.

Did he allow thoughts of home to dictate his actions? A home that truly wasn't his in the first place. Rather, it belonged to his wife, along with the vast estates left her by her late husband, the former Lord of Biaska. While Jacek now carried the title, he held no claim to its wealth. As a fourth-born son, he was, and always would be, a soldier. A damned fine one, but a soldier nonetheless. Then again, if he rekindled his dream of earning Crown lands in exchange for his battlefield accomplishments, he could finally contribute something of worth to her holdings.

His conversation with Filip before Wronski's arrival capered through his mind. He had reminded Jacek of a banty rooster—not unlike himself at that age—and Jacek couldn't blame the lad for his frustrations. Oliwia had always been protective of her younger brother, had fought fiercely to keep him from harm, and little had changed during the ten years Jacek had known her—except that now she was overly protective of his thirty-two-year-old person as well. As if the warrior in his blood had no idea how to take care of himself and protect her and hers to boot!

Like a bellows, he pushed an enormous breath in and out of his lungs. Nothing would be resolved tonight.

He stood and brushed the dirt from his backside. The men lifted their eyes at the motion. "I will take the first and second watches." He rattled off the names of the other guards tasked with the first rotation and where he wanted them posted before ambling toward his tent to gather his gear.

Henryk rose and fell in beside him. "Are you sure you're prepared for double duty? That's a long spell."

"If I am to command this crew, I had better be ready to do twice the work. Besides, I have plenty on my mind to keep me awake."

"Then count me in for double as well."

Jacek patted Henryk's shoulder. "Thank you, brother. Filip will take the final shift, beside the horses." He hesitated before confiding his reasons for this choice, but this was Henryk, so he went on. "He can get nearly a full night's sleep, and the position closest to the horses should keep him alert."

Henryk smirked. "Aiming for success on the lad's first go, yes?"

"Just in case."

Hours later, Jacek's unremarkable turns finished, and he lay upon his cot, his eyes traveling about the dim interior of his tent. Despite the familiar trappings, sleep was elusive. His bed was too small, too confining, too hard. Cold seeped into his back. The sounds of men snoring and breaking wind mingled with the night sounds and drifted about him, preventing him from descent into slumber.

He berated himself. He was *definitely* too soft.

Through the next rotation and beyond, he lay thusly. A rustling noise cleared his head, and he sat up, his ears keen for any telltale sound of imminent danger. Nothing. He swung his legs over the edge of the cot, prepared to rise and check on Filip, who was well into his shift, but stopped himself. The lad would see it as an intrusion, as Jacek not trusting him— and he would be right. Filip's ensuing resentment would not serve either of them well. So Jacek remained stock-still, perched on the edge of his cot, turning his head this way and that to listen. When no other sound came, he lay back down and finally floated into a restive sleep.

What roused him much later from his fitful slumber was not the gentle light of dawn. It was Marcin crashing into his tent.

"My lord! The horses have been taken!"

Jacek yanked on his boots, grabbed up his sabre, and sprinted behind Marcin to where the horses had been tied up. Judging by the number of figures, nearly every man in the detail was also present. Filip was conspicuously absent.

Many of the new warhorses remained—the thieves hadn't gotten them all—but a quick perusal told Jacek the sable was among those who were missing. His temper went off like cannon shot.

"How the devil did the brigands get past our sentries?" Even as he leveled the question at his men, he spun in place. The spot where Filip should have been was empty.

Marcin pointed toward Dawid, crouched beside the prone figure of a Biaska guard.

"Is he alive?" Jacek asked. Dawid gave him a grim nod.

Jacek's gaze probed the shadows and caught on a form some twenty feet away, partially covered by brush. Jacek raced over, Marcin on his heels, and found his brother-in-law on his side, trussed up and gagged. Gingerly, Jacek rolled him over, and Filip let out a moan. In the dim light, Jacek made out one lacerated cheek, puffy eyes squeezed shut, and a rivulet of blood running from the boy's hairline to his jaw.

"What the hell happened here?"

As Jacek loosened Filip's bindings, he ran his hands over the boy's body but found no other damage.

Filip began to whimper, and tears streamed down his cheeks. "It's m-my fault. I'm s-sorry."

Jacek sat back on his heels, braced his hands on his thighs, and hung his head. "So am I, brother. So am I."

Gabriel Wronski stroked the mare's neck in a bid to settle her. "There, there, my pet. If we are to become friends, you must trust me and I must be able to trust you, for you are mine now. Not to boast, but females generally enjoy my touch, and I have no doubt you will come to welcome it as well." He clucked softly, and the horse stopped straining but kept her large copper-brown eye fastened to him. "I may be aptly named for the archangel, but I have no vengeance to take on a lovely beast such as you."

Laughter erupted, pulling Gabriel's attention to the campfire, where men's outlined forms were shaking with glee.

Good, he thought. He enjoyed seeing his men at ease, for they had certainly earned the privilege. *His* men. They had always been his men, but it was official now that they had left their old commander for him. They were hard, certainly, but this was a hard country, and he trusted these battled-forged soldiers with his life—just as they now entrusted theirs with him.

Though the Crown needed him and his unit to carry out its dirty deeds, it refused to recognize their worth in word or compensation. Instead, the Commonwealth referred to them as the *Elear.* Lost Men. The Forlorn Hope. Mercenaries.

How forlorn the Commonwealth would be without the likes of him and his lost men darting in and out of the shadows!

No matter how others chose to describe them, they called themselves the Lisowczycy, a name taken after their commander, Aleksander Lisowski, had died nearly four years prior, and they wore it with pride.

As they were not recompensed like the regulars, the Lisowczycy were forced to gain their rewards by plundering. At first, Gabriel had been resentful of the Crown's dismissal, but now he was glad of it. He and his men made far bigger hauls than the wages they would have earned as the Commonwealth's regular troops—the *kwarciane* or quartz troops—and as long as the Crown continued to treat them as though they didn't exist, they could pillage at will.

The animal gave another tug, and Gabriel tugged back, bringing her nose alongside his head. She snorted; he soothed. "You are determined, are you not? Ah, but that is a fine trait. I like my horses animated, the same way I like my women." After a last pat, he headed toward his men and accepted the full cup handed to him.

CHAPTER 5

Hobbled Homecoming

Piotr stirred as Oliwia pulled him from her shoulder. His chubby arm tightened about her neck before easing once more. She rubbed her cheek against his silky hair, drawing comfort from the warmth his small body radiated. How much longer would this unbearable void linger? Between their uninvited guest, who had yet to make an appearance, and Jacek's delay in returning, Oliwia grew more anxious with every waking hour. Would he be home before his birthday on the sixteenth day of the month? Not that he celebrated the day—that revelry was saved for his name day in July—and it was during Lenten, which limited the merriment even further. Easter was only three days after.

Mary, Mother of God, please bring my husband home before the Resurrection of Your Son. And if you can, please conjure a miracle for the good people of Biaska.

In the hopes Mother Mary would hear her and grant her wishes, she had taken to visiting the chapel more often to pray with Biaska's newest priest, Father Cyprian. If he chose to believe her added piety was a reflection of the season, she would not shatter the illusion.

As she laid her son in his cradle, her thoughts strayed once more to the guest who was at this moment traveling toward Biaska. She caressed her son's head and whispered, "Never mind a battle that might pull him away.

I need his strength here, now, for soon we will face a firestorm of our own." Their tranquil life was on the verge of being turned on its ear.

Two days later, she stood in the south wing, inspecting the newly dusted and scrubbed guest quarters with Nadia. A faint trumpet call brought her to an abrupt halt. Nadia's eyes grew wide, and a smile lit her lips. "The heralds! They only use that call when—"

"When the lord is home!" Oliwia grasped the girl's thin arm in her excitement, though she didn't seem to mind.

"They must be returning at this very moment, m'lady!"

Joy bubbled in Oliwia's belly, and she threw up her hands and spun in a circle, unsure what to do next. Run to the forestairs or grab Piotr from the nursery first? She did neither, instead stepping to an oval mirror, where she pinched her cheeks, straightened her drab sage skirts, and frowned at the cap containing her braids. Off came the cap and down came the braids, dark strands slipping from their confines in the most unruly manner. She tossed the cap to Nadia, arranged the plaits, then flapped her hands at her own reflection. "Tcha! There is nothing to be done for it. I will not delay my reunion to make myself more presentable. Hopefully, Lord Dąbrowski will not notice how shabby his lady wife appears." Oliwia fought the grin tugging at her mouth.

Nadia folded the cap. "You are always beautiful, m'lady, especially to the lord. It is apparent in the way he looks upon you."

Oliwia's cheeks heated with the compliment, and she squeezed Nadia's arm once more. "You are very kind." Then she dashed from the room, calculating how long it would take her to reach the inner yard, where Jacek would ride in and dismount. No doubt folk would be thronging the space, and with her small stature, they would not notice the lady of the estate struggling to squirm between them. If Jacek spotted her swimming among the crowd, he would rail at them all—quite unfairly.

Better to remain atop the forestairs, then. Besides, she would likely be the last person to leave the keep, judging by how far behind she lagged. When she reached the great hall, she tore through it, ignoring the astonished servants working there, and skidded to a most unladylike stop before the oaken doors that led to the stone landing beyond. Here, she paused to catch her breath, grasp at the stitch in her side, and straighten her dress and her hair once more.

A cluster of dusty riders had just trotted in and were ringed by an exuberant crowd. Relief flooded her when she spotted her brother, Filip, laughing among the well-wishers. His face bore purplish hues—or was it the light?—but his limbs were intact. Behind him stood Henryk, his easy smile splitting his face. But where was her husband? She scanned the freshly arrived squad until her gaze settled on the one man she sought.

Jacek's eyes bored into hers with an intensity that made her heart race. Then he smiled, and a breath she hadn't realized she held whooshed from her. His gaze darted to two children streaming down the forestairs, shrieking for their papa. At six years old, Adam was the oldest of their brood, and he sprinted in the lead, abandoning his sister entirely to throw himself at Jacek's legs. "Papa! Papa!"

Jacek staggered backward with an "Oof!" and scooped the boy up, kissed his cheeks, and dangled him high in the air, making the child kick and squeal. "By all the saints, you're nearly as tall as your Uncle Filip."

"Strong like him too!" Adam boasted. He shouted with glee when he spied said uncle. Jacek lowered him to the ground so he could race for Filip, and just in time to catch Margaret, their four-year-old and the apple of Jacek's eye … because, he claimed, she so resembled Oliwia with her dark hair, fair skin, and light blue eyes.

Shooting Oliwia a tender look, he hugged Margaret to him and closed his eyes as he buried his nose in her hair. Joyful tears stung Oliwia's eyes, and she shook her head in a vain attempt to hold them in check. As if he read every thought, every emotion leaping inside her, Jacek opened his eyes and winked at her. Then he was bounding up the stairs with his daughter tucked against him.

Decorum kept Oliwia from throwing herself at him and hugging his neck. Instead, she gave him a shaky curtsy. "Welcome home, my lord. I am pleased you are back with us in time for Easter. You appear to be in excellent health. I trust all went well?"

His dark eyebrows shot to the cuff of his kolpak. "Over six sennights away, and this is all the greeting I receive from my wife?"

She pushed up to her tiptoes and cupped his face, letting the gloriously familiar scent of sweat, leather, and him wrap around her. She lingered a kiss upon each cheek before landing her lips squarely on his mouth. Pulling back, she took in his surprised expression and whispered, "I will show you a proper greeting later, my lord, when we are not surrounded by all of the citizens of Biaska."

A gleam lit his eyes. "I look forward to it."

The heated moment was broken when Adam crashed into his legs and demanded to be picked up. Oliwia bent and patted the boy's bottom. "Why don't we go and look at the horses Papa has brought home? There are bound to be some beauties among the lot."

The child whipped his head so fast he nearly butted her chin, his face a study in pure joy. "Horses!"

"Horses!" Margaret echoed.

Jacek's smile slid from his face. "Perhaps we can see them later. Papa is in desperate need of a meal and a wash." He picked up Adam with his free arm and nudged them all toward the keep.

Oliwia smiled up at him, worry receding like the tide. "I cannot wait to see the combat horses you brought." *And learn what they will fetch.*

His face fell, and alarm bells sounded in her head. "They are in good order, yes?"

"Those that returned with us, yes."

"How many did you bring back?"

"Come." He ducked his head to the side, avoiding her gaze. "I will explain later. Right now, I am hungry and need to fill my belly."

For now, she would allow his verbal feint to go unchallenged, but the sheepishness in his expression sparked a feeling of dread in her stomach she struggled to quell.

No sooner had they entered the great hall with Henryk, Filip, and Adam in their wake than the heralds sounded again—a different tone this time—and a sharp stab of realization brought her to an abrupt halt.

Jacek stopped beside her. "Who arrives?" He lowered the children to their feet and pivoted, ready to return the way they had just come.

Oliwia placed a restraining hand on his forearm. He swiveled his head and looked down at her. "What is it, Liwi?"

She raised her eyes to his and swallowed. "Just as you have news for me of the horses, I have news for you about an arriving guest."

His dark brows knotted together. "Who is it?"

Oliwia pulled in and released a small breath. "I hoped he wouldn't arrive for at least another day." *Or at all.* "It is the late Lord Antonin's son, Maurycy."

Confusion spread over his handsome features, followed by recognition, then shock. "Maurycy Wąskaski? Of Wąskadroga?"

"One and the same. The son of the man I killed, now a man himself."

Jacek's mouth dropped open and closed again. "Why is he *here?*"

Oliwia arched an eyebrow. "His missive claims he has business at his father's old estate—his estate now—but that it is in such disrepair he cannot stay there, and he is *certain* of our hospitality since we are kin."

"But you are *not* kin. You were related to the late Lord Eryk by marriage only. He, in turn, was the cousin of Maurycy's dead father. The blood ties were severed. And you did not kill Antonin, Liwi. You wounded him while defending yourself. It was Romek who did the killing."

Five years earlier, the covetous Antonin Wąskaski had ordered Oliwia's first husband, Eryk, killed so he could force her into marriage and thereby gain Biaska. The treacherous Antonin had then betrayed his captain, Romek Mazur. Romek had taken his revenge. While he might have dealt Antonin the final blow, Oliwia had first inflicted a mortal injury. Antonin would have died by her hand had Romek not hurried his demise along.

"Jacek, do you not see? By the nature of that relationship, Maurycy and Adam share the same blood."

His expression would have been comical under any other circumstance.

Jacek stood in stunned silence as Oliwia relinquished the children to the nursemaid, Anka. His first inclination was to intercept Maurycy and his retinue, but it was too late; the heralds had already announced their arrival. Why hadn't Jacek and his party been aware Maurycy was right behind them? *Because I was too eager to reach home, and that made me careless.*

"Henryk and the rest of the garrison must be alerted."

"Alerted about what, pray?" Henryk had been in conversation with several guards and now sauntered over.

While Oliwia rushed off to the kitchens, Jacek told Henryk of Maurycy's arrival. "I've little idea of his intentions or if he inherited his father's black heart. The last I heard, he had made his home in Austria serving the Holy Roman Emperor."

Henryk's brows knotted. "As a soldier?"

"I don't know."

"I will prepare the men and see to it that we get our answers." Henryk pivoted on his bootheel and hailed the guards standing where he had left them.

Striding toward the stairs, Jacek was caught short by the sight of Filip leaning against one of the ribbed pillars tucked into a corner in the great hall, his arm casually braced above a serving maid's head. She was staring up at him with wonder in her eyes. So intent on the maid was Filip that he hadn't spotted Jacek, and Jacek paused to listen, taking cover behind a large cabinet.

"They were ten brigands in all, and only I stood in their way." Filip's voice was filled with bravado. "They would have looted the camp for sure and probably slain everyone while they were about it, the curs!"

"How fortunate for your companions that you were on sentry duty that night, my lord! Were you frightened?"

Filip straightened, and his chest inflated several inches. "Frightened? Hardly," he scoffed. "I confess I was alarmed, for I had no time to run and warn the others, and the louts were stealing our horses. I had to act!"

"How did you ever find the courage to defeat them?" The girl's voice was high and breathy, and she fluttered her lashes at him.

Filip ran a hesitant finger along her jaw, eliciting a giggle. "I thought of you, Mary, and how like the sky your eyes are." Filip's voice had taken on a silky quality, reminding Jacek of Henryk. Jacek suppressed an eye-roll. "I wanted to look into them once more, and that desire drove me to—"

Jacek stepped out of his hiding place and clamped a hand on Filip's shoulder. The boy startled beneath his grip. "It drove him to attack them all and get himself knocked out for his effort." Jacek pointed at his face. "There is the proof."

She gasped and swung wide eyes to Jacek. Filip scowled. Jacek's grip tightened. "But he managed to hold them off. If not for his bravery, we would have lost every last wagon. Possibly our lives. Now, if you would excuse us, Mary ..."

"Of course, my lord." The girl executed a quick curtsy and scurried away.

Filip's chest deflated on an extended breath as he watched her go. Shoulders sagging, he turned to face Jacek.

Jacek crossed his arms over his chest. "At least I didn't tell her the truth. She won't hear from me how you fell asleep on your watch and let them sneak up on you, bash you over the head, and bind and gag you before you so much as squeaked. Nor how that led to us losing *three* warhorses." Jacek shook three fingers in Filip's face.

Filip balked. "I was simply trying to recount—"

"I know *exactly* what you were trying, and it had more to do with that maid's skirts than telling a true tale." Dear God, at least the boy was keen on a girl probably as virginal as he.

Filip seemed to lift himself—and his nose—to match Jacek's height. He had another four inches to go before he would reach eye level, but the mop of brown curls on his head nearly filled the gap as it was. "There is nothing wrong with having a bit of fun with a maid."

"Tell me, what is it you say to the brown-eyed girls? That their eyes bring to mind the dung heap you will be shoveling shortly in the stables? Do the green-eyed ones remind you of a scum-laden pond?" Jacek twirled his hand in the air with a flourish. "And now that we're about it, how do you keep from getting their eye color—and their names—confused?"

Filip's mouth thinned to a firm line, but Jacek wasn't done.

"You do realize the maids talk to one another, yes? That may not matter in a tavern in far-flung Halicz, but it very much matters here at Biaska Castle and the village beyond. First and foremost, you represent Biaska and your Armstrong clan."

"Who have all fled Scotland in poverty, disgrace, or both," Filip noted dryly.

And there it was, the boy's oddly hybrid background. "All the more reason to uphold the name. You may be the only able Armstrong remaining in Europe who can do so. Second, while you may fancy yourself an Ottoman sultan growing his harem, such a life is not in your future … for which you should be thankful, I might add. Pleasing one woman is more than one man is capable of. And third, if you are not very, *very* careful, you stand an even chance of populating Biaska with your bastard children. I would not wish to be in your boots if your sister—"

"I am of age. My sister has no control over me," Filip growled.

"Believe that at your own folly. Here, she is queen and she rules over you, me, and every man garrisoned here."

"Then before my sister returns and attempts to lord over me, I take my leave." Without so much as a dip of his head, Filip pivoted and stalked away.

One hand on his hip, Jacek rubbed his stubbly jaw with the other and watched the boy's retreating back. A boy no more, Jacek corrected himself, though not quite a man either. Filip was in that odd space between bursting fully into manhood with an ankle yet snared in boyhood, trying to find balance as he spanned the chasm between the two.

Handling Filip was a push-pull proposition. Either he was being held back from a grown man's world or thrust into it at the most inopportune times. The lad had been in training to become a warrior since the age of six, but did he have the right temperament? The fortitude? The ability to think and act when a false move meant death over life?

Jacek's anger over losing the horses still moldered in his gut. He was mad at Filip for succumbing to sleep and letting the curs do their devilry and furious with himself for putting the lad in that position in the first place. What stuck in his craw like a thistle was the loss of the sable. Jarosława had gone from gray to white, and for too long he had delayed finding her replacement so he could turn her out to pasture, where she would spend her days pulling up tender grasses and yellow dandelions. The sable, with her white socks, had inspired him to consider the switch. And now she was lost to him.

With these thoughts bombarding his brain, Jacek brushed himself off and made for the forestairs, bracing himself to confront a man possibly bent on exacting revenge.

CHAPTER 6

My Home, My Castle

Jacek surveyed the array of platters holding fish baked in dill sauce, roasted carrots in butter, and all manner of breads, dried fruits, and cheeses. Despite Lenten's reduced menu, Oliwia had outdone herself in welcoming Maurycy and his entourage to their home, especially under such strained circumstances. And his wife managed it all without appearing out of sorts. To the contrary, with her hair pinned up in loose braids woven with tiny pearls and her small form draped in a gown of ice-blue silk that matched her eyes, she shone brighter than anything or anyone else in the great hall—and this comparison extended to a young noblewoman named Lady Sabina who accompanied Maurycy and now sat beside him. Though not his wife, she conducted herself as though she held the station. Neither Jacek nor Oliwia had asked about the connection, and Maurycy had offered no explanation.

A sea of beeswax candles lit the table draped in white linen, their flames dancing jauntily with the drafts wafting through the great hall. A beautiful display, one that made his chest balloon with pride for his wife and his home, though the sumptuous scene could not settle his unease over their guest's appearance or the effect it had on Oliwia.

He fixed his eyes on the dark-haired man ten years his junior. What was the true purpose of Maurycy's visit? He claimed to have returned, at the king's behest, to determine whether his late father's estate could be restored to some semblance of its former self, but Jacek's instincts had him on alert.

Their guest at times seemed *too* affable, and as Jacek observed him, he noticed how Maurycy's golden-brown eyes roved over the great hall's adornments when he thought no one was looking. The same keen interest extended to their table, where Maurycy inspected a glass wine goblet as though weighing its worth.

Meanwhile, Lady Sabina's sharp gaze followed Oliwia. She quizzed Liwi about the myriad goings-on at Biaska, as if evaluating her suitability for the class of *szlachcianki*. If he knew anything about his Liwi, she was questioning her own suitability as a noblewoman and finding herself lacking. He reached for her hand beneath the table and gave it a reassuring squeeze.

Lady Sabina took a dainty spoonful of soup. "How long have you and your husband, been wed, Lady Oliwia?"

"Five years now."

Maurycy turned to Sabina. "They wed the very same year my father was slain."

The table fell silent. Before Jacek could marshal a response, Sabina offered Oliwia a wan smile. "I understand you breed warhorses, Pani Oliwia." Maurycy bent his head to his meal.

Oliwia cleared her throat. "Yes, when I can get them. I am very fortunate in my husband, who has just brought me a dozen and a half warhorses that I will show you on the morrow if you care to see them."

"I would." Sabina darted him a look he couldn't decipher. "You are indeed fortunate, Pani Oliwia. Handsome *and* a good provider."

Maurycy shot her a glare, but Sabina picked up her wine without giving him another glance.

The air crackled with unease. Unsure whether to thank the woman or ignore her outright, Jacek exchanged a questioning look with Oliwia, She patted his hand and turned her attention back to Sabina. "How kind of you to say so. I am in complete agreement."

She dropped her voice so low only Jacek could hear. "And so virile— especially for a man incapable of finding his voice." She gave him a subtle blue-eyed wink, the little imp.

"Well played," he mouthed, choking back a laugh. Deep in his chest, he glowed with satisfaction at Oliwia's praise, made all the sweeter by her devil's play. His wife had never let herself be restrained by decorum, and he loved her all the more for it.

Oliwia steered the conversation in a different, less prickly direction when she craned her head toward Henryk, who flanked her right side. "What news do you bring from the border?"

Henryk, who had been on the verge of devouring a morsel of meat, paused and lowered his eating knife. "I'm not sure 'tis appropriate dinner conversation."

Oliwia clapped her hands like a child about to be told a favorite story. "Of course it is! We all would like to hear, yes?" She nodded at her audience before turning back to Henryk. "Please, do tell us."

Setting his knife down, Henryk straightened and took a long drink of his wine. "Well, it seems the Crown thought it a good idea to send an envoy to Constantinople—"

"Which envoy, and why did the king think it necessary?"

Henryk gave her an indulgent smirk. "Samuel Otwinowski, a favorite at the sultan's court, was sent because relations at the border are in shambles," Henryk declared. "The Turks are angry because the Zaporozhian Cossacks continue to pirate Turkish vessels at will on the Black Sea, and the Commonwealth is angry over the Tatars' incursions onto our soil and the never-ending enslavement of our people. The region has been growing more and more unstable."

"It is far more complicated than raiding back and forth, is it not?" Oliwia prodded, though she was already better informed than most folk in the Jura Highlands—due partly to a keen interest in current events but also because among her land holdings was an estate called Silnyród that lay in the borderlands.

The designation "estate," however, was a generous one. The place was more of a collection of huts sheltered behind a shabby wooden fortress on the western edge of the steppe.

Henryk rolled his eyes. "I will either need to be exceedingly maudlin or deep in my cups to wade into the mess festering in Moldavia. Even those whose familiarity with the subject is vast struggle to explain the nuances. Let me only add that the king did not help himself by coming to the Habsburgs' defense—"

"More specifically, his brother-in-law's defense," Jacek cut in. Nor did it help the king's cause that he had married his late queen's sister, Constance of Austria. She, like her sister had been, was a Habsburg, but the country had come to embrace King Zygmunt's first wife, Anne of Austria, for her kindheartedness and piety. Her younger sister, however, was narrow-minded, severe, and disliked by the szlachta and the clergy, due in no small part to her encouragement of her husband's quest for absolute power.

It seemed the longer the king ruled, the more the thin thread of accord between himself and Parliament tautened.

With a bob of his head, Henryk acknowledged Jacek's remark. "In coming to Emperor Ferdinand's aid against Prince Bethlen, King Zygmunt sent in, among other troops, the Lisowczycy. Say what you will about the Lost Men, they are fearsome fighters. They crushed the Transylvanians and sent them running. Now Bethlen treats with the Ottomans for some sort of retaliation. Meanwhile, regiments of Lost Men are once more idle and ravage Podolia and its neighbors."

"A problem of a different sort, I imagine," Oliwia added, "but a problem nonetheless."

Jacek nodded his agreement. "One that fuels the foment in the area. Making matters worse is Gaspar Grazziani's shifting alliances."

Oliwia took a tiny sip of her wine. "The hospodar of Moldavia? But isn't he an Ottoman vassal?"

Across the table, Maurycy yawned and blinked. "They all sound rather backward."

Oliwia folded her hands together and placed them on the table, but Jacek sensed her body stiffen. "Pan Maurycy, I have been remiss as a hostess, and I apologize for the discourse. You see, the men returned just shortly before you arrived today. They have been gone well over a month, and we have not had a chance to catch up on these matters of grave importance that affect us all." She paused and seemed to pull in a covert breath. "Tell us of your plans for Wąskadroga."

Maurycy smiled at her, but it was without warmth. "I have no plans at the moment for I no longer have servants." He swiveled his head. "I see a number of them working here. Perhaps you would consent to give them back to me." His eyes regarded her with something akin to ice, and Jacek's hackles stood on end.

"That might be difficult," Oliwia replied evenly. "The people had no place to go when Wąskadroga was abandoned, so they dispersed lest they starve. A number came here seeking—"

"Wąskadroga was not abandoned, my lady," he hissed through clenched teeth. My father, its castellan, was removed from it and murdered."

Jacek and Henryk both stood at once, hands on their daggers. Maurycy raised his hands in surrender and chuckled. "My lords, please sit down. I meant no offense." To Oliwia, he said, "You will forgive me my poor choice of words, yes? It has been a long day of travel, and I fear fatigue has gotten the best of me." Jacek and Henryk retook their seats, and Maurycy continued. "As I was saying, without laborers willing to repair the defenses, fix rotten roofs, and patch damaged walls, it will be nigh impossible to render the castle habitable again. But tomorrow we shall travel there and assess." He turned his head to Lady Sabina. "That is our plan, yes?"

Sabina gave him a dip of her head.

Maurycy began inquiring about places and people from his boyhood, but a tense undertone ran through the ensuing conversation Jacek mostly eschewed in favor of continuing his observations.

During a break in the chatter, he leaned to Oliwia's ear and whispered, "Your virile husband wishes to know when this evening might end."

Resting her fingers lightly on his forearm, she raised her lips to his ear, her warm breath soft on his skin. "As soon as we can convince our guests to retire."

God grant me the strength to get through this accursed meal.

The accursed meal—which should not have been such, considering it was to be his homecoming and reunion with his wife—dragged on, and he had yet to tell Oliwia about the horses and face her disappointment.

Jacek drifted in and out of the stilted exchanges until Maurycy abruptly directed his attention his way. "Pan Jacek, I understand you have always aspired to have lands of your own. In your efforts to claim an estate of your own, did you picture yourself marrying into the lordship of Biaska?"

What the devil? Whether knowingly or not, Maurycy had just fired an arrow at Jacek's Achilles' heel. The subject of his lust for land was a volatile one and had been a topic he had shared with select others in the past. How had this whelp discovered it? The title "Lord of Biaska" had never been among his ambitions, nor was it his to claim now.

Henryk caught his eye, offered a sympathetic shrug, and raised his goblet in salute, shaking Jacek from his mind's wanderings. "Never. Though veritably, my wife is so capable that she acts as both lady *and* lord." He spoke the truth. Oliwia was more proficient at managing the estate than he would ever hope to be. He was a soldier, and he had neither the interest nor the talent to become a manager of domestic affairs.

He covered Oliwia's hand with his own. "And she does an excellent job of it."

Oliwia raised misty blue eyes to his. Her cheeks blazed pink, and her lips seemed to form a question.

Giving her hand a squeeze, he whispered, "It is true. Furthermore, I am proud to call you wife."

Her eyes welled, and she dabbed at them. "I seem to have a cinder stuck in my eye."

With a light touch, he chucked her under the chin, and she rewarded him with a lilting laugh.

Henryk excused himself, and Oliwia beckoned her brother, seated at the end of the table, to take up Henryk's seat. Their voices became low and strained, though Jacek couldn't make out what passed between them. Filip let out a derisive snort and abruptly excused himself. Oliwia appeared stricken for an instant but recovered and launched into a lively conversation with Lady Sabina, though her smile did not reach her eyes. Filip had wounded her somehow, and Jacek's anger ignited anew.

Left to his own thoughts while conversation burbled around him, Jacek revisited the missteps that had led to the depleted warhorses. How much to reveal to Oliwia? Obviously, he had to confess he had brought her half the stock she had expected, but dear God, he dreaded shouldering her disappointment. Why add to it by recounting Filip's blunder?

He dipped a finger and thumb into his sash and fidgeted with the small object he had bought for her. He let out a silent sigh. The offering would never make up for the lost warhorses. Perhaps she would be moved to forgive him more quickly, however.

He watched her from the corner of his eye, and his thoughts careened in a wholly different direction. Other activities he wished to engage her in pummeled any notion of talking.

CHAPTER 7

The Stench of Carp and Guests

Dinner dragged on like an overloaded cart in a bog, and Jacek now found himself ensconced with the menfolk on one side of the limestone fireplace nearly as tall as he. Meanwhile, the women gathered on the opposite side, chattering amongst themselves. Nobility spending idle time in polite, accustomed ways ... of which he presently wanted no part.

He had barely seen his children, and he had enjoyed no private moments with his wife. Filip's mysterious disappearance also niggled at him, but he had yet to discover what had passed between brother and sister in their curt conversation.

Henryk tossed back a measure of wodka and leaned in, his voice conspiratorial. "I take it you have not yet told Oliwia you brought her nine warhorses rather than eighteen."

"I have not had a chance," Jacek muttered. "Though I confess I am not eager to explain how I gave up the three." He had to tell her—tonight, before she learned about it elsewhere. Could that be what she and Filip had argued about?

"You are not the reason they were lost. That falls squarely on Filip's shoulders," Henryk pointed out cheerfully.

Jacek humphed. "A fact that will be infinitely harder to impart on Oliwia." He regarded his best friend. "Do you think I coddle the lad?"

"No, I think you are trying to please your wife by making sure he is not placed in harm's way."

"Does that not merely put him at odds with the men he so desperately desires to be accepted by?"

Henryk shrugged. "Possibly. Have you considered sending him to a different estate to finish his training?"

"Yes, but I think Oliwia will fight me on it. She cannot see beyond her duty to protect him."

Henryk jiggled the earthen wodka jug. "There is nothing for it tonight, my friend, so drink up. And quickly, man, so I can refill my own cup."

Jacek obliged him. Perhaps he needed more liquid steel in his spine to tell Oliwia.

Henryk nodded toward the women. "There's a handsome lot, yes?"

"Do you have your eye on one? I daresay you don't have many to choose from since nearly every single one is married … unless you fancy Lady Sabina and you think you might woo her with that honeyed tongue of yours." Henryk was nigh on impossible for any female to dismiss.

Henryk waggled his eyebrows. "Ah! You found me out."

"Did I?" Jacek whipped his head back to the cluster of females when one—his sister, Tamara—snagged his eye with a wave. Or had she intended it for Henryk? One of Jacek's hands balled into a fist.

Henryk cast his eyes toward a new serving maid. The girl exchanged a knowing glance with him and quickly looked away. He grinned wide. "I do believe my bed will not be empty tonight."

This both surprised and delighted Jacek. "Not Tamara, then?"

Henryk's eyes fairly bugged out. "Your sister?"

"Why? What's wrong with her?"

"Absolutely nothing. Tamara is lovely, but being interested in her would be akin to lusting after my own sister." Henryk pulled a face and quickly threw back more wodka as if to rinse away the thought.

Jacek burst out with a relieved laugh. He had known Henryk longer than he'd not known him. They had come to Biaska at the same time, from opposite ends of the voivodeship, and had forged a brotherhood stronger than Jacek enjoyed with his blood brothers. They had grown up together, fought countless battles at the other's side, and shared each other's triumphs and defeats.

But in one way they were quite different. While his skill as a hussar was Henryk's most noteworthy trait, his second most remarkable talent was charming the ladies. Henryk Kalinowski had bedded more women than the entire Biaska garrison put together.

The men exchanged tales of battle and glory, and Jacek took the opportunity to steal a glance at the women, his mind turning over what Henryk found appealing in an unending parade of lovers with whom he fell in and out of love. He did not envy his friend but rather pitied him at times. When he'd been younger, Jacek had fancied himself enamored of a number of maids, but that notion of love had been as pyrite was to gold.

His eyes lifted and locked with Oliwia's, and his heart broke into the gallop of an untamed horse. Though he could not make out every detail of her features in the dim light, he had no difficulty calling up her pale blue eyes, and the fire that sparkled inside them, or her smooth marble skin and rosy lips that tempted him beyond reason.

She smiled at him and turned back to the ladies, yet he stood transfixed. The lone bright spot in the evening's affair had been her; her strength and grace humbled him. Though her smile throughout the evening was forced, she showed their guests the esteem due their station—despite her discomfort in Maurycy's presence.

Fortunately, Oliwia had not arranged for dancing after supper—for the night would have gone longer still—but instead had hired an accomplished musician from the village to play the *suka*. As the man entertained them, Jacek leaned to her ear more than once, partly to pull in the intoxicating fragrance of lemons and newly picked herbs he so loved and partly to murmur his affection.

In return, she covertly stroked his forearm, shooting a shiver up his arm to his nape. He relished her touch. He needed it. He could not wait to get her alone … until he remembered the damned horses hanging above his head like an executioner's ax.

With a sigh, he sat back in his chair and waited for the suka player—and the interminable evening—to end.

When at last it did, they bid their guests good night. As he followed her up the stone steps to their quarters, his blood effervesced with anticipation. But when they reached the passageway leading to the nursery, a pang jabbed his chest.

"Liwi."

She turned. "Yes?"

He pointed to his left. "Might we stop and look in on the children? I have barely seen Adam and Margaret since my return, and I have not seen Piotr at all."

Oliwia hesitated, pulling her bottom lip between her teeth. Her eyes flitted to and fro, like a moth seeking the light.

Alarm rose inside him. "What is it? Is the babe unwell?"

"No, no, he is quite well. So well, in fact, that he is prone to bellowing. During your absence, you see, I made the mistake of allowing him into my bed every night, and now he is loath to leave it."

Jacek grinned. "He takes after his father."

"Yes, doesn't he, though?" she replied dryly. "Except you are less likely to caterwaul when it is time to leave."

"I try very hard to limit my caterwauling to only the iciest of mornings."

She gave him a headshake and a roll of her eyes, but a smile tugged the corners of her mouth. "I thought it best to break him of the habit starting tonight; therefore, I must stay away. The child has an uncanny ability to sense when I am nearby, and he may go into fits if I am about and not carrying him off for a cuddle. You are welcome to visit him without me, however." A pivot, and she continued her ascent, the hem of her heavy burgundy gown draping over the steps.

"Liwi?"

She glanced at him over her shoulder. "Mmm?"

"As Piotr will not be in bed with you tonight, may I be so bold as to assume you are expecting me to take his place?"

Oh so slowly, she turned once more to face him, and he waggled his eyebrows. Leaning down, she placed her hands upon his shoulders and hovered her lips inches from his. "I will be gravely disappointed if you do not. It has been far too long, my lord."

His heart threw itself against his rib cage. Then she kissed him soundly, heating his blood and sending his pulse to the heavens. She left him dazed, wanting more, and he stood rooted in place lest he take a tumble down the staircase. He watched her walk away. Finally, he shook himself from his trance and rushed to his apartments to perform his ablutions and exchange his posher garments for his nightshirt and robe.

Soon he was barreling down the tunnel that connected his bedchamber with hers. He pressed his ear to the door, and, hearing nothing, he pushed the door open. A squeal greeted him.

"It's all right, Nadia," came Oliwia's lilt. She sat at her dressing table in nightgown and open robe, her eyes catching his in the mirror. "His lordship once again forgot to knock. No doubt he hoped to catch his wife in some state of undress."

Jacek grinned at her reflection, but Nadia was not nearly so amused. The maid stood frozen in place, mouth wide open, Oliwia's partly braided hair looped in her palm.

Stepping into the room, he flapped his hand at her. "Leave it, Nadia. I will take care of your mistress's hair tonight."

Nadia's eyes bugged out of a face the color of beet soup. Her hands jerked upward, releasing the plait, and she turned a circle in place.

He had no wish to fluster the girl further, and gently as he could, he dismissed her. "Thank you. You need not check back on your lady this night. Rest well."

Nadia's eyes darted about like a hummingbird expecting a hawk's strike.

Oliwia gave her a dip of her head. "Until morning, Nadia."

"What of the fire? And do you not wish me to—"

"Good night, Nadia," Jacek fairly growled, and the girl scurried from the room, thudding the door behind her and catching her skirt in the process. It cracked open a heartbeat later, and the skirt disappeared.

He strode to Oliwia and began unbraiding Nadia's careful work.

Oliwia's eyes followed him in the mirror. "Poor Nadia will never get used to you barging in, I'm afraid."

"I do not barge." He tugged at a stubbornly tight weave that refused to come undone, then leveled his gaze at her reflected one. "Why the devil does she insist on braiding your hair when I am home? She knows her labor will simply be undone."

Oliwia glanced at him over her shoulder. "She feels it is her duty and that she's not serving me well if she does not fix my hair for bed."

He loosened the final weaves and pulled her strands apart, letting them sift through his fingers. "As I see it, she is preparing you for sleep, not bed. They are quite different."

Oliwia fluttered her eyes and gave him a flirty smile. "Which is it you now prepare me for, pray?" She tapped her forefinger against her cheek. "And while you're about it, remind me why you are in my bedchamber."

With a mild chuckle, he returned his attention to her thick, silky hair. "I have come to prove I am worthy of the praise you heaped upon me during supper." He canted his head and looked up at the colorful painted beams that spanned the ceiling. "What was it you said? Ah yes. 'Virile man.' Expectations are high, and I have much work to do before the night is over."

Oliwia stood and rose on her tiptoes as she looped her arms around his neck. His hands immediately found their way under her robe to her waist. "Well, then, should we not get started?" Her gaze dropped to his mouth.

Intent on covering her lips with his, he did not remember the gift until it rattled in the cuff of his robe.

She drew back. "What's that?"

"A gift I brought you." He extracted a bracelet made of slender gold links and instructed her to extend her wrist. When she did, he secured the bracelet and held his breath. Oliwia was not overly fond of displaying jewelry and wore only select pieces, such as the ruby-and-pearl ring and cross he had given her for their wedding. Hopefully, she would find this peace offering as enchanting.

She lifted her hand to inspect it, and her eyes filled with wonder. "What are these?"

"Charms. One for each child, and look, here's a horse and a tiny castle that could be Biaska."

56

"And a cart with moving wheels!" The delight in her voice made his heart soar. His actions had brought her joy.

"And more can be added," he rushed to say.

"It's lovely. Thank you." A quick peck on his lips and her look turned impish. "I can't help but wonder *why* you have brought me a gift. Is your conscience bothering you?"

"Can I not bestow a present upon my wife without arousing suspicion?"

She cocked an eyebrow, and he deflated.

"Well, ah, I do have something rather unpleasant to tell you."

Confusion clouded her features, and she took a step back, out of his reach. Too late. Inwardly, he admonished himself for the dolt he was. Men with greater sense than he would have delayed divulging bad news until *after* lying with a woman.

He made his expression as contrite and sheepish as he knew how. "This is about the warhorses we brought back."

"The ... horses?" The confusion etched itself deeper into Oliwia's features. "Does this have anything to do with what Filip was trying to tell me during supper before he hastened off in a state?"

Jacek straightened. "What did he say?"

Oliwia's hands perched on her lovely rounded hips. As much as they wanted to stray, he kept his eyes pinned to hers to help him concentrate on her words. "He rambled on about you not trusting him and him trying to prove himself and never being found worthy, so how on earth can he do anything right in your eyes. I pointed out to him that while you may be harsh, you are also quite fair and—"

"You think me *harsh?*"

Her hand flew into the air. "Well, not with me or the children, of course, but with your men, yes."

"And you consider Filip one of my men." Though it was a question, it came out as a flat statement.

"*Filip* considers himself one of your men."

Jacek chuffed. "First, he must be a man. Only then will he be considered one of *my* men." Suddenly, he was greatly vexed. About her brother. Again.

Oliwia seemed to sense his frustration, and she stepped into his arms and looked up at him with her big blue eyes. "Let us not speak of Filip right now. Tell me about the horses."

Her soft voice soothed and beckoned. Normally, he would be elated to leave the subject of her pigheaded brother behind, but doing so meant stepping off the precipice and landing in the thorny wicket that was the warhorses.

Her hands slid up his chest, and she pressed herself against him. Her scent filled his nose, and his mind did what it always did when she drew so close. It failed him.

"There are only nine," he blurted.

She blinked those beautiful crystal eyes. "Nine?"

"Nine. Not the eighteen you expected. The breeder only had twelve because Crown Grand Hetman Żółkiewski appropriated the rest."

Her mouth opened and closed twice before she finally said, "Never mind for now why the hetman helped himself to our warhorses. What happened to the other three?"

"They were stolen from our camp as we slept."

"*What?* How? When? Who stole them?" Once more, she stepped from his grasp. Cold rushed in where her body had been nestled against his.

"I do not know. That is, I suspect, but I have no proof."

She sank onto the cushioned seat before her dressing table.

He dropped to his knees and grasped her hands in his. "I am sorry. It happened on my watch, and I am responsible." His eyes searched her blank ones.

She seemed to come back to herself, and her blue gaze pierced his. "You stood at sentry and the thieves got past you? How could that be?"

He shook his head. "Not exactly. I had finished my turn and was in my tent trying to sleep."

"No, of course it would not have happened while you were on duty."

Her fierce faith exhilarated him but quickly thudded to the ground. "Your belief in me is appreciated but ill-placed, sweet."

She let out a great sigh. "It was Filip, wasn't it? *He* was at watch, but he didn't do his job, did he?"

"I cannot promise I will get the horses back, but I shall try."

She pinched his chin between her finger and thumb, her expression all fire. "You didn't answer me." As quickly as she'd grabbed him, she released her hold and eased back. "But you don't need to. I see it in your eyes. You're protecting him from himself, *and* you're protecting me from the truth. Why?"

Rubbing his nape, he pushed a breath through his lungs. "Your hopes were going to be dashed as it was. I saw no benefit in revealing your brother's hand in the loss. I know what that stock meant to you."

"Meant to *Biaska*. Mary, Mother of God, this turn of events compounds ... Never mind," she mumbled and looked away, but not before he caught the defeat in her eyes. It nearly gutted him.

Catching her chin, he turned her face toward him. "The truth, feeble as it is, is that I did not wish to disappoint you further. I will do whatever is in my power to make it right."

With a frown kissing her delicate brows, she cupped his face in her small hands. "I don't believe it is possible for you to disappoint me."

"Are you so sure?" Christ and all the saints, why couldn't he keep his big mouth shut? Normally, his tongue did not wag like an old woman's, but around his wife he could not contain the treacherous appendage.

Her eyes delved into his as her fingers traced the line of his scar. She followed their touch with light kisses. Desire pooled inside him, and a beat passed before he recovered his speech.

"You outdid yourself, sweet, accommodating Maurycy and his party. It wasn't easy for me to sit there, and I cannot fathom how much more difficult it was for you; yet you did it with the utmost grace." He ran a fingertip along her cheek. "Have I told you lately that you are more precious than any gem?"

"No, because you have been away," she sniffed.

"You are also the most adorable creature I have ever encountered."

"Adorable? Our children are adorable. I am not." Her pert nose inched up. "You may fancy yourself my elder because six years divide us, but I am no babe."

He stood, lifting her with him, and maneuvered them to the bed. "On this, you have my wholehearted agreement. You are a woman, through and through, and I missed that woman very much." He slid her robe from her shoulders, and she pushed up on her toes to return the favor. Firelight played on her sultry smile and in her eyes. Anticipation curled inside him, blooming low, and he lowered himself to the mattress, taking her hands in his. "Let me show you just how much I missed you. But first, you need to remove that chemise."

She arched an imperious eyebrow.

He raised his own. "Or would you prefer I do it for you?"

"Oh no, you don't. I have no wish to mend another chemise you have torn in your haste to remove it."

He gave her a salacious smile. "I will buy you another."

"And I will be mortified when Nadia questions why another nightgown has been tattered." Her cheeks pinked, but desire sparkled in her eyes.

How he loved that look.

Before he could conjure another rejoinder, she pulled the snowy garment over her head and tossed it to one side, leaving her in naught but the charm bracelet. His eyes ate her up greedily. Rejoinders and any thought of horses, thieves, or Filip flew from his head as she blew out the candle and fell atop him with a giggle.

In that moment, all was right in his world.

CHAPTER 8

Schemes

Tomasz blinked behind the round metal rims of his glasses. "Nine?"

"Nine." Oliwia held her sigh in check. Jacek had been home two days, and she was only now confiding the devastating news to Tomasz. She had managed to keep her disappointment at bay, but repeating the event now was akin to ripping a poultice off a fresh gash. The loss of the warhorses not only destroyed the future hope she had pinned on the herd, but it had dealt a real blow to the estate's treasury.

Tomasz shoved his glasses up the bridge of his nose and frowned down at his ledgers. "Hmm."

Another characteristic she usually cherished about her clerk was his sterile assessment of the estate's affairs. He was all tidy numbers and calculations; the messy unpredictability that humans brought to the equation was beyond his recognition. His dry approach helped Oliwia keep her own jostling emotions boxed up, but today his bland reaction grated, and the need to defend overtook her.

"When Pan Dąbrowski arrived in Halicz to take delivery of the stock, the breeder only had twelve."

"And yet he agreed to eighteen."

She explained how the hetman had claimed the warhorses for himself. "Then, on their journey home, Lord Dąbrowski and his party were set upon by thieves who stole three of those horses, leaving the nine."

Tomasz's eyes fairly bugged out. "That is a hanging offense!"

His outburst of emotion startled her. "Yes, it is, though in order to hang the culprits, one must know who they are and then track them down. And it doesn't get us back the warhorses we bought and paid for."

He sat in stunned silence for several beats before hurrying on. "Well, in that case, I must recalculate my estimations. The balance, I'm afraid, will be disappointing."

"It was already disappointing, yes?"

Nodding his answer, he produced a cloth and mopped his forehead.

Oliwia clasped her hands and leaned forward. "I might have a solution."

"Yes?"

"What if I were to sell Silnyród?"

"But you would be giving up a village and its revenue generation, my lady."

"Yes, but that revenue is hardly worth the worry, is it?" She had never even laid eyes upon the far-flung fortress estate she had inherited when her late husband was murdered. "We are talking about an estate located in the borderlands, one that's always susceptible to Tatar raids. Would the fortress not serve a magnate from that region better? He could add it to his defenses."

"Which magnate?"

"I'm still working that out." In truth, she had latched on to one name but wasn't ready to divulge it yet.

They tabled the discussion and concluded their remaining dealings, and Tomasz left her alone in the solar to ponder Biaska's predicament. She leaned back in the overlarge carved wooden chair, and her mind detoured to seeking Jacek's counsel on her idea. Though he insisted he wasn't a man of business, he had once lorded over Silnyród, transforming what had been described as a mud pit into something of a … lesser mud pit—with little to no funds—so he knew something of the place and its surroundings.

Traveling from Biaska to Silnyród took weeks, and that estimate assumed the roads were decent, but she had never considered the journey before. Currently, its overseer, Pan Lesław Nowak, managed the lands and tenants capably enough. Like Jacek, though, he was a military man, a hussar who had once served with Biaska's troops, and unless much had changed, he didn't have the means to purchase the estate himself.

If she sold it to another, Lesław could return to Biaska! The thought warmed her but then chilled as quickly. Lesław would bring his wife, which presented a completely different thornbush Oliwia didn't wish to dwell upon.

One problem at a time.

With the weather turning warmer, perhaps now was a good time to travel there—as soon as Maurycy and his minions departed. Much to Oliwia's consternation, Sabina seemed to hover constantly, like one of the hounds waiting for a scrap to fall from the table. As soon as Oliwia questioned her about their departure, however, the woman scurried away like a rat, leaving Oliwia with no answer as to when these "guests" planned to leave.

How to go about planting the seed in her husband's mind about Silnyród? He rarely questioned her management of the estate. The odd occasion when he did always involved defenses, such as hiring and outfitting men-at-arms and replenishing the armory. For the rest of it, he was content to let her handle Biaska's affairs, praising her efforts, telling her she ran the estate like a well-greased machine, and building her up when she thought to tear herself down. Letting her know how awed he was by his "talented wife." She gobbled up his tributes like a drunk consumed flagons of wodka, and she was likely as dependent on Jacek's words of admiration as the imaginary tosspot was on his drink.

Yes, she was an excellent manager, for she knew its workings as well as she knew her own name. Here, her confidence soared. But in the presence of a highborn woman like Sabina—even one whose status as mistress tarnished her reputation—it collapsed upon itself. Would traveling to Silnyród and meeting yet another noblewoman undermine it further?

A knock came at the door, and it creaked open the next instant. Tamara's face appeared in the crack. "May I come in?"

"Yes, of course." Oliwia waved her in.

Tamara's mouth curved into a grin. "Are you hiding?"

"Not on purpose. Tomasz and I have been reviewing Biaska's status, and I have more work to complete in that regard. I must confess I'm not chagrined to be locked away for the moment."

"You may want to go hunting instead of finishing your business."

"I—what?"

Tamara rolled her eyes. "Pan Maurycy insists on going hunting."

"Again? He went yesterday, and he's been here less than a sennight! Is he bent on killing everything in our forests?" Oliwia muttered the last bit.

"Or chasing it all toward Wąskadroga. I can envision it now."

"Perhaps I should ask Henryk to dispatch a contingent of guards to accompany Maurycy to be sure he doesn't kill indiscriminately and leave good meat behind. The game master found two yearling carcasses shot and left to rot."

"Maurycy?"

Oliwia sighed. "He doesn't know, and he has no way to prove who the wastrel was that did the deed, but I have my suspicions. I doubt it is mere coincidence that this has happened since Maurycy's arrival. If poachers were about, they would *take* the meat to feed their families."

"The plan to hunt today is only now being shaped. I have asked Dawid … um, Pan Dawid to join the party, though he's rather weary of the man."

The reference to Dawid piqued Oliwia's interest, but she put it aside. "As are we all. They consume our finest wine, run our serving maids ragged, and their guards eat copious amounts of food." Frustration bubbled like a boiling cauldron and spilled over. Only with Tamara did Oliwia feel at ease hurling such an insult, and she found herself grateful—again—for her sister-in-law's company. Here was one noble lady who did *not* put her ill at ease.

"Where is my brother anyway? I have not seen him all day."

"He left at dawn to inspect the tenants' fields and spend time in the villages talking to them."

"Jacek? Posing as the lord himself? I'll wager he's spending time in the village taverns talking to the tenants."

"What better way to escape? I wish I could have gone with him, but I could not delay my meeting with Tomasz."

Tamara stepped beside Oliwia, wrapped her arms around her shoulders, and laid her cheek against Oliwia's crown. "Do not despair, sister."

Oliwia closed her eyes and hugged Tamara's arm. "I am so glad to have you here." Her sister-in-law had, with just a small gesture, lifted Oliwia's spirits.

When Tamara left, Oliwia returned with renewed vigor to her plan for Silnyród. She dipped the quill into the inkpot and bent her head to the paper.

CHAPTER 9

Strike and Counterstrike

When Filip did not appear in the great hall for the morning meal, Jacek was obliged to track him down. "Go find him," Oliwia had snapped. Why, precisely, she had used such a terse tone made no sense to him. She had been playful and congenial when they awoke, and he had not left her wanting.

As he propelled himself across the bailey, his mind turned over what he could have done wrong, especially so soon after his return a mere sennight ago. He had kept Maurycy away from her, and a few well-timed instances of intimidation had prevented the scoundrel from bringing up his father. Jacek would soon apply more of the same to ensure the man and his retinue did not linger. But surely Maurycy was not the reason for Oliwia's sour mood.

At a loss to solve the thorny question, his mind moved on to a familiar overarching riddle: Why did women's moods turn more quickly than Poland's weather? Why couldn't they be as simple as men, as easily decipherable? Fill a man's belly with a warm meal and his bed with his woman and he was content. But women? Only God and the Virgin Mary knew what strange goings-on rattled about in their brains at any given moment, and possibly not even *their* higher powers could unravel the mysteries. Then again, perhaps it was those very unpredictable natures that kept a male tethered. Men were driven to take action, to solve problems; that the members of the fairer sex were unsolvable didn't stop a man from ramming his head against the ramparts of womanhood.

The entrance to the main quarters was sheltered by a sloped roof, and he ducked beneath the cover and burst into an interior chamber that led to a corridor and men's bunks beyond. The chamber also led to the squad leader's quarters—quarters he had once occupied when he had served as lieutenant.

He cleared the debris from his mind and entered the sparse chamber, where the squad leader, Stefan, and Marcin sat sharpening blades. They both whipped their heads up as Jacek rushed in. They were his brothers-in-arms and had endured many hardships and victories together over the years, and he was certain he knew their every expression. The surprised one they wore now was not one he typically saw; then again, they rarely witnessed him in such a ruffled state.

He paused to catch his breath. "Have you seen Filip?"

Stefan shook his head, causing his shaggy black hair to move with it. "Not since yesterday."

"Was he here last night?"

"Oh yes," Stefan chuckled. Mirth gleamed in his onyx eyes. "He earned the entire garrison's ridicule when we learned of his costly blunder with the warhorses." Stefan and Marcin exchanged amused looks.

Relief coursed through Jacek. Filip hadn't run off. "How did he take your mockery?"

Marcin bent back to his stone, the straight sable locks atop his head flopping into his face and hiding whatever was written in his chestnut-colored eyes. His hair was cut in the way of a hussar, with shaved sides and a mop on his crown. Where Stefan boasted a full beard that resembled a clump of black bristles dotted with white, Marcin was smooth-faced—not by his choice, but by nature's—making him appear far younger than his twenty-eight years. "He got into a bit of chest puffing with one of the other lads, and the two fought until they were too exhausted to land another blow. Nothing out of the ordinary."

Excitement replaced the relief coursing through Jacek. "Who won?"

Stefan threw his head back and laughed. "First of all, it was no fight—unless you consider two pups wrestling a fight. Second of all, there was no clear winner. Eh, Marcin?"

Marcin nodded.

"When a group of us left for the village," Stefan continued, "Filip removed himself to the bunk room, no doubt to sulk and lick his wounds." Stefan's dark eyes fastened on Jacek's. "He's a good lad. He'll learn. But he stands in a big shadow, yes?"

Jacek's shadow. Not that Jacek had brought him into that shadow. Rather, Filip had stepped into it himself and, with the impatience of youth, had grown frustrated that his prowess as a warrior was still being shaped. Rather than embrace the fact that he needed additional honing—not to mention an actual turn or two in battle—Filip chose to direct his rage at Jacek. Sometimes he arrowed that exasperation at Oliwia. Jacek could take—even understand—the venom Filip directed at him, but he drew a hard line when Filip vented his frustration on her.

Dawid, another of Jacek's brothers-in-arms and a stalwart of Biaska's garrison, sauntered into the barracks, pulling Jacek from his contemplations.

"Did someone die?"

One corner of Jacek's mouth quirked. "No, I was merely searching for Filip."

"Ah. I saw him in the tiltyard. I believe he is fighting an army of savage Tatars, from which he will save us all."

Jacek let out an amused snort. "Does he spar with others or with air?"

"Most likely air by now since he's bloodied every lad brave enough to take up the challenge."

Jacek's chest puffed with pride. He couldn't help himself. "Perhaps he'll give me a turn."

Stefan dropped his head to one side. "I daresay he's none too fond of you lately, lord-brother. Best watch your back."

"Why?"

"Says you don't treat him fairly," Marcin chuffed.

More likely, I treat him too fairly. "Well, then, I'll invite him to exercise his frustrations on me." Instinctively, Jacek's hand went to the hilt of his sabre.

"Perhaps I'll pretend I'm a Tatar and give him the chance to lop my head off."

Jacek exited the barracks with the men's laughter ringing in his ears and strode through the inner bailey that led to the tiltyard in the outer ward. Here, he came upon Filip, alone, thrusting and parrying with his sabre, his żupan discarded on the grass and his linen shirt stuck to his spindly torso with sweat. Not so different, Jacek imagined, from himself at sixteen.

Jacek stood a little behind Filip and to his left. The boy was so intent on his swordplay that he didn't realize he was being observed. An inner dialogue began inside Jacek's head as he shifted his weight to one leg and crossed his arms over his chest.

Don't bring the blade up so high. You're presenting a bigger target, and you'll be gutted by a more skilled swordsman.

Spare steps. You'll exhaust yourself taking giant strides like that, or worse, tangle yourself up in your own feet and end up on your backside.

That's it! Better.

No, no, no! What did I teach you about the thrust? Dart in, dart out! You're throwing your shoulder way too forcefully into the action and placing yourself in peril of losing your balance.

While Filip's left hand was his dominant one, he was swinging his sabre with his right. His motions were awkward, unlike the smoother movements when he grasped the blade in his dominant hand, but Jacek was encouraged by the boy's progress. He himself could fight with either hand, and the skill had saved his neck more than once.

Jacek bent his knee and braced his clasped hands upon it. The change in stance apparently caught Filip's eye, for he whirled.

"What are *you* doing here?"

"Watching you dance."

Chest heaving, Filip lowered his blade and leveled a glower on Jacek. "I am not dancing."

Jacek brought himself upright. "On this, we agree. While I am heartened to see you practicing, your movements would be more fluid if you *were* dancing."

69

The boy wiped a forearm across his sweaty brow, plastering his light brown curls to his forehead. "You make no sense, brother."

"Swordplay is a dance. Your steps should be nimble, light." Jacek took several strides toward him. "Think how your feet move when you dance with a maid. You do not take plodding, giant steps that will cause her to stumble."

"Are you saying my steps are too wide?"

"Too wide, too heavy. Your strokes are still too broad. Too dramatic. You offer your chest and belly as tempting targets to a foe."

Smirking, Filip jutted a hip and parked his free fist upon it. "I suppose you're here to teach me, or did my sister send you to fetch me?" The word "sister" fell from his lips with derision.

Schooling his features, Jacek advanced with deliberate steps, hands held out, palms up. "I have already taught you, as have others. Perhaps you need to put that training to better use."

The smirk flew from Filip's face, replaced by a grim line. He straightened and threw his shoulders back. "Fine. Let's go, old man."

Another two steps and Jacek was within arm's length. "Are you sure you want this? I have no wish to hurt you." They were dealing with real blades made of sharpened steel, not the practice sort crafted of wood.

"Oh, I doubt you'll have to worry about it." Filip switched the sabre to his left hand and held it to his side at hip height.

If it's a fight you want, then it is a fight you shall get.

Jacek closed his left hand over his scabbard, which hung to his left from belt loops. With his right hand, he reached over and slowly unsheathed the blade, giving Filip ample time to change his mind. The lad didn't. Too much pride inflated Filip's opinion of himself, and Jacek reckoned the arrogant pup was due for a deflating. Who better than his brother-in-law? Someone else might be so annoyed with Filip as to hurt him.

With a grin, Jacek tossed his hilt in the air, catching it with his left hand. "I give you the advantage."

He brought the blade to his face and made a small bow, never taking his eyes from Filip. His body went into a familiar stance, open at a forty-five-degree angle, knees slightly bent. Right foot leading his left, he held his blade in a ready position perpendicular to the ground and waited for Filip's first tell.

To his credit, his brother-in-law took his time sizing Jacek up. They had done this before, many, many times, so Filip was familiar with Jacek's style, but never before had their swordplay carried this gravity.

Curling the fingers of his right hand, Jacek beckoned the boy. "Come," he taunted, "show me how you are going to best me."

As Jacek had anticipated, fury flared in Filip's eyes and he sprang forward, shoulder down like a charging bull. Jacek pivoted to the side. With his free hand, he shoved the youth's shoulder harder than necessary, sending him sprawling in the dirt, facedown. Jacek rested the tip of his sabre against Filip's nape.

"Lesson one: Never let your opponent draw you into the first strike by goading you. Control your anger. Don't let it cloud your mind as you did just now."

"You know nothing of what was in my mind." Filip spat in the dirt.

"Perhaps not every detail, but you signaled your strike long before you launched it, giving me ample time to plan. Never announce your intention to your enemy." Jacek withdrew his blade and stepped aside so Filip could haul himself up.

Filip leaped to his feet and took up position once more. Blades of wet spring grass and dirt clung to his cheek, and Jacek suppressed a laugh.

This time, Jacek struck first, a quick thrust that caught Filip by surprise. The lad reacted swiftly, but Jacek had already backstepped out of reach.

"Ha! You missed!" Filip crowed.

"Did I? What happened to your right sleeve?"

Filip glanced down at the fresh slice in the fabric. Beneath it, a matching slice on his forearm welled with blood. Jacek took advantage of the distraction by pinioning Filip's left wrist and the sabre it clutched. Filip turned wide eyes on him just as Jacek touched the tip of his own sabre to the lad's throat. "Lesson two: Never assume your opponent is slower or less skilled than you, no matter his age or appearance."

Jacek released him with a little shove and retook his stance. Filip swallowed, his breaths coming rapidly. "You're not even winded," he protested.

"I'm delighted you noticed. Now try again. You're making this far too easy. I might add that warriors do not whine."

For the next several minutes, Jacek indulged him, and they exchanged parries, strikes, thrusts, and deflections. Though he anticipated nearly all of Filip's moves, he was nonetheless impressed by his brother-in-law's more tempered approach and quick feet. The lad had been practicing hard, and once he got his anger under control, his progress showed itself. At times, Jacek had to actually work to ward him off.

Filip's labored breathing and continual brow mopping signaled the time for the lesson was nearly at an end, so Jacek imparted his final message. "Lesson three: Never, ever speak with scorn about or to my wife, your sister." Jacek waited for him to lunge and disarmed him, bringing the point of his sabre to Filip's chest. "Especially not in my presence." Filip was gasping now, and while Jacek had barely broken a sweat, he too felt the need to catch his breath. Stepping back, he held his sabre upright in a salute before sheathing it. "We are done here. Good match."

With a nod, Filip fairly folded to the ground. Jacek flopped beside him. "How is the wound?"

Filip prized the rent in his sleeve open, revealing a line of crusted blood on his skin approximately three inches long. "Not much of a wound."

The moments stretched, and when Filip's breathing finally evened out, he muttered, "I simply wish to be regarded as a grown man, a soldier capable of taking charge of my own life. Yet I am treated like a clumsy child who will melt into tears over every blow dealt me, physical or otherwise. And that is my sister's doing."

Jacek arched an eyebrow. "You do know the men see you as being coddled by me because you're my brother, yes?"

The surprise in Filip's eyes told him this was news. "When? Who?"

"Shall we revisit the night you fell asleep while at sentry? I could have, should have, assigned that duty to a more seasoned soldier, one who would have taken advantage and slept for several hours so he could remain alert while on duty. The men knew I held that time specially for you. I nearly spared you from sentry duty altogether, which is what I should have done. Kept it to the qualified men instead. As it was, you—"

"I was careless and fell asleep despite the few previous hours of slumber. Yes, I know. I am constantly reminded how young and *unqualified* I truly am," Filip grumbled.

"Revel in the fact the men cajole you. Shunning you altogether would prove far worse, for it would show they have no respect and no further use for you. As it is, they may consider you a whelp, but you are *their* whelp."

Filip opened his mouth and closed it as if Jacek's remark stumped him. Then he opened it once more. "It is Liwi who holds me back from campaign. As it is, she barely let me go on this … this *horse* errand. Her protectiveness is too much. She stifles me."

Jacek's hackles rose, and he swiveled his head to give Filip a searing look. He understood the miseries Oliwia had endured for her brother—and for him—and he would give the youth no quarter when it came to her. "Firstly, we have had no campaigns to go on for many a year now. Secondly, and more importantly, that very protectiveness you complain about has saved your hide countless times. Mine as well. She, of all people, does not deserve your selfish ire. You say you are treated like a babe. Look inward and ask yourself if it is not because you *act* like a babe."

Filip met his gaze, narrowing his silver-gray eyes. "When has she saved my life?"

"Do you not remember when we first met? You, she, and Romek Mazur were the only living beings in a burning village in Muscovy. You were about to be slaughtered—or worse, sold into slavery—and it was her courage that kept either fate befalling you."

Memories resurfaced in Jacek's consciousness, and he smiled as he recalled once more the grimy-faced girl whose fierceness had caught him by surprise that day. She had been battling in vain with Mazur, yet she had been ready to launch herself at Jacek despite the fact he was armored and horsed. Indeed, she would have taken on his entire squad of hussars, who had happened upon the devastation. She had placed herself squarely in harm's way in order to save her six-year-old brother.

73

"And when you arrived at Biaska," Jacek continued, "she made untold sacrifices to not only see you safe but to ensure you were elevated to a lord's station. She is the reason you now train to be a hussar of Biaska. Your horse, your armor, your status are owed to her alone. You are where you are because of the very sister you find so much fault with."

"But I became *your* charge. *You* taught me what I know."

"Because Lord Eryk declared it so, and your sister implored me to look after you. It was not my choice." Jacek cast his eyes down and pulled up a tuft of grass, tossing it into the wind. "And apparently, I have not done a good job of it." He turned his gaze once more to his brother-in-law. "It may be time for you to continue your training elsewhere, as I did. Start fresh at an estate where no one knows you and you know no one." *Where my shadow does not exist.*

Jacek noted the alarm in Filip's eyes. It faded quickly as comprehension seemed to catch hold, and he gave Jacek a nod. He pulled up his own tuft of grass and tossed it to the side. "Go to another place, to learn from someone else, where I can build up my confidence."

"Confidence and pride you have, and they are important, but humility is equally important, as is the quest to learn. I must have failed to teach you those last two qualities, but perhaps someone else can do what I did not. I tell you now what I have found to be the most important rules to live by: Never assume you have mastered all the lessons, for you never will. Always strive to become better, wiser, stronger—not merely of body, but of mind." He tapped his temple with his forefinger.

Filip faced forward, staring at the vast field before them. "How did my sister save *your* life?"

She married a man she did not love.

"She …" Jacek hesitated. Was the story his to tell?

"I was under investigation for crimes I did not commit. She suggested to Lord Eryk that he send me to Silnyród, out of Sandomierz's deputy *starosta*'s reach, until they found and prosecuted the true culprit."

The first part was truth, but the second was fabrication. He covertly crossed himself and asked God to forgive him his lie. Preserving Filip's esteemed image of Eryk, he reckoned, was reason enough for the sin.

CHAPTER 10

When Family and Duty Collide

Jacek had been summoned by Erwin about one of the new horses, and he hurled himself down the main stairs into the great hall, where he was waylaid by all manner of staff pestering him with questions. Why hadn't he chosen the back staircase? He spotted Oliwia entering from the kitchens and sent them toward her, reckoning she would likely know the answers far better than he anyway. She actually *enjoyed* overseeing Biaska's affairs and was far more suited to it than he. In fact, her abilities rivaled most landed lords of his acquaintance. He, on the other hand, was a tactician, a leader of men in his prime, not a stately landlord who relished being enmeshed in harvest yields and villagers' petty squabbles.

She raised her hand to him and mouthed, "I must talk to you."

Waving, he mouthed back, "Yes, later." He was fairly certain he knew what the subject would be. Maurycy had been hounding staff about how they conducted their business, while his clergyman scribbled notes. He had been snooping around the guard house and armory with the same manner of questions, but Henryk had effectively shooed him away. Castle staff had no such luxury, for Maurycy was a lord and exploited his supremacy with intimidation, or so the servants had informed Oliwia. And Jacek and Oliwia both believed them, but they had no proof beyond the servants' words.

Moreover, he and Lady Sabina had been disrupting the entire household with various deceitful schemes during the week since they had arrived. Mary, the serving girl of whom Filip was fond, had, on one occasion, burst into tears and run to Beata after Maurycy's abuse. Beata was a mighty force whose temper gave even Jacek pause, but when she confronted Maurycy, he fed her with lies, alleging Oliwia had confided in him she was dissatisfied with Beata's service. He even planted a seed that much of Beata's help, some of whom had come from Wąskadroga, would be returning to that estate because Lady Oliwia was so displeased. Furthermore, he claimed Oliwia agreed Maurycy was entitled to these domestics and was arranging for the transfer even now. The "news" had nearly reduced the old cook to tears herself.

After an hour spent first calming then convincing Beata the claim was false, Oliwia had gone to Maurycy. The toad had feigned shock that such an "unjust accusation" had been leveled at him. He had then cleverly turned the tables on Beata, saying she and her staff were weary of Lady Oliwia's demands and fed up with accommodating him and his contingent; her resentment had motivated her to invent untruths about him. Oliwia had been stuck.

Lord, but he would be relieved when these agitators finally left— whenever that might be. Their plans were vague at best.

Deciding on a set of stairs leading to the solar's private entrance, he ducked out of the great hall and quietly ascended the steps so as to not alert the staff he was leaving. When he reached the solar's hidden door, he discovered it slightly ajar. He stilled at the sound of shuffling coming from within the chamber and peered through the slit. A woman, her back to him, was riffling papers atop the desk. One of Biaska's ledger books lay open, and several missives were strewn across one corner.

Recognizing the stranger, he stealthily stepped through the door. "What do you search for, Lady Sabina?"

She jumped, yelped, and spun all at once. Shock flashed in her eyes, and she hastily turned back to the desk and slammed the journal shut, then began tidying in a frenzy. "I was, um, your wife asked me to … I was searching for a, um, map so we can plan our departure."

"Which is imminent, I assume?" He kept his voice even.

"Y-yes."

He took measured steps toward her, his eyes scanning the documents. "How did you come to use the solar's private entrance? Only the castle's inhabitants know of its existence."

She whipped her head up and trilled nervously. "A maid showed me, but she did not warn me it was private. For that misunderstanding, I apologize. I-I was … It was quite crowded in the great hall, and I thought to use a different route."

He pulled himself up to his full height and crowded her. "There is no need for you to arrange the desk. Perhaps you should return to your quarters—through the *main* door."

She had been frozen in mid-fluster, but she seemed to recover. Her lips curled up in a feline smile, and her eyes glittered with devilry. Raising her forefinger, she rested it lightly beneath his chin. "You are a most attractive man. I was struck from the moment I laid eyes on you. I would enjoy becoming better acquainted."

The corners of his mouth twitched, as though he fought a grin.

She made a clucking noise and moved her body close to his. "My idea intrigues you, yes?"

He broadened the smile, though it lacked mirth. "Not in the least."

She stepped away, and her face shifted with dread. "You will not tell your wife, will you?"

"What? That you tried to seduce me to prevent me telling her I caught you going through her personal papers?"

Anger now commandeered her features. "I will deny it. I will say it was you who tried to seduce me."

"I venture my wife will see it for the lie it is, and she will be far less tolerant of your presence than I. Might I suggest instead that you and your party make preparations to leave as soon as possible? I daresay this is a good time to depart, with the weather turning."

She picked up her skirts, turned, and took the stairs rapidly.

Oliwia blew out an exasperated breath. Trying to snatch her husband's attention for a real conversation was like capturing mist in her fist. The only time she had him to herself was at night, when he was little interested in talk, but she had two serious matters to discuss: Silnyród—which necessitated summarizing the sad state of Biaska's finances—and Maurycy. Neither would be light conversations to anticipate with relish.

She marched to the kitchens and reviewed the menu with the old cook, Beata. When she exited, she made a quick sweep of the great hall, once more seeking Jacek, to no avail. She glanced out several windows in varying perspectives looking upon the gardens, the bailey, the gatehouse, the tiltyard. He was nowhere in sight.

Intent on ascending to the nursery to check on Piotr, Oliwia picked up her skirts and spun on her heel. Dizziness engulfed her. Nausea swept over her. Her vision dimmed, and she felt her body drift down, down, down. Concerned voices buzzed around her, but they were obliterated by the blood whooshing in and out of her ears. She latched on to one thread— Tamara's voice—that wafted through the cotton stuffing her head.

The air cleared, and Oliwia realized Tamara was holding her up and peering at her. "Are you all right, Lady Oliwia?"

Oliwia pressed a hand to her suddenly clammy forehead. "I-I think so."

Myriad voices now pierced the fog. "Mama! Mama!" Margaret cried, fat tears rolling down her cheeks. Adam watched Oliwia with owl eyes.

"I am fine, truly." Oliwia slid from Tamara's grasp, kneeled before her children, and opened her arms wide. "Children, Mama is fine. See?" Adam and Margaret rushed into her arms, and as she hugged them to her, she looked up at Tamara and whispered, "I spun too fast and made myself dizzy. Nothing more."

Tamara's eyebrows drew together in a skeptical frown. Oliwia discreetly swept a fine sheen from her forehead and looked around, masking her embarrassment.

"Children, why don't we go upstairs and see what Piotr is up to?"

Adam pulled back and pinched his nose. "Aw, he's naught but a boring baby. He cries all the time and smells."

"As did you, once," Tamara admonished. "We will go read some stories, yes?"

Margaret wriggled away and danced a circle. "I want to hear *The Princess of the Brazen Mountain*!"

Adam mimicked slashing a great whip through the air. "Ho! Magical Whip! To right and left skip! And do what I will!"

"Thank you," Oliwia mouthed to Tamara.

Tamara shrugged. "Of course. I am glad to see your cheeks are pink again. You resembled a specter before."

Oliwia rose, slowly this time, and was in the midst of excusing herself when a commotion came from the main doors to the great hall. In strode Jacek, with a young man on his heels whom Oliwia recognized as a messenger from Podolia. Her husband ground to a halt and turned toward her. Surprise flickered in his eyes, as if he only now became aware of his surroundings.

He sniffed the air. "Have I missed the meal?"

"I will have a plate prepared for you. You appear to be on urgent business."

"That I am. Thank you, my lady." He bowed his head and made for the solar.

Her mind awhirl with what that business could be, Oliwia fired off instructions to a nearby serving maid, determined to catch up to her husband. Any business involving Podolia was her business as well. She ignored the sour taste that had been coating the inside of her mouth since her dizzy spell. Time enough to deal with it, but now was not that time.

"I will read these quickly," her husband's voice boomed from the solar, "and let you know whether I need you to stay for a reply or whether you may be on your way."

"Yes, m'lord," came a disembodied voice.

The door was ajar, and Oliwia pushed her way through. Two pairs of eyes widened and swung to her.

"Hello, Gerard. I expect you would like a meal and a wash after your long ride, yes?"

Gerard removed his cap and gave her a deep bow. His toothy grin shone bright white in his grime-covered face. "Perhaps the wash first, then the meal, if my lady would be so kind? And if Beata has any extra—"

"Apple tarts? I remember." She gave Jacek a sidelong glance; his attention was fixed on a large red seal fastened to one of the letters. Mary, the serving maid, swept in with a tray wider than her frame, and Oliwia motioned for her to set it on the desk, behind which Jacek stood and scowled at no one in particular.

To Mary, she said, "See Gerard is fed something hearty. And if Beata has any apple tarts, tell her I said he should have at least two."

Mary curtsied. "Of course, Lady Oliwia."

"Thank you, m'lady." The grinning Gerard took an awkward goose step, trying to bow while simultaneously following Mary.

Oliwia closed the door and crossed the chamber to the desk. Jacek looked up and deepened his scowl. He clutched the open letter, his eyes wild and stormy, like a wind-tossed sea.

Oliwia squared her shoulders. "He must eat, Jacek, whether he awaits your reply or is free to leave."

His entire expression transformed, the scowl and storm falling away. "What? Oh, of course he must eat." He waved the letter in the air before depositing it on the desk and opening a second one.

Oliwia slipped into one of the carved chairs meant for visitors and craned her head toward the missive upon the desktop. It lay folded in on itself along its crease lines, and she couldn't make out any words. He discarded the next letter atop the first and opened the third and final one. To keep herself from fidgeting overmuch, she tugged the short lace ruffles attached to the cuffs on the sleeves of her indigo velvet gown. Then she inspected the intricate stitches woven into the gold braiding decorating her cuffs. She loved the gown. Jacek had purchased it during his travels several years ago, along with a partial bolt of the lace. After alterations to fit her small frame, she had taken to wearing it often when he was home.

80

The last letter fluttered from Jacek's hand and glided onto the desk. He raised his head and swallowed, his Adam's apple bobbing in his muscled neck. His eyes strayed to the flames wavering in the hearth.

All thoughts of gowns and lace and gifts raced from her head. "What is it?"

He swung his gaze to hers and locked on. "I have been recruited by the Grand Hetman of the Crown to fight the Ottomans. He is mustering every able-bodied hussar to come to our country's aid."

Oliwia's heart stuttered in her chest. "Have they declared war on the Commonwealth, then?"

"Not yet, but they are on the verge, according to Hetman Żółkiewski, and he aims to be ready for the invasion."

She pointed at the letters on the desk. "Is one of those from him?"

Jacek nodded. "The others are from Lesław and Klemens Matejko. They were supposed to arrive first and alert me that the hetman's recruitment letter was on its way."

"To what purpose?"

"To prepare me or convince me, I suppose. Though they needn't have."

Oliwia shook her head as if it would clear up her questions. "So the hetman has recruited you … That means what, exactly?"

"I go to the border. It is my duty."

"But why you?" she cried. "You do not live in Podolia."

His eyes softened. "Lest you forget, sweet, Silnyród lies not far from the border. He is recruiting whomever has holdings in the region, whether they live there or not."

"When are you to go? *Where* are you to go?"

"I am to leave as soon as I gather provisions and men."

Her heart sank. "What of our guests? Surely you will stay until their departure."

He proceeded to tell her an astonishing tale of discovering Lady Sabina shuffling through her papers. "I suggested to her now would be a good time to leave."

"What do you suppose she was looking for?"

"Information about the estate's finances that Maurycy might find useful? I put everything aside that she pulled out so you can see for yourself." He pointed to a stack of documents atop a ledger book.

"I thank you for that. I will review them myself. Now tell me where it is you are going."

"We are to meet north of the Dniester River, not far from Kamieniec Podolski. First, I will travel to Silnyród and join up with Lesław. I will assure myself the fortress is secured and adequately garrisoned, that the commander who takes over in Lesław's absence is competent."

"And if the fortress is not secure or the commander is not competent?"

Jacek lifted one of the letters. "They are. Command will fall to Florian and his squad. You remember Florian? He fought beside me when we wrested Biaska from Antonin."

She nodded dumbly. "What does Pan Matejko's letter say?"

Jacek blew out a breath. "He pleads with me to heed the call and come."

"Why should he have to plead? I thought you said you had no choice!" She hated the quavering, high pitch of her voice, for it exposed her fears and her soft underbelly.

Jacek stepped around the desk, sank into the chair beside her, and took her hands in his. They were so large as to nearly swallow hers. So powerful. So adept at showing tenderness yet able to commit terrible acts of violence. The man who was capable of folding a babe a fraction of his size into his strong arms was also capable of ripping out a man's innards while that man pleaded for his life … and showing no emotion while he did it.

She had witnessed both the loving side and the savage side of Jacek Dąbrowski.

But that was the way of the warrior, wasn't it? And he was a warrior. She had known this day would come. What she found surprising was that it had taken so long, though that fact made his going no easier to swallow with grace.

"Klemens pleads with me because he knows I have compelling reasons to stay here. He also knows that Stanisław Żółkiewski, for all his power and the title he carries for life, does not have the sway he once did, and many will not heed his call."

"I don't understand."

Jacek looked down at their joined hands and absently twirled her ruby wedding ring. "Do you recall talk of the Battle of Orynin back in 1618?"

"No." She had been busy grieving the loss of the child she'd been carrying in her womb. Though she had not been pregnant long, something had gone terribly wrong, and God had claimed the little one before it had ever been born. Even thinking on it caused tears to sting her eyes. Thank God for Piotr. And now …

"No, of course not. That was when … Well, suffice to say Żółkiewski no longer has the confidence of the magnates after losing that battle against Crimean and Budjak Tatars. Though the Commonwealth fielded fifteen thousand troops, those forces were divided because their composition was so diverse."

A familiar glimmer shone in his eyes. Her husband relished military facts and the minute details behind them, and that very attention made him so good at what he did. But while she loved to see the passion that drove him, she resented it at the same time.

He slid his hands from hers. "The armies, you see, were a mix of Crown quarter troops garrisoned at the border, a levy of knights—the *pospolite ruszenie*—provided by estates similar to Biaska, Zaporozhian Cossacks, and the magnates' own private armies. Those magnates did not wish to follow the hetmans' orders, so one large camp splintered into three smaller, quite disjointed groups."

He reached across her and helped himself to a few hunks of cheese heaped on the tray. "Five thousand Tatars under Khan Temir—or Kantymir—crossed the Prut and entered Podolia. Next came a ten-thousand-strong unit under a different Tatar leader. Both armies attacked, concentrating first on Tomasz Zamoyski's camp. Żółkiewski, who is no friend to Zamoyski, refused to come to his aid. The crown grand hetman is quoted as saying, 'First, he has to obey the old hetman instead of giving orders.'" Jacek popped a morsel in his mouth.

Oliwia let out a little gasp. "Surely he came to help in the end!" Żółkiewski was Jacek's idol and had been for as long as she'd known her husband.

Jacek pulled in and released a great, dejected breath. "Alas, no. Several other magnates sent hundreds of their own riflemen to save Zamoyski."

Oliwia was no student of military history, but the drama held her captive. "Then what?"

"The forces finally united under Żółkiewski. They prepared for a major battle the next day, but that battle never came. Instead, the Tatars slipped away and went north, pushing into the southeastern corner of the Commonwealth, where they ransacked an immense swath of territory from Sieniawa to Jampol." A haunted look flickered across his face. "They enslaved thousands of men and women, burned countless towns and villages, and captured a horde of plunder before returning to their homeland only weeks later."

The distress in Jacek's eyes was unmistakable, and her heart wept for him, for the memories of his own captivity that had left indelible scars upon his soul.

"Deserved or not—" His voice cracked, and he cleared his throat. "The, uh, the blame for the catastrophe came to rest on Hetman Żółkiewski. He was so dispirited that he offered the king his resignation, but King Zygmunt rejected it. I expect the old hetman still carries that guilt like a cloak of stone upon his shoulders." After a pause, he slapped his palms against his thighs and reached for a dried apricot. She slid the tray toward him.

Gathering up more bits of food, he winked at her, the sorrow erased from his expression and tone. "Then, of course, there is the matter of the festering cesspool that is Moldavia itself. The Cossacks' continued raiding and their burning of Constantinople suburbs does not help relations either," he said dryly. "Now there are tales of an Ottoman army building south of the border. That Samuel Otwinowski, Poland's envoy who has lived among the Turks for years, was sent packing by the new grand vizier with threats of war ringing in his ears is alarming. Those actions have convinced both Otwinowski and Żółkiewski that war is imminent." A gleam lit his eyes. "And the hetman has asked for *me*."

Had Jacek's chest puffed an inch or three?

Oliwia poured wine into two pewter goblets and handed him one. "What of Moldavia's ruler? Where does he stand in this mess?"

84

"Gaspar Grazziani? He is—or was—another Ottoman vassal. He has recently begun secret talks with King Zygmunt to bring that country under Polish rule. He's gone so far as to pledge tens of thousands of his own troops to fight the Turks. After weighing his alternatives, he must have decided that Polish rule is a much more favorable proposition."

She shook her head. "These leaders are behaving like children fighting over a toy."

Jacek chomped on a hunk of bread and washed it down with a gulp of wine. "Well, one of them *is* a boy: the sultan, Osman II. A very ambitious boy of sixteen years, who is compelled to show he is a man. After he ascended to the throne in 1618, he had the audacity to send King Zygmunt a letter threatening war *and* the burning of Kraków. This was how he chose to prove to his empire that while he had no whiskers to shave, and his testicles had only recently dropped, he had fully entered manhood." He let out a derisive snort and gobbled up a handful of almonds.

Oliwia leaned her elbow on the desk and rested her cheek in her palm. "Have you considered becoming a statesman so you can tell them all how to behave?" Though she said so in jest, she reckoned it wasn't a bad idea.

Jacek chuckled. "I do not have the patience. I would simply dispatch them all. No, you make a far better statesman than I. What a shame that women do not hold such offices." He bopped the end of her nose with his forefinger. "Then again, I'm selfish. I do not care to share my wife with the world and wave good-bye as she rides off on one diplomatic mission after another."

"Hmm. Perhaps you have an idea what I feel whenever *you* ride off." She released an extended sigh. "You wish to go, yes?"

He brushed crumbs from his hands. "It is not a matter of want. I must. Żółkiewski needs a turn at redemption, and he needs men like me. How can I refuse? It is my—"

"Duty. Yes, I do know, though I would remind you of your duty to Biaska and your family."

A scowl creased his forehead, and she rushed on. "And Filip?"

Jacek's uneasiness was evident in the way he shifted his big body. To his credit, he did not look away but fixed those startlingly blue eyes on her. "He will insist on going, and I do not intend denying him."

"And what of training at Pawel's estate?" Jacek had told her about crossing swords with Filip and how the two had discussed his going away to train at a different estate. The estate Jacek had in mind belonged to one of his comrades from the slave galley—a far safer place than Żółkiewski's expedition.

"He will get as much, if not more, training in the camp with the men."

She fought down the panic welling inside of her. "Then you want him to go! Jacek, he is only sixteen!"

He tenderly tucked an escaped strand behind her ear. "He's nearly seventeen, and this campaign will be a good opportunity for him, especially with me in charge of the banner. There is only so much a warrior can learn through sparring and practicing with soldiers who are also his friends. The rest of his mettle can only be honed in situations such as these."

"I do not find any comfort in your words," she grumbled.

He let out a sigh. "No, I don't expect you do."

This day had been coming, yet she wasn't prepared. "So you would take him away and lead him into a battle where he could be killed." Her tone carried no sting, merely resignation.

"I have no intention of leading him into battle. It likely won't even come to battle—just the signing of one more treaty. But, Liwi, it is time. He is ready. He wants this, and you will not be able to hold him back. If you try, you will only earn his contempt. He has grown up with this, been trained for this, and it is his most fervent wish."

She fought tears threatening to leak from her eyes. "I cannot lose you both," she whispered.

He cupped her chin and brushed his thumb over her jaw. "Sweet Liwi, you're not going to lose either of us." Tilting his head, he searched her eyes. "As God is my witness, everything will be all right."

She slid from his grasp. His hand fell away, and the air thickened between them until she thought she might not catch breath.

At last, he broke the choking silence. "Believe that I do not wish to leave you—"

Oliwia looked at him dead on. "You are not leaving me. I'm going with you."

He blinked—rapidly. "Pardon?"

CHAPTER 11

The Plan

Certainly, Jacek had heard her wrong.

Oliwia cinched her arms over her chest. "I said I'm going with you."

He shook his head vigorously. "No, Liwi. You will stay here. A soldier's camp is no place for a wife." She had lost all reason if she believed he would take her with him.

"But it is a place for camp followers, prostitutes, and *other* men's wives. Those women follow armies all the time."

"Not noble wives. Besides, as you well know, no women are *ever* allowed in a hussar camp."

"My mother followed my father." Apparently, she was choosing to dismiss the rule entirely.

"That did not end well." He cringed after the statement tumbled from him, but it was too late to reel it back in.

She seemed to realize the truth of his words, though, and changed tack. "I came from a peasants' village."

One side of his mouth quirked. "But that does not make you a peasant, Lady Oliwia Armstrong Dąbrowska of Carlisle and Biaska."

"Humph." She looked away.

The truth of it was he could refuse the hetman, but since getting the letter, the notion of charging back onto the battlefield had grown more shrill. The pull to test himself, to hone his dulled skills, the seductive call to adventure and its rewards thrummed inside of him. He might be elevated to a colonel! But he couldn't leave until they had rid themselves of that snake, Maurycy, and his spy, Lady Sabina. Podolia called to him at the same time the menace they presented compelled him to remain at Biaska. With Maurycy and his retinue gone, the castle would settle back to a normal, gentle rhythm that brought his wife contentment. Perhaps it was this very upheaval motivating Oliwia to insist on accompanying him.

"Is this to do with Maurycy?" he ventured. "Are you seeking a reason to escape his fetid presence?"

She raised her stubborn chin. "He has nothing to do with my decision. I wish to inspect my holding in Podolia."

"Silnyród?" he sputtered. *Why the devil ...?* No, this was a ruse.

Gently, he pinched his wife's chin between his thumb and finger and dragged her head back so she faced him once more. Fire and ice shone in her crystal-blue eyes, and he steeled himself for battle. "My sweet, I am a soldier. A good soldier. And one reason I am a good soldier is because when I am on campaign, I am focused solely on the mission and the men I lead. I eat it, I sleep it, I breathe it day and night. If you are with me, I cannot do that. I shall be split in two and will not be capable of doing right by you *or* the men I command. Do you not see that I shall be diminished by my worry for your safety more than I already am? If I am leading a charge, my thoughts will be with you and whether you are safe in camp and if my rightful place is back with you, protecting you from the enemy, who might swoop in and carry you off. I have seen formidable men falter and not do what's normally second nature to them in battle because their minds were elsewhere. They were too troubled by what was happening or *could* happen to their women. Besides, who will look after the children?"

"Tamara has offered to, and the children adore her. They won't even miss me." Was that hesitation in Oliwia's eyes? Surely she couldn't separate herself from her babes. No, he would count on them being the tether that held her here.

He resolved to forge ahead with logic. "You are still nursing Piotr."

"I am weaning him. He has teeth now."

A question that had been swimming in his mind surfaced. "Why is it you have nursed him this long? I don't recall you doing so with Margaret."

"The baba said it is good for the child." Oliwia's cheeks pinkened in a sure sign something else was afoot. "She also said that as long as a woman nurses, she cannot get with child."

"And you do not wish to get with child."

"No."

That one simple word trapped the wind in his lungs, though he shouldn't have been surprised. Childbirth was a dangerous proposition. While the birth of one child after another would have pleased *him* immensely, Oliwia was as fertile as freshly turned soil in a spring rain, and he understood her reluctance.

He came fully upright. "And should you become pregnant while following me on campaign?"

Her pretty mouth opened and closed, and calculations seemed to spool behind her eyes. Several beats passed before she said, *"Si non caste tamen caute."*

"If not chastely, at least with precautions?" he translated from Latin. "Are you suggesting abstinence? That, I am certain, would prove nigh on impractical."

"We will take precautions," she said primly.

He let out a guffaw. "The only precaution I can fathom is twenty leagues between us. At the very least." Putting several days of riding between them would provide a deterrent … most days.

"There are herbs and potions and methods and … ways."

His eyebrows shot to his hairline. "Potions and herbs are dangerous. As for 'methods and ways,' pardon me if I am not a believer. I have seen far too many babes born despite supposed precautions taken. Margaret is proof, not that I regret our daughter for one instant. But if—"

Her nimble fingers pinched his lips together. He had no doubt he resembled a fish. "Shush!" she hissed. "You are mocking me."

"No, I am not," came out in garbled fashion. She released him. "Liwi, I am trying to be pragmatic. For both our sakes." He infused a plea into his voice.

An obstinate set he knew far too well firmed her features. "I am being pragmatic as well. Silnyród is my responsibility. I am its lady and have neglected it far too long. It is past time I traveled there and evaluated it myself ... for a number of reasons. Therefore. I. Am. Coming."

Heat rose from his chest, up his neck, and set his face ablaze. "Over my rotting corpse are you coming." He wagged a finger at her. "Don't think I won't lock you up in the dungeon if you insist on this ... this madness. Do you realize how far it is?"

She rose to her feet, likely up on the tips of her toes, and puffed herself out like an owl in winter. "If you're insinuating that I am too delicate to travel such a distance, let me remind you of our travels in 1610 when we went from Vyatov—all the way inside Muscovy—to Biaska in Poland's far-flung western border. I am fully capable of the journey, and you cannot prevent me from taking it."

He stood and towered over her, glowering with every ounce of his being.

She let out another humph and swept from the solar with a swirl of her skirts, leaving the door ajar.

For long moments, he stood stock-still, glaring at the door. He was still imitating a statue when Mary re-entered the chamber to ask whether the messenger could go.

"Not yet. I have several replies to write."

He scrawled out three quick replies and had Gerard brought in. No sooner had the messenger departed, leaving the door ajar, than Maurycy poked his head through the opening. Jacek rose from behind his desk, his spine a shaft of unbendable steel, despite Maurycy's congenial air. Beneath that feigned affability beat the heart of a serpent.

"What can I do for you, Pan Maurycy?" His foul mood was in no small part due to this parasite's lingering presence at Biaska.

"I thought we could discuss the matter of Wąskadroga's recompense."

"I beg your pardon? Recompense for what?"

91

"Why, for its demise. Even a stranger to Biaska can see how rich it has grown. That wealth has been acquired at the expense my family's estate."

Jacek schooled his outrage. "How so?"

Maurycy crossed his arms over his chest, his expression transforming from cordial to menacing. "Your wife murdered my father—"

"Stop right there. My wife did not *murder* your father. She defended herself against a blackguard who had already abused her and was intent on doing more harm. Furthermore, it was his own man who ran him through with a blade. Your father was still alive when Romek Mazur killed him."

Maurycy's mouth twisted into a sneer. "So you say."

"I do not merely 'say.' Many bore witness to your father's transgressions, not only on that day but during the days prior when he took this castle by treachery and force."

"It was his birthright! Biaska belonged to his cousin and therefore should have belonged to him, not some female peasant who used her wiles to seduce—"

Jacek was on him in less time than it took to blink. His hand wound so tightly around the man's neck that Maurycy's words came out choked. "In the event she has not told you, I have advised Lady Sabina it is time for you and your party to leave. I now advise you of the same. Your presence here is no longer welcome. Is that understood?"

Maurycy's fear-filled eyes slid to the side. His hands scrabbled at Jacek's choke hold as his face turned the color of a pomegranate.

"I can't hear you," Jacek snarled. He eased up when Maurycy's eyeballs rolled back in their sockets, then released him and shoved him backward.

Gasping and coughing, Maurycy doubled over and grasped his neck.

Jacek gripped the handle of his dagger. "Well?"

"I understand," Maurycy rasped. His brown eyes darkened to onyx, and he glowered at Jacek. "But I will petition the king, and you and your wife will live to regret this."

Jacek's lips hitched in a smile, though there was no joy behind it. "I very much doubt it."

He stepped to the door and summoned Stefan and another guard. "Lord Wąskaski and his party are leaving. See they are properly packed and escorted beyond Biaska's walls."

"We will see to it." Stefan turned his attention to Maurycy, pinning him with a fearsome look.

Facing Maurycy, Jacek re-seated his dagger and swept his hand toward the door, where the guards both stood. "You have much to do, so I bid you good-bye."

Maurycy straightened and shot him a razor-sharp glare. Without another utterance, he turned and stalked out.

As Jacek watched him go, a dim voice inside him questioned whether Maurycy would one day prove a dangerous enemy.

Arms and legs pumping, Jacek fairly flew across the teeming bailey toward the stables. All manner of laundresses, stable boys, poulterers, and the like bustled about the bailey, interrupting Jacek's purposeful strides and fueling his temper. A pack of dogs barked and chased one another, nearly toppling him in their play. Christ! Why were people—and animals—putting themselves in his way? All he wanted in that moment was to vent his frustrations by working alongside the horse trainer, Erwin, or better yet, by convincing a worthy opponent to give him a go in the tiltyard.

As if he had conjured that very opponent, Henryk appeared, strolling into Jacek's path at an angle. He paused and waited for his best friend to reach him.

With one casual movement, Henryk slid his leather gloves off his fingers. He broke out in his familiar smirk. "You bring to mind a teapot with all that steam rising off of you, my friend. What the devil has you so vexed?"

"Besides Maurycy and his ilk? I just ordered Stefan to have him removed from Biaska."

"Problem solved."

"No, it is not because that's not the problem." Jacek jerked a thumb over his shoulder. "Women!"

Henryk's eyebrows crawled up his forehead. "Ah. What mischief is Oliwia up to now? Surely there's not trouble in paradise."

"She insists—*insists*—on coming to Podolia with us!" Jacek threw his hands in the air. A rumble deep down in his gut told him that by denying her, however, he might have unleashed a tornado.

Henryk's eyes bugged. "We are going to Podolia? When?" A small audience gathered. "Wait." He grabbed Jacek's nape and steered him away, dropping his voice. "I can think of a better place to have this conversation."

Jacek let himself be propelled toward Henryk's abode inside the castle walls. As captain of the guard, Henryk no longer quartered in the barracks, but rather in a spacious dwelling several dozen paces from the garrison. The squat wooden house was a bit large for the eternal bachelor, who no doubt rattled about within its walls when he was home … which explained why Jacek generally found him in the guardhouse, the barracks, or the tavern.

Henryk opened the door and gave Jacek a shove. Both men ducked to avoid cracking their crowns on a low white plaster ceiling spanned by heavy wood beams.

"This calls for something stronger than piwo or wine." He motioned for Jacek to sit in one of four chairs surrounding an oak table while he stepped to a painted cupboard and pulled down an earthen jug and two cups. The table took up the largest share of the room. Beneath Jacek's boots, the wide-planked wood floor creaked under his weight.

Jacek let his eyes wander about the space, re-familiarizing himself with it. The walls, like the ceiling, were of white plaster, and two surprisingly large windows washed the room in pale light. One corner was occupied by a bed and a cupboard topped by a cross and a painting of the Black Madonna. The space was clean and comfortable, and Jacek suppressed a smile.

Henryk poured out two generous measures of wodka. "What are you smiling about?"

"This domestic side you keep so well hidden."

Henryk plopped into a perpendicular seat and clacked his cup against Jacek's. "How can I entice a sweet, comely woman to share it with me if I keep it like a pigsty?"

Jacek gaped. "Don't tell me you're considering a life of marital bliss!"

Henryk took a sip. "Why not? It certainly has worked out well for you."

Jacek snorted and swigged. "You may not think so when I'm done."

"Fair enough, my friend. So tell me everything. Start with our trip to Podolia, and then explain to me how Oliwia came to lose her mind."

Jacek held his cup aloft. "I am heartened to know I am not the only one who believes my wife has taken leave of her senses." He went on to describe the letter from the hetman.

"And you say you also received missives from Lesław and Pan Matejko? What did they say?"

"Each letter was similar to the other. They wrote to alert me to the hetman's call to arms and added their pleas that I come to his aid. It seems Żółkiewski is plagued by an inability to recruit enough troops to defend against the Ottoman army despite the gravity of the situation." A renewed ambition burgeoned inside of him, and he grew practically giddy as he contemplated a rising rank within the small force.

Colonel Dąbrowski, second in command to the crown grand hetman.

He had bristled inside when Oliwia had spoken of his "duty" to his family and the estate, for he had been fulfilling that duty for years. Here was his chance, at last, to command troops and flex his militarily strategic mind once again for Poland and the king.

Henryk grunted. "Now I understand our mission. We will need to provision."

They spent the next while discussing who to enlist for logistics—Dawid—and which men to bring and which to leave behind in defense of Biaska Castle, all the while drinking deeply from Henryk's stores.

Henryk grinned. "Now that those decisions are made, please tell me about my former betrothed and her insistence on accompanying you. I have been far too patient as it is."

There had been a time, during Jacek's enslavement, when Oliwia had believed him dead. In order to save her from a forced marriage to her late husband's depraved cousin, Henryk had proposed. Seeing no alternative, she had accepted. Fortunately for all involved, Jacek had returned to Biaska in time to stop the nuptials and wed Oliwia himself. So while Jacek knew his friend's reference was a friendly jab, it didn't prevent him wanting to punch the grin off Henryk's face.

Resisting the urge, he went on to describe Oliwia's outrageous demand that he bring her on campaign. Henryk listened thoughtfully, nodding as Jacek recounted the discussion—minus the part about chastity and pregnancy.

"You explained that we do not allow women in camp, yes?"

"She already *knows* we don't from her travels with us in '10, and yes, I reminded her of that rule."

"'Tis one Żółkiewski will definitely enforce."

Jacek threw a hand in the air with a great flourish. "I think she has a ridiculous notion that she will trail behind with the other camp followers and somehow wiggle her way into my tent every night."

"Mmm. I see no 'somehow' about it. I wager the lady has the latter correct. After all, women wiggle their way into tents all the time. It could be an obliging stranger or your wife." Henryk's grin widened.

Jacek grunted in response.

Henryk tossed back the remainder of his wodka and refilled both cups. Long moments of comfortable silence passed between them. How many drinks had they shared now? Jacek's memory blurred around the edges, along with his rational mind.

"I have the solution to your problem," Henryk announced.

"Please. I need all the advice I can get, even if I have to suffer that advice at the hands of a man who will never know what it is like to tiptoe through the shards of glass that make up a marriage."

Henryk's eyes widened. "You sound as though your marriage is shattered, but that cannot be the case. I see how you two ogle one another. And don't be so quick to dismiss me when it comes to being wedded."

Jacek stared at his friend, trying desperately to catalog words he was incapable of deciphering at the moment. For the second time that night, Henryk's name had been linked to matrimony.

The implications of "shattered marriage" did pierce his muzzy mind, however, and he shook his head so vigorously as to make his neck pop. "No, no. I simply likened the state of marriage to a landscape where one has to step cautiously to avoid being sliced, no matter how drunk one might be on wedded bliss. Not that I am drunk, mind." Jacek brushed at a tickle on his nose. "Damned flies."

Henryk chuckled. "No flies here, my friend."

"Fine. So tell me, what is the solution? You have all of my attention."

A look of utter seriousness overtook Henryk's features. "Here is the plan: capitulate."

"What?"

"Agree to bring Oliwia. But deliver her to Żółkiewski's castle—or Silnyród or Matejko Manor, if you prefer. Somewhere you know she will be safe."

"Better that she remain at Żółkiew Castle. I have seen them all, and that is by far the most fortified." Jacek sat forward, resting his forearms on the tabletop. "But leaving her in any of those places means I still must bring her on the road, which places her in danger *and* leaves our children in the care of my sister. While it solves the problem of bringing my wife into a battle camp, it does not relieve me of taking her to Podolia in the first place."

"Face it, my friend. You are buggered no matter which way you turn. Bring your wife; make her happy. Then be prepared with a detail to escort her home as soon as she realizes what a bad decision she made. That's my advice."

An idea germinated in Jacek's wodka-logged brain. If they traveled to Żółkiew first, she might fall in love with the place and not want to leave. Then again, if they went to Silnyród first, she would be eager to leave the godforsaken fortress and return to civilization.

Henryk gave him another raise of his cup and drained its contents. Jacek followed suit, oblivious to time or space, while questions chased answers in his head.

CHAPTER 12

Storm Clouds Crowding the Horizon

Oliwia lay on her side, her hands pillowing her head as she watched Piotr sleep beside her. Though his baby features were soft, she recognized Jacek in them.

A squeak, like a footstep upon a wooden floorboard, had her sitting up and looking into the shadows beyond the pool of light cast by a lantern. Nothing moved in the gloom, and she released a disappointed sigh. Where was Jacek? He had not returned since she had announced she was coming with him, and that had been hours ago. Where was the man whose actions had set these emotions whirling inside her?

He had not been pleased when she had made her demand. In fact, he had been downright furious. But he never stayed that way long, and even if he had, he wasn't spiting her by sleeping in his own quarters. She had checked.

After reading the missives from Podolia, she reckoned she had a right to anger herself. Her husband had stretched the truth. The hetman hadn't required Jacek's service; he hadn't the right. His letter sought to cleverly coax Jacek to answer the call to arms. Jacek had fulfilled his obligation to country and king long ago and had no "duty" to do so again.

She questioned how competent the crown grand hetman was if he couldn't rally men to fight the enemy threatening their border. Was this merely a play at redemption? One last chance at glory to quiet his detractors and polish up his tarnished reputation? How many years was he now? Seventy-two? Seventy-three? Perhaps his faculties had gone missing. The thought of her husband risking life and limb for someone not wholly present sent shivers to her fingers and toes.

The boldness she had shown Jacek with her demand was not entirely real. She had feigned a good deal of that bravado, and now she contemplated whether the move had been a foolish one. Could she really linger in camp for interminable hours, wondering if he would return whole at the end of the day, like her mother had done? Oliwia had been old enough to remember the worry, the wringing hands, the sorrow when her father's broken body had been returned to them.

Reclining into her pillows, she let out a tired sigh. With so many thoughts crowding her head like sheep being pushed into a pen, sleep eluded her. Piotr began to fuss, and she lifted him into her arms. "Could I really bear to leave you, little one?" Tears suddenly closed her throat.

Eyes shut, tiny arms flailing, he turned his head toward her, his little wet mouth opening and closing, his tongue poking out as he rooted.

"Goodness, did I not just feed you? I'm not sure I have anything left." She tugged the laces of her chemise and presented her breast, and he latched on with vigor, his little fist coming to rest on her bare skin.

She stroked his downy cheek with the back of her finger. "I fear you will be disappointed." She should have relinquished him to Anka.

"Never disappointed," rumbled from the dark recesses, startling her, but Piotr remained where he was despite her jostling. As she looked up, Jacek appeared out of the shadows, a look of wonder on his face as he stared at his suckling son. The rest of him, however, appeared somewhat disheveled.

"Mary, Mother of God, you frightened me! I never heard you enter."

"Because I'm stealthy. He has a strong sucking reflex," he murmured.

99

A smirk tugged one corner of her mouth. "Like his papa." How long had he stood there watching without her knowledge?

He flashed her a proud grin. The smell of spirits wafted from him and hit her with the force of a wave.

She squinted in the dimness. "Are you sotted?"

"*Be*sotted, you mean? Yes, most definitely."

A ripple of relief moved through her. His ire, it seemed, was long gone—likely drowned in a vat of wodka, judging by the smell. "Where have you been?"

He sat on the edge of the mattress, and it folded under his weight, almost sending her and Piotr tumbling against him. "With Henryk, solving the problems of the world." He pulled off his boots and hose, then stood and unbuttoned his blue-and-silver brocade żupan. "We also laid plans for manning and provisioning the campaign. Dispatches have gone out for more men, and I hope to take a company of a hundred, possibly more, in total. Four score of those men will come from Biaska."

She tried not to gape. They did all this and got drunk too? "When will the company depart?"

"We should be ready in a month."

She watched and waited for any sign he was including her in these plans. Part of her yearned to hear him say she was coming, but another part wasn't so sure that was the answer she wanted to hear.

Tugging off the żupan, he looked around and finally flung it on a chair. "Biaska Castle will be garrisoned by a hundred and twenty men. Stefan will be in command." He gave her a sidelong glance. "He will call upon the militia from the village if the need arises, but neither Henryk nor I can see that it will. The estate will be in good hands."

Methodically, he tugged on his shirt laces. The air thickened between them.

"Thank you," she murmured.

"For?"

"For asking Maurycy to leave."

He pulled the shirt over his head, baring smooth skin over hard muscle everywhere her gaze landed. "I don't believe it was a matter of asking. More like threatening to kill him if he didn't."

She arched an eyebrow. "How did he take the threat?"

"It does not matter. All that matters is that he and his sycophants are gone." Standing in only his breeches, he looked from the shirt he fisted to her. Normally, he dressed in his own chamber—and he was completely sober—before making his way to hers, and tonight she was enjoying the display, so much so that he continued talking to her and she had no idea what he was saying.

"Hmm?" Piotr stopped nursing, and she transferred him to the other side. Jacek had grown quiet, and she raised her eyes to see why. He stood stock-still, staring, looking her over as much as she was eyeing him.

"Such a lecher. Enjoying your little peeks, are you?" she teased.

He seemed to come to. "Yes, very much. That is a sight I shall never grow tired of." He tossed the shirt onto a heap on the chair, followed shortly by his pants. He stood stark naked, save his gold cross, as firelight played on the hard planes of his body, wrapping them in a golden glow. She swallowed, trying not to look at him in an obviously predatory way. He was magnificent, and she wanted to let her eyes linger on him.

Perching his hands on his hips, his mouth curled into a smirk. "Such a wanton. Enjoying your little peeks, are you?"

"Very much." Piotr had fallen asleep, and she tucked his head into the crook of her elbow.

Jacek lifted the covers and clambered in beside her, pressing his icy legs to her warm ones.

"You are cold!" she yelped.

"And you are so delightfully warm." He purred the last two words, gave her a wink, and took Piotr from her, hoisting him onto his shoulder. Oliwia finger-combed her hair to loosen it from its braided strands while Jacek patted the boy's back. A little baby burp escaped.

Jacek lay back on the pillows and propped Piotr on his chest while she extinguished the lantern. He wound his free hand around her upper arm and tugged her to his side.

She snuggled against him and let out a contented sigh. "You and Henryk must have drunk everything in the tavern."

"We didn't go to the tavern," he replied, his voice low and gravelly. "But we did drink up every jug in his house and depleted a fair amount of Biaska's stores."

"I can smell it," she chuckled.

He caressed her shoulder, her arm, her head, and sifted his fingers through her hair. The touches relaxed her, and as she eased into the mattress, ready to drift off, his voice rumbled softly through his chest. "You will miss our little Piotr ... and Adam and Margaret. There's a good chance that by the time we return, Piotr will be walking and you will have missed his first step. You have considered this, yes?"

She stiffened beside him. Was he actually consenting to her coming? She lifted her head to peer at him. Staring back at her were two glittering orbs, too dark to make out their color. "Are you saying you will take me with you?" Her heart began hammering against her rib cage.

He ran the back of his rough hand along her cheek. "By Christ and all the saints, I must be soft in the head. But yes, if you wish so much to accompany me that you are willing to leave our children behind, then so be it. But you are only allowed two wagons."

Her voice came out in a rush. "I can make do with one."

"Then it's settled."

Stunned she had gotten her wish, she nestled back against him, though her body now hummed with excitement. Her mind followed, galloping through preparations until it screeched on the doorstep that was Lady Eugenia, Lesław's wife.

"I can hear your brain grinding, Liwi," Jacek mumbled. "Have you changed your mind?"

"No, I ... I was reflecting that soon I will meet the woman you nearly married."

"But didn't."

"Yes."

He craned his head, and she raised hers to meet his gaze in the dark. "Liwi, listen to me. I never loved her. I scarcely remember what she looks like. Until you brought it up, I had forgotten that she is part of Silnyród now."

"I wonder what that would have been like, you marrying her."

"It would have been like many other unions. I would have taken a mistress." His voice held a teasing quality.

"You would have?"

"Oh yes, and that mistress would have been you."

She scoffed. "I would never have consented to such an arrangement."

"Another sound reason for my not marrying her."

She propped herself up on an elbow. "Does this mean you will be taking a mistress now that you've married me?"

He cracked open an eye. "Is this a jest?" When she shook her head, he sighed and scrubbed a hand over his face. "Liwi, sweet, you are both mistress and wife. I want no other. Besides, I can scarcely keep up with your troublesome ways. I cannot imagine having two of you."

"I am not so difficult."

He grunted in response.

With her free hand, she gave him a playful push. "No sultan's harem for you, my lord?"

"God of mercy, no. I have neither the fortitude nor the stamina, no matter what rumors you might be spreading in that regard. Now go to sleep, you mischief-maker."

Settling back against his warmth, she began drawing figures on his chest. Jacek wasn't soft in the head, but he was soft in the heart. "Thank you."

"For what?" he muttered in a drowsy voice.

"For taking me with you. For being … you."

"Tickles," he mumbled as his big hand descended on hers, trapping it against his skin, stilling her caresses. "I'll wake you in the morning, and you can show me your gratitude then." She could hear the smile in his muzzy voice. How much had his inebriation to do with his concession? Would he regret it in the morning? Would *she* regret it?

Soon his breathing evened out, punctuated by drunken snores and Piotr's soft baby sighs. This, right here, might very well be heaven on earth, and she was about to upend it. As she lay curled beside her husband, she soaked in his warm strength, equal parts elated and terrified for the adventure that lay before them.

Filip strode through the great hall, head on a swivel for his favorite maid. The morning meal had been cleared away long ago, leaving a sprinkling of servants tending the fire and buffing pewter plates. Thank God and all the saints that oily Lord Maurycy and his entourage had departed. Now the keep bustled at a less frenetic pace, affording him more opportunity to coax Mary into a discreet alcove for some intimate, mutual exploration.

His buoyed hopes were dashed on the stone floor when his eyes landed on his brother-in-law's frame descending the staircase from above floors. Filip sidestepped, hoping to melt into the shadows and avoid Jacek altogether.

"Filip!" Jacek's voice boomed, echoing off the walls. "With me, in the solar."

Filip's shoulders sagged. As he followed the click of his brother's bootheels striking the floor, resentment bloomed low in his belly. He was being made to trail like an undisciplined puppy.

His eye caught on a flash of familiar fabric. Mary peered at him from behind a pillar, her eyes dancing with promise. "Wait for me," he mouthed. She covered her mouth to suppress a giggle, and he increased his pace. By the time Jacek entered the solar, Filip nearly barreled into his back.

"Close the door," Jacek called over his shoulder.

Yes, your royal majesty. Filip slammed it closed, and Jacek pivoted, his eyebrows drawn down.

"Save your frustration, little brother. You will need all the fuel it provides for far more meaningful pursuits."

"Such as?" Filip took up a soldier's stance. Feet eighteen inches apart, hands clasped behind his back.

Jacek fisted his hands and leaned them on the desktop. Crescent-shaped smudges below his eyes accented droopy lids and an uncustomary pallor in his cheeks.

Filip reined in a chuckle. "What happened to you?"

"I tussled with a bottle of wodka last night."

Filip couldn't contain his glee, and his face broke out in a wide grin. "It appears the wodka won the bout."

"It did. I'm pleased my misery amuses you," Jacek huffed. "Now sit."

Pressing his lips together to hold back his laughter, Filip flopped into a chair and waited.

Jacek poured and quaffed a partial cup of wine, letting out a belch that left him sighing. "Let me get straight to the point. The crown grand hetman has called upon Biaska—well, Silnyród—to join an army he is putting together to fight off a new Ottoman threat."

Certain his brother-in-law was going to tell him he would not participate, Filip opened his mouth to protest, but Jacek stilled him with a flick of his finger. "Wait until I have finished what I have to say."

"I already know," Filip grumbled.

"Do you now? If that is so, then why so truculent? I thought you would be delighted at the prospect of coming." Filip's confusion must have shown, for Jacek canted his head and smirked. "Ah. So you *don't* know everything, do you, little brother?"

Filip vaulted from his seat, his pulse racing. "I am coming? Truly?"

Jacek nodded.

"Does my sister know?"

"She does. In fact, she is coming as well."

Filip's mouth dropped open. He wasn't sure if he was more stunned by her letting him go or by her coming herself. "What? Why in blazes … ?"

"She has never traveled to Silnyród, and she wishes to see it."

"Now? Amid the conflict?"

"Now. Amid the conflict," Jacek repeated. "If you want to understand why, you will need to direct your questions to her." Filip could have sworn Jacek mumbled, "Because I sure as the devil do not understand."

Filip dismissed the remark for the joy ready to combust inside him. "Are we done?"

"Not yet. There are some rules you must follow. First, understand you will be housed among the pacholiks."

"Will I be in a charge?"

Jacek's jaw muscle jumped. "No."

"Why not? Marcin is a pacholik, and he takes part in the charges. Other pacholiks charge."

"Marcin is a hussar and more experienced than you, and he stays behind the first wave. As for the other pacholiks, they too are more experienced. Consider yourself a … junior pacholik."

The firm set of Jacek's jaw told Filip to go along with this gain for the moment. He could push the limits later, when they were on campaign.

"Fine," he groused. He endured more instructions, praying all the while for Jacek to speed up his delivery. When his brother-in-law at last paused, Filip blurted out, "May I take my leave?"

Jacek flapped a hand at him. "By all means."

Filip raced for the door and yanked it open, pausing briefly to look back at Jacek. "Thank you."

His brother-in-law acknowledged him with a nod.

Filip tore from the solar and down the steps. He had to tell the garrison! Nowhere in his thoughts was sweet Mary.

Under the cerulean April sky drenched in sunshine, a messenger appeared beside Gabriel's dilapidated manor gate. Gabriel strode toward him, and the man extracted a bundle of letters from his pouch.

"Anything of import?" he queried the courier.

The man tipped his kolpak. "I know not, sire, though one missive carries the crown grand hetman's seal."

Gabriel's eyebrows sailed to his hairline. "Żółkiewski?"

"Himself, m'lord."

Gabriel dropped a coin into the messenger's palm and hurried toward the shabby manor, where he locked himself inside the buttery—the cramped room doubled as his solar, and here, no one dared disturb him.

The humiliation of having to carve his private space out of the dark closet that housed victuals was at times too much to bear. A proper lord needed his own space to conduct his business, and someday, when he had accumulated enough wealth and built his new manor house, his solar would be the largest and grandest room of all. How else to impress business associates and tenants? Not that he had many of either, but someday he would.

He made his way to a stout barrel with a wooden top that served as his desk. He brushed away flour and grains and lit a tallow taper, pressing it into a pottery holder. Plucking up the first letter, he settled himself on an upended barrel. The seal confirmed the missive's author, and Gabriel snapped it open and unfolded the stiff paper.

He quickly scanned the hetman's message, twice. Reading the hetman's words once more, more slowly this time, he allowed a beatific grin to bloom.

The squeak of ancient hinges gave him a start, and he whirled to find Milena in the doorway. "May I get you anything, my love?"

"No," he barked. Her crestfallen expression made him soften his tone. "Not at the moment. I must answer these letters."

Tentatively, she crept into the space. "What does the hetman say?"

Jesus and Maria, the things he put up with! He mustered every drop of patience in his well and snapped the letter open. "He wants me to … Here. Read for yourself. I know you will anyway." It had always vexed him that she could read, and now he shoved the letter at her. "Read it aloud," he commanded.

Peeping at him from under her lashes, she handled the paper gingerly, her movements skittish. She cleared her throat and began in a shaky voice. "'My most esteemed Lord Wronski, I am once more obliged to call upon your military acumen and your loyalty to the Commonwealth.'" Gabriel snorted. Milena darted him a nervous look and continued. "'As you are well acquainted with the Cossack problem vis-à-vis the Ottomans, I shall not repeat the details here save to say they continue to violate the treaties between our nations. What you may not know, however, is that Samuel Otwinowski, the Crown's envoy, entered Istanbul late last year, where he was coldly received by the grand vizier. Now he is returned, having been sent off with threats of war from the grand vizier at the behest of the sultan himself. The king has no doubt they are true.'"

Milena paused, her eyes wide. "Shall I keep going?"

Gabriel rolled his hand for her to proceed, though he could by now recite the rest of the hetman's message.

The paper shook as she took up her reading once more. "'Adding more wood upon the pyre, the grand vizier is no friend to the hospodar of Moldavia.'" She lowered the paper.

"He refers to Gaspar Grazziani." Not that Gabriel cared about the politics. What most mattered to him was that opportunity once more stood before him, ushered there by God himself. Gabriel intended to grab it and prosper. "Continue."

"Ahem. 'Grazziani has befriended the king, but that friendship imperils not only his throne but his life. Rumors of the gathering Ottoman army run rampant, and these provocations hang above the Commonwealth's neck like a suspended blade. I have been charged with taking any action necessary to safeguard our sovereign border. To that end, I am assembling an army to repel the Ottoman threat.

"'The treasury is no fuller now than it was in 1619, and therefore I am turning to you and other trusted Lisowczycy. You may count on being recompensed in the usual way. As I write this, Crown Field Hetman Stanisław Koniecpolski has taken command of the quartz troops and concentrated them near Halicz. I wish to further surround myself with the most capable fighters from Podolia.'"

Milena finished with the hetman's closing before raising watery eyes to his. "What does this mean?"

Gabriel vaulted from his rickety chair and gripped her upper arms. "It means that, after years of meddling from afar, after years of allowing the crisis in Moldavia to brew, the Commonwealth is at last prepared to intervene. It means that our country is going to war against the Ottomans."

Milena's voice quavered. "Must you go?"

"I am called for a higher purpose. It is my duty. I am a servant of the king, who is as close to God himself as any man. Hetman Żółkiewski is an extension of the king, and therefore an extension of God. Would you have Gabriel deny God when he calls his archangel forth?" Giddiness as he only experienced right after victory, when the lust of battle had not yet ebbed and they were dividing their prizes, bubbled in Gabriel's veins. His skin turned to gooseflesh from the chills chasing themselves up and down his spine.

"Now go and let me pen a reply without delay."

CHAPTER 13

Podolia

If Jacek regretted his decision to let Oliwia come with him, he never let on. Oliwia, however, was bombarded with remorse she tried to wrestle back into an undersized cage. One of those regrets was trying to convince Filip to remain at Biaska. The campaign was all her brother would speak of since Jacek had informed him—without her knowledge—that he was to accompany the banner.

"If you are going, sister, why shouldn't I?" he had posed when she had asked him to reconsider and stay behind. In vain, she had played upon his devotion to his niece and nephews, insisting he was best suited for safeguarding them at Biaska Castle. His indignant self had retorted, "I am not one of the children to stay behind in the nursery." She could not muster a counterargument, for her brother was no longer a child, no matter how hard she wished it were so.

Her other regrets reared themselves when time came to depart. Leaving the children was far more difficult than Oliwia could have imagined. With her emotions balled in her queasy stomach and too-tight throat, she frequently turned from her perch upon her saddle and waved at them over her shoulder. Finally, their bodies grew too small to make out on Biaska's ramparts, and she forced back a sob. When would she see them again?

Dear Lord, what was she doing?

When they had exchanged their good-byes in the yard, Margaret had wept uncontrollably, causing Piotr to bawl. Even Tamara and Anka had shed tears. Adam, little lord that he was, had tucked his arms over his chest and struck a stoic pose, but his lower lip had wobbled and a tear or three had sneaked out of his eye, which he had angrily swiped away with the back of his hand.

Oliwia's heart rested inside her chest in tatters, but she couldn't let any of it show. This had been her idea, after all, though the reason she had latched on to it in the first place escaped her at the moment. Many details escaped her muddled mind lately. One thing was certain: her pigheadedness had carried the idea through to fruition.

Thinking back, she had never expected Jacek to agree. He had surprised her. But if he knew how bereft she was, he would march her right back home, and her pride wouldn't allow that to happen.

To marshal her strength, she looked toward Nadia, riding in one of the wagons with a look of abject terror on her face. The girl had never been beyond the walls of Biaska, and here Oliwia was dragging her away from everything she had known during her entire twenty-three years. Oliwia had to demonstrate strength for the girl, no matter that her confidence was feigned … and for Filip, who rode alongside Henryk in the vanguard … and for Marcin and Dawid and all the men who served the Lady of Biaska.

More accurately, they served the lord, whose strong back her eyes strayed to. She would feed on his understated power silently, draw from *his* strength. It was all she could manage. At times like these, she missed the days spent in the peasant village where Jacek had found her. Not that the living had been easy, but it had been far less complicated.

She quickly reminded herself that while decisions had been made for her, she had had no control over her life … including whom she married. As thorny as her daily affairs could be now, she had the ability—no, the authority—to make a difference in people's lives at Biaska, and to do so for the better. Biaska was one of the few estates that worked around the laws governing peasants, helping them move away if they needed to be with family elsewhere, and as a result, she found there were more tenants clamoring for a strip of land on her estate than she had strips to accommodate them.

She had forgotten how ponderous the travel could be, especially when they paced slow-rolling wagons plowing their way through rutted, sometimes muddy roads and shared cramped quarters with Nadia, Henryk, Marcin, and Dawid. She had also forgotten the discomforts of sitting astride for so long. Her backside, her hips, her abdomen, and her breasts ached. The latter she understood because she had rushed Piotr's weaning, and consequently her breasts were still tender. Her abdomen likely was related to the weaning as well. Of course, there was an altogether different reason why she might be experiencing these symptoms. The distressing fact that she had not had her courses in a long while was one she dismissed as best she could. Times of stress, like the sort Maurycy had brought on with his visit, could delay nature significantly.

Whatever the reason they had gone missing, Jacek seemed not to have noticed, for he hadn't questioned her. Then again, he was wholly occupied by military matters, and they had had few chances for intimacy. How would he know?

As they traversed the countryside, she recognized some of the terrain from their travels back in 1610. The farther east they journeyed, though, the less familiar her surroundings grew. They followed the ancient merchant road, and at times they were housed in an estate or an inn, while at other times, like now, they encamped just outside a town's walls. This day, it was in Rzeszów's shadow where they set up camp.

Eleven days had passed since they had set out from Biaska, and while Jacek was at times distracted, impatient, or both, he expressed pleasure with their progress. They had gained the halfway point, and Żółkiew was another fortnight, possibly less, depending upon the weather. Though it was mid-May, frequent rains not only turned travel cold and damp but could bog down the roads and make the going slower.

In Żółkiew, Jacek hoped to catch the hetman and his private army before they headed south for the border so he could gain more knowledge of the hetman's plans and receive his instructions. A detachment of Biaska's best soldiers would then ride with her and Jacek to Silnyród, a five-day trek if they traveled without wagons.

They set up camp in midafternoon, earlier than their usual pattern of stopping at dusk, affording Oliwia a respite from the saddle and a chance to wash and relax her sore muscles ... and eat to ward off dizzy spells and the gnawing in her belly. For all her discomfort in the beginning, Nadia seemed to have taken to the saddle. Where Oliwia would generally need minutes to get the blood circulating in her backside and lower extremities, Nadia was sprite-like as soon as she dismounted.

Oliwia's legs still wobbled when she entered their newly erected tent, and another bout of dizziness had her clinging to the opening. Jacek came up behind her, softly asking if she was all right.

Annoyed at herself for letting her unsteadiness show, she flapped an impatient hand at him. "Yes, yes, I am fine."

He flinched as if she'd slapped him.

She gave him a rueful smile over her shoulder. "I am sorry for sounding so harsh. I did not intend ... I think a wash in the stream is what I need." Hopefully, her statement hadn't sounded like a grumble. She had been very careful to bite back any complaints, for she neither wanted him to worry nor did she want to give him ammunition for sending her home. Although she was questioning—for likely the thousandth time—her wisdom in coming in the first place. Between aching for her children and being fairly certain another grew inside her, she had been moved to weeping more than once. So far, she had managed to hide the bouts from everyone. None could witness her weakness, especially not her husband.

He craned his head and frowned at her. "Are you sure you're all right? You're pale, and I don't recall seeing you eat today."

Because I will throw up if I do. She had never been sick with the other children, and she prayed her nausea was not a sign something was wrong with the babe.

She brightened her smile. "Truly, I am well. Nadia and I will head for the stream."

"I will accompany you."

"No, no. You have far more important matters to attend to."

"More important than protecting my wife and her maid? I think not."

Stubborn man. "Send someone else, if you must, but we wish to take advantage while the sun is high and before the men get there and muddy it up. We won't be far." She pointed toward a row of thickets, crowding into each other like children lining up for sweets.

He hesitated, seeming to run calculations in his mind. "All right, then, but do not go far. I will send Marcin and a man-at-arms." With a whistle, he signaled to Marcin, who was among the throng of men and horses.

Oliwia picked up her skirts. "Come, Nadia."

Nadia plucked a cloth bag from her pallet inside the tent and followed Oliwia through an aperture in the thickets.

They wended their way to the stream, and Oliwia paused, shading her eyes against the sun's reflection upon the stream, like so many diamonds strewn across its surface.

"Hmm. Too shallow and muddy here." The bank looked as through a herd of cattle had tromped through. Casting her gaze farther upstream, she spied a promising place. "Up ahead. That looks like a nice sandy spot that leads to a deeper pool."

When they reached the beach, it wasn't quite what Oliwia had expected, and she led them farther up the trail bordering the stream. The shrubbery on the other side transformed into dense woods, but still she couldn't find that perfect spot.

"M'lady? The lord did not want us wandering too far afield. Should we not retrace our steps?" The quaver in Nadia's voice alerted Oliwia that her maid was growing nervous, but then, Nadia was always nervous.

"Just a little farther."

Sure enough, another twenty feet and a perfect half crescent of fine gravel descended gradually into a gentle pool deep enough to reach one's neck.

"This is it," Oliwia declared. "Help me out of my traveling clothes, will you? I'll do the same for you."

Soon they were down to naught but their chemises, and Nadia was casting furtive glances toward the woods.

Oliwia's impatience bloomed. "What is it?"

"I thought I saw something move."

As Oliwia slid Jacek's ruby-and-pearl cross over her head and deposited it atop her gown, she peered into the deep spruce-green gloom, but all was still. Nadia had likely seen nothing. "Perhaps a rabbit or a squirrel scuttled along. Come on, then." Oliwia yanked her chemise over her head and headed for the water, unbraiding her hair as she went. She couldn't wait to dunk her head in the cool water and let it wash some of the sweat and grit away.

When Nadia didn't follow right away, Oliwia glanced over her shoulder. The girl stood frozen on the shore, still clad in her undershirt. "Are you coming or not?"

"I-I think I shall bathe with my chemise on."

"Suit yourself. Just remember that we haven't much time, and your chemise will still be wet when you get dressed. Wearing soggy clothing, I have found, is not very comfortable, especially as evening descends." Oliwia pushed off the bottom, vaulting her body into a deeper section, and gasped when the cold water hit her chest. She executed a short breaststroke, then flipped on her back to let the current run through her strands.

Another beat of hesitation and then Nadia discarded the garment and joined Oliwia, her teeth chattering from the cold. In her hand, she held up contents of the cloth bag: soap and linen squares for washing.

"Perfect!" Oliwia helped herself. Scrubbing away the grit and the grime felt heavenly. Before long, they were laughing and splashing, but the chilly stream encouraged them to leave it behind.

Back on shore, they let the water drip and dried themselves as best they could before donning their chemises.

Nadia's eyes darted about like a dragonfly. "I have not seen Pan Marcin and the other guard."

Oliwia twisted her hair to squeeze out excess water. "They are likely waiting just around the corner, giving us time and privacy."

Sure enough, something rustled in the woods behind them, and a man cleared his throat. Oliwia glanced over her shoulder and could just make out a masculine figure waiting on the trail.

She nodded at Nadia as she stooped to gather up her bodice and necklace. "See? What did I tell you?" To the figure, she sang out, "Just give us a moment while we finish dressing, Marcin."

"Oh, please don't do that, my lady," came a deep, mocking voice.

Oliwia whirled. Behind her, Nadia made a sound like a strangled blue jay as two masked men stepped from the shadows, blocking the trail. Each one brandished an unsheathed sabre.

Oliwia's heart nearly leaped from her chest as blood pulsed in her ears, making them ring. A wave of nausea and dizziness threatened to overtake her. *No, no, no! Not now!*

The men advanced, taking deliberate steps. The one who had spoken seemed to be in charge. "Please do not deprive this humble servant of the glorious sight that wet bit of silk clinging to your alluring figure presents. Though I must admit I enjoyed the view without the shirt much, much more." Besides the baritone depth to his voice, it was smooth, silky. And though he spoke in Polish instead of Latin, his words were crisp and elegant, as though he was of noble birth.

He tilted his head this way and that, as if appraising her. Oliwia clutched the bodice to her bosom in a bid to cover herself. She dared not look behind her at Nadia, for that meant taking her eyes off the twin threats moving toward them. Her dagger lay in the folds of her skirt inches from her feet.

The talking man quickly raised his blade and pointed it at her. "Ah, ah. Were you not listening? I understand you're frightened right now, but as long as you do as I say, you will not be harmed. Drop what you're holding and let me admire you." Out of the side of his mouth, he growled to the other man. "Grab the other one. Look for weapons and take whatever she has of value. And I do not mean her virtue."

In the blink of an eyelash, the other man moved around Oliwia and the leader stood within an arm's length before her. Behind her came a scream cut short, as though a hand had been clapped over Nadia's mouth, followed by the sounds of a struggle. Oliwia stood rooted in place, her eyes fastened on the tall, broad man before her, breath caught in her throat.

Where his companion wore a black mask, this man's was indigo and appeared to be a scarf tied about his entire face, obliterating his features except for hard, hazel eyes watching her through a slit about two fingers wide.

"I said—" He yanked the bodice from her grasp so hard she stumbled, and he tossed it into the stream. "Ah. Much, much better. What's this?"

He fingered the cross dangling from her other hand. She toed her way to her skirt, but her dagger wasn't there. Meanwhile, the struggle behind her continued, and then came a thump on the ground.

The man before her dashed his eyes over her shoulder. "Not yet, you oaf," he growled. "You'll have your turn when I am done with her. Meanwhile, hold her still. She's wriggling like a fish on a hook." He turned his attention back to Oliwia, and his voice turned velvety once more. "Which promises to be delightful once I have her under me. After that, I am all yours."

Oliwia locked out the muffled screams behind her and dipped her knees to keep her trembling under control.

The man dropped his gaze back to the cross and crooned, "Here now, let me see that."

"I will not relinquish it until you let her go," she gritted out.

The man let out a harsh laugh. "I don't see where you have a choice, my pet, do you? Although I must say, I like your fire." He ran the back of his finger down her cheek, her jaw, her shoulder, her arm. "Very much." With one swift motion, he jerked the necklace out of her hand and tucked it into his sash, patting it. "There now. All safe and sound."

Inching closer, he poked her flank with the tip of his blade and dragged it slowly down her body and back up to her heart. "Now be a good girl, or I cannot say what will happen to the maid," he whispered in a voice thick with honey. A whimper sounded at Oliwia's back. With his free hand, the man cupped her cheek and slid his fingers into her hair, entwining them in her tresses, and tugged hard. She balled her hands into fists and ground her back molars, willing away her fear while sending up a prayer to the Holy Virgin. It did little to keep her quaking in check.

He tsked. "You needn't be afraid, my lovely. As long as you do what you're told." His eyes locked on hers, mining them. She tried to turn her head, but his grip tightened and wrenched, and she bit back a cry. "Be still

117

now. Let me look at you. My, my. You have the most beautiful eyes I've ever seen. Like heavenly pools. No, more like precious gems. Brilliant. Fiery."

He loosened his hold and slid his fingers from her hair. She released a silent breath.

The mewls and rustles behind her had quietened, and she prayed the man hadn't choked the life from Nadia.

"You are a beauty. I'm saving you for last," the man before her said. "And trust me, you will love every minute." Though she couldn't see his features, she could hear the cold smile in his voice. "But first, I want a closer look at what I'm getting."

He switched the sabre to his left hand and trailed the fingers of his right slowly over her throat, her collarbone, her chest, pausing to cup her breast through the cold fabric. He brushed his thumb over her tender nipple. She was aghast when it stiffened under his touch.

He chuckled. "Ah, the anticipation. Patience, my pet. I know exactly what you want, but you'll have to wait. Then I'm yours for the entire night. I promise."

She pulled away, and he jerked her back by her wrist, so hard her fingers momentarily lost feeling. "Did I not say to be a good girl?" His smooth voice had taken on a menacing bite.

He continued his exploration, his fingers gliding down her rib cage, her hip, moving to her forearm and hand. Eyes still boring into hers, he wrenched the ring from her finger and tucked that away too.

"Pick up your clothes," he ordered, his voice suddenly pure flint. To his companion, he said, "We have to get out of here. Bring her and her garments."

"What do she need clothes for, sire?" He chuckled malevolently.

"Oaf! Be quiet!" the man raged. "As for the clothes, we can sell them." The man's attention was squarely on the oaf, and Oliwia seized the moment to kick the hand holding the blade, though she didn't dislodge it.

"Nadia, run!" she screamed.

The man roared and raised the hand still holding the blade as if to backhand her. She flinched, anticipating the hit.

But it didn't come. Instead, he whipped his head to the side … and then she heard it.

"Lady Oliwia? My lady!"

"Marcin! Over here!" she shrieked. "Hur—" The man struck her across the face with his free hand, knocking her to the ground.

"Let's go!" he barked to his companion.

"What of the women?"

"Leave them! They'll only slow us down."

Oliwia wrapped her arms around the man's leg, and he thudded to the ground. "Bitch!" he bellowed and landed a kick to her stomach that doubled her over. No breath remained in her lungs with which to scream, and she watched helplessly as the men lit into the woods.

She crawled to Nadia. The girl was shaken, her face red and streaked with tears, but she was unharmed, thank Mother Mary and the saints! Oliwia wrapped her up and rocked her in an embrace, stroking her hair. "It will be all right."

Oliwia stretched out her hand and snagged her overgown, dragging it to her to drape it about Nadia's shoulders. Marcin and Filip burst through the bushes. Puffing, panting, Marcin stopped short and bent to brace his hands on his knees.

"My lady!" he wheezed at the same time Filip cried, "Liwi!"

She pointed toward the woods. "They fled that way. Hurry! Stop them!" Then she dug her forearm into her stomach in a vain attempt to control a sharp, pulsing pain.

CHAPTER 14

Foibles Beget Frustrations

"**M**y love, you will wear a hole in the carpet if you continue tromping about."

Jacek came to an abrupt stop and looked at his wife, who was wrapped in layers of blankets as she sat upon his cot. His emotions tilted and whirled. He had swung from being livid with her to wanting to crush her against him and hold her there forever. Right now, the sight of her swollen purple cheek enraged him. He wanted to plunge a blade into the man who had done this to her. Or wrap his hands about the bastard's neck and watch the light fade from his eyes as he choked the life from him. Or shove the brute's head beneath the stream and watch him flail and kick until he stilled. Or—

"Marcin and Filip should have reached you sooner!" *I should have been there!*

"Jacek, this is not their fault. And as you can see, I am unharmed."

He fastened his eyes on her bruised face. "Not exactly unharmed." She looked so small, so vulnerable. He never should have countermanded his initial instinct to leave her at Biaska. "You've told me everything you can recall?"

"Yes. As I said, the one man seemed to be educated, of noble birth, while the other was rough, as if he hailed from the peasant class. And he called the noble one 'sire.' Do you suppose they were hajduks? I've heard of them robbing people along the merchant road."

"Hajduks only attack Ottomans, and they do so to keep Christians safe. These men were highwaymen, brutal and treacherous. Land-bound pirates who do not care whom they hurt as long as there is a prize to be had." He flung out an arm, his frustration erupting. "Why didn't you wait for Marcin? Why did you wander so far away without guards?"

Her face crumpled, gutting him. A beat later, he was on the cot with her on his lap and encircled in his arms, his voice soft. "Damnation, but how I wish I had the rancid pieces of … I would have carved them up, bit by bit, and shoved each piece in their faces for what they did to you." But Marcin and Filip had done the right thing to stay with the women and protect them. Had he sent enough men to the stream, as he should have, perhaps they would have captured the curs.

"Filip tried."

"Tried what?"

"He chased them, but they fled on horses they had tethered." Jacek stiffened, but she seemed not to notice. She flattened her palm against his chest and rested her head on his shoulder with a resigned sigh. "I am so sorry."

His mind dancing with what the devil Filip had been thinking, he rested his cheek atop her crown. "What could you possibly be sorry for?"

"For being foolish, careless, for not waiting as I should have. And now I have lost the cross and ring you gave me." Her shoulders shook as she wept.

He stroked her hair. "Shhh. They are mere objects."

She raised watery blue eyes to his. "They were more than objects, Jacek. They were—"

"Replaceable. You and Nadia, however, are not."

"How is Nadia?"

"She is well, darting about in her usual mouse-like way, only now she is surrounded by at least six guards everywhere she goes. I daresay she is either vexed or delighted by the attention. She will sleep in our tent tonight, as will Marcin, Filip, and Dawid."

Oliwia let out a sound that was part sniffle, part giggle. "It will be rather crowded. Another night of intimacy thwarted."

"I can't imagine that is what you desire at the moment."

With a snuffle, she raised her head and patted his chest, offering him a weak smile. "Lovemaking will wait until we reach Żółkiew."

"Agreed." He pulled her in tight and squeezed. Too tight, apparently, because she winced. He dropped his arms to his sides. "I'm sorry! Did he hurt you elsewhere?"

Biting her lower lip, she tugged on his arms and gathered them about herself, as if she were pulling up a quilt. "He kicked me in the stomach. It's tender, and if I move the wrong way …" A painful chuckle escaped her. "Another reason to avoid lying together."

Jacek wrapped her up in his arms again, gently this time, though inside he seethed. "I will kill them. I will find them, and I will kill them." First, though, he had another piece of business to deal with.

When she finally settled and he saw her comfortable on the cot, he went in search of Filip. The boy had not shown his face since his return, not even bothering to come check on his sister, and his absence fueled the fire raging inside Jacek.

Marcin appeared in his line of sight, and Jacek made for him.

His retainer froze and swallowed, his Adam's apple bobbing noticeably. "How is Lady Oliwia, my lord?"

"She will recover. I wish to ask you about Filip's actions when you reached the women."

Marcin blinked.

"Did Filip take off after the scoundrels?"

Marcin looked around, as if formulating an answer.

Jacek decided to help him along. "My wife says he did."

Marcin bobbed his head. "That he did. Tracked them through the woods, but they were prepared. They had picketed their horses and were able to mount and flee."

"Did you tell him to stay put?"

"I, uh …" He scratched the back of his neck.

Jacek arched an eyebrow. "Sounds to me as if you did."

"I did, my lord, but you know how impulsive one can be at his age. He likely wanted to avenge the assault on his sister and didn't stop long enough to think."

And there was the problem: Filip didn't stop long enough to *think*.

Jacek grasped Marcin's shoulder in a gesture of thanks before renewing his search for his brother-in-law. He followed the sound of laughter and found Filip seated among the men around a cook fire, playing cards. The whelp was laughing and whooping among them, as if he hadn't a care in the world, as if his sister did not lie injured in their tent.

"Filip!" he boomed. The men's lively banter came to an abrupt halt, and all eyes turned to him. All eyes except Filip's. "Brother, I would speak with you."

Filip took his time looking up from his cards. His reply? A lazy blink. "Now!"

One of the guards elbowed the lad and jerked his head toward Jacek.

With a disinterested grunt, Filip rose from a rock where he'd been perched. Rangy, he was, and Jacek could have sworn the boy had added another few inches of height overnight. He was taller at sixteen than men twice his age, though that fact made little difference right now.

Filip folded the cards in one hand and brushed the back of his żupan with the other, his movements casual.

"Hey," one of the men complained. "You can't take those with you."

Filip shot him a grin over his shoulder. "I'll be back soon enough."

That's what you think. Jacek led him into the mess tent, shooing out the servants preparing *bigos*—hunter's stew—for their supper.

The lad leaned against a table and crossed his arms over his chest. "What is it I have done to aggrieve you *this* time?"

Jacek pulled in a steadying breath to keep his simmering blood from erupting into a boil. "I wish to discuss what happened today."

"What happened? You mean my sister being attacked by those devil dogs?" Looking down, Filip flicked a piece of lint from his chest.

"Yes. Marcin says you chased them into the woods."

Filip cast his eyes to the side. "So?"

Jacek's hands balled into fists. "Did it occur to you to stay put and protect the women, to have Marcin's back?"

Filip's nonchalance evaporated. "What did you expect me to do? Of course I went after them! Not only did Oliwia urge me to, but that scum needed to be brought to justice! Surely you can't fault me for trying to catch them!"

"I can, and I do."

Filip snorted. "Had I caught them and brought their hides back to camp, you would be praising me right now instead of doing whatever the devil you're doing. Telling me how inadequate I am. Again."

Jacek scrubbed a hand down his face. "I am not telling you you're inadequate. What I'm saying is that it was one of you against two of them, and they could have easily ambushed you. Then what?"

"But they didn't, did they? Instead, they mounted up on steeds they had hidden in the forest, and they lit out. It appears they know these woods far better than I."

"Exactly. They are familiar with this area; you are not. You left Marcin alone with the women. Those scoundrels could have doubled back, overpowered Marcin, and taken your sister and Nadia. Did you consider that?"

Filip's face was a dusky dark red, his mouth a bitter line. "Don't tell me you wouldn't have chased them. That was *your wife* the brutes abused."

"I would have secured the women first. I would not have left my brother-in-arms alone. You want to be a hussar, an elite soldier, and these are the very situations where you will be tested. The decisions you make could mean the difference between life and death for your lord-brothers. Hubris can spawn one act of foolishness that will get them killed."

"All right, then," Filip gritted out. "Since you are so perfect, tell me what I should have done."

"After returning the women safely to camp, I would have gotten on my horse, taken men with me, and pursued them."

Filip flung an arm into the air. "But they would have been long gone! You would have missed your chance completely!"

"Maybe, maybe not. Men in a hurry leave a trail that can be tracked. At least on horseback I would stand a chance of hunting them down. On foot, alone, none. If I could not find them, I would have questioned everyone who was about. People pay attention to two masked men galloping in earnest, especially with all the reports of highwaymen on the road."

A look of contrition flashed in Filip's eyes.

"You did not consider that, did you?"

The lad shook his head.

"You need to accept your limitations, Filip."

Just as quickly, the contrition disappeared, replaced by a blaze. Filip cinched his arms across his chest.

"Well?" Jacek prodded.

"Well what? What the hell do you want me to say? Nothing I do is right. It's never enough. I could have caught them and brought them back—or better yet, cut them down—and still you would find fault with me."

This was going nowhere. Jacek blew out a ragged breath. "Did you at least get a good look at them? At anything that could help identify them?"

"No. Other than the horse who looked like the sable that was taken," Filip muttered.

"There are lots of horses that resemble the sable."

Henryk poked his head in just as Jacek prepared to hurl another reprimand. "The starosta of Rzeszów is here with several of his men and would like to speak with you about the attack."

Jacek frowned. "How did you know where to find me?"

Henryk's eyebrows flew to his hairline. "Do you jest? Everyone in this camp can hear the two of you going at each other."

Jacek rolled his shoulder and tilted his head side to side, popping his neck. "Filip, you haven't gone to see how your sister is faring since you returned, and she is asking after you. Go see her now while I accompany Henryk."

Filip scowled like six-year-old Adam being told to wash before sitting down to eat.

Henryk held up a hand. "Actually, Jacek, they would like to talk to Filip as well."

Jacek leveled his gaze on Filip. "Let's go."

Jacek stood back while Filip repeated the story to the town officials. Marcin had gone first, both recounting nothing Jacek hadn't already heard. But one detail resurfaced and poked at him. The horse. Chances were it was not the same one, yet what if it was? What if whoever stole the warhorses were today's highwaymen and one of them rode the sable now? No, it was preposterous. Besides, Jacek still suspected Wronski had been involved in the mounts' theft.

Suddenly, Oliwia's description of the men's voices streaked through his head like a comet lighting the night sky. *The one man seemed to be educated, of noble birth.*

Wronski was of noble birth.

The starosta addressed himself to Jacek, bringing Jacek back to the tent where they were conducting their interviews.

"Naturally we will note all these details, Lord Dąbrowski"—he glanced over his shoulder at a clerk who sat at a small table, writing busily—"but you do understand it is hard to capture someone who keeps his face masked. And as we receive reports of various types and colors of masks, we can't even say it is the same men."

"Have you arrested anyone for any of these crimes?"

"One old man who, frankly, is no highwayman. He merely acted the part to get enough coin for drink and was easily caught."

"My wife believes one of them is szlachta. If she could listen to a voice—"

"Would you have me parade every nobleman in town past her? Not only is that impractical, it would be nigh on impossible," the man sniffed. The thought occurred to Jacek that the starosta could be the educated highwayman Liwi described, but he quickly discarded the idea. As a starosta, the man made plenty of money and did so without endangering himself.

With promises to inform Jacek and his party should they catch any suspects, the starosta and his deputies left. Frustration and defeat whirling inside of him, Jacek had his and Oliwia's dinners brought to their tent. That night, she clung to him fiercely as she slept, certainly more than she ordinarily would, especially with the other bodies cluttering their tent. But he wasn't complaining. In some small way, it soothed him to know she felt safe in his arms, even though he hadn't done a damned thing to protect her.

As he lay beside her, his mind turned over plans and routes. Tomorrow, he would select a detachment to help him see her and Nadia safely behind Żółkiew Castle's fortified walls. Without the cumbersome wagons slowing them down, they would easily reach the town in three days.

Now that he had solved that problem, he turned to his next thorny issue: what to do about Filip.

CHAPTER 15

Silnyród

Though the next days brought fair weather and no brigands, Jacek remained on high alert, at times riding with the vanguard, at other times with the rear guard, but always swiveling his head to and fro. Oliwia and Nadia's chatter as their eyes took in new sights belied the fact they had nearly been raped and possibly murdered a mere three days prior. Filip, however, acted as though Jacek had berated him mere minutes ago, and the lad cloaked himself in a brooding, dark sullenness that kept him from interacting with most everyone.

The worried glances Jacek occasionally observed Oliwia casting her brother's direction sat like a rock in Jacek's chest, but nothing could be done for it. The boy had to come into his own, on his own. He certainly wasn't going to accept direction from Jacek … or anyone else, for that matter. Even Henryk's cajoling thudded flat.

Jacek rode between Dawid and Marcin in the vanguard and was searching behind him, eyes finding Oliwia so he could reassure himself she wasn't laboring to keep up.

"Rider up ahead," Dawid announced.

Jacek whipped his head to the front. "Does he ride alone?" He squinted, finally spying movement in the distance; the minuscule outline of a horse and rider approached. "He appears to be in a hurry." He reached into a leather pouch attached to his cantle and extracted the looker he had been gifted by Gian, his benchmate on an Ottoman slave galley many, many years ago.

He slowed Jarosława to a near standstill and raised the looker to his eye. "Do you see anyone else?" asked Marcin.

"No, but he is carrying a blue-and-white pennant, and I think I can make out the Lubicz coat of arms with the upside-down horseshoe between two knight's crosses."

"Żółkiewski's coat of arms," Dawid remarked.

"Could be anyone from that clan," Henryk countered.

Jacek lowered the looker and urged Jarosława into a trot. "Let's meet him and find out, shall we?" He signaled behind him for three men-at-arms to replace them at the vanguard.

The rider drew closer, slowing to a trot, and Jacek made out a man in his early twenties. His chest heaving with exertion, he pointed at one of the Biaska banners snapping behind them. "Red and yellow. Are you of Biaska?"

"Who wants to know?" Jacek replied.

"I have a message for Commander Jacek Dąbrowski from the Grand Hetman of the Crown, Stanisław Żółkiewski."

Jacek pressed his knees into Jarosława's sides, urging her forward. "I am he."

The messenger looked him over, his gaze landing on Jacek's jagged scar. "So you are. The hetman has left for Lublin, but he will be back in two sennights. He asked that you not proceed to the border until you receive further instructions. You may await his return at your border estate, or, if you prefer, Pani Żółkiewska offers guest quarters at Żółkiew Castle." His eyes scanned the troops stacked behind Jacek. "And your men may encamp in the ward. You are all welcome to remain there until the hetman's return."

"Jacek." Oliwia's voice came from behind him, and he turned his head, annoyed. When had she worked her way up to the vanguard, and why the hell wouldn't she stay put? "Since the hetman is not presently at Żółkiew, why not proceed to Silnyród? If he's assembling his army just north of the Dneiper, the trip between Silnyród and the staging area would be shorter."

"She makes sense, Jacek," Henryk offered.

Jacek ignored them both and addressed the messenger. "You look as though you've been riding hard. Would you care to take some refreshment while I work out my reply?"

The young man nodded. "At your service, my lord."

Before a half hour had expired, the messenger was on his way back to Żółkiew with a reply, and the entire Biaska caravan, minus a score of soldiers, had turned and was plodding in the same direction the messenger had gone.

The remainder, which included Jacek, Henryk, Filip, Dawid, Marcin, the women, and two packhorses, veered eastward to Silnyród.

He'd never thought of visiting this godforsaken landscape again, and yet here he was, treading toward a place that held nothing he wanted to recall. What awaited them—a vast, empty landscape that had little regard for human life—left him dreading every approaching inch.

The farther east they went, the sparser villages and settlements became. Forests bursting with unfurling leaves thinned, giving way to squat shrubs dotting a scrubbed landscape of undulating ground. Fields that had once been plowed lay fallow.

An eeriness settled heavy on Oliwia's shoulders, like a mantle lined with lead ingots. The land was desolate and still and menacing, as if eyes watched them. Hairs prickled along her neckline, and she felt as though she walked through a silent graveyard under the watchful presence of specters. Who would live—let alone build an estate—in such a hauntingly empty place as this?

She asked Jacek that very question one night as they huddled under a lean-to being torn asunder by the relentless wind. The question kept her mind from wandering to her warm feathery bed at home and her little ones, who often filled it. It also kept her from dwelling on the highwayman's kick to her stomach and what damage he might have caused. So far, the blow had produced no grave consequences, and the pain had abated.

"Many more people used to live here before the Tatars began their raids. Back then, there was reason to have a fortress among the settlements, someplace safe where people could flee for protection if they were attacked. It also served as a center of commerce, drawing people in to sell or trade their wares. Then those blasted Tatar whoresons began setting fire to villages in the middle of the night and capturing terrified people as they escaped the flames. From a military standpoint, it's a rather brilliant strategy. Smoke out your prey and funnel them right into your net. From the view of all that is godly and decent and merciful, it is brutal. Far too many who came to the steppe to farm and raise a family were enslaved, marched along the Black Trail far, far away from everything they know and everyone they loved, to be treated as poorly as insects one might squash under one's boot. Dogs are treated better."

He had held her tight as he had calmly explained, with her fighting the quakes shuddering through her body. Later, she had practically burrowed into him, as if doing so would keep him safe from dark memories, sleeping little for thinking of all those people, thinking how lucky she was that her husband had escaped a similar fate. Later, she would fall into a deep sleep free from Tatars and other nightmares.

On the third day after they had detoured toward Silnyród, the nightmare become real and the Tatars' cruelty revealed itself. They came upon the blackened skeletons of structures where men, women, and children had once lived, toiled, and loved. An entire settlement had been wiped out.

Jacek and several guards dismounted and crept toward the ruins, ever vigilant, while Henryk and Dawid lingered behind to watch over her and Nadia.

When he returned to his mount, his face was grim. "This happened long ago." Yet he was visibly shaken—the entire party was shaken. A pall descended over them, and each step seemed to grow more weighted than the last, as though a heavy shroud had been dropped upon them and was entangling them within its folds.

Jacek rode apart from them the rest of that day, and she left him alone to wage war with the ever-present demons haunting his soul, demons that had lain dormant for years and had only sprung to life since leaving Rzeszów in their wake.

Why, oh why had she insisted on this journey? All of her yearned to turn and flee. Instead, she drew her cloak tight about herself despite the sunbeams shining down and warming them on this fair May day.

The burned-out settlement overwhelmed her thoughts. It brought to mind the ghosts of Vyatov, the village where she had lived before Jacek had saved her and Filip. So much violence had befallen their home that day, with her and Filip the only survivors. That horrible destruction had been wrought not by Tatars or Lost Men, but by Polish soldiers. Lost Men, sometimes called the Forlorn Hope or Elears … the Lisowczycy.

How could man be so cruel to fellow man?

The party ate their meager meals in silence and camped rough. She found herself longing not for her soft bed, but for protective walls and simple straw pallets to rest their aching bones upon.

More days of riding passed until, at last, Jacek twirled his arm in the air. "Silnyród ahead!" He had been stock-still astride Jarosława, the looker to his eye as he had surveyed the landscape.

A whoop rippled through the troop, and her heart leaped in her chest when she made out a dark, symmetrical shape on the horizon she had first mistaken for a hummock like those so plentiful in the Jura Highlands where Biaska lay. Far off yet, but the fortress began to take shape in the open landscape where it sat, its looming stone walls promising shelter.

As they drew closer, the fortification appeared larger and sturdier than she had envisioned, its stone walls forbidding and unscalable. The surrounding flat ground was broken up by breastworks and spiked trenches and a dry moat spanned by a wooden bridge. To the right, on the fortress's eastern flank, thatch-roofed houses huddled together, the smoke from their chimneys drifting into the sky. Beyond them lay a crescent of dark woods that swept east to south.

The promise of shelter soothed her after days being exposed on the steppe. But now a new concern swam through her mind: she would soon come face-to-face with the woman Jacek had once asked to marry him. Perhaps Silnyród would not be so accommodating, after all.

She had little time to ponder the wayward worry, for a fresh buzzing undulated through the column, this one lifting the hairs on her nape and arms.

At the front of the line, Jacek unsheathed his sabre with lightning speed. Stabbing it at the sky, he bellowed, "Tatars! Make for the fort as fast as you can!"

Off to the right, at as yet a distance from the fortress, a thick, locust-like swarm was emerging from the woods on the south side. The trajectory would bring the enemy right into their path!

Jacek spurred Jarosława into a spin. Horse and rider flew to her and Nadia, even as guards were urging them forward.

"How many, Jacek?" Henryk shouted.

"Three score. You and Dawid protect the women." In her peripheral vision, Henryk nodded and dropped back, drawing even with her and her maid.

Oliwia's mount, Apolonia, danced in place, no doubt absorbing Oliwia's own distress, and when Jacek reached her, he took the reins and brought the horse under control.

Intensity blazed in his sapphire eyes when he looked directly into hers. "Liwi! Take Nadia and run like the wind. Do not delay, and don't look back."

Panic swelled inside her, choking her, stealing her breath. "What about you?" she squeaked.

"I will be with you shortly. Now go!" He whacked her horse's rump with the flat of his sabre and repeated the motion with Nadia's mount. The horses vaulted into motion, racing ahead with guards flanking them like a protective wall. Too short a wall. Behind her, Jacek yelled, "Run as though Lucifer and the hounds of hell are at your heels!"

Because they were.

Spirit of God! Had Jacek not been scanning the horizon with the looker, he would not have noticed the Tatar cavalry before it was far too late to make the fortress gates. Though the raiders were still at some distance, they were without question those accursed whoresons. The Tatars' style of riding was distinctive, as were the size of their mounts, and he had seen far too many of the flea-infested devils to mistake them for Cossacks or Commonwealth quartz troops. Why were they riding for Silnyród? They had to be attacking!

Jacek and his band had a chance to reach the fortress before the enemy, for the Tatars were as yet unaware of their presence. But that would last for one or two breaths, no more, and any advantage they had would vanish.

His thoughts jumped to safeguarding Oliwia and Nadia. If they fell into the Tatars' hands …

Jacek pivoted in place until he reassured himself everyone was moving with haste. Henryk and Dawid rode on either side of the women, with Filip and Marcin just behind. Setting the pace, Jacek raced ahead, his heart hammering in time with Jarosława's hoofbeats. He knew the land, knew where the divots and rocks lay, and he would guide his group to the safety of Silnyród's defenses.

Beneath him, Jarosława labored, lather collecting on her coat. God of mercy, but she was getting too old for this! In his head, she retorted that *he* was too.

"You remember this terrain, old girl, so let's show them how fast you can go." He leaned over her neck, daring a glance behind him. The wind tore his kolpak from his head, but he didn't care. What mattered was that everyone was riding on his heels in tight formation. *Good!*

The Tatars had spotted them and were closing fast. *Bastards!* It didn't take a looker to know how outnumbered his squad was. To the Tatars, they were easy prey. Overpower his band, and the enemy was assured gold, horses, and slaves.

Oliwia! No, he would not let that fate befall her. He urged Jarosława into a gallop. "We are on the battlefield at Kłuszyn, and we're charging into the enemy!" he urged. "You and I, in the front, and we will smash their line."

Had the horse understood him? She surged forward, hooves digging into the earth and sending up a spray of dirt clods. Silnyród rose higher, bigger. Soon they would be at her gates and behind her palisades.

He cast another sideways glance at the Tatars. They were matching pace, getting nearer. Then he saw something that turned his blood to ice.

Bows!

Tatars were skilled archers, able to nock an arrow and send it to its mark while galloping at top speed on a horse's back. And right now, he could make out several riders doing just that.

"Arrows!" he yelled behind him. He caught a glimpse of Oliwia's dogged expression, eyes bright with purpose, mouth clamped in an unforgiving line as she too took in the Tatars. He loved that fierce look, and his heart levitated for a beat.

An arrow whizzed past him, sobering him. No matter how much determination and fire she possessed, it would not stave off capture or death at the Tatars' hands.

Now loomed the fortress walls, and hope surged inside Jacek. Lesław had carried on Jacek's work, reinforcing the wooden palisades with stone. Yes, yes! They just needed to fly through the gates and—

The gates were barred! There was no other way in. His heart plummeted to his stomach.

More arrows whizzed behind him. A man cried out. At this distance, wheel-locks would fall short of their targets, and Jacek had no time to ready his own bow.

He dug his heels into Jarosława's flanks. More arrows flew, but they went in the opposite direction.

They're coming from the fortress! They've seen them! Thank Christ!

More shrieks. The sound of horses crashing propelled him toward the gates, and he stood at the bridge, shouting, "Open up!"

Figures peered over the ramparts.

"For the love of God, open the damned gates!" He roared in Latin, then in Polish and Lithuanian.

"Jacek?" someone cried.

"Lesław! Let us in!"

The gates creaked open enough to allow no more than two riders through at a time. Jacek's guards fell back, and the women were across the bridge and through first, and he puffed out a relieved breath.

The gates creaked open a little wider. Windmilling his sword arm, he urged everyone through until only he, Henryk, and Dawid remained. The gates began a slow, rolling close.

"Hurry!" the guards on the wall urged. "They're almost here!"

"Jacek!"

He snapped his head toward Henryk, his gaze darting to where Henryk pointed. In the turmoil, Jacek had lost sight of Filip. And there was the foolish boy now, loosing arrows on the oncoming enemy as he rode *toward* them!

Jacek shouted Filip's name, to no avail.

"Go, go!" he urged Henryk. "I can't leave him out there!"

"But—"

"He is my responsibility!"

Grim as Jacek had ever seen him, Henryk saluted him with his sabre. "May God protect you, my friend." He turned his steed toward the gate as Jacek urged Jarosława toward the fray.

He crossed himself. *May it be swift. May Filip and Jarosława survive.*

The Tatar cavalry bore down.

Filip shouted a string of curses at the oncoming enemy. Thrills charged his bloodstream as he nocked and shot one arrow after another. His movements were smooth, confident, and accurate. He was a well-oiled siege machine, and he had already felled three of the vile vermin! Now Jacek would see—no, they would *all* see—that he was worthy of being more than a *junior* squire.

One of his arrows missed and skidded impotently in the dirt. The next embedded itself into flesh, sending a horsed rider crashing to the ground. They were drawing closer now. Joy thumped in his chest. He reached into his quiver, groping when his hand closed on only four shafts. How could that be? Had some spilled out as he rode?

Panic shot from his stomach and filled his mouth, corrosive and bitter. He swallowed it down and nocked the next arrow. A wall of Tatars surged toward him.

One, two, three. Breathe. Breathe! When had they become so many and drawn so close?

"Filip!" Jacek's voice thundered behind him, and Filip spun his horse toward the sound. Thank God the squad hadn't deserted him!

His elation fled when he realized Jacek raced toward him alone. Behind his brother-in-law, the fortress gates groaned into place. Silnyród was closed.

Filip spurred his horse toward Jacek, the panic welling, spreading, driving his limbs and thoughts.

When he reached Jacek, his brother-in-law shoved his own quiver into Filip's hand. "You invited this fight! Now fall back to the gate, and pray they let us in! Otherwise, that is where we take our last breath."

Filip swallowed but could muster no moisture to coat his burning throat.

Jacek's sabre dangled from its lanyard, and Filip unsheathed his own as his brother-in-law slid his primed pistols from their holsters. Jacek had two shots. Filip had dozens of arrows. How many foes could they defeat before they were swarmed?

"Go!" Jacek barked, fury etched in his features.

Filip fled, an image branded on his brain of his brother-in-law backing his horse, facing the enemy armed with naught but two wheel-locks and a sabre.

Hooves thudded behind him, but Filip dared not look as he flattened his body and urged his horse to go faster, faster, faster. He clattered onto the bridge spanning the moat.

The boom of a cannon startled him, rumbling through the walls before him like God's angry voice. Then came another volley of shot and arrows sailing overhead. Chest heaving, Filip stopped partway on the bridge and dared a glance over his shoulder.

A series of war whoops pierced the din of battle, and a volley of arrows struck one of the Tatars in the back, even though that enemy was bearing down on Jacek, now many yards from Filip's position. How was it possible an arrow had hit the enemy's *back*? It happened again, wounding a half-dozen more foes.

Jacek fired his wheel-locks, and two Tatars toppled, blood and matter blooming on their earth-dull tunics. One fell while the other dangled from his saddle, and his horse turned broadside, causing a jam among the Tatars. Jacek scrambled *toward* them but was swallowed up in smoke, thick and acrid, that obscured the field beyond the dry moat. The smell of blood joined the unholy mixture.

The smoke cleared as more arrows slithered across the sky, and artillery rained down from Silnyród's ramparts, tearing through tissue and bone. The Tatars had turned away, seeming to engage a swarm of soldiers not their own. Filip shook his head as if to shake off his confusion.

What was happening? Should he ride to his brother's aid?

Torn between following Jacek and hurtling across the bridge to safety, Filip felt as though he were caught in a bog of molasses, unable to move. His head rang, and his ears were muffled from gun and cannon fire. The screams of dying horses and men pierced the cottony affect. Hesitation paralyzed him.

A familiar voice yanked him from his stupor. He looked up. The gate was ajar, and there stood Henryk on his warhorse, waving his arm and bellowing, "Get in here! Now!"

Filip raced toward Henryk as Silnyród's gates groaned open and horsemen poured through the opening.

"What's going on?" he shouted at Henryk.

"A relief force has appeared. God's archangels, perhaps." Henryk prepared to ride out.

Filip hesitated. "Should I go too?" He didn't want to go, and his tone reflected his exhaustion and cowardice and filled him with shame. More than anything, he yearned to be enveloped by solid stone walls.

Relief waved through him when Henryk laid a hand on his shoulder. "No. You've caused enough trouble. Now get inside and stay there!"

138

Filip nodded and hung his head, unable to muster an ounce of anger at the rebuke. Instead, he moved to the side and weaved his way through the gate, avoiding the brave troops flying out to meet the enemy. He would not be among them today. He didn't deserve to be.

CHAPTER 16

Aftermath, the Hereafter, and Afterthought

J acek heaved in breath after breath as he watched a knot of Tatars flee in the direction from which they had ridden. Others turned and ran as soon as the other force joined the skirmish. He had suffered only minor abrasions and bruises, but his arms were like heavy oaken limbs, dragging at him, stooping his shoulders. Though he still sat in his saddle, his legs were no better. His thighs burned from the strain of keeping himself in said saddle, and his calves shook with fatigue.

Catching his breath, he surveyed the battlefield strewn with bodies and horses and gear and blood. So much blood. Its copper tang filled his nostrils, along with the pungency of smoke, earth, death, and shit.

He noted with grim satisfaction that more Tatars littered the ground than any of his own or those who had ridden in and added to their numbers.

Right now, those mystery men were stripping bodies of garments and belongings, digging through pockets and folds of clothing, cutting off hair or ears or fingers that displayed any shiny object, no matter how insignificant. They carried out their looting smoothly and swiftly, seeming not to consider or care if a body was dead yet. The plunderers treated the dead and living with equal disregard, wrenching a coat from a man with a crushed arm or ribs, or boots from one with torn legs, heedless of their screams of pain. And if the wounded man struggled too much, the pillagers casually plunged a blade into a kidney or neck to stop the noise.

"You there," Jacek yelled at one of the men nearest him, "leave some of them alive."

The man stopped his rooting about long enough to level an amused look on him. "What for?"

"So we can question them and find out where they're camped. So we can track down their companions and finish them off. And they may have knowledge of other raids being planned even now." Or Ottoman plans—possibly even the Empire's troop movements and the strength of their armies.

The man bent back to his work. "They're Tatars. That's all we need know."

Out of the side of his mouth, Jacek hissed to Dawid beside him, "Let's get our own behind the walls before this carrion takes everything from them as well. And bring in a few of the enemy who appear hale enough to interrogate."

A handful of the mysterious fighting men helped themselves to tack and saddles and saddlebags, some even leading off horses. To Dawid, he added, "Grab any horses you can too."

A familiar figure with a straight back and broad shoulders steered his mount across the field and headed for Jacek. Where had Jacek seen him before? As the man drew closer, Jacek took in the mustached face, then his eyes drifted to the man's horse. Jacek's breath caught. A sleek, beautifully built mare, with a coat of rich sable, had all his attention.

The man spoke, and now his identity crystallized. "So we meet again, Pan Dąbrowski." Gabriel Wronski tilted his head in a small bow.

The thanks Jacek had planned to bestow upon his rescuers stuck in his craw. "Gabriel Wronski, well met. Your arrival was most timely."

Wronski flashed him a grin. "My men always enjoy a bit of sport with these Mongol bastards." He jerked his chin toward the man Jacek had exchanged words with, the one who continued liberating corpses of their

141

treasures. "You must excuse Arek. He has no use for any living Tatar since they carried off his wife and son."

Jacek nodded his understanding. They watched the activity for several silent beats before Jacek canted his head at the horse. "That's a beautiful mare you have there. How did you come by her?"

Wronski did not hesitate. "From a different band of heathens we encountered as they fled back to Crimea with their ill-gotten goods." He stroked the mare's glossy neck. "She's a beauty, eh? I wager she was not one of theirs but likely once belonged to a szlachcic." He sent Jacek a knowing wink. "But I didn't let the kumis-sucking bastards live long enough to tell me."

Wronski scanned the scene before them as if he were at a town fair. "Did you lose any men?"

"No, and no horses that I'm aware of. You?"

"We lost two mounts, but no men. Mercifully."

Jacek reckoned Wronski was accompanied by thirty men-at-arms. Who the devil was he? "Your arrival was most fortuitous. I speak for my men and the good people of Silnyród when I say we are grateful you came when you did."

Wronski nodded. "Are you Lord of Silnyród?"

"The fortress is one of my wife's holdings."

"So you *are* the lord." Wronski smirked, and Jacek felt an inexplicable urge to wipe it from his face. Instead, he nudged for more information.

"What brought you to this place?" He waited patiently, his eyes trained on the man as he watched for any telltale twitches, but Wronski's face was as blank as one of the corpses before them.

After several long moments, he met Jacek's gaze. "We were hired by a Lithuanian magnate to track down his wife."

Mercenaries, then. "So you and your men hire out? Which magnate?"

"Only occasionally, when there is great need." Wronski dropped his voice conspiratorially. "As for the magnate, I'm not at liberty to say. Seems the lady was seduced by the son of a voivode, a young man fifteen years her junior. You can understand why the magnate does not wish his name known. It could prove rather, ah, humiliating."

Instinct told Jacek Wronski was lying. "And were you successful?"

"Pardon?"

"Did you find the lady in question?" What was it about Wronski that set Jacek's teeth on edge?

"Ah. Yes and no. That is, we found her, but her lover paid us a great sum to hide that fact from her husband. For now."

"Information to the highest bidder, yes?"

"Isn't that how it always works?" Wronski let out a hearty laugh, though it held a greasy quality to it.

"So how and why did you happen upon Silny—"

"Jacek!" Jacek snapped his head up to Oliwia's voice. She stood on the ramparts, a hand in the air, and an unexpected wave of relief flooded him. Upon its crest rode unbridled joy.

Anticipating her question, he waved back. "I am well."

"I shall come out—"

"No! Wait until I come to you." He didn't want her close to the carnage. Though it was on full display from where she stood, distance kept its full impact somewhat contained, he reasoned.

Wronski turned his head leisurely toward her voice only to bring it abruptly forward. The smugness disappeared from his visage. "The lady is …?"

"My wife, Lady Oliwia Dąbrowska." When Wronski didn't reply, he added, "The Lady of Silnyród."

Wronski cleared his throat. "Your wife is … quite comely. Unusual eyes, those. So light. I expect you do not tire of looking at them."

"I am blessed in my wife," Jacek agreed, intrigued by the change in Wronski's demeanor. "I should go to her. You and your men will stay and be Silnyród's guests, yes? The manor house is not large, but we will accommodate you and find room for your men in the village."

Wronski's eyes traveled the battle scene once more. "That is a generous offer, but my men and I must move along."

Surprised, Jacek reared back. "Surely you can stay long enough to share a meal. Your men must be famished—"

Shaking his head, Wronski held up his hand. "We are due, ah, at the magnate's court and must deliver our news with all haste. Before that, though, we have fleeing Tatars to track down and kill." He barked several commands at his soldiers.

One of them returned an astonished look. "But, Captain, we're not done—"

"Now!" Wronski bellowed. As contrary as a raging storm to a sun-filled day, Wronski's expression transformed with a beatific smile. "Fighting alongside you has been an honor and a pleasure, Commander Dąbrowski. Would you please give your lovely lady wife my heartfelt apology for leaving so abruptly? I hope we may meet at some other time, under less … bloody circumstances." A grin curved his mouth, and he gave Jacek a small salute before backing his horse and pivoting.

Bemused, Jacek merely nodded as he watched man and mount trot away—the mount intended for *him*, Jacek was sure of it. He studied the captain, studied the men who served him, until his attention was snagged once more by his wife's voice drifting from the wall as she exchanged heated words with someone.

Jacek looked up at Oliwia's dark outline against the bright sun; the form beside her was tall and lanky with curls atop his head. *Filip*. The boy turned and raced out of sight, and she started after him, stopped, and started again, disappearing from Jacek's view.

His mind shifted from Wronski to the bits and pieces that made up the mosaic of his life. Though he could see Oliwia was unharmed, the overwhelming urge to pull her into his arms and reassure himself burst inside him. As he rode through the gate, scanning the chaos for her, two things occurred to him: He had not learned what had brought Wronski to Silnyród's aid, and how the devil could the man have seen Oliwia's eyes? Her features were concealed in the muted shadows that had been playing over her.

Bringing Jarosława to a standstill, he dismounted, his attention glued to his wife's slight form darting toward him. His heart caught in his throat. He opened his arms in time to catch her as she leaped into his embrace.

144

"Oliwia!" he croaked. Tears stung his eyes, and he gave himself over to the warm, sweet kisses she rained over his cheeks, his jaw, his neck while his fingers dove into the unbraided hair at the back of her head. She murmured his name, murmured she loved him, murmured she was grateful he was whole. In that moment, life roared through his veins like it hadn't done in years. The questions swirling—about Wronski, the Tatars, the attack—fled from his head.

Cradling his face, she drew back, tears spilling from her crystal-blue eyes that swept him from brow to chin. "Jacek, I thought I'd lost you! Praise God, you are unharmed."

He crushed her to him, indulging himself a moment to breathe in the citrus-and-herb-fresh scent of her he loved so dearly. This was his home.

She hugged his neck fiercely, pressing her body to his before separating herself from him. Clinging to his hands, she made a quick perusal of his body with her gaze.

He laughed. "I am whole, Liwi, thanks to Captain Wronski and his men. We all owe him a debt of gratitude."

"I would like to thank him myself."

"He sends his apologies, but he and his men could not stay." It occurred to Jacek that Wronski's abrupt departure mimicked the last encounter, on their return journey from Halicz. The captain and his men had disappeared like so much smoke then in the same manner they did today.

Oliwia's mouth parted, and her delicate brows drew together in a tiny frown. "Oh."

"But you and Nadia are well? And Filip?"

Without answering, she glanced over her shoulder when Henryk joined them and clapped a hand on his shoulder. "You look as though you could use a wash."

Jacek took in his friend's face, freckled with blood, and grinned. "As do you. Thank you for joining the fight."

Henryk gaped at him. "What, you expected I would miss the chance to rout Tatar curs? As for Filip"—he jerked his chin to the side—"he is in one piece, miraculous as that is. He was white as a sheet and his tongue seemed to have left him, so I put him in charge of our horses. I reckoned it was best to give him something to do rather than to leave him alone with his thoughts."

Jacek glanced down at Oliwia. "Or to fight with his sister. What was that all about?"

She flapped a hand. "Nothing. I simply told him to take in the scene below because *that* is what it means to be a soldier, not merely impressing a maid with one's shiny sabres or spinning spurs."

"Although those do help considerably when it comes to the maids." Henryk winked at her, and she rolled her eyes in return.

Jacek's mood was too dark to let himself be buoyed by the levity. Leaving Filip alone to turn over his sister's words might serve him well, he thought bitterly. In his eagerness to "prove" himself, the reckless lad nearly gotten them killed!

"Jacek!" boomed Lesław. Quick strides brought his old friend to his side, and they shared a teeth-jarring clinch. "I am delighted to see you, my old friend, but I cannot for the life of me comprehend why you thought to invite the Tatars." Lesław beamed him a wide smile. The creases framing his friend's brown eyes had deepened, and strands of gray hid among the dark ones in his bushy beard. They were *all* getting older.

Lesław smacked his shoulder, yanking Jacek back to present. "Like old times, yes?" *Too much like old times.* "Although you could have taken shelter behind our walls and not engaged. We were prepared for them."

Now it was Jacek's turn to gape. "So this attack was no surprise?"

"Only the timing of it. Several of our scouts spotted them days ago, but then the bastards—" Lesław seemed to remember Oliwia was in their midst and mumbled a quick apology while giving her a dip of his head.

In response, she smirked. "If you are speaking of Tatars, I am in full agreement that they are bastards. Please do go on."

Henryk chuckled, but Lesław paled before pink engulfed his cheeks. "Of-of course, my lady." He cleared his throat. "As I was saying, our men caught sight of the Tatars, but as they are wont to do, they disappeared like a mist on the river. Our scouts continued their daily reconnaissance missions, but they saw no evidence of the raiders and we all assumed they had moved on." Lesław shook his head. "Obviously, their appearance today shows we were mistaken." He paused to sweep a hand about the place, like a proud father showing off his newborn son. "As you can see, we continued your improvements, Jacek. Silnyród is well fortified now, and unless they bring siege engines, we can withstand a raid or two. Unlike Matejko Manor. Pity, that. Eugenia is quite distraught," he tsked.

Jacek's head spun, but before he could ask what had happened to Klemens Matejko's estate, Lesław raised his gaze. His eyebrows pinched together. "Those men who fought with you, who were they?"

"A troop commanded by a man named Captain Gabriel Wronski. Do you know of him?"

Lesław's eyes widened. "They are Lisowczycy! The devil's spawn!"

"I suspected they were mercenaries, but …" Why hadn't Jacek made the connection? Because Wronski had been *too* polished, too much like Jacek in his bearing. And Jacek had let that blind him. But now he questioned if Wronski had truly intended to come to their aid, or if his arrival had been sheer happenstance, and his gratitude became tinged with suspicion and distaste. "Don't tell me the Forlorn Hope are up to their old tricks here?"

"That is a mild description," Lesław growled. "They are the scourge of Podolia, Slovakia, the Holy Roman Empire, wherever they travel. Like cockroaches, we cannot rid ourselves of them. Ever since they defeated the Transylvanians at the Battle of Humienne last November, they have been turned loose by Emperor Ferdinand and King Zygmunt to plunder whomever, wherever, killing even children and dogs."

"Did some not remain in the employ of the Holy Roman Empire?" Henryk asked.

"They did," Lesław confirmed. "Their army split up, with some remaining in the service of the emperor. Others returned to Poland, and they've been pillaging their way across the countryside." He let out a mirthless laugh. "They are no longer the 'Forlorn Hope.' They have a new name now: Riders of the Apocalypse. And the name suits."

In far-off Biaska, Jacek had heard little of the Lost Men's exploits. A few rumors from travelers or during their recent visits to Halicz, no more. Lesław's next comment caught him like a *nadziak*'s breath-stealing blow to the chest.

147

"We suspect it was the Forlorn Hope who attacked Matejko Manor."

Every hair on Oliwia's body lifted as though charged with electricity. The Lost Men, here! The same men who slaughtered everyone in her village before setting it ablaze in 1610! She looked at Jacek, whose mouth hung open as he, along with everyone else, fastened his eyes on Lesław.

Henryk hissed, "The devil, you say!"

Jacek seemed to recover himself and drew in a lung-filling breath. "What of your father-in-law and his household?" Of course he would be the first among them, besides Lesław, to be concerned for his old friend and commander, Klemens Matejko. Why, the man had nearly become *his* father-in-law.

Lesław grimaced. "He was not present. He departed for Kamieniec with half his force weeks ago. Had he been there, or had I had any warning, we could have repelled the attack and kept the damage to a minimum. And killed a fair number of the brigands at the same time. They got little plunder, but they catapulted firepots over the walls and burned part of the place down."

"Your wife, is she there or here with you?" Oliwia blurted out, unable to contain her concern for a woman she didn't know.

"She and our children were to travel to Matejko—she still manages her father's estate—but, thank the Virgin, they had not yet set out when we received word," replied Lesław. "They are here and safe."

Oliwia arched a brow at him. "Safe depends upon one's perspective, yes?"

Jacek shot her a warning glare. Lesław looked stricken, and a pang knifed through her. She immediately wanted to reel back her harsh words. "I am sorry, Lesław. I did not mean … You are performing admirably here, especially under the circumstances. I should be more appreciative of all you do for Silnyród." She pressed one hand to her temple and another to her belly. "I believe the day's events have gotten the better of me. Will you please forgive me?"

A flush of embarrassment spread from his neck to his forehead. He dipped his head. "Of course, Lady Oliwia. Perhaps I should escort you inside—"

She wasn't quite ready for that yet, and she told him so. "A few more minutes in the outside air will help clear my head." Even though that air was filled with the sharp smell of gunpowder and the pungent scents of humanity, it would be far worse in the confines of the compact manor house. And in there waited Lady Eugenia …

The men had restarted their discussion, and she fisted her hands, digging her nails into her palms to clear her head.

"I'm not alleging they are one and the same," Lesław was saying, "but Wronski's band is well known in these parts as being rather indiscriminate when choosing their victims. While he has never been accused of raids near Silnyród, any number of Matejko's men-at-arms swear the Lost Men were involved in the attack. Their attire, weapons, and style of fighting are the same. Much as you witnessed in the fight today."

Beside her, Jacek rubbed his nape. "Can those witnesses identify these men they believe to be the same Elears?"

"Doubtful," Lesław replied. "They say their faces were entirely masked with scarves. Couldn't even see the color of their hair, it was so completely disguised."

Icy cold chattered up Oliwia's spine, and Jacek discreetly reached for her hand and squeezed.

When next he spoke, his deep voice rolled through her, soothing her. "Tell me, Lesław, have you had reports of highwaymen?" Lesław gave him a puzzled look, and Jacek continued. "Just a few men, but masked as you've described."

Lesław shook his head.

Jacek quickly summarized Oliwia and Nadia's encounter with the two marauders.

Henryk glanced up at the sky. "So what *were* Wronski and his men doing here? Are the attack on Matejko Manor and what happened here today linked, or are they mere coincidences?"

Jacek seemed steeped in thought, his eyes trained elsewhere as he tapped his chin.

"Jacek?" Henryk prodded.

"Possibly very convenient coincidences." Jacek met Henryk's gaze. "I have the same questions as you, plus one more. What if Wronski and his platoon's appearance was not a stroke of providence?

"I'm not sure I follow."

"What if their mission was actually to raid Silnyród themselves? Surely they knew of its existence."

"Probably even stopped here a time or two," Lesław agreed. "Passing themselves off as something other than the Lost Men, of course."

Jacek nodded. "Assuming they were the ones who attempted to plunder Matejko Manor, they would be driven to find another prize to take. Silnyród is not so far away. Perhaps they turned their thieving plans in this direction and were surprised to find Tatars with the same notion and a few steps ahead."

"If that's the case, that didn't work very well either," Henryk remarked dryly.

A headache began blooming behind Oliwia's eyes. "Wouldn't they have scouted first and been aware of the fortress's defenses? To not do so seems unnecessarily reckless."

"Desperate men *are* reckless," Jacek said, "but it's likely they were already familiar with the fortifications. They could have passed themselves off as merchants or travelers and gotten past the gates. Once inside, they could have easily sprung a trap."

Oliwia hugged herself. "How could one so cunning and ruthless ever be trusted?"

Henryk humphed. "Thank the saints none here has to be concerned with trusting them. It would be akin to trusting a hungry wolf to not sup on you."

"All this speculation could be just that," Jacek added. "After all, they could have still ridden in and wreaked more havoc. As it turns out, trusting

Wronski just now saved my life … and Filip's. They may be brigands and scoundrels, but they are formidable fighters."

The reminder of Filip's foolhardiness had Oliwia seeing in shades of red. She had approached him with an embrace and a few choice words when he had appeared on the battlements, and he had had the temerity to shrug her off before giving her a chance to bestow him with either. Her reckless brother had nearly gotten himself—and her valiant lord husband—killed. And for what? To show the world he could strike a few Tatars with his arrows?

To show the world that he could be killed, more like.

An involuntary shiver moved through her, and she placed a protective hand over her belly. Jacek must have noticed, for he arched a questioning eyebrow at her. "I believe it's past time you were inside with the other women," he rumbled.

Lesław gave her a polite bow. "I shall escort you inside to meet my wife. She will take care of you."

Her mind flashed to the broken bodies on the plain before Silnyród's gates, and she made up her mind.

Jacek must have mistaken her silence for hesitation. "Would you like me to accompany—"

She darted him a look and touched Lesław's arm. "That will not be necessary. You are both needed here. I will find your wife on my own, Lesław."

Taking in Jacek's look of mild surprise, she spun on her heel, picked up her skirts, and made for the manor house with her shoulders straight and her hammering heart rushing blood through her veins.

CHAPTER 17
Shackled Men Tell No Tales

A cacophony of women's voices greeted Oliwia when she stepped beneath the lintel, leaving the bright day behind and entering the murk of the manor house. The interior was dim and smoky, crowded with numerous shifting shadows. Movement stopped, and so did the chatter. Oliwia squinted, adjusting her sight.

A familiar feminine form appeared out of the shadows and took her hand. "Over here, m'lady. We have been so worried about you."

Oliwia thanked Nadia and let her lead her deeper into the manor's hall. Soon the shadows took shape, their features sharpening. Another form advanced on her, but before Oliwia could get a good look at the woman, she dropped into a deep curtsy.

"Welcome to Silnyród, Lady Oliwia," the bowed head before her said.

"I am honored to be here among you." *Whoever you might be.*

Silence charged the air, leaving Oliwia unsure what to do. At last, the woman straightened from her reverence. Clasping her hands in front of her, she looked Oliwia square in the eye. Several inches taller, the bowing woman had to look down to do so. "I am Lady Eugenia Nowakowska."

Oliwia lowered into a reverence of her own. "Lady Eugenia, it is a pleasure to meet you at last." Bringing herself upright, Oliwia pushed up on her toes. Her eyesight had adjusted, and she got her first close look at the lady.

To describe Eugenia as plain was an understatement, and Oliwia came to the conclusion without prejudice. Eugenia possessed a face devoid of any remarkable feature whatsoever, and her few adornments were modest. She was lithe of frame, with golden-brown hair caught in two braids. Guarded hazel eyes set close together stared out of a milky face scattered with faint freckles. Pale pink lips made up a tight mouth and completely disarmed Oliwia when they tipped up in a smile.

"I daresay greeting you in the midst of an attack was not what I had anticipated."

Oliwia burst out with a relieved laugh, and the entire place resumed buzzing. Soon a wizened woman with bony fingers stood before her. Like gnarled old grapevines, those fingers gripped Oliwia's hands.

About a head shorter, the crone tilted that head this way and that as she examined Oliwia like a cabbage she intended to chop. "So you are Captain Dąbrowski's wife." The woman's voice grated like ancient iron hinges.

Oliwia darted her eyes to various women's faces, but no one offered aid. Instead, they seemed to be holding a collective breath. She bobbed her head. "Yes."

"Such a tiny thing, and him so big. I hope you have the wherewithal to keep him walking in a straight line."

A snorting laugh escaped Oliwia. "Was he so badly behaved here?"

"Tchah! I could never get that one to wipe his boots. He dragged the outdoors in with him all the time, whether it was the stables or the black mud from the steppe—sometimes even vile Tatar blood—and no amount of haranguing stopped him doing it. Naughty like my grandsons, but too big for me to pinch his ears." Expression stoic, the woman patted Oliwia's hand before relinquishing it and tottering through a doorway that appeared to lead to the kitchens.

Tittering broke out in her wake, reminding Oliwia of a tree limb laden with chirping birds.

Eugenia positioned herself beside Oliwia. "You must forgive Bogna, Lady Oliwia. She has been Silnyród's master and commander since before the rest of us were born, and while I couldn't run the estate without her, she is more forceful than a gale."

"Biaska has Beata, who rules supreme over the kitchens. One never wants to be on her bad side, but I would be lost without her."

"Then you understand." Eugenia grasped her arm. "Come. Let me show you to your quarters so you can wash and change. I'll have one of the boys bring in your trunks." Eugenia led her to a heavy plank door that opened right onto the hall. "I wish we had more luxurious accommodations for guests, but your husband's old quarters are comfortable and fairly private."

A frisson of horror flamed Oliwia's cheeks. "Oh, we could not take your rooms—"

Eugenia slid her a sidelong glance. "You are not. My lord husband had more spacious quarters added soon after we were married." Eugenia's cool demeanor suddenly seemed to crack. "That is, you understand, before I knew Pan Dąbrowski had not perished."

Oliwia wasn't sure if she liked the woman or not—she needed more time in her presence to decide—but one thing was certain: she didn't enjoy watching Eugenia twist herself over something that had passed a long time ago. "Of course I understand. And I daresay I can speak for my husband when I tell you so does he."

Well, now we have that out of the way.

Eugenia pushed open the door and led Oliwia inside. She came to a stop at the footboard of a simple wood-framed bed covered in furs and began wringing her hands. "Do you think he has forgiven me?" Her voice came out in a hush so rushed Oliwia wasn't sure she had heard her correctly.

Stepping deeper into the chamber, she faced Eugenia and gathered the woman's hands in her own. "I am sure of it. Would you like me to speak to him on the matter? Or perhaps you would rather speak to him yourself—"

Eugenia's eyes widened. "Oh no, I could not! And truly, if you are sure he has recovered …"

Jacek's words about never having loved Eugenia—which he'd spoken more than once—bobbed about in Oliwia's brain. As Bogna had done with her, Oliwia gave Eugenia's hand a reassuring pat. "I am sure. I hope this is not awkward for you, us being here."

Appearing flustered, Eugenia slid her hands from Oliwia's grasp. She looked about to say something when a golden-haired whirlwind tore into the room and latched on to Eugenia's leg, its head reaching her hip.

"Mama, mama!" a little boy cried.

"Manfred, use your manners! We do not barge into a guest's private chamber as though we are uncouth little barbarians."

Oliwia crouched in front of the boy and looked into big green eyes. "Manfred? I am Pani Oliwia. How old are you?"

The little cherub held up four soggy fingers.

Oliwia feigned surprise. "Such a big boy! I have a daughter that very age and a little boy not much older." She poked the boy's belly, quelling the pangs lashing her heart.

Manfred stuffed a fist into his smiling mouth before hiding his head in his mother's skirts. Oliwia rose.

"Have you brought them with you?"

"Not this time." *And it is probably for the best.*

Sympathy softened Eugenia's features. "You must miss them terribly."

Like a fist, tears suddenly jammed Oliwia's throat, and she swallowed around the knot making it hard to breathe.

Eugenia uncoupled Manfred from her skirts and gave him a little pat on the bottom. "Shoo, now. Let me finish up with our guest."

Manfred dashed to the door and paused a moment to look over his shoulder. He gave Oliwia a beatific smile, sending a fresh wave of yearning crashing through her.

"He is a lovely child," Oliwia rasped.

"When he is not acting the hellion." Eugenia smiled softly and gestured about the chamber. "There is fresh water for washing. I will send in your maid. I hope you don't mind, but I arranged for her to share my maid's chamber. If you would prefer she stay here, I will arrange for a pallet to be brought in."

"No, your arrangement suits perfectly." *More* than perfectly. The idea of spending a few hours alone with Jacek was one she relished more than Father Cyprian would have approved of.

Eugenia left Oliwia alone to survey the sparse contents of the chamber where Jacek had once lived. Besides the bed, the room held a table with a single chair beneath a shuttered window. A pitcher and bowl stood upon a washstand, and tucked into one corner was a shrine of sorts that held a candle with a short, charred wick. Above it were a carved crucifix, a depiction of the Black Madonna—Our Lady of Częstochowa—and a faded painting. Drawing closer, she squinted at the image and let out a squeak when she realized it was one she had made of Jarosława and gifted to Jacek during her and Filip's first Christmas at Biaska.

Her eyes probed the wood-walled chamber for more vestiges of Jacek, and unsurprisingly, she found none. If not for the clutter of life brought by Biaska, her, and their children, her spartan man would leave few traces of himself anywhere.

She lowered herself upon the bed, her mind flipping through page after page of memories—some wondrous, some heart-wrenching. Life. Death. Love. So much love, like that which manifested itself in her belly at this very moment and had stood in the face of the evil that had visited Silnyród mere hours ago.

Yes, she carried new life inside her, a life the highwayman's viciousness hadn't dislodged. Of that she was certain. What she was not sure of was where that child would be born and whether it would be in the midst of calm or the storm of war. Nor was she sure how much longer she could keep its existence from its father.

Jacek fell in behind Lesław as he led them up the winding wooden staircase to the guardroom atop one of Silnyród's four watchtowers. Outside Silnyród's walls, guards dispatched mortally wounded Tatars and hauled off bodies to be buried in a pit. Few remained alive and mostly unscathed, and that handful was presently under lock and key in the guardroom. Many had fled, but with any luck, Wronski and his squad had tracked them down and dispatched them. Whatever else Wronski might be, at least they were in agreement on this particular enemy. A dead Tatar was one fewer to fight.

"You have transformed this shabby old fort into a true fortress, Lesław, and a thriving one at that." Jacek's voice echoed off the tower walls. "In truth, I feared Silnyród may no longer stand when we finally came upon it."

Lesław glanced over his shoulder as he trod the steps. "It is little used for its original purpose because so many have fled or been captured, leaving these lands devoid of humanity. Where there are no people, there is no need for a fortress to house them in times of attack. But what we've become accustomed to instead are travelers needing a refuge. Where else can they hide out here on the steppe?" He paused and beamed. "We are up to five whores now. And four have all their teeth! Henryk, you will likely enjoy them all."

"Likely," Henryk chuckled. "What sorts of visitors do you get?"

"Mostly military—detachments from the quarter troops or magnate armies—and the odd merchant or family traveling to visit loved ones." Lesław banged open a heavy wooden door reinforced with bands of iron, surprising two men-at-arms bent over a table. In one corner, three shackled prisoners slumped on the floor.

The soldiers looked up, and one broke out in a huge smile. "Ah! Look what the wolves have dragged in. If it isn't Kapitana Kamen-holova himself!" He skirted the table and pulled Jacek into a fierce embrace. Jacek laughed inwardly at his old nickname—Captain Rockhead, earned when he had survived being bashed in the head by Tatar raiders.

When the man released him, Jacek returned a grin of his own and clasped the man's shoulder. "Florian, you flea-infested mongrel! How do you fare?" His old friend's hair was still a riot of raven curls, though threads of silver glinted among the strands, and creases cut deeper grooves around his mouth and eyes.

"I am well. God and the Blessed Mother see some purpose in keeping me on this earth, so they protect my hide."

"And a job they have of it, no doubt."

A sharp bark pulled Jacek's attention to a three-legged, pig-like dog at Florian's feet. "Jesus Christ! Is that Statyw? Or is it his ghost returned from the dead to haunt us all?" The dog had once been the bane of Jacek's existence at Silnyród.

"It is he in the flesh," Florian laughed. "Best Tatar hunter I've ever known."

Jacek crouched and held out the back of his hand for the dog to sniff, ready to snatch the hand back in case the mutt decided to taste rather than smell. "And how is my favorite tavern maid?"

The only sound was the shuffling of legs, and Jacek glanced up at Florian, whose face sagged. Jacek shot to his feet.

"Luiza died in childbirth several years ago," Lesław said quietly.

Jacek grasped Florian's shoulder once more. "I am so sorry." The vision of a pretty, dark-haired, dark-eyed maid floated through Jacek's consciousness. Full of vitality, always smiling, always flirting—though she had only ever had eyes for Florian. He swallowed around a knurl in his throat.

Florian nodded. His grim face quickly lightened. "She left me two daughters who are every bit as beautiful as their mother. They will always be a reminder."

"And he has another babe on the way," an amused voice called behind Jacek.

Jacek wheeled, his gaze landing on the other man they'd surprised when they had entered. This soldier also had a familiar face, one that beamed at him. Jacek would recognize that smile anywhere. "Benas?"

The Lithuanian boy-soldier who had come to Silnyród to study the ways of the hussar under Jacek and Lesław, who had fought at Jacek's side when they had reclaimed Biaska, was a boy no more. Jacek pulled him in for a hug and clapped him on the back. "It *is* you!"

"That it is. And don't feel too sorry for Florian. He has gone and married my sister and wasted no time getting her with child." He held up two fingers. "Twice!"

Jacek feigned shock. "How many children is that, Florian?"

Florian shrugged sheepishly. "Three in all—Darya gave me a son last summer, and God and the saints willing, we will have another child by the Feast of the Assumption of Mary."

158

"By Christ, you've been busy!"

Florian pointed an accusing finger at Benas. "As has he! He has three already!"

"God of Mercy, when were you wed, Benas? And who would want to marry you in the first place?" Jacek joked. "Did you drug the poor girl?"

"No, she seems to like me. Only girl who ever has, so I married her."

Lesław jerked his head toward the prisoners. "Speaking of coercion, what have you discovered?"

Levity was sucked from the room as though Zeus himself drew in a great breath, replaced by the grim reality sitting bloodied upon the floor. Hand resting upon the hilt of his sheathed sabre, Jacek turned and took in the raiders, whose pitiable state nearly wrested a thread of sympathy from him. Two appeared to be in the middle of their twenties, while the other was perhaps of an age with Filip—a mere boy.

Suddenly, memories, harsh and jagged, lanced him, and pictures he never wanted to see again unfurled in his mind, reminding him how other Tatar raiders had once abused him and his fellow captives—decent Christian men, women, children, some mere babes. An ever-present rage heated from a simmer to a slow boil, leaving the bitter taste of hatred in his mouth. His grip on the hilt tightened, and temptation to finish these three off himself sprang to the fore.

Florian's voice startled Jacek back to the guardroom. "Benas, lock them up." They had all been speaking Polish, and Florian switched to Latin as he explained to the others. "At least one understands Polish. Probably Lithuanian and Russian as well."

Chains rattled and bloodied men grunted as Benas hoisted them to their feet, one by one, and shoved them into a dark cell in one corner of the tower. The youngest of three was the last to be manhandled, affording Jacek a long look at him. Blood crusted his face and neck, and an ear hung from the side of his head by a fragile flap of skin. One quick yank, and Jacek could have easily held it in his palm. It must have hurt like the devil.

He ran his fingertips over the jagged scar on the left side of his face, a reminder of Tatar treatment he would carry for the rest of his days.

The sullen youth turned his head and spat. Benas sidestepped the glob with surprising grace. The Tatar then tried to head-butt his jailer, but Benas placed a boot on the youth's backside and kicked him into the cell and thudded the heavy door shut. Through a small metal grill, the young Tatar leveled a black look at Jacek and the others.

Benas sauntered back into their midst and lowered his voice. "They say they traveled from Crimea with a company whose mission was to bring back slaves. They claim to know nothing of an Ottoman army gathering south of the border."

"Do you believe them?" asked Henryk.

Florian smirked. "I do. Benas's methods are very, ah, effective, and besides, the young one—after cursing us to hell and back—added that if the sultan was gathering an army, he would be joining it now to help rid the world of infidels such as us."

Jacek glanced over his shoulder at the sullen young man, whose nose still pressed against the grill. "Just because they didn't encounter any armies doesn't mean one isn't mustering."

"True enough, but this lot is part of the Dobruja Horde, and they are usually the first to know when the Ottomans are organizing because they travel through the horde's territory and call them into service. So far this season, they have heard the usual rumors, nothing more, and they have seen no activity that leads them to believe war between the Ottoman Empire and the Commonwealth is coming."

Questions bombarded Jacek's brain. Could they be believed? Their news flew in the face of what the Crown Grand Hetman Żółkiewski maintained. So who was right? "Lesław, what do your patrols say?"

"Of an army, nothing. Of raiding Tatars, they have seen an increase in their mischief, but one must ask if it's caused by more unrest or if it is simply the time of year when their incursions into Podolia, Ruthenia, and Muscovy grow bolder. Before today's attack, Silnyród has been spared for a very long while."

"What prompted them to attack *now*?"

Lesław shrugged. "Perhaps it was one of the only targets remaining."

"Any ties to Wronski and his bunch?"

Only Lesław showed surprise at Jacek's question. "Do you suspect they had some kind of pact? The Lost Men took Matejko Manor in exchange for the Tatars getting Silnyród?"

Before Jacek could answer that he was considering all possibilities, no matter how outrageous they seemed on the surface, Benas piped up. "I don't think so. They've said they would sooner throw their children into the Dniester and watch them drown than ally themselves with the Elears or any other Commonwealth soldiers."

"Jacek," Lesław began, "after the attack on Matejko Manor, I was planning to take Eugenia and the children to Żółkiew. Now I am that much more intent on getting them there quickly. I suggest you accompany us and do the same with Oliwia. They are not safe here."

Jacek gave him a grim nod. "I am in total accord with you." He now had a solid reason for taking Oliwia somewhere safe, far away from Silnyród and the border. The question that loomed, though, was whether she would come willingly.

CHAPTER 18

Life at the End of a Thread

Jacek fell in behind Lesław and the other men, bringing up the rear as they entered the dark confines of the manor house's hall. He scanned the hazy space, on alert for two different women. One, his wife, he very much wanted to see. The thought of seeing the second one, Lesław's wife, was causing beads of sweat to pop out on his upper lip. While he had no problems controlling his fear when it came to confronting an enemy, coming face-to-face with the woman he had once been engaged to sent signals to his feet to turn and run in the opposite direction.

It never occurred to him that a *third* woman, one he had given nary a thought over the years, would shriek his name, throw her arms about his neck, and burst into tears.

Bogna so surprised him with her greeting that he nearly pried her from his torso before realizing who she was. Instead, he stood stock-still while she pulled away from him, recovered herself, and cupped his face in her knobby hands. Though she pushed up on her tiptoes, he had to stoop so she could kiss his cheeks.

"M'lord, I never thought to see you again. Welcome back to your old home."

He returned the kisses to her leathered face. "Bogna, it warms my heart to see you again. Obviously, Silnyród cannot do without you." He couldn't tell if she had aged, for she had always looked as ancient as the torches hanging on the inner walls of the fortress. He was quite convinced she had left the womb looking thus.

People pressed closer as Bogna ran on about his days at Silnyród, spending an inordinate amount of time on his muddy boots for reasons he could not comprehend. She pointed to said boots. "Are you tracking mud inside this clean abode yet again?"

His grin broadened. "No, I took great pains to scrape them off before entering." *Because Lesław made me.*

Laughter waved through the assembled group. A feminine figure emerged, and he backstepped. When her face came into view, he executed an awkward series of bows that likely made him resemble a bobbing chicken.

Eugenia dipped into a deep curtsy. "Welcome to Silnyród, my lord." She straightened and grasped his wrists. "It does my heart good to see you alive and breathing."

Dear Lord up in heaven! Were those tears shimmering in her eyes? He tugged at the collar of his żupan, fighting for the right words. "You are looking well, Lady Eugenia. Lesław tells me your union has been blessed with two children. I am delighted for you both."

"Yes, just as I have heard from your lovely lady wife of *your* children back in Biaska. You must be quite the proud father."

"That I am." Where the devil was Oliwia?

As if reading his inner thoughts, Eugenia swiveled her head, fastened on one particular form lingering at the back, and held out her hand. "Lady Oliwia, come. I expect you will want to show your husband to your quarters and help him get comfortable before the meal."

As Oliwia stepped from the shadows, he held his breath. Her placid expression gave no hint as to what thoughts streamed through her mind. She merely dipped her head in greeting and gestured for him to follow her. People parted as they made their way through the hall.

Trepidation tripped through his chest as they entered his old chamber and he latched the door behind him.

163

She pivoted to face him and swept a graceful hand in the air. "Does it look the same?"

His gaze traveled about the familiar room. "Uh, it appears so." His eyes landed back on hers. "No, there is one marked difference. It is brighter now, for you are in it."

She smirked, and several bands of tension loosened their grip in his chest. "Flatterer."

"Is it flattery if I am merely speaking the truth?" He snaked an arm around her waist and pulled her to him, gratified when she came willingly.

She raised her eyes to his. "Feeling guilty, are you?"

"I have nothing to feel guilty about," he pointed out rather logically. He dropped his free hand to the small of her back and pressed her closer still.

Looking away, she smoothed the fabric covering his biceps with an idle touch. "Actually, that's not true."

He cocked an eyebrow at her. "How so?"

Resting her hands on his shoulders, she darted her eyes back to his, latching on, boring into him, fire blazing in their icy depths. "Watching you out there, battling such a vicious enemy ..." A strangled sigh escaped her. "You nearly got yourself killed out there today."

"Trying to save your brother."

"I could not bear it if anything happened to you." Her eyes turned glossy, and his heart lurched in his chest.

"Nor I you. Which is why we leave tomorrow for Żółkiew."

Surprise flickered in her crystal orbs. "You are coming with me?"

He pulled in a breath. "Yes, I am escorting you there. Lesław will also accompany his wife and children."

Her brows crinkled. "We all travel together?"

Anticipating the question, he was able to deliver the answer smoothly. "It is safer that way."

"I see. And what happens after we reach Żółkiew? Do we embark for home?" Hope flashed in her eyes.

Casting his gaze to the wood-beamed ceiling, he drew in a lungful of air.

She dropped her head, seeming to find great interest in one of his pewter buttons. When she spoke, her voice was a defeated hush. "There is no need to answer, for I already know what that answer is. Will you leave me there, or am I to travel to Biaska alone?"

He caressed her upper back in small, soothing, circular motions. "You will stay at Żółkiew. I must take the company to wherever Żółkiewski sends me, whenever he tells me to go. Therefore, I will not have enough men to see you home safely. You are better off behind Żółkiew's fortified walls, with the hetman's army defending it."

He searched her eyes, finding only fresh tears. "I know it is far from ideal." Pulling her flush against him, he murmured into her hair. "I miss them too, my sweet."

As he held her against him and let her sob away the day's ordeal, his mind wandered to a different place. Was it possible for a father to miss his children as much as the mother? He had no idea about such things. He had spent hours upon hours talking with men around campfires, taverns, and great halls, covering a vast array of subjects. While these conversations touched on family, he had found that most men, when discussing their offspring, were brief and boastful. Tender feelings belonged solely in the realm of their women.

Were he to pose such a query to his own sire, the father would likely ridicule the son for lacking a man's strength. And there was the crux of it, the reason the question vexed him so. He had traveled in a full circle back to whether his rich family life had turned him soft. Well, then, here was his opportunity to prove to himself—and anyone who cared—that he was as formidable a warrior as he had ever been. No, *more* formidable, even … because his physical prowess had not diminished but instead had been enhanced with the wisdom that only came with age.

Pulling out of his grasp, Oliwia swiped at her moist cheeks. "Stupid, stupid tears!" She brushed her fingers across the spot on his żupan now drenched from her crying. "What a mess I have made. I am so sorry."

He ran his hands up and down her arms. "I was already a mess. I tried to clean up in the guardroom, but it wasn't nearly enough. I must complete the job before we sit down to dine with our hosts." He bent at the knee and peered into her tearstained face. "Will you help me?"

She bobbed her head and gave him a wobbly smile. "Yes, of course. I had Nadia pull out a fresh change of clothes for you, and they are on the pegs over by the washbasin." Her nimble fingers went to work on his buttons, and soon he was shrugging the garment off. As she helped him with the rest of his clothes, she began to chatter. Lost in his own thoughts, he didn't pay close attention at first, but soon his ears pricked up.

She untied his shirt and helped him pull it over his head. "Lady Eugenia is quite discomfited by your presence. It seems she believes your heart might not have recovered from her marrying Lesław."

His eyes flew wide. "Really? And what did you tell her?"

"I assured her you've quite gotten over it and have forgiven her." Oliwia beamed him the first genuine smile he had seen since before the attack. Then she pointed at his feet. "Sit, so we can take care of those boots and pants."

"I admit it was somewhat awkward for me as well. I'm glad we've gotten that out of the way." He lowered himself to the edge of the mattress. "And what do *you* think of the lady?"

She gave a little feminine grunt as she worked a boot free. "I confess I was rather surprised when I first laid eyes on her—especially after seeing the beauties who used to revolve around you when I first came to Biaska. I found myself wondering what it was that drew you to her in the first place."

"Her father," he blurted as he stripped off his breeches. "He approached me with the idea first and ended up planting a seed. With my mother's voice inside my head telling me it was past time I settled down and started a family, I reckoned Eugenia was as good a candidate as any. Besides, I would get her father in the bargain."

Oliwia plucked a fresh linen shirt from a peg and held it out for him to wriggle into. "It sounds as though you should've married the father."

He yanked the shirt over his head. "Begetting children would have proved impossible, especially as I felt no attraction to him whatsoever." He sent her a wink and muttered under his breath, "Then again, I felt none for her either."

Rising to his feet, he spun and lifted his arms behind him so she could slide on his żupan.

"Well, I for one am eternally grateful that God saw fit to intervene so that the right couples married. Turn around." She began fastening his buttons when he faced her, pursing her lips in concentration.

He was overcome by a sudden surge of affection and, unable to stop himself, swept her into his arms and kissed her with a fervor fueled by the emotions that had been whirling inside him.

She gasped when he broke the kiss. "What was that for?"

"To show you that you are, by far, the most excellent wife a man could ask for."

A knock sounded on the door. "What is it?" he bellowed, annoyed at the interruption.

Nadia's quaky voice was muffled by the wood. "I was told to fetch you and Lady Oliwia for supper, m'lord."

His stomach rumbled in response, sending Oliwia into a fit of giggles. He pecked her lips and released her. "I am not yet done with you."

Oliwia glanced around the dusky hall, its confines bursting with all manner of citizens and soldiers feasting while serving maids jostled to deliver platters laden with food and whisk away empty jugs to refill. The description that popped into her head was chaos with a cadence.

She had offered to lend a hand, but Lady Eugenia had shooed her away, so here she sat, sharing a bench with Jacek on her left and Filip to the right of her. Beyond her brother sat Henryk, Marcin, and Dawid. Still vibrating from the ordeal they had endured earlier today, she anchored herself in a slice of blissful normalcy … normalcy like her menfolk gobbling food and talking amongst themselves.

The joviality lifted her spirits, affirming that she was a part of something bigger than herself. People celebrated the fact they were alive, and the sounds of life thrumming through the hall warmed her inside. But for

Providence, today's outcome could have been a tragedy had the Tatars succeeded. She discreetly crossed herself.

Jacek was in deep conversation with Lesław, so she shook off the shivering that made the small hairs stand up on the back of her neck and turned toward her brother. Between stuffing his mouth and gulping his wine, he was relaying some story with a great deal of exuberance. She cocked an ear.

"… and at the end of the fracas, Captain Wronski clapped me on the back and told me that I would have a place in his company anytime I pleased." He lifted his cup in salute to his audience of three.

Henryk leaned back, crossed his arms over his chest, and slid Filip a look Oliwia had rarely seen from the affable libertine. "And you believed this man you had never met before today."

"Why shouldn't I? 'Tis only you and my brother who still look at me as a child."

Henryk humphed. A ghost of a smirk tugged the corners of his mouth, but his hazel eyes held an uncharacteristic flintiness in their depths.

Filip put down his eating knife, and his voice took on an indignant tone. "And I expect that will never change." He jerked his chin at Marcin. "What say you, Marcin? You too were held down for a long time before you were treated as an equal by your brothers-in-arms."

Marcin spoke not a word, picking up his cup and taking a long, slow sip as he eyed Filip over the rim. His expression was inscrutable, but beyond him, Dawid rolled his eyes.

The atmosphere within this bubble of conversation shifted, taking on a decidedly icy quality. Henryk sat forward and placed his forearms on the table with startling abruptness. He canted his head toward Filip. "It is statements like that one that prove you are still a boy." This was Henryk the warrior, the man, not the carefree merrymaker.

Filip flicked out his hands, palms up. "Why? What did I say?"

Henryk's voice dropped to a near growl. "It is not so much the words you use as it is the audacity with which you use them."

Oliwia held her breath for fear any movement she made would interrupt the conversation that held her spellbound.

"I fail to see how you make any sense," Filip scoffed. "Perhaps you should explain yourself as I am a mere child who understands nothing."

She winced and braced herself.

This time, it was Marcin who spoke up. "What he means, young pup, is that your foolishness not only nearly led to *your* death, but to the death of your brother-in-law."

And now Dawid stepped into the fray. "And in case you hadn't noticed, we are in rather short supply of valiant warriors."

Henryk raised an expectant eyebrow, but Filip seemed to have lost his voice.

"Have you considered," Oliwia ventured softly, "that you owe Jacek a word of thanks as well as an apology?"

Filip whipped his head toward her and glowered. "I didn't know you were eavesdropping."

"Your sister is right," countered Henryk. "If Wronski and his men had not arrived—or had arrived a mere quarter of an hour later—you and your brother would either no longer be drawing breath or would be marching to Crimea in chains, *wishing* for death." Henryk paused and pointed an accusing finger at Filip. "And *you* alone would be to blame for that miserable circumstance." Straightening, Henryk slapped his hand on the tabletop. "Think on that, pup." He practically spat the last word.

Oliwia took a quick peek over her shoulder, but Jacek was still deep in conversation with Lesław, oblivious to the drama unfolding beside her.

Probably best that way.

Marcin stood. "And let me correct your misconception. No one in this company—especially not your brother-in-law—has ever treated me as a lesser man than I am. I hail from the lowest rank of szlachta as one can get without being part of the yeoman class, and I knew my place. I lived to serve. I still do, and I take pride in it." He lifted his chin at Oliwia, his gaze meeting hers, both startling and pleasing her. Heat flooded her face.

Marcin returned his gaze to Filip. "If not for your sister, I would likely not have been elevated to the station I now enjoy. For that honor, I am immensely grateful. I do not presume—like some seated at this very table—

that I am entitled to it or guaranteed it will continue for the duration of my life." With a head dip in Oliwia's direction, he excused himself.

Filip turned to her, eyes wide, mouth pinched at the corners. "Surely you do not agree, do you, Liwi?"

His query plucked at twin strings of her heart—compassion and the ever-present desire to protect him. But she put aside the twanging and marshaled her steel. "To an extent, yes, I do. In order to drape yourself in glory, you put two lives I care about as much as my own at peril today." She maintained a gentle, even tone. "You have known the men around you to be honorable your entire life. The fact that you are at this very table and not sitting among the squires is proof of how they favor you, yet you show them scorn.

"Why you do not try harder to emulate them puzzles me. Instead, here you are, singing the praises of a man you do not know. I would feel shame were I you, and I would thank these lords and ask their forgiveness. If I know these men, that forgiveness would not be withheld." Henryk and Dawid were riveted on her. Filip fidgeted with his cup. "I pray it is hubris born of youth and inexperience that makes you think and behave thusly, for to believe this is who and what you are in your heart would break mine."

Her brother looked down, his long curly lashes fluttering against his flushed cheekbones. "I-I didn't realize … I …" he trailed off, the bravado absent from his tone. He turned on the bench and, without another glance or word to anyone, fled from the hall.

Henryk cocked an eyebrow at her. "That took courage. I expect it was quite difficult."

She gave him a mirthless smile. "Yet it had to be said, and I have been guilty of holding my tongue far too long. Whether he will listen and learn, however, is up to him."

Henryk and Dawid both nodded and quietly picked up their cups. She hadn't realized her shoulders had been hitched around her ears until they sagged. She let go a sad sigh.

A warm, rough hand covered hers and squeezed, and she absorbed its strength. Jacek leaned to her ear. "I hope I haven't been ignoring you, but

Lesław and I were planning our departure tomorrow." He peered over her head. "What has become of Filip? He left the table rather abruptly."

She sucked in her bottom lip and sawed it between her teeth, then raised her gaze to his. "I gave him a new narrative to think on, one that does not agree with his own. I pray he will take my words to heart."

Jacek's eyebrows inched up his forehead. "He will, Liwi. He loves and admires you, even if he doesn't show it. He is like a young bull trying to find his place in the herd. In order to do that, he must fight the established stags. Had he a father, he would likely direct all that frustration at him. Instead, he spreads it among those he most wants to be like."

She covered his hand with her free one. "Speaking from experience?"

He nodded. "Oh yes."

Fiddle music started up, and soon people were moving tables and benches aside to clear space for dancing.

Jacek winked at her. "'Tis time to forget the day's trials and lose ourselves in revelry. Would you do me the honor of dancing with me, Lady Oliwia?"

Hope floated in her chest and, like a tide, raised her heart several inches. "I would love nothing better, my lord."

CHAPTER 19

Borderland Flight

Henryk reined in his horse beside Jacek, joining him in the vanguard, his expression one of cautious amusement. "We travel on this warmest and most beautiful of spring days," Henryk waved a hand about him as if presenting their surroundings, "and yet you scowl as if we are in the dead of winter, freezing our balls off."

Jacek smirked. "Some of us have serious matters on our minds." The journey to Żółkiew, now in its fourth day, had so far been mercifully uneventful. Another four or five days stretched ahead of them before their arrival at the hetman's fortified city.

"Such as?"

"Such as the miscreants who thought to harm Oliwia and Nadia. How I would love for them to appear now so I could exact revenge upon their worthless hides."

Henryk nodded. "And I would help in that endeavor. No doubt every man here would like a piece of those devils." Henryk beamed him a smile. "But they are not here, are they? Nor will they appear unless God wills it. So put your woes aside and take joy where you can."

"I suppose you shared *the joy* of a maid's bed last night and are here to bore me with the details." Jacek exaggerated a yawn.

"I shared no one's bed," Henryk scoffed.

Now Jacek feigned surprise. "Have you fallen ill?"

"No! Can't a man sleep alone without his companions mocking him?"

Jacek turned in his saddle and stared at his friend. "What has come over you? No, don't tell me. I never realized before, but it must be difficult for you to stand in the shadow of such a virile force."

Henryk laughed. "Surely you're not referring to yourself! No, you must be talking about me, and yes, it's nigh on impossible to stand in my own shadow."

"Who here has fathered two healthy children? Those are big boots to fill." He had, in fact, impregnated Oliwia three times, but she had lost one babe early on. Why she wasn't pregnant right now gave him pause until he recalled her comment about nursing Piotr.

"Oh, believe me, I do not need to sire a child to prove my virility. Although I sometimes wonder ..."

"Wonder what?"

An unaccustomed seriousness overshadowed Henryk's smile. "I see you and Lesław, and I find myself wondering what it would be like to have sons of my own."

"Who says you don't already? The way you—"

"I'm serious." Henryk's hazel eyes pierced Jacek's.

Henryk's surprising confession had Jacek squirming in his saddle. "First, you, ah, need to find the right woman, and I don't believe she lives in a tavern."

Jacek ransacked his brain for the right words as they rode along in silence.

Mercifully, Henryk seemed to recover his affable self. "Ah, well, if I devoted myself to one, I would have to fight off the rest. It would be positively exhausting."

"Hmm. I see you're as delusional as ever."

Henryk's grin returned. "And you should know, what with those ridiculous claims of your *virility*. Not only do you suffer hallucinations, but you are as bigheaded as ever. Or is that pigheaded? Likely both."

The awkwardness passed, and Jacek's mind wandered to whether a woman existed on this earthly plane who could become the puppet master of his cavalier friend's heart. Before Oliwia, Jacek thought that woman didn't exist for him either, yet he was proof such miracles did happen.

A smile touched his lips as memories of the night before played through his mind, when he and Oliwia had at last found themselves alone and curled up beneath the furs in his old bed. His wife had asserted her desires boldly, and he had been only too happy to oblige her. They had gotten little sleep for reveling in the fact that they *lived* after the day's melee. Christ, they had probably awakened the entire fortress with the thumping of the bedframe. If he hadn't gotten her with child *last* night, perhaps he wasn't as potent as he fancied himself. Then again, if she were to become pregnant … No, that would not do with their present circumstances. Soon enough, he would be gone on campaign and that danger would pass.

Henryk glanced over his shoulder. "Speaking of the fairer sex, the women are getting along."

Jacek turned his head, glimpsing Oliwia riding beside Eugenia, her arms wrapped around Lesław and Eugenia's young daughter seated before her in the saddle. She and the child chattered as they pointed to this or that, and the glow reflected in her smiling face was undeniable.

He silently thanked a merciful God the two women had come to share a surprising easiness in one another's company. At times, their heads were bent together as though they plotted some dastardly plan, while at other times they rode together in comfortable quiet. Perhaps it was sharing the care of children that bonded them, but whatever the reason, Jacek was glad for it—not only because it relieved the guilt he had carried for so long, but because his wife was distracted from dwelling on missing her own children or the trouble that simmered between her and her brother. And it was no small matter that in Eugenia's presence Oliwia had not resisted departing Silnyród.

Facing forward once more, he scanned the horizon, on alert for unwelcome surprises. "Yes, and thank God for that. There is only so much interest I can feign over domestic matters. Liwi is canny about most things, but what woman can grasp the commitment of a soldier preparing for war?"

"And do you believe there will be a war?"

"I don't know. I confess that when I first received Żółkiewski's request to join him on campaign, it did not occur to me to question whether the hetman had the correct intelligence."

"And now?"

Jacek was astride one of his spare mounts today, Heban, and when the young gelding stopped to sample a tuft of tender grass, he yanked on the reins, admonishing the black beast. "While I'm still convinced the Ottomans are gathering and that war is imminent, I cannot discard what we learned from the prisoners or what Lesław's patrols reported."

"Or what we've been learning in taverns and inns along this journey."

Jacek nodded in agreement. Though they had ventured farther from the border in the last few days, they had encountered a number of travelers at the various establishments where they had stopped. Those travelers had also come from the border, some as far south as Wallachia. While most were cognizant of increased dangers, none among them had seen or heard of this vast army the Turks were said to be assembling. Was a war brewing or not? The narratives did not mesh, and doubt that hadn't been there before planted its seed and began to take root in his mind.

Oliwia relinquished the little girl to her nursemaid, both bereft to lose the weight in her arms and relieved to remove the pressure that had been leaning against her abdomen. Taking in a few breaths to quell her sudden nausea, she stroked her horse's neck. "Thank you for being such a patient girl." Apolonia had been destined to become a warhorse, but when she failed her final tests, she became Oliwia's mount. The turn of events should have been cause for chagrin, but Oliwia couldn't bring herself to regret it. Besides an even temperament, the horse was as handsome an animal as Oliwia had ever seen, with a glossy ivory coat, a mane of ebony, and symmetric black splotches on her front legs.

Oliwia took the opportunity to check behind her, reassuring herself of Filip's presence in the middle of the caravan, where he rode between Marcin and Dawid. At least he seemed to have mended his rifts with the other hussars; he had likely earned back some of their respect by working as hard as the other retainers and keeping his lips clamped.

She and her brother had had a rough go of it, and though she couldn't see clearly through the layers that made up a sixteen-year-old boy's rebellious nature, she had agreed to heed Jacek's advice and leave Filip to his sullen moods.

Eugenia trotted up beside her. "I am sorry my daughter caused such a fuss."

"She was no bother. I am delighted she allowed me to hold her as long as she did."

Eugenia's delicate brows crinkled with sympathy. "You must miss your children terribly. I can't imagine being away from them for so long."

"That I do." Oliwia stole a glance at Jacek, riding beside Henryk in the vanguard, several horses' lengths ahead. For not the first time, he wrestled his wayward steed into behaving. She drooped with the thought that yet again a mount destined to be a warhorse would not measure up. Ah, but what could she do about Biaska's finances at this moment? And with Klemens Matejko's time and treasure being turned to repair his own estate, she had no hope of selling him Silnyród.

Eugenia gave her an appraising look, opening her mouth as if to say something but quickly shutting it again.

"What is it?" Oliwia prodded.

The lady's cheeks flushed red. "I was just thinking … I wasn't sure what to expect when my lord husband told me you would be coming to Silnyród. He's always spoken so highly of you, and I should have felt more reassured, but I confess I was … I was quite anxious."

Oliwia gave her a head dip. "As was I. And now?"

"And now I understand." She cast her eyes away, a shy smile curving her mouth.

Warmth rushed to Oliwia's cheeks. "Thank you. You are very kind." Had anyone told Oliwia she would strike up a friendship with a woman once betrothed to Jacek, she would have scoffed. Where at first Oliwia had expected a siren, Eugenia had proved somewhat bland—not at all the type of woman she could picture Jacek proposing to—but she had many qualities to recommend her. Intelligence, a keen eye, and steadfastness. Even though Eugenia's high station cast a dark shadow on Oliwia's own plebeian upbringing, Eugenia had done naught but make her feel as an equal. Oliwia had no doubt that—passion aside—Eugenia would have made Jacek a serviceable wife.

The notion stirred a pang inside Oliwia, but before she could dwell on her own shortcomings, Eugenia began speaking again. "The way your husband looks at you, the affection he shows you … All I can say is it's obvious you two belong together, and I'm pleased for you both."

"I am very fortunate in my husband." Oliwia flitted a hand across her belly absently.

"As he is in his wife. I am curious about one thing, however." Eugenia seemed to hitch a breath.

"Yes?"

"Why is it you traveled so far from home, especially as you had to leave your little ones behind?"

"I … Well, I had never laid eyes on Silnyród, and I thought I should do so."

Eugenia blinked. "Now? With war ready to burst over our borders?"

Oliwia turned her gaze to the sky. Today, clouds scudded across the azure vault in an orderly stream of white fluff. Would they bunch up, turn leaden, and drench them all? It was too soon to tell.

With a deep inhale, she met Eugenia's eyes. "In truth, while I did want to see the fortress, I … I was hoping to meet with your father and see if I could interest him in buying it. It's so far away, you see, and I … Well, Biaska has experienced a bit of misfortune and could use the income."

Eugenia's eyes widened.

Oliwia recoiled inside. "I hope I have not offended you with my frankness. Jacek often tells me I speak my mind too freely." Her hopes had been dashed days ago with the news of Matejko Manor; what was the point in holding back the truth? She shook her head. "It hardly matters now, though, does it? Your poor father will be preoccupied with restoring Matejko Manor."

177

"That is true."

Long, silent moments stretched between them. The trilling of birds and soft rustle of tender grasses filled the void. Prayers marched across Oliwia's mind, prayers that her outspokenness hadn't soured this good woman's opinion of her, along with a spate of prayers for Biaska's survival.

"You know, though," Eugenia mused, "I may have a solution to your problem."

Oliwia's heart lifted. "You do?"

"I don't know for certain yet. Let me think on it a while."

Before Oliwia could press Eugenia further, another bout of queasiness spiked and swept through her. It must have showed all over her face, for Nadia was suddenly beside her. She handed Oliwia an uncapped skin. "Drink this, m'lady."

Oliwia shook her head, only worsening the nausea.

Nadia shoved it at her. "One sip."

Men-at-arms were coming to a stop, eyeing her curiously. Waving them on, she grabbed the skin, took a quick drink, and handed it back to Nadia, her eyes trained on Jacek's frame the entire time. *Please don't turn around.*

"Deep breaths," Nadia encouraged.

Oliwia wiped the back of her hand across her mouth and nodded after several beats passed. "Thank you." Alarms began to sound inside her head. Each time she had carried a child—even the one she had lost—she had never felt the sickness other women suffered from. Was this an omen that something was terribly wrong with the babe?

Nadia held up the skin once more. Olivia took another sip of the watered-down wine mixed with herbs and recovered barely enough to urge her horse into a walk. Nadia capped the skin and fell back in line.

"Better?" Eugenia murmured.

"Yes," Oliwia rasped. When Eugenia scrutinized her, Oliwia mustered a wobbly smile. "Once we reach Żółkiew and I am not swaying on a horse the day long, I will be fine."

A beat passed. Eugenia's eyes flicked to Oliwia's stomach. "Does your husband know?"

Early June, the weather had favored them, and they reached Żółkiew by midafternoon on the ninth day of their journey. The hetman's fortified town sprawled before them, its towers and domes stretching to the sky. Jacek had sent Henryk and Lesław ahead to the main gate and now sat astride Jarosława, Oliwia beside him, while they waited upon a rise before a wide-open plain under a sun-drenched sky. A restless wind snapped Biaska's red-and-yellow banners and tugged at the pheasant feathers pinned to Oliwia's kolpak as if it wanted to pluck them for itself.

She crushed it to her head with one gloved hand. "What a formidable place! I have never seen ramparts outside of curtain walls. They come to a point, like triangles."

He suppressed a grin. "They are called ravelins. They are a detached outwork of two walls that abut the curtain wall and so create a triangular shape."

"Like a giant version of a broad arrowhead."

"I suppose," he chuckled. "They are the most integral part of a castle's bastion fortification system. Their function is to protect the gates and the inner bastions. Unlike Biaska," he explained, "Żółkiew does not have the advantage of placing itself against a rock mountain, so it must fortify itself using other methods." Żółkiew's stone ravelins matched its inner fortifications in materials, though the walls were lower.

She continued gaping at the sight. "How do they work?"

"Within each ravelin's walls is an open yard where the castle's troops and guns can be arranged to fire upon an attacking force. Its shape also divides that enemy force as it approaches. Plus, it prevents besiegers' artillery from breaching the curtain wall. What you can't see from this vantage is the ramp that connects the ravelin to that inner curtain. That allows the defenders to move troops and artillery from the inner works to the outer works."

"Oh! And those gardens. What lovely designs." She pointed to her right. "Those four long buildings arranged in a square, with towers at each corner.

Those make up his residence, yes?" Before he could answer, she ran on. "Is that … Do I see bison moving in the gardens?"

"Yes, that is his castle, and those are his gardens. And yes, you see live bison. One of those gardens is a zoo of sorts." He found her exuberance contagious, and the prospect of showing her the grounds invigorated him. "Besides bison, it contains chamois and deer. Moreover, the town itself is an asymmetrical heptagon, designed in the fashion of an 'ideal city.' Rather impressive, isn't it?"

"Oh yes. I can't wait to get inside." Her eyes surveyed buildings and walls, sweeping from right to left. "Has it changed much since you were here ten years ago?"

The wind lifted his cloak, and he snatched it back to himself. "At least one new tower and several more ravelins. It appears they've also added to the walls and built some wooden galleries. I believe the moat is fuller and wider than when I was here last."

"It looks like a river wrapping around the town. So many buildings!" She pointed excitedly to the left. "Is that a church rising up behind the walls?"

His gaze followed her finger. "Yes, that is St. Lawrence's, and beyond it is a Basilian monastery. Both are quite grand." A signal from the gatehouse caught his attention. "Come. We can enter now, and soon you will see for yourself."

They descended the rise and crossed the plain. Leaving the men-at-arms behind to encamp outside the town walls, their party crossed the drawbridge and passed through the main gates. There, Henryk and Lesław joined them, and together they were led by four guards toward the castle to their right. To reach the castle, they wound their way through an interior ravelin, a gate within a large guardhouse and barracks, and a final gate beneath a massive arch that opened onto the inner bailey, which was surrounded by the four buildings and towers Oliwia had observed.

Before them sprawled a majestic building that held the hetman's apartments. To one side stood the stables and armory … and several wagons filled with *kopie*. How long had the lances been there? Had King Zygmunt sent them in anticipation of war? A hussar's kopia was the only weapon the Crown provided, and the fact there were so many right here … Well, it brought Jacek to one conclusion.

He envisioned himself leading a company of hussars against the enemy, and a thrill charged his bloodstream.

Smartly attired stable boys swarmed them, and Jacek helped Oliwia dismount, chuckling inside at her head swiveling in every direction but backward, like a ball on a skewer. As she swung down into his arms, her cheeks reminded him of polished apples, pink and shiny, and her blue eyes sparkled as she took in Żółkiew Castle. His chest ballooned with pride that he could call this beautiful, lively creature his.

Behind them, Henryk helped Nadia clamber off her horse. The little maid had surprised him with her tenacity. Oh, she still behaved like a timid mouse, but Jacek was beginning to wonder if it was an act, or if, as Oliwia had predicted, the adventure had brought out a different side to her.

"Isn't it stunning?" Oliwia enthused to Nadia. They began jabbering about the columns and arches and flourishes.

Henryk sidled up beside him and cupped his mouth with one hand. "No wonder you didn't want to leave here."

Those words poked at a tender wound acquired long ago. Jacek had wasted many weeks at Żółkiew, hoping to ingratiate himself with the hetman and thereby pave his way to an eventual gift of his own lands. The errand had been foolish, futile, and costly. While Jacek had played at courtly pastimes, lingering in Żółkiew and then Warszawa far longer than he should have, Oliwia had become trapped into marrying Lord Eryk Krezowski of Biaska. Jacek hadn't been there to prevent it. By the time he had returned to claim her, it had been too late.

He looked at the splendid facade that so captivated his wife, but his recollections of the place rekindled dark memories he would just as soon leave in the dusty recesses of his mind.

"'Tis not the place that kept me anchored here," he grumbled.

Oliwia glanced over her shoulder and grinned. "No, I expect it was the very charming countess."

Had he spoken so loudly as that? Beside him, Henryk placed a fist to his mouth to stifle a laugh.

"'Twas not her either. I was here to complete a mission." Even as the words tumbled from his tongue, Jacek recognized the petulant child in his tone.

"A foolish one, I daresay," Henryk quipped.

And one I failed at. Jacek puffed out a frustrated breath. "Perhaps, but it was the *only* reason that compelled me to stay."

Oliwia removed her gloves. "Well, fortunately for you, I do not have to meet the lady and find out just how much she had to do with your staying." She winked at him, the little imp.

Before Jacek could open his mouth to defend himself—and likely sound far guiltier than he was—a familiar steward and several servants rushed out to greet them.

The man, whom Jacek recognized from his previous visit as Brajan, bowed deeply before bringing himself upright. "Welcome to Żółkiew Castle, my lords and ladies." He brought his gaze back to Jacek. "Pan Dąbrowski, how wonderful to see you again. It has been far too long since your last visit."

Jacek disagreed but kept the ungracious thought to himself, instead introducing Oliwia.

While the stable boys and servants busied themselves with horses and gear, Brajan gestured them toward the castle's entrance. "Please. Follow me."

Boots crunched on gravel, and Brajan announced a feast was being held in their honor that evening. "We have several other guests that will attend as well."

Interest in a far more urgent question quickly replaced Jacek's fleeting curiosity over the "other guests." "Has the hetman returned from Lublin?"

"Yes, he arrived only yesterday after his meeting with the king."

Jacek and Henryk exchanged a look with Lesław. So Żółkiewski had been meeting with the king. The answer behind the mystery of the kopie crystallized. They must have accompanied the hetman, and a fresh spring found its way into Jacek's step. Soon he would discover all he needed to know about the coming war.

CHAPTER 20
Zamek Żółkiew

Oliwia smoothed and re-smoothed her pale blue silk overgown. Her hand flew to her upswept hair, pinching a pearl earring here, taming an already tame tress there, straightening the aquamarine-and-pearl comb Jacek had given her years ago.

Nadia flitted about her, trying to tuck what Oliwia's nerves untucked. "Is my lady unhappy with this dress?"

Oliwia peered at herself in the mirror. Nadia came to a stop and canted her head at the reflection.

Oliwia rearranged the neckline—again. "Your lady is unhappy with herself!" Though Oliwia had managed to conceal the growing swell of her stomach from everyone—including her distracted husband—she overfilled this and nearly every other garment she had brought to the point of discomfort.

"I will go fetch the crimson, shall I? I'll hold it up in the mirror so you can decide if you'd prefer it over the blue." Nadia lit from the chamber before Oliwia could tell her it would do no good.

Ever since entering Żółkiew Castle, Oliwia had struggled to keep her composure. She'd had to concentrate on keeping her mouth clamped shut lest anyone in their party catch her gaping at the grandeur surrounding them. Even Nadia appeared less ruffled by the opulence than she. After traveling for more than a week, Oliwia had fancied herself ready to spend time at a luxurious estate, but as they had trod after Brajan and an army of servants through mirrored halls and gilt columns to their quarters, she came face-to-face with a hard fact: she was an impostor. She didn't belong here among the highborn gentry.

She had stolen glances at Lady Eugenia, whose regal bearing fit seamlessly with their elegant surroundings. Even the hussars, soldiers she'd observed in rough camps, strode the halls with confident ease, while she hankered for the cozy fustiness of the inn where they'd spent the previous night—despite its resident rats. In this moment, her peasant roots reigned supreme, and she prayed she could keep them hidden.

Like his lord-brothers, Jacek was used to a world filled with places like Żółkiew Castle. He had spent his life among nobles of the highest class. No wonder he moved about as if he belonged here. He did.

Sapphire-blue eyes bored into hers in the mirror, startling her from her unhappy thoughts. "Liwi, 'tis past time we left," Jacek rumbled from the doorway separating their chambers. When had he appeared there?

"I-I ... Yes, I'm almost ready."

Nadia dashed in with the red dress, her eyes bouncing between Oliwia and Jacek. She subtly draped the garment over an armchair.

Oliwia appraised herself one more time. "I so want to make a good impression." One more smoothing would do it ... maybe two.

As Nadia fluffed the lace draping Oliwia's forearms, Jacek's eyes roved over her. "You are perfection. You will be the envy of every woman and the object of every man's admiration." He cocked an eyebrow. "First, however, we must get there."

She expelled a noisy breath and turned to him. He dropped his voice to a smoky timbre. "If Nadia weren't here, I would show you just how appealing you are right now."

Behind her, Nadia let out a squeak and began tittering. Her cheeks suddenly aflame, Oliwia stepped to her husband and presented her hand, which he dutifully kissed. Then he whisked her from their rooms, through a high-ceilinged corridor, down a sweeping staircase, and along a tiled arcade to a glittering hall teeming with people and noise. She reminded herself not to rotate her head about her as he led her along, or else she would become dizzier than she was.

He smoothly weaved his way into the crowd, steering her along as he did so, coming to a stop in an oasis of fresh air. Unable to help herself, she peeked at the great hall's resplendence, its gilt mirrors reflecting dozens upon dozens of beeswax candles in candelabras and girandoles.

Her attention was yanked back when she heard a woman's voice cry out, "Pan Jacek!" Oliwia looked toward the source. A short, plump blond woman with arms held wide was quickly gliding toward them as if she floated on a swift current.

"My Lady Magdalena!" Jacek smiled wide and extended both hands to her. Shocked at her husband's rare show of public excitement, Oliwia appraised the woman. Older, attractive, sumptuously dressed, with a showy bosom cresting her neckline, an aura of sultriness encapsulating her. Her brilliant smile and twinkling blue eyes focused solely on Jacek.

Lady Magdalena? Von Rohan?

Familiar pangs of jealousy lanced Oliwia as she watched him grasp the woman's hands and lean down to buss her cheeks with far too much familiarity. The delight on his face was undeniable. "I had no idea you would be here! What a wonderful surprise!"

They pulled apart, and Lady Magdalena turned her attention to Oliwia, her smile just as dazzling.

Jacek cleared his throat and clasped his hands behind his back. "I wish to present my wife, the Lady Oliwia Dąbrowska. Liwi, this is Lady Magdalena von Rohan, the dear friend who selected your comb." He waved a vague hand toward Oliwia's hair, presently adorned with said comb.

Oliwia's mind jumped to the circumstances—born in this very place—that had led Jacek to send the gift in lieu of returning himself. He had meant it as a peace offering, but it had instead served as a wedge between them. That wedge had resulted, in some large part, to her first marriage to Lord Eryk.

As dismal, unwanted memories swirled inside her, Oliwia swallowed around a lump of self-doubt stuck in her throat and straightened her shoulders. She gave herself over to her curiosity for this woman she had once suspected of being her rival—of being Jacek's lover.

Lady Magdalena grasped Oliwia's arm. "Oh, your lady is more beautiful than you described, Pan Jacek. I'm so pleased you finally used your brain and won her." Her words were warm, sincere, and full of amusement. Oliwia's steeled shoulders relaxed a fraction.

Jacek chuckled. "I confess it took some effort on your part, Lady Magdalena, but I finally listened. Unfortunately, I had other obstacles I found necessary to clear out of my path before she would consent to wed me." He gave Oliwia a sidelong glance and winked.

"I am sure once you set your mind to it, she had no choice." Magdalena peered into Oliwia's eyes, making Oliwia squirm like a bug being inspected under a glass. "Those stones are dull indeed compared to your eyes, my dear." Over Magdalena's shoulder, Jacek grinned like an imbecile.

Oliwia couldn't decide whether to be embarrassed or flattered. What she was, though, was an outsider to whatever history or bond they shared, once again percolating the doubt-fueled jealousy that simmered just below the surface of her self-assuredness.

Sparked by nervousness, Oliwia flapped her fan—also a gift from her husband—in front of her face a little too vigorously and groaned inside at her inelegant movements.

Magdalena waved a graceful hand in the air, and three goblets of wine magically appeared. Jacek asked about her travels, how long she planned to visit Żółkiew, and on and on, and Oliwia wanted to be swallowed up by one of the many potted palms.

Jacek sipped at his wine. "Are you here alone?"

Oliwia nearly snorted her own drink up her nose.

"I am." Magdalena fluttered her eyelashes. "Why? Have you a companion in mind for me?"

"I might. Many women find him charming. Isn't that so, Liwi?"

Magdalena arched her perfectly plucked eyebrows at Oliwia. "Do *you* know this gentleman?"

"Enough to know that he is no gentleman." Oliwia's hand flew to her mouth. Dear God, what was the matter with her? Why had she blurted such a thing?

Magdalena, however, erupted in laughter. "Then he sounds like someone I must meet. And you, my dear, sound like someone I wish to spend more time with." She turned to face Oliwia and flipped her fan in Jacek's general direction. "Shoo now, Pan Jacek. Go find your friend while we ladies discuss matters of the highest importance."

Jacek excused himself, and Magdalena's expression became earnest. "My dear, I hope you do not mind my monopolizing your husband for a little while. He was a great friend to me and sacrificed much more than his time when he accompanied me to Warszawa." She grasped Oliwia's wrist. "I heard of your travails, and only later did I realize the favor I asked of him cost so dearly. For that, I want you to know I am truly sorry."

Unexpected tears rushed to Oliwia's eyes, and she blinked to keep them in check. Had Magdalena not detained Jacek for so long, Oliwia would have likely married him before Eryk could press his advantage. Then again, she wouldn't have Adam.

She cleared a quaver from her voice. "I believe God has a purpose in everything he does, my lady, so please do not trouble yourself. All ended as it should."

A mischievous twinkle shone in Magdalena's pretty eyes. "Now tell me the truth about this friend of Pan Jacek's. Is he a gentleman or a rogue?"

In spite of herself, Oliwia let out an errant giggle. "Most definitely a rogue. But a charming one."

Magdalena covered her heart and looked toward the ceiling. "Oh, be still my heart. Now. Who do you know here?"

Oliwia chuckled. "Absolutely no one besides Lord and Lady Nowakowski."

"Well, we shall change that." Magdalena began a visual tour of the room, holding her open fan to her mouth as she whispered conspiratorially about this person or that. She had not gotten far in her narration when an array of noblemen began queuing up to greet her and the "mysterious woman in blue."

187

Oliwia endured a half-dozen kisses upon her hand by as many gentlemen, and more awaited their turn. A commotion rippled through the line, and the reason soon became clear.

Jacek barged his way through and appropriated her arm. He gave Lady Magdalena a tip of his head. "The companion I spoke of, Pan Henryk, is temporarily detained but will find his way to you shortly. In the meantime, if you will excuse us, I would like to show my wife the ... zoo." The words "my wife" blared from him as he eyed the line.

Magdalena smirked and indicated the room with her fan. "I doubt that zoo will be more interesting than this one, but I understand your desire to change, ah, shall we say, venues."

With a possessive grip on Oliwia's arm, Jacek propelled her away from the men who had been jostling one another. Picking up her skirts, she scurried to keep up with him. "Was that not rather impolite, husband? I believe those gentlemen wished to introduce themselves to Lady Magdalena, and I have abandoned her."

"No, Liwi, their interest was in you," he huffed. "Not that Magdalena does not warrant their attention, but—" He pulled up short when a man with a shock of white hair, surrounded by an entourage of szlachta, materialized before them. Relinquishing her arm, Jacek bowed deeply, and Oliwia followed suit with a deep curtsy.

Her husband brought himself upright, his back rod straight, as the man addressed him.

"Pan Dąbrowski, I am delighted to see you here at Żółkiew." His voice reminded her of gravel being crushed under the iron wheels of an overladen wagon. He turned his head slightly in her direction. Chestnut eyes crowned by bushy white eyebrows regarded her.

Jacek gestured toward her with a sweep of his hand. "Lord Hetman Żółkiewski, may I present my wife, Lady Oliwia Armstrong Dąbrowska."

Several beats of silence charged the air. "And now I understand why eager suitors began to form a line. Young woman, the descriptions of your beauty were not exaggerated."

A fierce blush spread over her décolletage and crept up her neck to her scalp until she thought her skin might burst into flame. "Thank you, Crown

Field Hetman, er, Crown Field, um ..." Jacek darted her a horrified look. "Forgive me! It is truly an honor to finally meet you, Crown. Grand. Hetman. My husband has spoken highly of you for as long as I have known him."

The man's mouth, which was surrounded by a neatly trimmed, snowy beard and mustache, twitched with a smile. "Thank you, Lady Oliwia. It is gratifying for an old soldier to know his presence can tie a beautiful young woman's tongue." The hetman was tall, though his stooped shoulders belied his stature. Grooves radiated from the corners of his eyes, and his lids drooped with age, but a gleam shone in their dark brown depths. He took one of her hands between his two warm, weathered ones. "As for your kind compliment, I will tell you what I tell my own daughters: do not believe everything you hear." He patted her hand. "Armstrong. How very interesting. Are your people from Scotland?"

"My father was, yes." She ran on, her nerves jangling. "In fact, he fought with the Poles."

Żółkiewski's wise eyes seem to appraise her. "Someday, I would like to hear more about that. In the meantime, let me express how chagrined I was to learn of your unfortunate encounter with the highwaymen. Rest assured, the starosta of Rzeszów and our own starosta here in Żółkiew are doing everything they can to catch the villains."

Apprehension spiked inside her. Her fingers sought to twirl the wedding ring that was no longer on her left hand. "Are there reports of them here?"

"Nothing meaningful. One witness, someone who was robbed himself, swears he recognized one of the men. He claims to have gotten a good look at him when he yanked at the brigand's mask right before the lout knocked him out. When he came to, he followed their tracks and believes they led here. But you need not worry. Żółkiew is well guarded by the finest army in these parts. If they are here, we will capture them."

Something in the hetman's eyes and voice coaxed Oliwia into trusting him, and she clung to his promise. With a knowing nod, he released Oliwia and introduced the men in his party, which included his son, Jan, and a corpulent, mustached, and bearded man dressed in red and furs. The name

Stanisław Koniecpolski barely resonated; her mind gamboled to how the man's horse supported someone of such rotund proportions.

She would have to do better, she reminded herself, but her fatigue and the corset pinching her abdomen were driving her to distraction. If only she could curl up on that featherbed and drift …

The hetman's hoarse voice yanked her from the warm mattress. "Let me present my wife, Lady Regina Hubert Żółkiewska, and my daughter, Lady Zofia Żółkiewska Daniłowiczówna."

The hetman's wife appeared younger than he—or perhaps the ravages of war did not show in the lines of her face as they did in her husband's. Where his hair was stark white, hers was dove-gray threaded with strands of gold and chestnut. Of a height with Oliwia, the woman's bearing and matronly figure made her appear taller than she was. A placid visage held the eyes of a hawk. No doubt the woman was a force to be reckoned with.

"It is a pleasure to welcome you to Żółkiew, Lady Dąbrowska. And, Pan Jacek, it is wonderful to see you again." Jacek bowed over the woman's hand and brushed his lips against it. "I trust your quarters are suitable?"

A marble fireplace and ornately carved four-poster covered in silk bed linens floated through Oliwia's brain. "More than suitable, my Lady Żółkiewska. You are most generous in the quarters you set aside for us."

The woman dipped her head. "You must allow myself or Zofia to show you all the wonders of Żółkiew during your stay with us."

"That would be delightful. Perhaps you could teach me some of the history of the area. I only know it was once called Vynnyky before King Zygmunt bestowed the Magdeburg charter and the name Żółkiew upon it. The rest is a mystery to me." In her peripheral vision, Jacek's mouth parted and quickly closed again. Time spent with Eugenia had not been in mere idle chatter.

Lady Regina's eyes lit. "It would be my pleasure."

Oliwia pressed her advantage. "When was the castle built?"

The hetman's eyes crinkled with amusement. "It was started in 1594 and completed—mostly—in 1606 under the guidance of a rather esteemed architect." He enunciated the man's name, and others nodded.

Oliwia had no idea who that might be, but she followed suit and bobbed her head as if she too knew the man.

Lady Regina placed a staying hand on her husband's forearm. Her gaze bounced between Jacek and Oliwia. "As you likely observed on your way in, several projects are yet to be completed. But we are nearly there. Why, we even have a source of fresh water piped into the town from a spring in the mountains—not unlike the Roman aqueducts of old, but much improved. Our water system employs wooden conduit." Pride shone in the lady's expression, lifting her cheeks and erasing some of the lines bracketing her mouth.

To Jacek, Żółkiewski said, "As you can see, we take a great deal of pride in our 'ideal city.'" He slid his wife a sidelong glance, and she gave him a head dip in reply. "After the feast, a select few of us shall retire to discuss military matters. You will, of course, be present among that group, Pan Dąbrowski. We shall leave the ladies behind to enjoy the dancing and revelry."

Jacek gave him a curt bow. "I look forward to it, my lord Hetman."

They watched as the hetman limped away; it was the first Oliwia had noted of a wooden cane he leaned upon.

Jacek steered her toward the doors that led outside. "Come, before we are waylaid yet again." They stepped into a vast garden where other guests already strolled along its many paths.

Her arm was looped through the crook of his elbow, and he covered her hand with his. She looked up at him. Jacek was the most handsome man Oliwia had ever seen, and she could stare at him for hours, what with his towering height, strong jaw, powerful shoulders, hair streaked gold from the sun, and eyes the color of polished sapphires. Those fine masculine attributes, unfortunately, appealed to other women as well and had for as long as she had known him. How lucky she was that he was all hers.

But she couldn't resist teasing him. "God of Mercy, my lord, is there nowhere on this earth where we can go without encountering a former paramour?"

He blinked in rapid succession.

She prodded him with her elbow. "I am speaking, of course, of Lady Magdalena."

"She is not a former anything. A friend only. Was she rude?"

"On the contrary, she was quite charming. It explains much." Spending time with Magdalena had dissipated Oliwia's envy, but she was deriving far too much pleasure from his discomfort to let him off just yet.

"I did not realize she would be here," he muttered, "or I would have warned you. What did you think of the hetman?"

"He is … That is, he possesses a remarkably commanding presence." She could not recall seeing Jacek quite so reverent before.

"What else?"

She tried, in vain, to form the right words.

He glanced down at her. "What is it, Liwi? You look as though you are distressed."

"It is simply that I did not expect the hetman to be so … advanced in age." *And feeble looking.*

"I told you he was seventy-two, did I not?"

"Yes, but it is one thing to hear it and quite another to see it. Does he possess the vigor to lead another campaign, especially one as large as this one is reported to be?"

Oliwia's mind revisited the battle with the Tatars outside of Silnyród. They were ferocious warriors, capable of unspeakable atrocities. What level of damage would an even greater force aligned with trained Turks inflict?

An errant shiver caused her skin to break out in gooseflesh. "For that matter, you are not getting any younger either," she blurted—unwisely.

His glower told her she had gone too far. "I am two score years the man's junior. Many would say I am in my prime, but apparently my wife thinks I'm a broken-down old horse to be put out to pasture."

"That is not what I meant. I am … I am worried for you." Tears suddenly stung her eyes—again—and she whispered, "I do not want to lose you."

He stopped them both in their tracks and turned to face her. "Liwi, we have been over this many, many times." His tone communicated his exasperation. "I have no choice. Even if I did, I would still go."

"Why?" Yet she knew the answer: duty. The word infuriated her. When the creases between his brows deepened, she continued. "That is not intended to be a challenge or a slight. I am genuinely curious. Why would you want to follow a man who is clearly beyond his best years?"

"He is an accomplished general. He possesses a brilliant strategic mind. He is deserving of my respect and everyone else's."

She dared not voice her next thought: What if that mind was no longer as clear as it had once been?

Jacek seemed to sense her doubt. "He has many capable commanders under him, starting with his own kin, whom you just met." This gave her no confidence. "I count myself among those accomplished commanders."

"As you should." And he was. But what if he was only one of a fistful of competent leaders? Would he be overridden? Outvoted by those with higher status than he? Her head pounded with the scenarios traipsing through it, tying her tongue in knots. If she opened her mouth, there was a high likelihood she would say the wrong thing and spiral their heated discussion into a full-scale argument.

Once more, he seemed to divine her thoughts. *"Amor patriae nostra lex."*

"Love of country is our law," she repeated.

"Yes. My country calls, and I must go, no matter the consequences. It is that simple."

Stubborn man. She was in a losing battle, yet she persisted, fisting her hands and resting them upon her hips. "It is *not* that simple. What of the consequences of our children growing up without their father?"

His eyes darkened, reminiscent of a storm whipping up frenzied waters. Before he could counter her, they were called to the dining tables.

The feast went on, course after succulent course, but Olivia had no appetite and soon was stuffed like one of the many exquisitely prepared capons. Beside her, Jacek had no such problem and ate enough for them both. They barely spoke as they supped, for the lively conversations around them kept them otherwise engaged. When the meal finally ended, gentlemen and ladies mingled in the music hall, anticipating a pianist who would soon begin his recital. Jacek tugged her into a corner beside a palm.

"Liwi, this may not be the ideal time or place, but once I am behind closed doors with Żółkiewski and the others, I may not emerge until the birds are serenading the dawn. We must settle this."

She crossed her arms and arched an expectant eyebrow.

The firm line of his mouth told her a belly full of food and wine had not softened his side of the argument. "I would finish the discussion we were engaged in before the meal."

She braced herself for battle. But before they could exchange a word, a man's voice, silky as a satin ribbon, pricked every pore and raised each small hair at the back of her neck.

"Commander Dąbrowski? The hetman summons us."

Whirling, she came face-to-face with a handsomely dressed, well-built noblemen whose hazel eyes narrowed when they landed on her. They darted to her bare décolletage, where her ruby-and-pearl cross should have rested. His expression puzzled Oliwia almost as much as the familiarity of his voice and the chord of terror it struck inside her.

The surprise flashing in Jacek's eyes was also evident in his deep baritone. "Captain Wronski, allow me to present my wife, the Lady Dąbrowska. Liwi, this is Pan Gabriel Wronski, the man who saved us at Silnyród."

CHAPTER 21

The Pułkownik and the Forlorn Hope

Jacek quickly checked his surprise. What the devil was Wronski doing here? More troubling, why had he been dispatched to summon Jacek to the meeting? Jacek's mind flipped through every possible reason for his presence, and one in particular had dread oozing through him like a leaky pail of tar as he strode beside the Elear. Żółkiewski had marshaled the Lost Men to fight this war.

"Jacek!"

He turned at his name, his irritation climbing when he spotted Filip hurrying toward him. Schooling his voice, he asked what Filip wanted when the lad reached him.

"I wish to accompany you to this gathering." Filip's hopeful gaze bounced between Jacek and Wronski.

Jacek turned to Wronski. "I must speak to my brother-in-law. Do not let me detain you."

Wronski smirked. "You are not detaining me. I shall happily remain."

Gritting his teeth, Jacek addressed his brother-in-law. "We have instructions that only one may accompany us to this council, and that one is Henryk. Moreover, an untested squire of sixteen years does not belong at such an assemblage."

Filip's mouth swung open, and his features quickly twisted with anger.

Wronski tilted his head. "Who's going to be policing the number of attendants? Why not let the lad observe the council? What better way to learn?"

Gratitude commandeered Filip's expression, and he directed all of it to Wronski. "Thank you, sire."

"I believe a formal introduction is in order." Wronski sent Jacek a sidelong glance and proceeded. "I am Lord Gabriel Wronski."

Filip gave Wronski a formal bow. "And I am Filip Armstrong of Carlisle, England, and Biaska in the Silesian Voivodeship. At your service."

"At my service, eh? Excellent, Pan Filip, and well met." Dismissing Jacek entirely, Wronski continued. "My second is not joining me. Perhaps you would care to take his place? Not as my lieutenant, of course, but as my guest."

Filip's eyes widened, reminding Jacek of a puppy about to receive a scrap of pork. "Would the hetman allow it?"

Wronski's chest seemed to expand along with his self-importance. "Of course he will, for you will be there at *my* invitation."

Filip exclaimed that yes, he would attend, and the two proceeded side by side. Falling in behind the newly forged friends, Jacek ground his back molars and clenched and unclenched his fists. Henryk appeared beside him, mumbling words Jacek didn't completely catch but whose meaning was clear: Henryk wished to place his boot against Wronski's posterior and send him sprawling. He would have to wait his turn behind Jacek.

Soon they joined other nobles and were ushered into a spacious salon decorated in dark woods and navy velvets. The door closed, shutting out the soft tinkling of a piano echoing from the music hall.

Filip's innards leaped like frogs fleeing a flock of cranes, and he struggled to keep a smile from sprouting on his face. Pan Wronski believed he belonged among some of the Commonwealth's most influential leaders!

He looked around the buzzing, overflowing room at the magnates gathered here, some old, some young. The informality of the space surprised Filip. He had expected a war room, complete with a large table surrounded by rows of chairs and grim-faced men. Not a morning room where one might deal with correspondence or grant an audience to a handful of courtiers … not that Filip had seen much of such spaces.

A modest wooden desk occupied the right side of the room, and behind it sat Crown Grand Hetman Żółkiewski, flanked by two men.

Filip swiveled his head toward Pan Wronski. "Who are the men with the hetman?"

Pan Wronski leaned down to his ear. "The man on the hetman's right is his son, Jan, and the other one is the great hetman's protégé and former son-in-law, Crown Field Hetman Stanisław Koniecpolski."

Poland's highest-ranking officers were here, in this very room, and so close Filip would only need a few strides to stand before them. "Why do they refer to the crown field hetman as a 'former' son-in-law?"

"He was once married to the great hetman's daughter, but she died and he married into a different family. A son-in-law to Hetman Żółkiewski no more, though the relationship is thicker than ever."

Had Filip detected a note of scorn in the captain's voice? Surely not. Filip continued scanning the room.

Pan Wronski laid a hand beside his mouth and whispered, "Over there is Samuel Korecki. Beside him is Stefan Chmielecki, the so-called 'Tatar conqueror.'"

"'So-called'?"

"Never mind. Now stay quiet and out of sight." Pan Wronski's affable demeanor had turned chilly, and Filip flushed with embarrassment. The captain lifted his chin toward a back corner. "Become one with the wall, boy."

Filip pushed his way through a barricade of grumbling men and found a vacant space along the wall he could press his back against. His gaze sought and found Jacek and Henryk a row or two behind the most important-looking potentates. Jacek turned toward him and gave him a silent nod before turning his attention to the front of the room. The small gesture gave

Filip a modicum of reassurance and soothed the sting of the captain's rebuke.

Żółkiewski began to speak, and the room hushed. In a voice weighed down with exhaustion, he thanked them for coming. "We are grateful for your presence, whether you are here representing your own interests or representing your commanders." Here, he gave a nod to Pan Wronski, who seemed to stiffen as though he had been affronted.

Filip had little time to ponder the odd shift because the crown grand hetman announced those he had selected to report directly to him, and Jacek's name was among the dozen or so mentioned. A frisson of joy rose inside Filip for his brother-in-law. For so long, Jacek had sought the recognition the old hetman was bestowing in front of all these prominent men. He darted a look to his brother-in-law, whose back was to him, so he couldn't see his expression. But the set of his shoulders told Filip Jacek stood as stoic as ever—an irritating habit that quashed Filip's tendril of joy for him. The man showed little emotion. Then again, neither did the hetmans.

Żółkiewski canted his head toward Koniecpolski. "The crown field hetman left his post at Mohylów and journeyed here for the sole purpose of taking part in this council. Tomorrow, he returns. Some of you assembled here will accompany him to the border and serve as his support."

Where the devil was Mohylów? Filip wasn't the only one wondering, for in the hubbub someone asked that very question.

"It's a fortified border town on the north side of the Dniester," came the response.

One of the potentates spoke up. "What of the movements of the sultan's army?"

Żółkiewski waved a hand at Koniecpolski and tented his fingers, thereby giving the floor to the field hetman. "As-as of th-this moment," the man stammered, "what we know is that he has dispatched Iskender Pasha to remove Gaspar Grazziani from Moldavia's th-throne. We have some idea of their numbers, but Gr-Grazziani has been prolific in his information gathering, so we expect t-to have a more accurate count s-soon. Meanwhile, we are confident the r-resistance will not be as fierce as we first believed."

Was the crown field hetman nervous? Filip looked over the crowd, but no one seemed surprised by the man's manner of speech.

A magnate called out, "Is it necessary, then, that we all go? If, God forbid, the same travesty takes place as it did at Orynin, our estates will be in grave danger. We must defend them." Those surrounding him nodded their affirmation of the question.

Koniecpolski's booming stutter quieted the murmurs. "Wh-what happened there took place because far too many f-fancied themselves in charge and served their own interests to the d-detriment of the campaign. That w-will not happen again. Remember, we also have interests in Podolia that we must protect. Th-those interests include Grazziani's. The hospodar is fearful for the fate of his crown and his life."

Someone grumbled that the Commonwealth did not need the likes of the two-faced Grazziani and that he was getting what he deserved. "He has been sitting astride the fence since he began ruling in Jassy last February. With one hand extended to the Commonwealth, palm open as if he is offering up Moldavia, he keeps the other hand tight behind his back, and with it he strokes the Sultan." The assenting murmurs grew louder.

"He is our ally and our toehold in M-Moldavia. Lose him, and the country falls into Ottoman hands. The Commonwealth n-needs Moldavia as a buffer between Christendom and the Muslim curs. Without Grazziani on the throne, the border becomes a sieve through which the infidels will easily flow," Koniecpolski roared back.

"But he cannot be trusted! He only came to power because the Porte put him where he is in the first place! He is naught but an Ottoman puppet," a man in the audience cried.

Żółkiewski's tired eyes locked on the man. "He has realized the error of his ways and is aligned with the Commonwealth. He has pledged fifteen thousand of his own troops in support of the effort. His force will double our numbers, and we can repel any threat from the Ottomans. If we refuse him, and lose those vital military resources, defeating the Ottoman Empire is a much more difficult task."

The din grew louder. Though Filip listened keenly to the conversation, the politics escaped him and therefore left him confused—such affairs were foreign in Biaska—but he cataloged his questions and would ask someone more knowledgeable than he. Perhaps Lord Wronski would enlighten him. Yes, it would offer an opportunity to engage with the man who thought he belonged here.

"How confident are we in the intelligence that's been gathered?" The burble halted, and heads turned toward Jacek. Filip's brother-in-law commanded ears when he spoke, and now Filip felt a sliver of pride thrumming in his chest.

"V-very," Koniecpolski replied. "In this, Grazziani has been an invaluable source of information."

"What of the Zaporozhian Host?" Jacek continued.

Żółkiewski's fingers bounced against one another. "They will not be part of this campaign."

Though Filip could not see Jacek's expression, he recognized the incredulity in his tone. "Have they been invited to join the fight? The Ottomans are as great an enemy to the Cossacks as they are to the Commonwealth. They will wish to take—"

Żółkiewski cut him off. "They are part of the problem that has led to this confrontation. They cannot be trusted to heel, and unleashing them will lead to more raiding and bloodshed, which will only make diplomacy more elusive."

"Diplomacy," one the magnates—Chmielecki, the "Tatar conqueror"—repeated. "What are the chances of diplomacy after the expulsion of Samuel Otwinowski by the Grand vizier and the escalation of warmongering?"

The exchanges between the crown grand hetman and Chmielecki ramped up, and so did the tension, for reasons beyond Filip's comprehension. Glancing about the room, he noted the exchange had captured the audience's full attention, and many a frown crinkled a forehead—all of them directed at the crown grand hetman. An undercurrent he didn't comprehend simmered and brewed, and his confusion gave way to boredom. Truly, how much did he care about politics among powerful men in an unfamiliar region?

His mind wandered to a pretty serving maid he had traded glances with earlier. Would Captain Wronski notice if he slipped out? He looked toward the exit and expelled a sigh. A cluster of men stood in front of the door whispering among themselves. Then the captain himself turned around as if looking for him and gave him a head bob. Filip was captive until the meeting came to an end.

The crown grand hetman regarded Jacek with a narrow-eyed look that gave him pause. He had asked his questions out of genuine concern and curiosity and hadn't anticipated the asking would cause the great hetman to chafe. Nor had he expected igniting a firestorm between the magnates and the hetmans.

What the potentates weren't saying aloud, but was couched in their words, was that diplomacy, which Żółkiewski had pursued in favor of aggression at Orynin, had weakened the Commonwealth. According to Żółkiewski's many critics, he had given up far too much over the years in exchange for peace with the Turks. The hetman's courage was spent, he had grown feeble, and a steadier, steelier leader could have extracted more and lost less. Though Jacek didn't agree, the undertone of failure was unmistakable among the men assembled in the chamber, and the atmosphere troubled him. They should have shown more respect for the crown grand hetman.

Żółkiewski held up his hand, and the room quieted. "War, if it comes, will not last long. As the crown field hetman explained, we expect little resistance from the Ottomans."

Jacek pulled in a deep breath and braced himself. "Do we know the composition of their army?"

Koniecpolski's famous stutter continued to punctuate his speech. "Iskender Pasha l-leads the Turkish troops. Our intelligence r-reports Khan Temir and his Budjak Tatars may join him."

"The same damned Tatars as at Orynin!" someone spat.

Żółkiewski waved a tired hand. "We are uncertain of their numbers, but initial reports of a large army gathering are no longer valid, correct?"

To Jacek's surprise, Wronski cleared his throat and took a step forward. He canted his head toward Jacek. "You may recall, Pan Dąbrowski, after the tussle at Silnyród"—he paused and looked at the expectant faces as he explained—"Commander Dąbrowski's force was pinned at the gates, and my men and I came to their aid." Wronski went on to describe the event, casting himself and his men in the most valiant terms.

When he was done, men who had regarded the Lost Man with distaste bobbed their heads grudgingly. Others, who likely had no idea who or what he was, clapped. Wronski's chest ballooned. He seemed to fight a self-satisfied smile. "As I was saying, I informed Pan Dąbrowski at that time that those reports were incorrect. My men and I saw no evidence of a great gathering. What mustering we observed was a smattering here and there and appeared disorganized." Wronski lapped up the attention like a cat lapping at milk, presenting himself as a humble servant the whole while. Jacek nearly clapped himself at the man's convincing performance.

Then Wronski coolly turned back to Jacek. "I suppose relaying such details to the crown hetmans would have slipped my mind as well had I ridden in with caterwauling women and babes." Gabriel smiled at him. "How easy it must be to momentarily take one's eye off military matters when the family occupies one's priorities, which is why I never allow mine to accompany me. You, Pan Dąbrowski, are a far better man than I."

Jacek clenched his teeth but kept himself rod straight. Beside him, Henryk let out a subtle snort.

Żółkiewski turned his eye on Wronski, and the flintiness the hetman had shown Jacek faded. "I would like to publicly commend Pan Wronski for risking his life and those of his men to bring us these vital details."

Wronski acknowledged the mumbles of appreciation with a bow of his head.

Żółkiewski held up his hand, once more commanding the floor. "Since their strength is less than originally anticipated, our own forces need not be as large as we originally thought."

Talk then turned to the composition of the troops, and Koniecpolski took over. "A large number of quartz troops are stationed at Mohylów.

They, along with several private armies, will comprise the majority of our force."

"And what of the Lisowczycy?" Henryk piped up. A few gazes darted to Wronski.

"We will be supported by many Lisowczycy b-banners," Koniecpolski replied.

Murmurs waved through the assembled men. Wronski swiveled his head and narrowed icy eyes on Henryk, who seemed not to care a whit. Jacek put a fist to his mouth to suppress his amusement.

A question was raised about infantry, which spurred more discussion.

"Will there be enough to support the cavalry?" an aide asked.

"We have several hundred German infantrymen and reiters available to us as well." The irritated edge in Żółkiewski's tone was unmistakable, and no further questions regarding infantry came to the fore. The crown grand hetman was a staunch advocate of heavy cavalry, and that preference showed itself often in battle.

Other queries were raised and answered, and Jacek shifted his gaze and his attention to Filip. His brother-in-law fiddled with his knife, obviously uninterested. What the devil had Wronski been up to when he'd invited the lad in the first place?

Koniecpolski signaled the end of the meeting, and the men began to disperse, funneling out the door, while the hetmans and Jan Żółkiewski bent their heads together in animated conversation. Jacek hung back, catching Filip's eye and gesturing for him to join him. His brother-in-law darted hesitant eyes to Wronski; expectation and a plea for approval lurked in them. Alarm and resentment spiked inside Jacek, and he told himself it was merely because the lad was moldable and he didn't want him falling into Wronski's hands.

Before Jacek could wrest his brother-in-law from the Lost Man, Żółkiewski's voice rang with a command. "Commander Dąbrowski and Pan Wronski. A word in private."

Filip fell in with Henryk, and together they quit the chamber and shut the door behind them. Jacek strode to the desk and stood at attention, his hands clasped behind him, while Wronski took station beside him.

Żółkiewski fell into a coughing fit, and Koniecpolski poured him a measure of wine. The old hetman waved it away and leveled his gaze on Wronski. "Pan Wronski, until your colonel and his banner arrive, you and your men will report to Commander Dąbrowski."

Wronski's body seemed to vibrate. Jacek glanced down, noting Wronski's clenched fists and knuckles nearly bursting from his skin.

Żółkiewski then turned to Jacek. "And you, Pan Jacek, are elevated to the rank of colonel. As I stated earlier in the meeting, you will report directly to myself or Hetman Koniecpolski. Now you do so as a *pułkownik*."

Jacek blinked. *Pułkownik!* Had he heard right? He was to serve as colonel? His heart didn't dare believe his ears, yet it leaped in his chest anyway.

Rousing himself from his stunned state, he bowed his head and placed his hand against his heart. "I thank you, Hetman Żółkiewski, and I look forward to serving you, the king, God, and my country. I am humbled and honored by the faith bestowed upon me, and I vow it will never be misplaced."

Żółkiewski dipped his head. "And we are all fortunate to have you." Jacek's stomach churned with the beating wings of a thousand butterflies. One moment, he had felt Żółkiewski's disapproval, and the next his greatest dream had been fulfilled by the man himself. A pułkownik!

His elation was such that he had forgotten Wronski beside him until the Elear was dismissed by the crown grand hetman.

To Jacek, Żółkiewski said, "Colonel, you will remain here with us so we may further discuss our plan." The hetman indicated a hand-drawn map Koniecpolski had unfurled upon the desktop.

Wronski shot Jacek a look that would have sliced him to ribbons had it been made of blades before crisply turning on his heel and leaving them behind.

Gabriel stormed from the chamber and hurtled down the hallway, choking on the bitter bile of his fury.

Why Dąbrowski? Gabriel was as deserving as that insufferable son of a bitch. *More* deserving! God's blood and all his teeth! Goddamn the man!

This was the fault of those idiots in charge. They had no business being in such lofty positions, and this decision proved it. Żółkiewski was frailer than an old crone—more addled too—and as for Koniecpolski, how could a stuttering fat man be the military commander second only to the crown grand hetman?

"Because that crown grand hetman pulled his puppet's strings for his son-in-law, that's how," Gabriel growled as he made his way to the ramparts. There, he paced, back and forth, pounding his fist into his palm.

Gabriel should have been put in charge of the Lisowczycy, not an outsider like Dąbrowski. Dąbrowski had no idea what he was doing. It was Gabriel they should have shown the respect he deserved and the command he had earned. Well, he had no intention of following any of these imbeciles—Dąbrowski included. Gabriel *knew* the power he wielded and wield it he would. Żółkiewski needed him and his banner.

As for Dąbrowski? His new pułkownik indeed! A Lisowczyk was not subordinate to a hack commander from the western border and never would be simply because he wore a pair of wings on his armor.

A thought occurred, brightening Gabriel's sour mood. He stopped pacing as a plan crystallized. Soon a vow pounded in his head.

This day would only be the beginning of leaving the Lord of Biaska in his wake and taking his brother-in-law with him.

CHAPTER 22

Tidings

Oliwia gulped air after a vigorous mazurka with a dashing young soldier whose name she did not remember. He was one of a myriad of faces that had been dancing about her. Now she stood beside Eugenia, who clapped and swayed in time to the music.

"It appears the meeting is over." Eugenia pointed across the ballroom. "There go our husbands."

Oliwia's gaze chased Lesław and Henryk, but where was Jacek? She stood on tiptoe, trying to catch a glimpse of his broad shoulders. Rather than dancing with strangers all evening, how she would have preferred dancing with him.

The meeting participants trickled in and returned to the revelry, and she was told Jacek had stayed behind in the war room. She let out a little sigh. Jacek was in his milieu, his attention captivated by all matters soldierly. She would not be surprised to discover he only recalled her presence when he crawled under the bed covers later—assuming he did not spend the night discussing military strategy with like-minded lord-brothers.

And where was Filip? Perhaps Jacek had forgotten him as well.

No sooner had Eugenia excused herself to go check on her children than Magdalena filled the empty spot beside Oliwia. Oliwia welcomed her with gratitude. With Magdalena, however, came Lord Wronski, and a series of shivers snaked from Oliwia's tailbone to her nape. Why did the man discomfit her so? Perhaps it was his military association. That he was a Lost Man brought up horrifying memories of other Lost Men and tainted her opinion of him. What else could explain her aversion? Between his attractive features, sophisticated manner, and his bravery defending Silnyród, she should have been charmed. Instead, her blood ran to ice.

Lord Wronski caught her off guard when he appropriated her hand, lifted it to his mouth, and gently pressed his lips to her skin. She fought the urge to tug the hand away and claw at the spot his mouth had brushed.

"We arrived at Silnyród at the same time during a most unfortunate circumstance a fortnight ago, my lady," he said in a velvety baritone, still bent over her hand and grasping it in his with a familiarity that verged on inappropriate. "Had I known such a beautiful lady was secreted behind the fortress's walls, I would have lingered."

"Lord Wronski." The name stuck in her throat like a hedgehog's hide.

He brought himself upright, and she had to cant her head to look up at him. He was nearly of a height with Jacek. His smile slid wider. "Please, my lady, call me Gabriel. I feel as though we are already well acquainted." His gaze skimmed her body, and he tightened his hold on her hand.

Was she imagining this behavior, or was Magdalena aware of it too?

She wrestled the hand away. "I was not afforded the opportunity to thank you for the lives of my husband and my brother. I am indebted to you, sir."

"Perhaps my lady would care to show her gratitude by bestowing me with the next dance."

Magdalena arched an eyebrow. "You are rather bold, Lord Wronski. And possibly reckless."

"No one has ever accused me of being timorous, Lady Magdalena."

Eyes dancing to another side of the ballroom, Magdalena broke out in a coy smile. "You may wish to rethink that strategy. The lady's husband approaches."

Olivia's eyes caught on a blur moving toward them, and relief flooded her veins. A heartbeat later, her hand was engulfed in Jacek's possessive one. He shot daggers at Wronski. "If you will excuse us, it is past time I danced with my wife."

Wronski bowed his head. "Of course, Pan Dąbrowski. I would never dream of coming between a man and his wife."

As Jacek escorted her toward the other dancers, she glimpsed a smirk spread over Wronski's face. On Jacek's face, however, an uncharacteristically beatific smile sprouted.

She fluttered her fan. "Proud of yourself?"

"Immensely."

"I suspect your self-satisfaction stems from more than claiming your wife."

They joined a promenading couple, and he grasped Oliwia's hand in his. "You know me too well, wife. I shall tell you my news when we are alone, which will be shortly."

They had taken a mere two steps when Jacek whisked her from the dance floor, out of the grand hall, and toward a quieter wing of the castle. Steely arm about her waist, he hurried her forward.

A laugh bubbled up inside her, and she forgot Lord Wronski. "You must have good news indeed, my lord. Where are you taking me in such haste?"

"To our bedchamber," he growled, "before another man can employ the excuse of a dance to put his hands on you."

She halted in her tracks, her momentum spinning him to face her. "You were watching!"

"Of course I was watching!" He glanced up and down the passageway, lit by the flames of countless candles suspended in wall sconces. He dropped his voice. "And when your last prospect approached, I decided I'd had enough." With a waggle of his eyebrows, he resumed his determined march, dragging her alongside him.

Amusement gamboled through her. "And where were you lurking as you watched? I grant you the palms are large, but not so large as to hide one of your stature." A vision of Jacek peeking from behind a bush nearly launched her into peals of laughter.

He slid his arm from her and tucked her hand into his elbow. "I was here and there. Everywhere. You need not know all my secrets."

"Oh, I disagree on that score."

Before long, he banged open the door to their apartments, and a sleepy Nadia jumped from the armchair she had been occupying in front of the fireplace.

"M'lord, m'lady," she gasped and executed a half curtsy that nearly tangled her feet.

Before she could recover herself, Jacek asked if the other fires were tended. To his credit, he mustered the gentlest voice Oliwia knew him to possess.

"I shall check, m'lord," she squeaked and dashed off.

Oliwia reached up and brushed a tiny leaf from his shoulder. "Confess it. You merely glimpsed me now and again as you rushed from one meeting to the next. Or you had Marcin watching, and he came rushing when Lord Wronski approached."

Jacek humphed.

Now she ran her hands over both shoulders, straightening his emerald brocade żupan. "Whichever way it happened, thank you for rescuing me."

He looked down his nose, his eyes alight with surprise. "Did you *need* rescuing?"

Stepping away, she smoothed back a wayward lock. "I'm not sure. I only know something about the man unnerves me. We've only just met, yet something inside me recoils when I am in his presence. I feel as though an eel has pressed his slimy, oily skin against me, and I am compelled to wash."

"Interesting that he elicits such a reaction. He does in me as well, though I'm not sure he brings to mind a slippery eel. A snake, perhaps, or a cunning fox. And circumstances are about to become more interesting still. Crown Grand Hetman Żółkiewski just placed Wronski and his banner under my command."

Oliwia's eyes widened as a breathless Nadia emerged from the bedchamber, and their discussion of Gabriel Wronski came to an abrupt end. "I added wood to the fire and prepared a warmer for the bed. When would you like me to return to help you dress for bed, m'lady?"

Jacek flapped a hand at the maid. "I will help your mistress with her lacings and whatnots. You may retire for the night."

A thank you, followed by a smoother curtsy, and Nadia darted away like a mouse evading a cat.

"Why is it she is so afraid of me?" He shook his head once Nadia had secured the door behind her.

Oliwia picked up two goblets of wine Nadia had prepared and handed one to Jacek. "Perhaps because you tower above her and she worries you will fall over and crush her?"

He accepted the drink. "Ridiculous! My children are far smaller than she, and they do not run from me."

"That is because Adam fears nothing and no one, Piotr is incapable of running, and Margaret is extremely adept at plucking her father's heartstrings. I do believe you should be afraid of *her*, my love." Oliwia sipped her wine, but it soured when it reached her stomach.

"I wonder what our next child will be." He grinned. "Besides Polish, that is."

Had that sip of wine still lingered in Oliwia's mouth, she would have expelled it.

Jacek's grin slid from his face. "Are you well?"

"Yes, of course. I am merely uncomfortable after that feast." Her corset had been digging into her all night.

"Yet you ate nothing."

She rolled her eyes at him. "I sampled every dish. Consider that a woman's corset presses on her stomach and makes it difficult to eat. Besides, you were so busy eating every morsel on the table, how would you have noticed?"

He gave her a sheepish smile. "I was hungry."

"You are always hungry," she chuckled. Unable to contain herself, she asked the question that had been blaring in her mind. "What is the news you have that made your face look like Adam's when he bites into one of Beata's apple tarts?"

"Hopefully, it was not as messy," he quipped, then grew solemn. "The crown grand hetman has named me colonel. I shall command my own pułk."

"You already command a pułk."

"I command my own pułk now, not one comprised of other banners as I am now charged to do. Think of it, Liwi. A rank of colonel—a true colonel—in charge of an entire regiment! It is a great honor I have only ever dreamed of."

Despite his serious demeanor, his elation broke through. How ironic that his excitement over his military accomplishments served to weigh down her own happiness. Reality was here. He would soon leave. He and his men were going to war.

"When do you depart?" Her voice came out in a strangled hush.

He tipped her chin up and delved into her eyes. "We'll speak of it later. Right now, I have a wife to seduce if I am to live up to the scandalous thoughts Nadia harbors."

Oliwia shed her foreboding and headed for the bedchamber. "We cannot disappoint Nadia. Now will you kindly help me with my 'laces and whatnots' so I can breathe once more?"

He set down his goblet. "Gladly, my lady." His bootsteps increased in pace as he approached her. His fingers went straight to her skirt ties, but he growled in frustration when they didn't yield. "This infernal garment isn't sewn on, is it?"

"No," she laughed. "In your impatience, your clumsy fingers are simply overworking the fabric."

"Clumsy fingers? I will show you how nimble my fingers can be … if I can ever get this damned thing off." With that, he loosened the ties, and the skirt slid off and puddled at her feet. "How many layers have I yet to conquer?"

She glimpsed him from the corner of her eye. "Shall I call Nadia back? I daresay she is more efficient than you, and she doesn't complain."

"No need. I am up to the challenge." He undid the ties holding her sleeves and moved to her bodice.

"I have no doubt." Her eyes traveled the sumptuous room as she slid the sleeves from her arms. "Such an elegant place. I had no idea Żółkiew would be so … so opulent. It puts Biaska to shame."

"Don't tell me you are of a mind to redecorate," he rumbled from behind her.

"No, I love our country estate just as it is." Pulling in a breath, she steeled her nerves. "Tell me about the council. Were any strategies laid out?" He had begun an even rhythm of unlacing but stuttered to a stop at her question. "Did I ask about matters of a sensitive nature?"

He returned to his work, mumbling, "No."

"Are you able at least to tell me the date you're leaving or where you're going?" She didn't want him to go, but she put the sentiment aside.

"We make for Mohylów in several weeks' time. Żółkiewski will remain here while he marshals more troops and awaits more shipments of kopie from the king. Eventually, we will travel south to Jassy to secure the Moldavian throne for Grazziani."

"Kopie? So he is expecting a skirmish."

"No, he's expecting to treat. His scouts report that the grand vizier's declarations of war were bluster. They have seen no decisive preparations for war. This campaign has more to do with rescuing the hospodar. But should their spies see wagons of kopie, they will know *we* intend to use force if we must."

She bit back her exasperation. "Mohylów. How far is that?"

"Roughly two hundred and seventy miles."

So far! It would take him forever to get there and forever to return home. "How many fight on behalf of the Commonwealth?"

"I do not know. I do know the Zaporozhians are not invited to take part, but the hetmans are counting on a number of Elear banners to add to the numbers."

"Which explains Wronski's presence here—and why he retired to the council with the rest of you."

"Yes, exactly."

"So he *is* a Lost Man."

"Mm-hmm."

A few more tugs, and the laces gave at last. She let out a long, sweet sigh of relief as he pulled the offending garment over her head and tossed it beside the dressing table. Turning to face him, she unwound the sash from around his trim waist.

While she discarded her shoes and disencumbered herself from her petticoats, he sank onto the edge of the mattress and pulled off his boots and pants. "Another thing I do know is that you will be returning to Biaska shortly."

She gaped at him. He frowned in return. All too well, she recognized she was on the losing end of this verbal battle. Besides, she yearned to see her children … and there was that other small detail she had yet to divulge. Lady Eugenia's words capered through her brain: *Do you think it wise—or fair—to send a husband off to war without the knowledge he has fathered another child? That comfort might be all he has to cling to during the bleak, cold nights.*

Oh, how she did not wish to think of Jacek on a battlefield or lost to a bleak, cold night, though he seemed confident neither would come to pass. She drew comfort from that. "I expect Filip will be going with you."

"I do not think it possible to stop him doing so."

She smoothed her chemise over her hips. "May I at least stay until your departure?"

One corner of his mouth twitched. "I believe that can be arranged."

Tendrils of relief and gratitude twined about her heart. At least she would have him a little while longer.

After unfastening the buttons of his żupan down to his abdomen, he yanked it over his head, leaving him seated on the bed in only his undershirt. "Might we leave the subject of war behind for the moment? I have far more important—and pleasant—thoughts on my mind." He reached for her and pulled her between his legs, his eyes drifting to her breasts, covered only by the gauzy fabric of her chemise.

"I have my hair yet to do."

He released her and, scooting backward on the bed, beckoned her with his hand. "Come, and bring your brush."

She snatched it from the dressing table, climbed onto the mattress, and settled her backside between his muscular thighs. While she undid one braid, he worked on the other, and when her hair hung free, he drew the coarse bristles of the brush through her strands. She dropped her head back, giving him easier access, and hummed in ecstasy.

213

He put the brush down, wrapped an arm around her middle, and cinched her closer, surrounding her in his scent of cedar and leather and man. She inhaled deeply. With his free hand, he gathered up her hair and tilted her head to the side. Warm lips landed on her neck and laid languid kisses along her skin. Liquid lightning sparked in her veins, shooting chills to every part of her body. The hand spanning her stomach glided up and cupped a breast.

As he massaged her tender flesh, he murmured against her throat, "Either you are finally putting on weight or my hand shrank."

She pulled away and craned her neck to look at him. His hands remained right where they were, and his lips curled salaciously. "I am not complaining, mind."

"Um, well, I have something to tell you."

He stilled, and the mischief fell away from his features. "What is it?"

"Do you remember a short while ago when you were contemplating what another child might be, besides Polish? If I am counting correctly, you will know in another five months." She gave him a watery smile.

His mouth swung open. "You are with child again? How did this happen?"

Oliwia looked as if she was about to burst into hysterics, and no wonder. "Yes, I am with child. As for how it happened, you should know. After all, you were present. I did not do it alone, Jacek."

His idiotic question proved he was an utter clodpole. In his defense, however, he had been delightfully distracted when she had dumbfounded him with her announcement. What little brainpower he *had* possessed at that moment had been wholly dedicated to fulfilling his baser desires. Those desires were wilting faster than a plucked wildflower under the summer sun's rays.

She moved away, taking her body heat and all that softness with her, and sat beside him, curling her legs beneath her as she rearranged herself and the chemise clinging to her.

He glanced down at himself and rearranged his own posture and clothing. "Of course I understand *how* it happened. What I meant was, I thought you were nursing Piotr, and there was the matter of, ah, our returning to being more disciplined of late." *Disciplined* was Oliwia's word, and it meant accommodating her wish that he withdraw and spill his seed outside her body. But the word "disciplined" evoked thoughts of war-making, and he preferred it not be invoked as part of *love*making. Moreover, he favored eschewing *discipline* altogether, for he delighted in his wife's pregnancies—her ripe shape when she carried his child, the fact he was at liberty to empty himself inside her, and most especially her lusty abandon when they coupled.

Holding to her wishes was no hardship, and only God knew they joined for more reasons than procreation. The Lord, he was certain, would forgive them their sin. He had more important matters to manage than a husband and wife indulging in their enthrallment with one another.

With her crystal-blue eyes drilling into him, he dipped an eyebrow. "Are you sure, Liwi?" Too late, he realized how ridiculous *that* sounded.

Her delicate eyebrows rode up her forehead. "Oh, I am sure. Did you not just now discover proof of it yourself?"

"Well, yes, but … I mean, such things could be due to other … things." He waved his hand lamely at her chest. "And frankly, I was more diverted by enjoying the … things than considering how they came to be." He raked his fingers through his hair.

Why hadn't she told him sooner? How had he not recognized the signs? His mind swam with calculations—and emotions. The thrill of welcoming another child spiked in him but quickly gave way to wondering when it had been conceived and its future while they languished in Podolia.

She let out a series of girlish giggles that had his heart flipping in his chest. "Are you pleased?"

"Yes, of course I'm pleased!" He narrowed his eyes at her. "But how long have you known?"

Her eyes skated about the four-poster. "Only a little while."

"Liwi?" He lowered his voice to a warning growl. "Did you know before we set out from Biaska?"

215

"I, um, suspected it *might* be possible. But I wasn't certain."

"And now you are."

"Now I am." She seemed to fight an imp's smile.

Despite a want to be stern with her, to express outrage over her deception, he couldn't even muster a sham glower. Instead, he pulled her into his arms, his heart hammering with joy, and whispered that he loved her. He drew back and saw tears glistening in her eyes. One lone drop rimmed her lower lashes and spilled down her cheek.

"This changes everything," he murmured.

Her brows knotted together. "What does it change?"

"You must stay here at Żółkiew."

"But—"

He pressed a finger to her lips and shook his head. "No. I will not have *my* wife, who bears *my* child, traipsing through the countryside where brigands and Tatars wait to pounce on the innocent. Unless I am there to protect you myself, you will remain here where I know you are safe. That way I need not worry over your and our"—he covered her stomach with his hand—"child's well-being. Say you agree, Liwi."

He removed his finger. When she said nothing, he arched an eyebrow. "You may wheedle me as much as you please, and while I am normally amenable to giving you whatever you desire, on this I will brook no argument."

Her tears fell in earnest. "But I miss our children so."

You should have considered that before. Selfishly speaking, though, he could not say he regretted bringing her with him. She was his heart, and being away from her left him hollow. How, then, to reconcile the draw of the battlefield with the lure to her and the home she embodied? A question to be revisited at a different time.

"Yes, I know. I miss them too," he soothed. "But think on this. They are in good hands with my sister and the dozens of ladies who fuss over them, and this child will need all of you. Moreover, I will not have to wait as long to be reunited with you when this confrontation is over. I will return to you here at Żółkiew, and together we will travel home."

"Can I not convince you to stay behind? I worry for you." Her voice came out in a soft hush.

"As I do for you, sweet, which is why I will not take you with me. And we both know my staying is impossible." Especially now that he had been elevated to such a lofty rank.

Her small shoulders sagged with defeat, rending the fabric of his soul. He gathered her in his arms as much to comfort himself as to comfort her.

Later, he made love to her, but the passion that had blazed inside him before had transformed into the steady heat of a banked fire, full of emotion and pieces of his heart. He took his time, moving inside her languidly, deeply, savoring the feel of her, putting silent affirmations of his love for her in every stroke, until they climbed that peak together and cascaded in shards of pleasure. Serenity enfolded him as he drifted back to the corporeal world.

Afterward, he watched her sleep in the dimness, watched her chest rise and fall with each sweet breath, and he imagined the babe growing within her. Would he be there when she gave birth? Would he hold his child in his arms and hear its first feeble cries?

Emotions swept over him, so many and so vibrant he couldn't separate them all. He lifted a lock of her hair and pressed it to his nose. His heart overflowed with love for this woman, for the children she had given him, for their life together. As overwhelming as that devotion was, though, it held another equally powerful side. Where devotion was lightness and love, this side was dark and filled with fear wrought from one question that would not relent.

Would they survive childbirth?

CHAPTER 23

Tremors

When Oliwia stirred the next morning, Jacek had already left for yet another council meeting. He had warned her there would be many to come before his departure for the front. At least the nights would belong to them, or so she hoped.

She entered the dining salon at breakfast, and Lady Magdalena motioned her over and patted the seat beside her. Oliwia gladly accepted the lady's offer, for she felt more comfortable in Magdalena's company than any of the unknown noble ladies seated at the table.

"My, but don't you have a rosy glow about you this morning, Lady Oliwia." She leaned to Oliwia's ear and dropped her voice conspiratorially, her heavy floral fragrance invading Oliwia's senses. "Please tell me it's due to a night of delicious pleasure spent in your handsome husband's arms."

Oliwia choked on half-formed words lodged in her throat. Heat overtook her face, no doubt lighting it like a beacon.

Magdalena let out a melodious laugh and grasped Oliwia's forearm. "I am sorry, Lady Oliwia. I did not intend to embarrass you. Well, maybe just a little." She waved her graceful hand about her. "As any of the ladies here can tell you, I can be rather outspoken at times."

A raven-haired woman seated across from them scoffed. "*Can be?* Really, Magdalena, you are too modest."

Magdalena plumped her blond curls. "Why thank you, Lady Struś. Allow me to introduce Lord Dąbrowski's wife, the Lady Oliwia Dąbrowska of Biaska." Magdalena proceeded to make introductions to the dozen or so women seated around the table. Pleasantries exchanged, they turned back to their own conversations, freeing Oliwia to ask Magdalena a question that had been dangling from the tip of her tongue.

She helped herself from a platter of hard-boiled eggs and cheese. "How well do you know Lord Wronski?"

Magdalena tilted her head, and the air between them thickened. "Not well at all, and that is certainly more than I would like to."

Stunned, Oliwia could do no more than stare at her.

The lady twirled a half-empty cup on the tabletop. "My answer surprises you, yes?"

Oliwia nodded dumbly.

"While he exudes charm by the platterfuls, he is a lecher and as oily as an eel, and the more of our sex who know the truth and avoid him, the better." She shook her forefinger at Oliwia. "You stay away from him, do you hear?"

"Forgive me, but do … do you know this firsthand?"

"No, thank the Virgin and all the saints." Magdalena crossed herself. "But I have heard enough stories to know what treachery that one is capable of, and it turns my stomach. Consider this: any man who makes his living by terrorizing and victimizing others is not beyond stealing a woman's virtue while he is about it. Leopards do not instantly don new spots, and I don't care how skilled he is at soldiering. Lying, stealing, cheating—even murder. His depravity knows no bounds, and he will employ any means possible to gain what he desires. He is truly a Lost Man, devoid of morals or scruples."

Oliwia's head spun. This man was free to move among the other nobles? He was to report to her husband? A shiver racked her body. "I thought I was alone in the unpleasant effect he has on me," she murmured.

"Oh no, my dear. We women need to stick together and defend ourselves against the likes of men such as him."

Oliwia breathed an inner sigh of relief when Eugenia approached the table. Magdalena urged the woman on Oliwia's other side to make space.

Smiling demurely, Eugenia slid into the seat and met every woman's eye until her gaze came to rest on Oliwia. "How are you feeling this morning?"

"I told him," Oliwia blurted. "Last night."

Eugenia's mouth opened and closed, and her gaze darted over Oliwia's shoulder.

Magdalena leaned in and whispered, "Now I understand your rosy glow, my dear. Congratulations to you and Lord Dąbrowski. When is the happy event to occur?"

Now that she had admitted her pregnancy to Jacek, her excitement fueled her runaway mouth. "Early November, as near as I can tell. Perhaps it will coincide with All Saints' Day. I hope it is another boy."

"How delightful for you." Sincerity shone in Magdalena's eyes, but a hint of sadness crept in. "My husband and I tried for many years, but alas, we were not so blessed. And then he died." She nibbled at a pączki; red jelly oozed out, and she licked it up with a little moan. "Lady Żółkiewska's cooks make the finest pastries."

Magdalena's age puzzled Oliwia. In the glow of candlelight, she had appeared to be of an age with Oliwia—in her mid-twenties. However, in the salon bright with morning light, creases surrounding the lady's eyes and mouth were visible beneath meticulously applied powder. Was she even of childbearing years? "But if you were to marry again—"

Magdalena shook her head. "No, no. I was married off at a young age to Count von Rohan, and while he treated me with kindness, I was never in love with him. I promised myself that next time I would only marry the man who captured my heart. Unfortunately, I have not met one who wields the net." Her rouged mouth twitched with a smile. "As for children, I'm afraid I will never know the joys." She patted Oliwia's hand. "Not all of us are as lucky as you, my dear. Treasure what you have with your man."

Memories of Oliwia's own loveless first marriage assaulted her, and a beat or two passed before she spoke. "I do, believe me. I suppose that explains why I am so distraught over his leaving on campaign."

Eugenia leaned forward. "I know exactly how you feel." Her lips tipped up with a hesitant smile. "So will you be returning to Biaska?"

Oliwia chuckled. "Oh no, my husband insists I remain here until the baby arrives and he returns."

Eugenia's eyes lit, and her smile broadened. "I'm delighted to hear it! I too am to remain. We will help each other pass the time until our husbands return safely home."

"I have no one to wait for, though I am here to aid Lady Regina while her dear hetman is away. Perhaps I can be a companion to you both as well." Once more, Magdalena laid her hand upon Oliwia's forearm, though Oliwia did not mind. Oddly, she found the gesture reassuring. "And, I might add, I have helped many a noblewoman through childbirth. Consider me at your service."

Oliwia arched a quizzical eyebrow. "Do you force garlic and onions down her gullet while she labors?"

Magdalena flung her hands wide. "Heavens, no! I've always found that bit of folklore rather disgusting. Chase away the evil spirits bringing you difficulty indeed! The woman is suffering enough, is she not?"

Oliwia threw her head back and laughed. The release felt wonderful! "You are hired for the job, my lady." She turned to Eugenia, who fought laughter of her own. "And you, Lady Eugenia, shall be tasked with barring anyone—*especially* babas toting elixirs, onions, and any noxious herbs—from entering the birthing chamber."

"It is settled, then." Eugenia gave a decisive bob of her head. "We are your sisters and are united in this endeavor."

Warmth washed over Oliwia. What an odd trio they made, she and these two women who had orbited Jacek once! But Oliwia could not deny that their presence here at Żółkiew buoyed her spirits. Her new friends could not replace her husband, but she would count on them for every bit of comfort and friendship they could offer in the difficult months to come.

Oliwia burst into the quarters assigned to her and Jacek after yet another rejuvenating breakfast spent among the ladies, disappointed when she found only Nadia folding clothes. What had she expected? Waking up without her husband and returning to quarters devoid of his presence during the daylight hours had been the way of it since their arrival at Żółkiew four days ago.

"Have you seen my husband?"

Nadia paused her folding. "No, m'lady, not since he left early this morning."

Oliwia glanced about the sitting room. "Perhaps I shall go find my brother and see how he is faring."

As it had the last four days, her eye caught on a delicate writing desk with beautifully turned legs. It sat before a multi-paned window pierced by the sun's rays, making the furniture fairly glow, inviting her to sit. She had managed to ignore it, but this morning her mounting guilt proved too much.

"On second thought, I am behind in my letters." She needed to let Tamara know about the change in plans and send instructions to Tomasz. Then she would pen simple messages to Adam and Margaret, who were learning their letters.

Her heart stuttered in her chest. Were her little ones all right? Had they suffered any illness or injuries? Did they miss her? How much had Piotr grown? If she had to fly to them, how long would it take to reach them?

She vowed that after her missives were written, she would take herself to St. Lawrence's Church and plead with the Virgin to keep them—and their father—in Her care.

Nadia pulled her back to the present. "If my lady would be so kind, when do you expect we will leave Żółkiew?"

Oh dear! How had she overlooked telling her maid? Of all the people who needed to know of their extended stay, it was Nadia. "Pan Dąbrowski has ordered that we stay until his return from campaign."

Nadia's pebble-brown eyes widened. "Are we to stay until after the child comes, then?"

"You've known this whole time, haven't you? That's why every time I felt ill on the journey from Silnyród you were there with something to calm my stomach."

A look of bewilderment replaced Nadia's surprise. "Of course, m'lady."

"You are a treasure, Nadia. And what irony. I was able to keep the babe secret from my husband, but not my lady-in-waiting."

Nadia's cheeks blazed red, as they always did when Oliwia referred to her as a lady-in-waiting. Though the girl had been elevated from a scullery maid by the previous Lady of Biaska before Oliwia's arrival, she still thought of herself as that lowly maid.

"If I may be so bold, there is very little I do not see where it concerns m'lady." With that, she dropped her head, hiding her face from Oliwia, and went back to her folding.

Apparently, Oliwia had had it wrong: Nadia knew full well the position she had grown into. Oliwia indulged herself in a covert smile.

Bending at the waist, Jacek propped his hands on his thighs and sucked air into his lungs. He had been running drills for hours in the tiltyard, which was nothing unusual, yet he could not recall being so winded before. He took advantage of the men-at-arms' attention being diverted to catch his breath in private.

Relative private.

Henryk strolled up beside him and whacked him between the shoulders. Jacek stumbled and groaned. Hinging forward from the waist, his friend peered at him, a grin plastered on his idiotic face. "Youngsters getting the best of you, my friend?"

"Piss off," Jacek grunted. He picked up his blade and brought himself upright, though his breath hitched as he did so. The men would not see him struggling, by Christ!

Henryk matched his movement. With his sabre, he pointed toward the field where two men sparred. "Filip seems to be acquitting himself quite well against Marcin. Impressive."

"I taught him everything he knows," Jacek panted.

Henryk pursed his lips. "Of course you did. And I taught him nothing, I suppose."

Jacek glared at him and for one instant deliberated knocking the smirk from Henryk's face, but he was too spent to follow up on the inclination.

Once he recovered his breath, he whistled at Dawid. Training was at an end—mostly because *he* was at an end, though they would never know that—and Dawid needed to lead the men back to their encampment outside the city walls. Jacek needed a drink and a rest and a reprieve from the ache shooting from his fingers to his shoulders. When had he turned to the consistency of porridge anyway?

Another group of men continued to thrust and parry on an adjacent field, wielding weighty wooden swords with aplomb. He arched an eyebrow. "Who are they?"

Henryk turned his gaze in the direction where Jacek's was presently pinned. "They are part of Wronski's squad."

"They're good."

"As they proved at Silnyród."

Marcin trotted over with Filip trudging behind. The lad walked forward while his head was swiveled toward Wronski's bunch. When he reached Jacek and his group, he jerked his chin forward. "Pan Wronski invited me to join them."

"Then by all means, join them," Jacek encouraged. "More practice won't do any harm."

Filip narrowed his gaze at Jacek. "No, I mean he asked me to *join* them. As in, join up with their banner."

"You cannot be serious," Jacek spluttered. Before he could rail that absolutely not, the lad was only sixteen, he took a Henryk elbow to the ribs and expelled a loud, "Oof!"

Filip's gray eyes turned steely. "I am perfectly serious. Contrary to how some regard my skills, Pan Wronski praises them. He is down several men and says I would be a worthy addition to his company."

Jacek fisted a hand on his hip. "So you think you are ready to step into his hardened soldiers' boots?"

"No, of course not! All I'm saying is that he is short a man, and he is recruiting for that post. I am his top pick." Filip's chest puffed.

Jacek bit back his dry retort that of course Wronski had selected Filip as his top pick—he needed a squire to wipe his boots on. What the devil was Wronski up to anyway? In Filip, he had an untested, sixteen-year-old soldier-apprentice. He was angling for something else, but Jacek couldn't decipher what that something else might be.

The four of them—Jacek, Henryk, Filip, and Marcin—stood clustered together as they watched Wronski's men run through their drills.

"They leave in a few days," Filip added quietly. "I wish to go with them."

Jacek crossed his arms over his chest. "Absolutely not."

Filip whirled, fists clenched at his sides. "Why not? At least with him I'll have greater opportunity than you'll ever permit me to have."

"Greater opportunity for what, exactly?"

"To prove myself!"

Marcin shifted uncomfortably from foot to foot, but Jacek pressed on. "How are you to prove yourself? By joining them in sacking a village? By stealing what little possessions a poor peasant has to his name and, in doing so, starving out the man and his family? By raping his daughters? His young sons?"

Filip reared back as though he'd been struck with Jacek's fist rather than his words. His mouth swung open, and the color drained from his face. "That's not what they do! They kill Tatars and Turks and enemies of the Crown!"

Jacek quashed his rising temper, grinding his back molars until he got his voice under control. Despite his effort, it came out as a low rasp. "And when they're *not* killing Tatars and Turks, they are pillaging and plundering their own countrymen. Ask anyone in Podolia. Hell, ask anyone in Żółkiew, if you refuse to believe me or Henryk. These men are the scourge of the earth, feared as much as the terrorizing Tatars. I wager a year's earnings that they are departing Żółkiew before everyone else because they are intent on raiding before they reach Mohylów. Yet these dogs have earned your admiration, so much so that you aspire to be like them." His voice climbed in volume, charged with emotion. "Are you merely unworldly, Filip, or have you completely lost your sense of honor? Have you learned nothing in all the time you have been at Biaska? What the devil has become of your sense of right and wrong?"

"You are …" Filip sputtered. He drew in a great breath and regained his momentum. "You are an arrogant, self-righteous, imperious son of a bitch, and I want nothing to do with you!" he screamed.

The men in the tiltyard paused, turning to look at the drama playing itself out like an overacted play.

"And you are a spoiled brat." Jacek jerked his head in their direction. "One who is making a spectacle of himself."

"I cannot believe my sister married you! Well, I for one do not have to bend to your tyrannical ways. I shall go where I please and do what I want!"

Jacek stabbed a finger in his direction. "You enjoy a great deal of freedom, far more than most in your circumstance, so that may be true to some degree, but you will not join the Lost Men—unless you do so over my corpse." His flaring temper hung by the slenderest of threads.

Filip barked out a mirthless laugh. "And you will stop me?"

"Test me and find out, boy." Jacek spat the last word, and it rang harsh even in his own ears.

The color of Filip's face matched the red of Biaska's pennants. He spun on his heel and stormed away. At least he wasn't making for Wronski's men—yet.

Henryk gave Jacek a sidelong glance, a sardonic expression on his face, as they watched the lad stomp away. "Well, that was well handled."

Jacek released a gust of air. "And you could have done better?"

"Doubtful."

"I just hope he doesn't go running to his sister."

"No, having Oliwia mad at me … Brrr!" Henryk exaggerated a shiver.

"That's not what I meant. I meant it's the sort of behavior that will only make him appear weaker, and he will use the disdain to fuel whatever gnaws at him."

"He's had a burr up his backside for months now," Marcin remarked. "I doubt his head can be turned by anyone who rides for Biaska. He listens to none of us. It seems, in fact, that he goes out of his way to defy us."

Which meant Filip *could* be turned by a villain like Wronski. Jacek found no solace in Marcin's words.

Was life not complicated enough without having to corral this bad-tempered bison of a boy who had no earthly idea what was good for him?

Oliwia had donned her cloak and exited the castle walls, making for St. Lawrence's vaulted vestibules, black-and-white marble-tiled floors, and high windows that threw down prismed light. She should have arranged for a male escort, but said males in her party were engaged in the tiltyards. Besides, Nadia walked beside her, they were within the walls of the city, and the sun was high in the early afternoon sky.

They scurried across Viche Square into the welcoming embrace of the cathedral's walls. Nerves that had been jangling off and on for days suddenly calmed as she dipped her fingers in the font's cool water, genuflected, and crossed herself under the watchful eyes of the archangels high above the glorious altar. She had come to love those angels.

The place was stunning … and mostly empty, which gave her an opportunity to linger as long as she pleased. She lit candles for each of her children, her brother, and Jacek before selecting a pew close to the front. Kneeling, she bent her head over her hands clasped in prayer, dimly aware that Nadia sat several pews back.

Mary, Mother of God, I beseech you, please protect …

How long her prayers ran on and how much she repeated them, she could not say. When she lifted her head, shadows moved across the high windows. Glancing over her shoulder, she glimpsed Nadia sitting rather than kneeling, and the maid seemed to be asleep. Oliwia suppressed a smile and sent one last prayer heavenward. She made to rise, but her knees and lower legs had gone numb. Eyes cast downward, she rearranged herself and grasped the pew to heave herself to her feet. A looming shadow, followed by a rank smell, had her eyes flying fully open. A man she did not recognize stood beside her, broadside to the altar so that he faced her side.

He crowded her. "Ain't this a fortunate coincidence?" Breath fouled with the smell of decaying teeth and spirits blasted her, and his raspy voice sent alarm bells clanging in her head. She knew that voice! She turned to run, but a viselike grip clamped down on her arm. "Such a fine, fine lady. I have been dreaming of you ever since our encounter, my pet. Let's go somewhere quiet where we can become better acquainted and tend to our unfinished business."

My pet?

Terror seized her, and she kicked out, landing a blow to the man's inner thigh. She had missed her mark, but he howled nonetheless, giving her a split second to whirl and run to the main aisle. Nadia startled to life and took off in the opposite direction toward one of the chapels. Behind Oliwia, the man thumped his way along the pew, though his steps were clumsy, uneven.

Finally unhampered by the pew, Oliwia ran shrieking down the aisle. "Help! Highwayman! Help!"

A stunned priest and several worshippers were congregated in a portal. The priest shouted for a guard, and Oliwia slowed enough to look over her shoulder. Her would-be attacker was headed for the sanctuary with all haste, but Nadia … Where was Nadia?

CHAPTER 24

Timely Ends

Gabriel sprang from his cot, refreshed the moment the morning's first rays touched the eastern horizon. He tossed a boot at his squire. "Get up. We're moving out tomorrow, and we have a lot of work to get camp ready." The answering groan buoyed Gabriel's mood further.

An hour later, Gabriel stood in the middle of camp, watching with great satisfaction as men scurried about like cockroaches. His lieutenant, Arek, had overseen camp logistics and kept men in order, but Arek was gone, and Gabriel was performing the task himself. By Christ, it was impossible to find a disciplined deputy! He needed more men.

One of the sentries approached cautiously. "Begging your pardon, m'lord, but there's someone here to see you. Says you asked him here so's he could join our company."

Ask and ye shall receive. Once again, God was showing His deserving archangel His generosity, though Gabriel couldn't recall who this fellow might be. "What's the man look like?"

"He's a young pup, curly brown hair, all noble like."

Recognition sparked inside Gabriel. "By all means, bring the lad here." Yes, God certainly did favor His archangel—not with a new lieutenant, but with a chance to get even. A smile lifted Gabriel's cheeks.

Moments later, Filip Armstrong strutted into the camp. Gabriel couldn't help but admire the boy's starch, but the pup had some hard lessons to learn.

"Welcome, Master Filip." Gabriel swept his arms wide.

Filip glanced around, taking in the activity. Bemusement settled into his features. "Are you packing up?"

"That we are, lad. I have orders to pull out, and we depart in the morning." Gabriel folded his arms across his chest. "Now what's this about you joining up?"

The lad hesitated. "You mentioned you had some openings that needed filling in your company and that I should consider ..."

"Ah! So I did. And how fortuitous. I am indeed down a few men. I find myself in need of a lieutenant, so I'll be elevating someone from within the ranks, which leaves a hole. I'm also considering replacing my lazy squire."

Armstrong looked at him warily. "What happened to your lieutenant?"

"Probably drank too much and got carried away with one of the whores and she stuck him with a knife. Either he's bled out by now or he's holed up somewhere getting repairs."

Filip's eyes widened, and Gabriel erupted in peals of laughter. "I'm only joking, boy! I have no idea where the lout is. All I know is he's no longer part of this company."

"Did he resign?"

Gabriel bit back his annoyance. Why was Arek any of this boy's affair? "No one resigns from my outfit. It's like this, lad. I've had a hard time keeping lieutenants, and he's the latest in a long line of subordinates who find the work too demanding. Like the others, he deserted. Vanished without a word, like the coward he was. But that's not you, is it, lad?"

Filip shook his head.

"Play your cards right, and maybe *you* can serve as my lieutenant someday."

The boy shifted his weight from foot to foot.

Gabriel regarded him. *First test.* "Though I don't expect your brother-in-law would condone it."

The boy went rigid, as if someone had just shoved a lance up his ass. "What my brother-in-law condones or does not condone is of no import to me. I am my own man."

Gabriel arched an eyebrow. *Second test.* "Is that so? Where is your purse?"

"I'm not sure I understand."

"In order to join our company, I ask everyone to pay an … entry fee, shall we say. Victuals must be purchased, feed for the horses, and so on. These things do not simply appear as if by magic."

"I've never heard of a soldier buying his way in."

"But then you've never been a soldier, have you?"

The lad hung his head. "No, sir."

"Have you any coin at all?" How desperate was this lad, and how far was he willing to go?

Filip raised his head. "A little. I have other funds, but they are currently … out of reach."

So the boy actually had funds? How interesting. "And who is keeping them from you?"

The boy hesitated, calculations flitting behind his eyes as he obviously sought the right words. "My sister runs the estate's finances, including those funds that belong to me."

Third test. "So she has a head for business. And here I thought your sister was merely an attractive adornment for your brother-in-law's arm."

Filip's eyes narrowed, and his mouth thinned into a grim line. Apparently, Gabriel had struck a protective nerve—which could be good or bad. Good because the boy demonstrated innate loyalty, and Gabriel could direct that loyalty toward himself. Bad because if that bond was a powerful one, Filip might turn on Gabriel in favor of his fealty. He had seen it before—not often, for most men were loyal only to themselves—but a few upheld their vows, and it never ended well for them. Not in Gabriel's banner.

"Tell you what, boy. Bring what funds you have and a prize and return in the morning when the sun is fully above the horizon."

"A … prize? Like what?"

Final test. "A pair of hussar's wings would fit the bill."

231

"Wings? I have no wings."

"No, but your brother-in-law does, yes? Bring me those, and you may join my banner and leave with us."

"But I can't! Those are his. They're priceless."

"And replaceable." Gabriel gave him a hard stare. "That's my price, boy."

The lad's face fell. "Yes, um—"

One of the sentries appeared. "Begging your pardon—"

"Commander," Gabriel barked. "You address me as Commander."

"Begging your pardon, *Commander*, but some official gents here to see you."

Over the man's shoulder stood a trio of guards and two dandies, one of them the starosta of Rzeszów, whose acquaintance Gabriel had already made—unfortunately—when the pompous windbag had asked Gabriel and his men to leave his city months ago. The other was Żółkiew's starosta, Paulius Bosko, a capable sheriff, though he too had asked Gabriel and his men to leave—hence their current packing. This demand seemed to be a contagion among self-important starostas. A dose of apprehension put Gabriel on pins and needles.

He grasped Armstrong's shoulder. "I must attend to these men. Are we in accord?"

"I, um, yes. Commander."

"Good. And tell no one of your plans. Understood?"

"No, sir. Thank you, sir." The eagerness in the boy's eyes had Gabriel chuckling inside.

"I had better not be disappointed." Gabriel pivoted on his heel, his step a little lighter at the prospect of collecting Dąbrowski's brother-in-law *and* his prized wings.

Straightening the cuffs of his żupan, he plastered on his most charming smile and headed for the sheriffs he needed to rid himself of.

Filip plodded away from Lord Wronski in a daze, willing his hammering heart to slow its breakneck pace. He lifted the kolpak from his head and swiped a hand across his sweaty brow before resettling the cap. Jacek's wings? How could Lord Wronski ask for such a prize? And why?

A voice inside his head questioned whether the lord was worthy of Filip's admiration, but another voice shot it down. *"Of course he's worthy! He's the captain of a banner!"*

"Ah," countered the first voice, *"but he is a captain of Lost Men, and they are not honorable. As their leader, might he not be even less virtuous than the rest?"*

Losing track of his surroundings, Filip came to a stop and muttered, "But I will be given the chance to prove myself with a commander who recognizes what I can bring to a company of soldiers." And truly, when was the last time Jacek had used his wings? Not for years. Would he miss them? Had he even brought them with him?

"Of course he did," the first voice warned, *"for there's a chance he will lead men in a charge on the battlefield."*

The second voice piped up, *"But commanders do not don wings."*

And so the inner argument raged until Lord Wronski's voice snagged his attention. He looked to his right, surprised that through the bustling camp he heard the captain's voice as clearly as if he stood beside him. The captain was turned at an angle away from Filip and toward his guests, who in turn faced Filip.

"Arek? Missing? Oh no, no. You gentlemen must have received bad information. He resigned. Came to me and said he had to leave. Some family matter or other called him away. What could I do but pay him his final wages and wish him well? Good man. I'd welcome him back anytime."

Filip froze. Had he misheard the captain?

One of the officials—the starosta of Rzeszów—jotted a note. "When?"

Captain Wronski tapped a finger against his chin. "Hmm ... let me think. It has been a sennight since we first arrived, and he left three days later. Four days now, I reckon. What is this all about?"

The second official, Paulius Bosko of Żółkiew, addressed the question. "A body was discovered by the river this morning. The man was badly beaten, and we had heard of your lieutenant disappearing. We wondered if the two might be the same man."

Gabriel held up a finger. "Not disappeared, resigned."

"Resigned. Yes, of course," chimed in Rzeszów's starosta.

"I pray it was not my man. But what makes you think he could be Arek? Did someone identify the body?"

"Impossible." Rzeszów's starosta shook his head, and Lord Wronski raised a quizzical eyebrow.

Starosta Bosko said, "Animals ravaged the body, but beyond that his face had been bashed in with a viciousness I have never witnessed. He is unrecognizable."

"So how—"

"One of our officers recalled the man's cloak and boots."

Lord Wronski clasped his hands behind his back. "And is this officer acquainted with my former lieutenant?"

Bosko offered, "It seems they had a bit of an altercation over a, ah, woman of easy virtue."

Wronski's tone showed his surprise. "I had no idea. Did it come to blows? Is it possible this officer was the one who did the beating? As I'm sure you gentlemen know all too well, many a man has been known to lose his mind over a wench—"

"No, no. They resolved their differences with a jug of wodka—purchased by the officer—while the two remained at the brothel."

"And the strumpet? How did they come to an accord about her?"

Rzeszów's starosta dropped his voice, and the only words Filip made out were, "… interviewed the lady in question … verifies the story."

Lord Wronski's clasped hands seemed to tighten. "I see. And you are sure the officer could not have—"

Paulius Bosko shook his head. "We are sure. He returned to his barracks, and any number of soldiers in the garrison have vouched for his presence. There is more."

"More?"

"We discovered a piece of notepaper inside the dead man's pocket with a name written on it. We also found something of value that was stolen from a noble lady …" The wind caught Bosko's voice, and Filip craned his head to better hear. The movement caught the starosta's attention, and he lifted his gaze to Filip.

The captain turned and locked eyes on Filip. Recognition and surprise transformed the captain's features. He seemed to quickly recover himself, and disregarding Filip's presence, he cupped both officials' elbows and steered them toward his open tent flap. "Let's go into my tent, where we have more privacy."

Heat flooded Filip's face, and he pivoted and hurried from the captain's camp, one question after another circling in his head. He needed to find someplace quiet and sort through all he had just heard. Where did the truth lie?

If only he could present his dilemma to someone he trusted. In the past, he would go to Jacek or his sister with matters of such gravity, but they thought poorly of Lord Wronski and would never offer the objective counsel he sought. Henryk, Marcin, and Dawid were no better. As for the squires he shared a tent with, they were mere boys. Idiots, most of them. No, this was a man's problem to unravel. It was time to rely on his own reasoning and make up his mind for himself.

CHAPTER 25

Treasures Lost, Treasures Found

"Lady Dąbrowska?" An impeccably dressed gentleman Oliwia recognized as Paulius Bosko, the castle starosta of Żółkiew, stood outside her sitting room door, presently being held open by Nadia. His expression told her he was not here on a social call.

She was seated at the desk, where she had been penning a series of notes she would tuck randomly among Jacek's belongings before his departure—simple missives with prayers, blessings, and words of love to lift his spirits during the campaign. She had a stack for Filip as well, but he had been ruder, sulkier, and more sullen of late. Her generosity toward her brother steadily dwindled with each passing day until she felt few of the words she'd scrawled, and she was sorely tempted to withhold the notes altogether.

Scolding herself for her petty thoughts, she rose from the desk and greeted the man. "Welcome, Starosta Bosko. Are you looking for my husband? He is training with—"

"No, my lady. It is you I seek."

What on earth did the sheriff want? A peek over his shoulder revealed a man-at-arms. Her pulse began to race. Had something happened to Jacek? Filip? "Won't you come in? How may I be of service?"

Bosko, a middle-aged man of a height with her and nearly double her girth—even with the child in her womb—removed his kolpak, entered the chamber, and ordered the guard to remain in the hallway. He began worrying the cap between his hands. "I wonder if I might ask a rather … delicate favor of you."

Oliwia gestured for him to sit down. "May I offer you a glass of wine?"

"No, thank you, my lady." He reached into his *pas* and extracted a small object she couldn't make out, for his sausage fingers hid it from sight. He placed it in his palm, which he extended toward her. "Do you recognize this?"

Before Oliwia fully comprehended what she beheld, Nadia gasped. "M'lady, your wedding ring!"

In the man's palm lay the ruby ring Jacek had brought from Genoa and gifted her for their wedding. It had to be hers. Never before or since had she beheld such an exquisite ring. Not an impractical, gaudy affair, it nonetheless caught the eye and fit as if crafted solely for her hand: a gold band with a dazzling ruby at its center surrounded by dainty pearls and diamonds that sparkled with light.

Oliwia's mouth dropped open. "That is the ring the highwaymen took from me several weeks ago. But wherever did you find it?"

"It pains me to say we found it on a body discovered early this morning near the river. We believe the deceased was one of those two highwaymen."

Horror vied with curiosity inside her. She plucked up the ring, her mind vaulting to her necklace. "Did you discover any other items? I lost a necklace too."

He shook his head. "No necklace, my lady."

"Who did the body belong to?"

"We, ah, are not sure. We might never have known of the corpse had the animals not dragged …" He paused to clear his throat. "The body is in rather poor condition, and the face is, ah, unrecognizable. That, my lady, is where the favor comes in." She raised a querying eyebrow, and he ran on. "I thought perhaps if you would be willing to take a look at the man's garments—"

237

"Yes, of course."

"—on the man's body."

"Oh! Oh yes, I see. It would be easier to identify the garments on the person rather than folded or neatly laid out, wouldn't it?"

Jacek stalked into the sitting room, causing them both to jump. "Starosta Bosko, to what do we owe the pleasure?"

The starosta rose to his feet with a speed and grace belying his roundness. He canted his head. "Lord Dąbrowski. I am here on business. I had some questions for your wife."

Oliwia stood too. "The starosta needs my help identifying someone he believes might have been the man who accosted me at the church. And look! They have found my ring!"

Jacek looked from the ring pinched between her thumb and forefinger to Bosko. "So you have apprehended this man?"

"Not exactly. A soldier from one of the encampments discovered the body of someone we believe is the fiend who tried to attack your wife yesterday. I was hoping she could tell us whether our dead man is the same one from the church."

Jacek's eyebrows shot to his hairline. "You want her to identify a decaying corpse?"

Oliwia moved beside Jacek and rested her hand on his forearm as she addressed the official. "Just the clothing upon his body, yes? And it sounds as if the body is fairly … fresh, but the face is … beyond recognition." Her husband's muscles tautened beneath her touch. She glanced up at him, whispering, "I am not unaccustomed to gruesome deaths, Jacek, and I feel compelled to help the starosta in any way I can."

Said starosta gave her a dip of his head. "Thank you, my lady. I understand that this is not easy."

"What of his accomplice?" Jacek demanded.

Bosko rocked on his heels and rearranged the collar of his żupan. "We have some ideas. If we could address this man first, I can give you more information about the other suspect."

"Fair enough, but I am coming too."

Bosko gave Jacek a nod of tacit agreement.

Oliwia glanced at the ring, and the places it could have traveled and the grubby fingers that might have handled it streamed through her mind. She handed it off to Nadia, who was already reaching for it. "Nadia, if you would—"

"Allow me to clean it, Lady Oliwia."

Suddenly overcome with emotion, Oliwia grasped the maid's upper arms and bussed her cheek, completely startling the girl.

She donned her cloak and allowed the two men to escort her along passageways and down flights of stairs. As they walked, Jacek asked the starosta if any other items were discovered on the body.

The man shook his head. "Not a weapon, not even his belt. The culprit who committed this crime removed everything. Well, nearly everything."

Jacek's forehead furrowed. "So why take a man's belt and leave behind a valuable piece of jewelry? Are you sure the perpetrator wasn't trying to make a murder look like a robbery gone bad?"

"At this moment, we are not sure of anything. But I will tell you that the ring was secreted in a tiny pocket that could have been easily overlooked by a thief anxious to leave the scene of his crime."

They followed the starosta and his guard deep into the bowels of the castle, where they arrived at a storage room at the end of a long stone passageway. Holding a lantern aloft, the guard swung open a door, and there, upon the dirt floor, beneath a tarp, lay the unmistakable shape of a man.

The starosta kneeled at the corpse's midsection and ordered the guard to bring the lantern closer. Gingerly, Bosko lifted the tarp, exposing a section of tunic and the man's trousers.

Crouching, squinting, Oliwia inspected the fabric. "Is that spruce-green?" The color was hard to discern in the gloom.

The starosta affirmed that it was, and Oliwia flipped up the hem, careful not to brush the stiff corpse. Even in the lantern's dim light, the lining as bright as a canary's feather came to life, and polished wooden buttons carved in the shape of a snail's shell glowed. "Is his hair dark brown with coarse curls?"

"It is, my lady." Bosko seemed to hold his breath, as if he dreaded her asking to see said hair.

She glanced up at Jacek, who leaned over her shoulder, then brought her gaze back to Bosko. "This is the same man."

"You are sure?"

"I am."

The starosta's shoulders visibly relaxed, and he re-covered the body as Jacek helped her to her feet. She leaned against his hard planes and steadied herself. As if to reassure her, he held her hand several beats longer than needed.

Wordlessly, the group retreated from the storage room and hurried above floors, where the sun splashed prismed light across white walls. Jacek's voice floated through her foggy consciousness; he was pressing the starosta for details about the dead man's accomplice.

"Let us retire to your apartments," Bosko suggested.

Back in the sitting room, after they had settled into chairs and the guard had once more taken up station in the hallway, the starosta began fidgeting in his seat as though he had lowered himself onto a bed of thistles.

With Jacek scrutinizing him like a wolf sizing up his next meal, the man seemed to squirm even more.

Never one to dance around the rosebush, Jacek arrowed right in. "What is on your mind, Starosta?"

"Well, Commander, it is like this. When you asked earlier about the dead man's accomplice, I did not disclose another piece of evidence that was tucked away in his pocket." Bosko produced a slip of paper from inside his *ferezeya*, a sleeveless cloak in royal blue trimmed in the finest fur. He unfolded it and handed it to Jacek.

Oliwia drew closer and peered over her husband's shoulder. Her brows stitched together. "Dawid Pawelski? Why, he is one of Biaska's most celebrated hussars. Why does his name appear on this piece of paper?'"

The starosta retrieved the slip from Jacek and tucked it back into his garment. "Why indeed? We have been asking ourselves the same question and can only draw one conclusion." Bosko's gaze fixed upon Jacek, as if Oliwia was neither present nor sentient. She quelled her irritation.

Jacek tented his fingers, his cool gaze boring into the starosta. When he next spoke, his voice was equally icy. "Are you implying that Pan Pawelski, who has been in Biaska's service for as long as I have known him, had something to do with this highwayman?"

"Not that he had something to do with the villain, but that he was in fact the ringleader." The man plucked out a linen square and mopped his brow.

"That's impossible," Oliwia cried.

Again addressing himself to only Jacek, Bosko continued. "He is a nobleman and therefore fits your wife's description of the highwayman's voice. We are questioning him now."

Oliwia sat forward, at last winning the official's attention. "Is it possible you have forgotten, Starosta, that following the attack, you asked my maid and I if we could identify the perpetrator's voice, and we both said no, that it was unfamiliar. Surely if this highwayman were Dawid Pawelski, we would have recognized his voice."

"He could have disguised it," the official sniffed.

Anger rose inside Oliwia, firing her cheeks. "Is he under arrest?"

The starosta deigned her with a blink of his eyes. "Merely detained, madam. For now."

"But you have no right! He is szlachta, and according to the Privilege of Jedlnia and Kraków, you may not imprison him without a proper court-ordered verdict. He is protected by *neminem captivabimus*."

Beside her, Jacek held very still, his fingers still tented. He slid her a sidelong glance, as if to convey that the floor was entirely hers.

Confusion commandeered Bosko's features. "But he is not imprisoned!"

She threw out a hand. "Detained, held in custody—whatever you wish to call denying him his freedom—flies in the face of the very acts set down by King Władysław Jagiełło two hundred years ago. You are starosta of Żółkiew. Surely you are aware of nobility's right of due process."

"I have violated no due process," Bosko huffed.

Oliwia held out her hand, palm up. "Then may I see your warrant?"

"Warrant?" He darted pleading eyes to Jacek, as if to say, *"Can you not control your madwoman of a wife?"*

Jacek's lips quirked. "As Biaska's adjudicator, my wife is quite precise about the law, and in this, I have no doubt she is correct. Might I also suggest that you acknowledge her authority rather than looking to me." A slow smirk spread. "Trust me when I say it will go smoother than if you ignore her."

Sweat popped and beaded on Bosko's forehead, but Oliwia was moved not a whit. "Yes, of course. Begging your pardon, my lady," he stammered, looking at the floor before seeming to remember himself and raising his gaze to hers.

Oliwia folded her arms across her chest. "How long do you intend 'questioning' our man?"

"Until we have the answers we need."

"And when, pray, is that?" she challenged, tilting her chin imperiously. "Will it be when you gather the answers you need to issue the warrant you do not have? Do your plans include resorting to torture so he will confess what you want him to confess? And when can my husband and I see him?"

The starosta's eyes popped wide. "That is not possible, my lady."

"Is that so? Shall I take it up with the crown grand hetman? He may see it quite differently, especially when he understands how these items—and little else—were so conveniently left on the body."

A knock at the door garnered all their attention. Jacek called for whoever stood on the other side of the door to enter; the guard stuck his head through the gap just as Nadia tore from a different chamber to admit him.

"I beg your pardon, my lady, my lords." His eyes settled on Bosko. "One of your deputies needs to speak with you, Starosta."

Bosko launched from his seat and pressed himself through the opening. Fierce, undecipherable whispers passed between the two men. Within moments, the starosta was back in the sitting room. Nadia began withdrawing to the adjoining chamber, but the starosta bid her stay. To Oliwia, he said, "Your lady-in-waiting, she accompanied you to the stream that day, yes?"

Hugging a corner of the chamber, Nadia darted wide eyes between Oliwia and the starosta.

Oliwia nodded, puzzled. "Yes, she did."

The official arranged his garments, a triumphant smile adorning his chubby face.

What was the sheriff about?

The answer was not long in coming, for he held up his hand, and between a sausage finger and his thumb a shiny object gleamed.

Jacek sat forward, and Bosko dropped the object into his open palm. "What is this?"

"Why not ask the maid?"

Jacek beckoned her and held out his palm. Oliwia craned her neck to see what he held.

Nadia gasped. "My clasp! I lost it that day at the river!"

Oliwia's confusion grew. "You never said anything, Nadia."

"M'lady was so distressed. I d-did not want to add such a trivial matter to your worries."

Jacek handed her the object and turned back to Bosko. "Where did this come from?"

A smugness settled itself about the starosta. "One of my deputies recovered it during a search of Dawid Pawelski's belongings. Now how do you suppose it got there?"

The boldness that had surged inside Oliwia mere moments before receded like a tide chasing its lowest ebb.

Oliwia paced the sitting room, pivoting whenever her path ended at an immovable object—such as a stone wall. The space seemed to shrink with each pass. Jacek had left hours ago with Starosta Bosko, and being alone with her galloping thoughts had disquiet frothing in her bloodstream. Why hadn't Jacek returned?

As if the saints listened in, Jacek re-entered their quarters, pausing as he came through the door.

She stuttered to a stop and blurted, "I should have gone with you."

His movements deliberate, he closed the door behind him. "Where is Nadia?"

"I sent her off to deliver letters to the messenger." Oliwia flapped her hand in the air, dispersing a modicum of her nervousness. "How is Dawid?"

Jacek stepped to the fire and rested his arm on the mantel as he looked down into the flames. "He is hale. Somewhat confused, much perturbed, and greatly worried. He claims he never saw the clasp before today. I believe he's telling the truth."

"Of course he is! They are trying to convict him of a crime he didn't commit! Have they shackled him in a dark cell somewhere?"

"No. The room where he is housed has a guard outside it, but the space is light and comfortable." He glanced over at her, and one side of his mouth curled up. "He is not as concerned about what he is accused of as he is worried about what *you* think of him, Liwi."

"You told him I believe he is innocent, yes?"

Jacek nodded.

She resumed pacing. "Dawid would never … Someone has arranged this to make him appear guilty. The damning details are far too convenient."

"I agree. Unfortunately, no one remembers seeing Dawid during the time we stopped."

"But he was there," she cried.

He reached out and touched her shoulder as she strode past him. "Actually, he wasn't. He needed to take care of something in Rzeszów, so, with my permission, he left the company. He caught us up in Silnyród, which gave him enough time for an assault when we stopped at the stream."

Her mouth swung open. "I didn't know … I never noticed his absence." She shook her head. "I stand by what I said, though. Dawid is not the man who stole my valuables while he leered at me. *That* man was taller. How could Dawid have grown several inches in height? And honestly, Jacek," she scoffed, "how could the starosta believe he would do such a thing?"

Jacek regarded her for a beat, as if deciding what—or how much—to say. "Starosta Bosko has a theory that Dawid needed money. In addition, he is convinced Dawid coveted you after admiring you for many years."

"That's preposterous!"

"You and I know it, but the theory fits Bosko's requirements quite neatly. With a man safely under guard, he escapes the demands of his superiors and pressure from the townspeople." He ran his fingers lightly across the mantel's surface.

"You say the dead man was fraternizing with one of the guards before his demise, and that the two fought in a nearby bordello, yes?"

"Yes, but they settled their differences. That is what Starosta Bosko relayed to me."

Tapping her finger against her chin, she let her mind wander a path of possibility.

One of Jacek's eyebrows dipped. "What is racing through that brain of yours?"

"The only word we have of the highwayman's encounter with a potential suspect comes from the starosta or one of his men, which fits the starosta's narrative nicely indeed, and which also makes me wonder ..."

"Wonder what?" His eyebrow assumed a skeptical slant.

"If I should not investigate myself. After all, Dawid belongs to Biaska, and as you so adroitly pointed out to the starosta, I am the adjudicator. I do not believe I thanked you for that, my lord."

His second eyebrow crashed into the first. "Investigate? How, exactly?"

"By going to the ... establishment myself and speaking with the, er, workers who might have witnessed the exchange."

He gawked at her.

"Why do you gape at me thusly?"

"If anyone should question the 'workers,' as you so amusingly put it, it should be me."

The thought of her husband among a bevy of perfumed and powdered women set off a tinkling bell of unease inside her head. "I disagree. I can speak with them, woman to woman."

"You cannot be serious," he spluttered.

She felt herself stepping into shifting sands, but her stubbornness kept her on the precarious track toward danger. "I am very serious."

245

"I have a somewhat better understanding of brothels and the women who ... live in them. Trust me when I say your presence would be far differently received than mine."

Her nose inched into the air. "Because you are handsome, that's why."

His mouth quirked. "I will take that as a compliment. But truly it has little to do with my—or any man's—looks. Rather it is the look of his coin that matters ... how much it shines. But I have a better idea than either you or I conducting an investigation for which neither of us is equipped."

"Henryk!" they both exclaimed at the same time.

He straightened his cuffs. "I will speak to him now. That way, I might be able to help prove Dawid's innocence before I leave. Besides, I need Dawid with the company."

She came to a stop before him. "What do you mean, before you leave? Have you had news of your departure?"

"I have. Just now, in fact."

The gravity etched in his features caused a well of dread inside her to fill. "And what is the news?"

"The crown grand hetman received word from King Zygmunt an hour ago that, after a meeting of the Sejm, Żółkiewski is authorized to do whatever it takes to rescue Moldavia's hospodar. Therefore, we march with Hetman Koniecpolski."

Tightening her fists, she dug her nails into her palms. "But I thought the latest reports confirmed no large Ottoman army is gathering at the border."

"And that is still true. However, the Sejm is gravely concerned for Grazziani's fate."

The dread that had been building inside her snapped, and tears pricked her eyes; she rested a protective hand on her belly. "How soon must you leave?"

He flicked his sapphire eyes her direction, their intensity sending jolts through her. "We leave three days hence."

His words stole the breath from her lungs. *So soon!* Dear God, but that was no time at all!

She mustered a steadiness she did not feel and swung her attention to Dawid. "Then I shall take up the fight. I will appeal to anyone who will listen. The hetman's wife, if I must. Jacek, I swear upon all that his holy it was not Dawid who spoke to me at the stream that day. In fact, I think—" A shiver rippled through her before she could stop it.

He arched an eyebrow. "What is it, Liwi?"

"I should not say without knowing for certain."

"This is between just us." He crossed his heart. "I swear I will not divulge your secret."

No, of course he wouldn't. "I think ... But it makes no sense! The man's voice sounded oddly like ... Pan Wronski's."

CHAPTER 26

Preparations Reap Separations

Jacek frowned at the exquisitely crafted pistol he seldom fired as he ran his fingers over the inlaid butt. It was one of a prized set given to him in Genoa, but what was he to do with it? Leave instructions to split the pair, gifting one to Adam and one to Piotr? Bequeath them both to Adam, who was the oldest but not of Jacek's loins? And what if the babe growing inside Oliwia's womb was another son?

Such were the questions churning in his mind since Żółkiewski's order to muster two days ago. Readying men—and himself—for battle was a feat he could accomplish with minimum contemplation. Readying his wife, however ...

As he carefully laid the pistol back in its velvet-lined case beside its twin, he considered how thoughts of safeguarding a wife and children should he never return daunted him more than preparations for any campaign had ever done.

The world around him glowed, wrapped in a false blanket of serenity, for even as he sat before a window overlooking a garden bursting with color, Oliwia beside him fussing with a piece of embroidery, his mind was restive and worried—just as he knew hers was preoccupied with affairs back at their estate, where he would not allow her to travel.

He slid her a glance, his eyes drifting to the swell of her belly hidden beneath her skirts.

She let out a little squeak and nearly stabbed her finger with the needle. Before he could ask what was wrong, she grabbed his hand and placed it on her abdomen. The day was warm, and she wore light silks. Consequently, the fluttering beneath the taut skin of her belly was unmistakable, and he was overcome by an awe that rendered him speechless. Worries melted away.

"Goodness," she laughed, "but this one is like a fish on a hook, flipping and flopping and kicking my ribs with his tail."

Jacek laid his ear beside his hand. Did the child make a noise he could hear? The lightest tickle against his jaw, like the brush of a butterfly's wings, had him breaking out in a smile. "Is the movement uncomfortable?"

"Not yet. He has tiny elbows, but they will grow bigger and sharper."

"If the babe is moving about that much, it's a girl. And if it *is* a girl, she will be a beauty like her mother." He lifted his head and kissed her, busying her mouth before she could accuse him of false flattery. Pulling back, he explored her face with his eyes, memorizing every line, every curve. His fingers traced the same path.

A delightful shade of pink dusted her cheeks. "Your tongue is becoming as honeyed as Henryk's. I cannot help but deliberate what schemes are hatching in your head."

He blinked. "Why do you not take my compliment for what it is, an expression of admiration for my wife?"

She looked away, her eyes riveting on some distant, unknown target. "Perhaps it is because when I look at you, I see what other women see. The years have made you no less attractive. However, when I look in the mirror, I see that the years have not been so kind to me."

He brought himself fully upright in the chair and plucked her free hand from her lap, cradling it between his own. "Either your mirror is in disrepair, my sweet, or you have taken leave of your senses."

Her eyes darted back to his, and he marveled at their crystalline hues ringed in indigo. He had never seen more beautiful eyes than hers, nor did he tire of delving into their depths.

She puffed out a breath. "There are creases around my eyes that never used to be there, and with each child my body grows rounder and is more reminiscent of an overripe pear than a maiden's shapely figure."

"Then you *have* taken leave of your senses. I find your shape more alluring than ever; it is full in all the right and best places. As for lines around your eyes"—he feathered the tip of his finger at the corner of her eye— "what little is discernible adds character to your flawless countenance." Before she could speak, he pressed the finger to her lips. "And do not accuse me of flattery when I merely speak the truth."

She cast her eyes down like a shy maid.

He grasped her chin and raised it. "Besides being the most enticing creature I have ever laid eyes on, you have a sharp mind. How else could you manage Biaska so skillfully—"

"Not so skillfully," she protested, "or we would not be in the financial straits—"

"Do not interrupt. I was about to say, and how else could you maneuver Starosta Bosko into releasing Dawid?"

She shrugged.

"You may think it no major feat, but both Dawid and I are indebted to you. He has told you so, yes?"

"Many times. And I will tell you what I told him: the starosta had no right."

"I agree, but getting the hetman to intercede at a time like this, when his attention is wholly focused on the border, is nigh on impossible. He has far more consuming matters to deal with than one hussar's freedom."

"More like the hetman's wife." Her brows knotted together ever so slightly before returning to their neutral state.

"What just flew through your brain, wife?"

"Are you certain the hetman … knows what he is doing?"

"Of course he does," he scoffed. "Why ask such a thing?"

"Naturally, I do not know him so well as you do, especially not in a military sense, but I cannot help wondering if his poor health clouds his mind. The talk among the magnates' wives is that his prime left him long ago. Is he too old and too ill to be leading men into battle? Should you be following him blindly?" Her questions were tentative and quietly posed—and irritating as the devil.

Jacek released her chin and frowned down at her. "You are correct in that you do not know him. You are incorrect, however, that I follow blindly. Therefore, on this subject, you have no standing to question as you do. I, who know the hetman and his capabilities well, have all the confidence in him." While Żółkiewski might have fallen out of favor with his fellow magnates, he remained a brilliant military leader that Jacek had served under and greatly admired. The fact that the man was in his seventies and continued fighting the accursed Tatars was reason enough for Jacek to bestow his respect. "Why do you insist on raising this specter of doubt?"

"I'm sorry. It's just that I—"

"Yes, I know. You don't want me to go." He rose abruptly, the midsummer spell shattered. "You are trying everything you possibly can to keep me beside you."

"Better that than hurrying you along so I can run into my lover's arms!" she snapped.

He wheeled. "What the devil does that mean? *What* lover?"

She rolled her eyes to the ceiling and back. "You are as thick as a castle wall at times. I have no lover but you, and you well know it. I was simply making a point."

"Point *not* well taken."

"Obviously." She picked up her sewing and bent her head to it, showing great interest in an activity he knew her to loathe while hiding her face from view.

How had the mood turned from a warm summer breeze to an icy-cold blast? "Now if you'll excuse me, I have—"

"Preparations and separations to make. Yes, by all means, my lord, do not let me delay you from your *duties*." Ignoring him, she muttered to herself in heated whispers.

Slamming the lid of the pistol case harder than necessary, he stalked from their apartments, utterly flummoxed about what direction his feet should follow.

The opening door made a telltale squeak, but Oliwia kept her head down, struggling with a simple stitch she had no interest in sewing. "Back so soon? What did you forget?" Surely it wasn't an apology Jacek had forgotten, was it? Stubborn man!

"Liwi?" Filip's brown curls preceded his sparkling gray eyes through the opening. "I would speak with you for a moment, if I could."

Her heart took flight. Discarding the embroidery, she waved him in with an excited hand. "Of course! Come in, come in." She offered him refreshments.

He slid into the chair Jacek had vacated minutes before. "No, thank you. There is much to do, and I cannot stay long."

"Will you not be dining with us in the great hall later?"

His curls bobbed as he shook his head, tempting her to reach out and put them into some semblance of order, but she reined in the urge. "No, we leave at sunrise, and there is much to do before we go."

She forced the disappointment from her voice. "I see. Well, duty first." She was learning to loathe the word.

As he sat beside her, straight as the trunk of a young pine, she marveled at how much he had grown.

He darted her a look. "How is my next niece or nephew doing?"

"If his spirited mazurka steps are any indication, he will emerge from the womb a ready dancer."

Filip threw his head back and laughed, breaking some of the tension that had wedged itself between them these past many weeks. "That is a good sign, then."

They stared out the window for several silent, yet comfortable, beats. Finally, Filip broke the quiet. "I came to tell you that I'm sorry we have been at odds lately. I want to be sure there is no discord between us before I go."

She reached for his hand, surprised when he not only grasped it, but gave it a firm squeeze and held on. "I am so glad you did. It has hurt my heart to

feel this chasm between us. It was never my intention to push you away."
Though she wasn't certain how much it was her pushing as it was his pulling.

"I know." He paused to straighten the hem of his żupan in an obvious
bid to delay an uncomfortable conversation. "I, uh, also know I have been
at times guilty"—his voice cracked—"of blaming you for disappointments
and slights that were, um, not always of your doing."

Inside, a protest rose up that she was the cause of nary a disappointment
or slight, but she chose to keep the opinion to herself lest she snap the olive
branch he was clearly handing her. "Do you speak of Jacek?"

"Not only him. Let us just say that there are others who make promises
they have no intention of keeping."

Puzzled, she canted her head. To her knowledge, Jacek had never made
a vow he had not kept. "Of whom do you speak?"

"Just some soldiers I was becoming acquainted with in another camp."

"Why were you spending time in another camp?"

"I was spending time in another camp because they did not treat me like
a stupid boy," he spat.

"Yet they did something to upset you. What was it?"

"It does not matter, Liwi." Irritation charged his voice. "Please stop
asking questions."

Unsure what else to say, she blurted what was in her heart. "I have asked
Jacek to look out for you, and I want your promise that you will take care
of him as well. For me."

A sheepish smile curled his lips. She reckoned it was as much of an
apology as he would offer for his harsh tone. "I will watch his back, just as
I will watch my other lord-brothers' backs and they will watch mine."

Bravado seemed to seep from him, and his broad, bony shoulders folded
forward.

Clutching his hand tighter, she murmured, "Do you fear what lies
ahead?"

For several long moments, he did not say a word, and she worried she
had tripped over yet another tender spot that would cause him to close
himself off. At last, he expelled a gust of air. "I am not sure whether it is

apprehension or excitement, but I do find myself visiting St. Lawrence's more often."

Admitting as much must have weighed heavily upon him, and she merely nodded.

He leaned to her cheek and kissed it. "Be well, sister."

Refusing to give up possession of his hand, she caressed his cheek with the back of her free hand. "I shall. You as well, brother." *Please come back to me. I couldn't bear losing you.*

Unable to stop herself, she rose when he did and threw her arms about his neck. "Stay safe." He wound his spidery arms around her and pulled her in for a fierce hug, long enough for her to discern his lanky limbs but short enough that he need not compromise his emotions more than he already had. Knowing her little brother still lived inside the man struggling to break through his shell warmed a space deep inside her chest.

As he disengaged from her embrace, his movements were awkward and his cheeks blazed red. With a quick bob of his head, he pivoted for the door. She choked back the tears clogging her throat as she watched him disappear.

Jacek stood, waiting for Oliwia to come to him and help remove his clothing. Confounded that she didn't seem to notice him, he was even more surprised when he realized he stood stock-still, as if he was incapable of the task himself.

"Helpless fool. You've gone soft. Good thing you're heading back on the road," he muttered to himself. As he pried apart the fastenings on his żupan, she dashed about the chamber, her nightgown and robe flapping behind her as she went. The sight reminded him of a confused bee, and he thought to stop her frenetic movements.

"Liwi," he called softly.

She continued careening about the space, gathering up his belongings for his morning departure as if she hadn't heard him—or was ignoring him.

"Oliwia." Louder this time, but again she did not acknowledge him. It was as if he stood in the chamber alone. In a huff, he wrangled the żupan off his body and dropped onto the edge of the mattress and tackled his boots.

Boots removed and placed beside the bed so he could pull them on in haste if an emergency required it—at least some part of the soldier still lived inside him—he stood and yanked the linen undershirt over his head in exasperation. He fisted his hands on his trouser-clad hips and watched in disbelief as she darted from trunk to table, laying out clothing only to remove it again.

"Wife! Stop!" he bellowed.

She did stop—and froze on the spot—swinging wide crystal eyes to him as if only now recognizing his presence.

"Come. Now." He pointed a finger to the space before him. While he was used to commanding armies, he was not used to commanding her, and he held his breath as he waited for her reaction.

Seemingly stunned, she stepped to him, her owl eyes glued to his. "What is it, my love?" Her voice was soft, soothing, and quite the opposite of his.

"Your frantic flittings are driving me to distraction."

She gaped at him.

He encircled her in his arms and drew her close, cradling her face in one hand. "Everything is prepared," he murmured. "There is naught for you to do."

"That's not true. I must tend to a few more details."

"They can wait. There is something far more important that needs your attention."

Her sable brows pulled together.

"That something is your husband." He leaned down and kissed her tenderly, whispering against her mouth. "I need you, Liwi. I need you before I go." He kept his tone gentle but insistent.

He pulled back and delved into her eyes, searching for her thoughts. In turn, her gaze ignited and scanned his. Oh so slowly, he untied her dressing gown and pulled it from her shoulders, letting it flutter to the floor. He ran both hands in her hair, cradling the back of her head.

"I need to get my fill of you," he murmured and then moved his mouth over her neck, trailing soft, lingering kisses, tasting her skin.

Her body came to life, chasing away the dazed state she had been suspended in mere moments before. She skimmed her hands along his shoulders and plowed her fingers into his hair, spilling chill after chill down his spine. He raised his head to find a seductive smile playing over her lips.

"Are you trying to seduce me, my lord?"

"Indeed, I am. I am heartened you recognize the effort."

She arched an eyebrow. "I daresay it's a welcome change after your imitation of a growling bear the day long."

With an extended sigh, he rested his forehead against hers. "I am sorry, sweet."

"As am I. I believe we are both on the edge of a knife, growing ever more so as your departure draws nearer."

"I know of only one way to solve this problem."

Her lusty smile transformed into a smirk. "Judging by that familiar look in your eyes, I know what solution you propose. It is the same one you offer time after time."

He wound his finger in a tress and tugged. "What 'look' do you speak of?"

Narrowing her eyes, she pointed an accusing finger at his face. "The one where your eyes gleam with determination. The one that leads to this." Her finger turned downward, toward her stomach protruding through the nightgown's gossamer fabric.

As if of its own accord, his hand slid from the small of her back to her belly, where he splayed his fingers over its smooth, melon-like surface. He gave her his most innocent smile. "I merely suggest it because it has proved effective time after time. You and I have solved many a difference together this way in our years of marriage, and it has led to a very happy union. At least for me." When her expression did not change, he rushed to add, "It has been happy for you too, yes?"

She pursed her lips and tilted her head as if in contemplation.

"Liwi?" Alarm rose inside him. His wife was the only person capable of compelling strong emotion inside him with a mere look, and she was using it to great effect right now.

"At times you pontificate too much, husband." Her eyes dropped to his mouth and suddenly blazed like a wildfire in dry grasses. She slid from his grasp.

Confusion and disquiet—for she hadn't answered him—stormed into his mind, but then she began to disrobe. His body always reacted to hers with a mind of its own, and as he watched her, said body expelled all doubt from his mind and instead let itself be lulled into enchantment by the lovely form in front of him.

They lay entwined in one another's arms later, his fingers stroking her strands as her head rested on his bare chest. "You never answered my question."

She raised up and peered at him, her hair gliding over his skin like a silken curtain. "What question?"

"About being happy in our marriage."

She nestled back against him. "You need ask? Of course I am happy … except at times like this, when war threatens that joy." The last bit came out with a hitch.

This too was a familiar refrain. He would never, could never, sway her to his side of the argument. "Liwi, you know—"

"Yes, Jacek, I know the man I married. But that was five years ago. Everything is different now. You are the father of two sons and a daughter, with another on the way. Let the Crown find another commander. The king is not the only one you owe a duty to." The anguish in her voice cleaved his heart in two and threatened to undermine his resolve.

Their joining had taken him to a euphoric plane, but the return from that journey had come too soon and had done nothing to dim the specter of his leaving.

257

The telltale softening of her body and her contented sighs as he held her told him she had drifted off, leaving him to ponder the looming shadows alone. Tomorrow night, he would lie on a hard cot in a cold tent, the prospect of home stretching long into the future. When would he return? When would he see her again? See Biaska and their children?

She had lost one child and had been devastated by that loss. What if she miscarried this one and he wasn't there to console her? What if she died in childbirth and he in battle, and their children became orphans? Who would oversee the estate for Adam without robbing him blind? What would become of Margaret and Piotr?

His thoughts wandered back to the baby. Part of him soared with the knowledge another child grew in Oliwia's belly, but another part despaired he might not be there for the birth. Though the hetman had assured them the conflict would be over quickly—save the hospodar's throne, sign a treaty, and leave Moldavia—Jacek had been through too many campaigns to count on a swift return.

He cradled her in one arm and pulled her closer, pinning her against him as if he might safeguard her. By all the saints, he would give his heart's best blood to behold Oliwia safe and happy.

With his free hand, he crossed himself in the dark, kissed his pendant, and sent the first of many prayers heavenward.

Virgin Mother, hold my wife and the baby within her safely in your hands.

CHAPTER 27

Camp

Heat shimmered on the horizon, making the Dniester River appear as though it had overflowed its banks in places. Into the fourth day of their journey now, the banners were at the halfway point between Żółkiew and the village of Śledziówka, the Commonwealth's muster site nine miles northeast of Mohylów. Jacek should have been pleased with their progress, but his insides felt as though thistles embedded themselves in them. A restiveness he had not experienced before coursed through him, like an undercurrent of dread, tamping down his excitement about being on campaign once more. Not long ago, he had yearned for the camaraderie he shared with his lord-brothers in the evenings after setting up camp, swapping stories of past glories and battles yet to come. But now he had no patience for storytelling or dicing or card games. A tune being plucked by a fellow soldier on a fiddle was as likely to grate as to soothe, no matter how expertly the musician plied his instrument.

Further vexing him was the "why" of his unease. Was it the summer heat? The disjointed companies his banner traveled with that didn't seek interaction with their fellows? Or was it the worry for his wife and unborn child that constantly tickled the back of his brain?

He could have sought solace in his brother-in-law's company, but Filip refused to be cajoled from his sour mood. After years spent speaking of nothing but his first campaign, the lad should have been elated. Instead, he clung stubbornly to his sullenness and kept his distance from Jacek.

The priest accompanying them, at the behest of Żółkiewski himself, might have eased his soul, but the man was distant, with the cold glint of judgment in his gaze. His curt interactions only came when he hounded Jacek for his confession—something Jacek couldn't fathom doing yet, especially as it meant admitting to fornicating with his pregnant wife before his departure. Perhaps on the eve of battle he would consent to reconciliation … or if the campaign grew desperate. In the meantime, he kept his sins to himself.

There were always Lesław and Henryk, his brothers-in-arms in so many other campaigns, but the former was similarly distracted—no doubt by thoughts of his own young family—and the latter's incessant cheerfulness ofttimes stretched Jacek's patience to a thread on the verge of snapping. Like now.

Riding beside him in the middle of the caravan, Henryk swiveled his head and smirked. "You bring to mind a mourner at a funeral. Why so gloomy, my friend?"

"I have important matters on my mind."

"As do I." Henryk leaned forward over his pommel and shot Jacek a knowing look. "Last night, for instance. This one tavern maid could not stop flirting with me. I have seen far prettier faces, but she was witty and had very ample assets." He waggled his eyebrows. "So I let her lead me upstairs and—"

Jacek puffed out a noisy breath. "These are the important matters weighing heavy on your mind? Must your idle talk always be about the latest whore you bedded?"

Henryk straightened in his saddle and looked down his nose. He feigned a frosty tone. "She was not a whore. She was a barmaid."

"Are they not the same?"

"Not at all! I didn't have to pay this one. In fact, I'm fairly certain she would have paid *me* to plow her field."

Jacek raised a skeptical eyebrow. "And you left her no coin? Nothing with which to buy herself a bauble or trinket?"

"She needed a new shawl, and I saw no reason to deny indulging her," Henryk grumbled. "You are merely envious because you have returned to your monkish ways."

"And I should behave like you, I suppose."

"Absolutely not. If you did, I would be obliged to trounce you on Oliwia's behalf." He threw his head back and laughed. "Seems you have little choice but to pray for a hasty return, my friend. Hopefully, the hetman is correct and we need only show our might before the Ottomans surrender, returning us home before the Feast of the Guardian Angels. Any delay will make you more intolerable than you are now."

Snippets of conversations between the magnates in Żółkiew bubbled up in Jacek's brain, like an overheating pot of bigos. Frantic whispers had included concerns about the size and readiness of Żółkiewski's army, whether they had been too hastily pulled together, and whether their numbers were large enough to defeat the enemy. As he had done since he had first overheard the talk, Jacek rammed the dialogue deep down. Hetman Żółkiewski knew what he was about. The man would never lead troops into a dire situation such as the one the magnates fretted over. They were merely old, fat men inventing reasons to remain in their too-comfortable manors, where they could gorge themselves on delicacies and drink.

Oliwia's remarks about the hetman's advanced age and poor health surfaced in his mind, and he reflected on different episodes at Żółkiew when he'd witnessed the hetman's coughing fits or his need to depart a supper table early for his fatigue.

"There, you see! This is exactly what I was talking about. I try to make light conversation, generously recount my bedchamber adventures with you since you have none of your own, and you plunge yourself into an abyss of bleakness. What has you vexed now?"

Before Jacek could open his mouth to dispatch the next verbal barb—namely, telling Henryk he had no interest in being regaled with his bawdy tales—a stirring at the front of the column caught his attention. He put his heels to Jarosława's flanks and sped ahead. When he gained the head of the formation, he pulled up beside Dawid and refrained from gawping at the sight of Gabriel Wronski and his squad facing them.

Wronski raised his arm in greeting and flashed Jacek a broad smile. "Hail, Pan Dąbrowski. What a pleasant surprise encountering you here." Wronski's expression communicated the surprise was more distasteful than pleasant.

"I thought you would be encamped at the muster site by now." After all, Wronski had preceded them by weeks.

Wronski waved a dismissive hand in the air. "We found other adventures which distracted us for a time."

"Trying to join up with us, no doubt, seeing as how you and your men now report to me. How fortunate. We can now make our way to Śledziówka together, and I can impart the ways of Biaska's banner." Jacek fought a smirk, enjoying the abhorrence that flickered in Wronski's expression before he quickly schooled it.

Wronski dipped his head. "My plan exactly."

The clopping of hooves behind him had Jacek swiveling his head. Filip reined in his horse, his eyes fastened on Wronski, his expression unreadable.

"Ah," Wronski greeted, "and here is my favorite lad come to say hello." Wronski's grin widened, lending him a slightly mad look. "Well met, Master Filip."

The scene poked at Jacek's suspicions—nearly everything Wronski said or did poked at Jacek's suspicions—but he kept his wariness in check.

Jacek watched with curiosity as Filip's cool expression transformed with a narrowing of his eyes at his hero Wronski. An uncomfortable, palpable pause thickened the air like a rain-laden cloud, punctuated only by the sounds of horses whinnying and pawing at the ground. Had something transpired between the two? If so, when had it occurred?

Finally, Filip nodded in Wronski's direction. "I trust you are well, my lord."

"Never better." Though Wronski's smile did not waver, a hard glint shone in his eyes. It brightened as he turned to Jacek. "Lead on."

The sun had reached its apex when the vanguard spotted the encampment outside of Śledziówka days later. Jacek held the company back and waited on a scouting party he had sent ahead nearly an hour earlier.

Two of those scouts, Dawid and Marcin, now rode hard toward him, their horses kicking up puffs of dirt in their wakes. As they reined in their mounts, Marcin panted, "A site has been set aside for Biaska, Commander."

Jacek removed his cap from his sweaty head and waved it toward the duo. "Show us the way."

Beside him, Wronski sauntered forward astride his horse, scoffing, "What kind of site? What of us? Do we have a special 'site'?"

Wronski's presence in camp had started as a pricker beneath Jacek's saddle but was now a fully developed thistle head burrowing its way into his tender backside.

He perched his kolpak back upon his head. "We will make do with where they assign us. As for you, Captain Wronski, perhaps you should send your own men to check with the camp quartermaster." Spirit of God, but the man was insufferable!

"I will do that. And I will request—no, demand—a space at the southernmost edge of camp so we lead the army into Moldavia."

Jacek smirked. "Leading the army falls to the hetmans, not to me and certainly not to you." He picked up his reins and nudged Jarosława forward, leaving Wronski to fume in his own bluster.

As the servants and retainers were setting up camp, a message arrived from Hetman Koniecpolski, bidding Jacek and his senior officers to join him in his command tent. So Jacek wiped the grime from his face and hands with a damp cloth and dusted off his żupan. Then, accompanied by his four top men—Henryk, Lesław, Dawid, and Marcin—he trudged to the hetman's tent.

Like other tents in the encampment, it was a white conical affair, adorned with flags displaying the Koniecpolski clan coat of arms—a knight's cross atop a horseshoe, similar to Żółkiewski's—and colorful pennants whipping in the wind. For all its size, it could have held three regular tents.

Jacek and his men entered the cool, dim interior guarded by several men-at-arms, but Koniecpolski was nowhere in sight. Jacek took in thick Turkish rugs, ornate chests, and a large shrine devoted to Our Lady of Częstochowa. The shrine featured a painting of the Madonna in heavy gilt with a kneeling bench and candles before it. In the center of the tent stood a table covered in maps and surrounded by numerous folding, cushioned armchairs. The opulence fit the hetman himself, Jacek noted, as said hetman swept into the tent.

Koniecpolski caught Jacek off guard when he gripped his arms and bussed his cheeks in a warm greeting, his belly so large it brushed Jacek's. He was dressed in bright blue silk and, despite the warm summer day, a cloak trimmed in rich fur. Hair shaved on the sides in the hussar fashion, he wore a bushy beard that was longer than the hair atop his crown. "Welcome, Colonel Dąbrowski. I have been anticipating your arrival and am heartened to have you and your men here at last."

When the hetman released him, Jacek bowed at the waist. "My officers and I are honored to be here."

With the hetman came an entourage of colonels, magnate commanders, and scouts. Mikołaj Potocki, whom Jacek had heard referred to as "Bearpaw," was one of the louder and more flamboyant among them. His behavior was expected, if not wearisome, for he was a Potocki, one of the most powerful families in the Commonwealth. The man's disdain and heavy-handedness toward the Cossacks likely contributed to Żółkiewski's decision not to call said Cossacks to his aid for this campaign. But had Żółkiewski picked Potocki over the Zaporozhians of his own volition, or had the choice been foisted upon him?

Koniecpolski bid them sit and gestured for wine to be served before sitting behind the table himself and calling for the latest intelligence on the Ottoman army.

"Their numbers to date are unimpressive but growing," a scout reported, "with most gathering near the fortress at Tehinia."

"And what if they grow beyond our own?" a commander rejoined. "We are not a large force ourselves."

Koniecpolski tented his fingers. "Grazziani has promised at least fifteen thousand troops to supplement our own."

"As he should," grumbled a different man. Jacek looked toward the voice, recognizing another magnate who had brought his private army to the fight. "After all," the man continued, "at peril to ourselves and our estates, it is *his* backside we have come to rescue."

"As we should," blustered Potocki. "The hospodar serves the Commonwealth."

"The hospodar serves himself," interjected a different potentate. "You Potockis have been meddling in Moldavia for so many generations you seem to have forgotten that until recently he was allied with the Porte."

Voices rose in argument, and soon the din made it impossible to hear aught but an angry buzz. Henryk swiveled his head toward Jacek at the same moment Jacek turned to face him. Henryk's troubled expression mirrored Jacek's own.

Christ and all the saints! *These* were the leaders to whom Żółkiewski had entrusted the campaign? Solidarity was crucial if they were to defeat the enemy; conflict within their own ranks only served the Ottomans.

Koniecpolski's shout brought them all to heel.

"We accomplish n-nothing by fighting amongst ourselves," the hetman thundered. "We can debate all we like about w-what Grazziani has or has not done, but it does not change that the hospodar is in need of s-succor. Nor does it alter the fact that should we f-fail, the consequences are grave. The Porte will install its own leader, and Ottomans will swell our b-border, presenting a threat to the Commonwealth and Christendom such as w-we have never seen."

The silence that followed was deafening.

Someone seated several feet away from Jacek turned and regarded him. "You are the commander from the west, yes?"

Jacek didn't recognize the man. "From Biaska, yes."

"I am Teofil Szemberg. Though I have never witnessed your leadership on the battlefield, Hetman Żółkiewski holds your acumen in high regard. You have said naught, and I am curious. What think you of the situation?"

Jacek straightened in his seat as all eyes fastened on him, marshaling diplomacy. "Intelligence is everything. Continued scouting is crucial to laying our plans, including accurate reports of the topography. We are mostly cavalry, which lends itself to the flat terrain I have heard of but not yet seen, which could balance our smaller force should they outnumber us. However, adding infantry can only benefit us."

Koniecpolski nodded in agreement. "And f-foot soldiers are exactly what Grazziani has promised us."

"Given those numbers added to our own, we should prevail." What he didn't say was that Grazziani's fifteen thousand were crucial if they hoped to intimidate the enemy and force them to the negotiating table, as Żółkiewski was counting on. Without the added troops, the enemy might decide to test them; no one could predict that outcome.

More discussion followed, with Koniecpolski reiterating the promise of Moldavian support, until at last the magnates calmed.

One of the men, a prince named Samuel Korecki, turned to Jacek.

"As you are newly arrived from Żółkiew, Commander, I wonder whether you might have crossed paths with any brigands."

Jacek's eyebrows rose. "No, nor did we see signs of any. Why do you ask?"

"We have heard rumors of a group of bloodthirsty marauders raiding the countryside. Sometimes it is a small army, and at other times it is a handful of masked highwaymen. We cannot ascertain whether crimes are being committed by one large pack of curs or numerous unassociated criminals."

Henryk leaned into the conversation, and the prince darted him a suspicious look. Jacek tilted his head toward his friend. "My second, Henryk Kalinowski."

Surprise flared in the man's eyes. "Are you related to the colonel from Kamieniec?"

"Not that I am aware of," Henryk drawled.

Jacek urged the man to continue.

266

"What we do know is the villagers being victimized are not making false reports. The investigations conducted by the starosta of Kamieniec, Colonel Walenty Kalinowski, and his deputies have uncovered one atrocity after another against people whose only fault is that they inhabited the path of these scourges." The man's dour words led Jacek down a familiar path teeming with images of the horrors man was capable of visiting upon the innocent.

"How many villages?"

"Eight, at the very least, some in my voivodeship. They swarmed through like a rapacious plague of locusts, jumping from one fertile field to another, destroying everything in their path before we could give chase. At first, the starosta believed them to be Tatars, for they behaved as brutally, but that notion was quickly dispelled by the eyewitnesses."

Jacek clenched and unclenched his fists. "I only wish we *had* crossed their path." He and his men would have relished wiping them from the earth and sending them to meet Satan.

The man gave a grim nod. "As do we all. But we have other missions we must direct our attention toward, yes?"

Jacek could not help but entertain the thought of hunting the miscreants during the idle time they would surely spend in the coming weeks. One corner of his mouth curved wickedly. "That we do, but with God's grace, we may yet have a chance to avenge the villagers."

CHAPTER 28

Play Fair with a Viper and Suffer His Fangs

A bedraggled guard looked up at Filip astride his horse. "The commander will see you now." Filip suppressed a grin as he dismounted. He had anticipated this meeting since Captain Wronski had humiliated him back in Żółkiew.

He picketed his horse and followed the man to a large tent in the center of the camp. Seated on a bench outside the tent, Captain Wronski looked up from wiping down the barrel of his wheel-lock with an oiled cloth.

Unexpected delight played over Wronski's features. Setting the firearm down, the captain stood and spread his hands in welcome. "Well met, my friend. To what do I owe the pleasure of seeing you here in my camp?"

Filip invoked a flat tone, steeling himself to the man's potent charm. "I bring a message from Colonel Dąbrowski."

Wronski let his arms drop to his sides. "Ah. Following orders, yes?"

Filip extracted a folded paper from his kolpak's cuff. "Commander Dąbrowski did not order me. I volunteered."

"That shows pluck, boy. I like that. It's an admirable trait and one that's lacking in most men."

A modicum of pride swelled inside Filip's chest. Wronski took the note and unfolded it. As he scanned Jacek's words, his brows crashed together. Then he raised his head and broadened his smile; all vestiges of anger vanished. "It appears your brother-in-law has summoned my men and me to take part in his company's drills."

Filip nodded, keeping his gaze level with Wronski's.

"Please inform Lord Dąbrowski I have already drilled my men today. Perhaps another day?" Filip detected naught but solicitude in the captain's voice.

The captain picked up his wheel-lock and pocketed the cloth. He looked down the barrel of the gun. "Do I detect an air of hostility on your part, Lord Filip? If so, I must admit I am baffled by it."

Heat flooded Filip's face. Had he been so obvious? His eyes darted to the weapon before swinging back to Wronski's, and his lips thinned into a hard line. He had questions begging answers. "You invited me to join you but left before the appointed time."

And there it was, the crux of Filip's anger. For long, tormented hours, he had grappled with switching to Wronski's banner. In the end, he had convinced himself that, though not the ideal circumstance, seizing the opportunity was in his own best interest if he wished to advance his military career. He had even pilfered Jacek's wings, an act that still caused his stomach to turn over. But when he had appeared at Wronski's camp, the entire troop was gone. The only evidence they had been encamped there were the flattened patches of ground that had held tents and the heaps of rubbish. When Filip had inquired at the next camp over, they told him Wronski and his men had pulled out long before dawn—and long before Wronski had instructed Filip to be there. Had Wronski misled him on purpose? If not, why hadn't he sent word to Filip that their departure had been changed? The slight had stung like a swarm of angry bees. Mercifully, Filip had replaced the wings before Jacek or Marcin had noticed them missing, but that was the only positive he could claim about the entire episode.

"Ah. Yes, I understand your disappointment." Wronski lowered the wheel-lock and gave him a look of genuine contrition. "I was disappointed as well, for I was looking forward to your company on our journey."

The answer knocked Filip off balance for an instant. "Why did you not send a message telling me you were pulling out early?"

The captain's mouth dropped open. "Your brother-in-law did not deliver my message?"

"What message?"

Wronski gestured toward his tent. "Join me for some refreshment, yes?" Wronski seemed to sense Filip's hesitation. "You are safe here, and none of my men will divulge your presence to anyone in your company. Come. Let's go where we have privacy."

A tug-of-war played inside Filip, and the equivocation rooted him to the spot. Wronski clapped a hand on his shoulder, and Filip let himself be steered toward the tent. Once inside, Wronski poured equal measures of wine into pewter goblets, handed one to Filip, and raised the other. "To the defeat of the Ottomans!"

Filip lifted his cup. "Na zdrowie." He took one drink, then a second, longer one. Wronski had poured the good stuff. The strong stuff.

Wronski swiped the back of his hand across his mouth. "First, may I say how delighted I am that you are here. Had the choice been up to me, you would have joined us that day instead of coming upon an empty camp. What I wouldn't give to have saved you the disappointment." He paused to drink more wine. "It began when some idiot got himself murdered. Apparently, folk wanted to place blame on my men and me, and the starosta came to see me not long after you had been there. Your brother-in-law was with him, and we were asked to leave immediately."

This made no sense. "Why would my brother-in-law appear in your camp with the starosta?"

"Draw your own conclusions. I assumed he did so in his capacity as the commander of our company. That is the logical explanation. Although now that I think back ..." He cleared his throat. "You see, at first I thought he meant to intervene on our behalf as any commander might do, but ... Well, it does not matter." He waved a dismissive hand.

Filip swallowed more wine. "What exactly did my brother-in-law do?"

The captain let out a long-suffering sigh. "I suppose you will find out eventually. Your brother-in-law, you see, was the one who urged *the starosta* to urge *us* to leave with all haste."

Filip blinked, more off balance than ever. "Did he explain why?"

"Something about keeping us safe from angry townspeople, though I'm a bit baffled as we saw no hostility from any of the folk. To the contrary, they seemed quite happy to have us spending coin in their town." Wronski shrugged. "Now that your brother-in-law is a pułkownik, I suppose he wishes to keep a tight rein over his troops. In any case, I handed him a message and asked that he deliver it to you. The missive explained what had happened and invited you to join us when we arrived here. Perhaps he opened it and … No, no. I can't imagine your brother-in-law doing such a thing."

More questions circled in Filip's brain. Might Jacek have accepted Wronski's message and destroyed it? "You're sure you gave it to him?"

An offended frown creased Wronski's brows. "Yes, I'm sure. Shall I produce witnesses to vouch for me? Several of my men watched the exchange. Better yet, ask the starosta."

Guilt stabbed Filip, followed by a spike of anger as reality dawned. *Why, that meddling, overbearing goat turd! How dare Jacek—*

The captain interrupted Filip's inner railing. "I understand you might be tempted to confront your brother-in-law, but I caution you against doing so."

A muted alarm rang at the back of Filip's mind, and he narrowed his eyes. "Why?"

"Because you will show your hand. Sometimes it's wisest to keep such tidbits close to one's chest, to be used when they garner one the best advantage." Filip wasn't sure he understood, and he began to say so, but Wronski continued. "Besides, he will likely only deny it, and it will create more ill will between you. Best to keep peace in a camp."

Was Wronski trustworthy? A different question Filip had harbored sprang to the fore.

"Why did you lie about your lieutenant? You told me he had deserted, yet you told the officials that he'd been forced to leave to take care of his kin and you had paid him his wages."

Gabriel sighed. "The truth? It won't put me in the best light. You see, I lied. I didn't want to make the man look bad. He served me well. If word got out that he abandoned the company ... Well, that wouldn't look good, now would it? All the poor sod ever knew was soldiering, and if he had wanted to join a different company—"

"You speak of him as if he's dead."

"Do I? Dead to our banner, I suppose, though you can see how much I care for my men. Even though he abandoned his company, I didn't want him to suffer not being hired elsewhere, so I lied to protect his ... reputation." Sadness overtook Lord Wronski's features. "You've no doubt heard we Liscowczycy referred to as the Forlorn Hope, but we fight for Poland and we take pride in our allegiance. We have as much honor as a hussar banner, yet we are unfairly vilified because we are not knights of their lofty level—"

"And because you sack and pillage—"

Wronski's placid features now took on the look of a whipping winter storm. "Only when necessary, and only the enemy," he growled. "We are much misunderstood."

"So you have nothing to do with the raping and looting that has occurred lately in these parts?"

"Ha! The raping and looting has gone on for centuries, but only now is it getting noticed by the magnates because only now do they bother to travel to this part of their country. These crimes are not at our hands. Never at our hands. We are merely the most convenient target." The captain refilled their cups. "Why, if I were to come across the brigands, I'd slit their throats myself! They are no better than the Tatars that attacked you and your party the day you arrived at Silnyród."

Filip's mind streaked back to Wronski and his squad riding in and rescuing him, Jacek, and the fortress itself. He took another long drink and let his contrition show in his tone. "I do not believe I ever thanked you for coming to our aid that day."

Wronski raised his cup. "Think nothing of it. We stick together, yes? And frankly, it was that day that convinced me I wanted you in my company."

The wine was muddling Filip's brain, his thoughts crossing over one another, blurring. "How so?"

"You were taking on the entire enemy cavalry." Wronski reached over and gave Filip's shoulder a friendly shake. "Your courage impressed me. You're the kind of man I want fighting beside me."

Embarrassment at the praise crept up from Filip's chest along with pride, flushing his entire face.

Wronski refilled Filip's cup, though Filip didn't remember finishing off the last cup. The captain flashed him a beatific smile. "Now that you are here, let us talk about your role in the company."

Eagerness shot through Filip. "What role do you have in mind, sir?"

"That depends upon what you will bring in payment."

Where the devil was Filip? The drudgery of setting up camp, arranging the horses in their temporary stables, and cleaning gear had been accomplished over the days since their arrival at the encampment. The men had at last settled into a somewhat normal routine of drilling with lance, sabre, pistols, and bow—all of which Filip should have been present for, and normally relished, but had been strangely absent from since they had arrived.

"Have you seen Filip?"

Henryk looked up from where he sat shuffling playing cards, his żupan discarded beside him on the bench. Jacek was tempted to strip down to his own linen undershirt and escape the heat clinging to his torso in beads of sweat, but being pułkownik meant setting an example for the men he led.

Henryk shook his head. "Not since the morning meal."

Marcin sidled up beside them. "Are you searching for Filip?"

273

"Yes. Have you seen him?" Jacek gripped the hilt of his sabre reflexively as a lavishly attired nobleman accompanied by two hussars entered his peripheral vision.

"I noticed him in Wronski's camp, engaging in some swordplay with one of the soldiers." Marcin jerked his head in the general direction of said camp.

Jacek's attention swung to the newcomers. The nobleman smiled. "You are Colonel Dąbrowski, yes?"

Jacek squared himself up. "I am."

The man's smile broadened, and he clasped Jacek's arm with his own. "I am Walenty Kalinowski, and I am delighted to meet you." He glanced around the camp. "We are neighbors."

Jacek had been surprised when, upon their arrival, the encampment's quartermaster had guided him to a space that been saved specifically for Biaska's men. Pecking orders within camps were well established, with commanders radiating out from the hetmans like ripples on a pond in waves of importance. That Jacek and his men were in the second row was a position he'd only ever dreamed of, and he swelled with pride at the arrangement.

"It is a great honor to meet you." *And be encamped next to you.* "How may I be of service?"

"On the contrary, the honor is mine. I have heard many compliments bandied about where your name is concerned, sir. As for how you may be of service …"

Jacek cocked an eyebrow.

Kalinowski chuckled. "I hope to convince you to lead my troops. You would be very well compensated."

Jacek spluttered. "I am extremely flattered, but I am obliged to lead the troops from Biaska, my own est—" Except Biaska *wasn't* his estate. The truth rankled at times.

Kalinowski clapped him on the shoulder. "Well, there is plenty of time for me to persuade you, yes? Meanwhile, you would do me a great favor by leading my men in some drills, if you can spare the time. My captain"—he gestured to the hussar beside him—"will be at your service."

Jacek glanced at the captain, expecting an aggrieved expression, but the man gave him a nod of agreement. Jacek cleared his throat. "Of course. It would be my pleasure."

Kalinowski grasped him on the shoulder with a familiarity that caught Jacek off guard. "I hoped you would say as much. Other companies will join the encampment bit by bit until the crown grand hetman himself arrives, and I want to ensure you are not appropriated by any other magnate."

Appropriated? An image of Jacek astride Jarosława, barking out orders to hundreds upon hundreds of hussars danced through his mind, puffing his chest further. Jacek itched inside with Kalinowski's unexpected admiration.

The magnate turned to leave but pivoted on his heel. "Prince Korecki is leading a gathering in the war council tent this evening. I have it on good authority he has brought some of the finest Hungarian wine available. You should join us and help us lighten him of his supply." He winked conspiratorially.

Jacek dipped his head. "It would be my privilege, sir."

Henryk had stood and yanked on his żupan when the man first appeared and now gaped, along with Marcin, as they watched Kalinowski's retreating back. His fur-trimmed silk cloak fluttered to perfection about his buttery yellow boots. How the man looked so cool in the sweltering heat was beyond Jacek, but perhaps it marked one of the many characteristics that separated a magnate from lowly nobles like them. The notion that wealth prevented one from sweating under the blistering sun streaked through Jacek's mind before he tossed it out like the rubbish it was.

Henryk chuffed. "That was my kin, yet he neither acknowledged me nor handed me a fat purse."

"I thought you weren't related?"

"We aren't, though I reckon we share some of our ancestors high up the family tree." He turned to Jacek and grinned. "Meanwhile, we have a celestial star in our midst. Tell me, my friend, will you continue to dignify us mere mortals with your presence at mealtime? Will you acknowledge us on the practice field?"

275

Jacek shoved him and told him what he could do with his mealtimes and practice fields. He strode from his companions with their laughter ringing in his ears. Despite their teasing, he could not keep the quirk from his lips. Lord Kalinowski had bestowed an honor so great Jacek scarcely had words. Him! Jacek's boots floated several inches off the ground.

When he trotted Heban into Wronski's camp and dismounted, however, his heels struck the hard-packed earth. A group of rough men in their shirtsleeves sat clustered outside a large tent, tossing back liquid from battered tin cups. One of their number held up an earthen jug and tipped its contents liberally into the cups now being held aloft.

Arm draped about the fellow beside him, a man urged his companion to empty his cup. "Drink up! *Na zdrowie!*"

As Jacek drew closer, he recognized the instigator as Wronski and the drinker as none other than Filip. The lad finished his drink in one go, then darted a sheepish look at Wronski and laughed.

Wronski's gaze snagged on Jacek, and surprise overtook his features before he shifted into an oily smile. "Welcome, Pan Dąbrowski. You are just in time to join us in a toast to your brother-in-law."

Filip's eyes widened as they landed on Jacek.

Jacek came to a stop, planted his boots a foot apart, and clasped his hands behind him. "No, thank you. I am not thirsty." He inclined his head toward Filip. "I have come to retrieve my brother-in-law, who apparently forgot to inform any in our camp of his plans."

Filip's wide-eyed stare transformed into a glower. "I do not owe you an accounting of every place I go," he grumbled.

"And so we differ on our opinions. In a war camp, it is not only polite but prudent to inform your brothers-in-arms of your whereabouts so they do not waste their time searching for you, fearful you've been abducted by an enemy."

Rooted in fuming silence, Filip did not budge until Wronski elbowed him. "He's right, young Filip. Best go with him and, if apologies are merited, bestow them upon your camp fellows, for one day you may be spending precious time looking for them too."

Reluctantly, Filip rose. He thanked Wronski and every man in the group before stomping over to his horse. He weaved his way to the Biaska camp— a horse's length ahead of Jacek. On its outskirts, he stopped and waited for Jacek to catch him up, his face a study in fury. "How dare you embarrass me in front of my friends."

"And how dare you go sneaking off to another camp without letting anyone know your intentions."

"You are jealous because I prefer Commander Wronski's company to yours," the impudent lad scoffed.

"Jealousy has nothing to do with it. Looking after your well-being, on the other hand, has everything to do with it."

"I do not need any looking after. I am a man and fully capable of the task myself."

Jacek crossed his arms over his chest.

Filip flung out a hand. "I know you do not think so, for you have made it plain enough. But Commander Wronski believes in me! Which is why I feel more at ease in his camp than in my own." He stabbed an accusing finger in Jacek's direction. "You have no faith in me, and he does. He has invited me to join his camp, and I wish to go."

Jacek's eyebrows hit his hairline. "We will discuss it at another time."

"There is nothing to discuss!" A vein on Filip's temple throbbed, and his face shifted from red to violet.

Biting back the exasperated words dancing on his tongue, Jacek infused a feigned calmness in his tone. "On the contrary, brother, there is much to discuss when such a grave decision as this is in the balance. So important, in fact, that it begs a calmer demeanor." *On both our parts.*

He would have wagered his life's blood that he heard Filip hiss, "I loathe you," between clenched teeth.

After seeing Filip back to the tent he shared with the other squires, Jacek paced the camp, his mind flipping through various solutions. His own men were clustered together, some napping, some preparing their weapons. Others exchanged war stories over piwo, diced, or played cards. They had no need of him, so he mounted Jarosława to have it out with the viper

Wronski. Camps were still sparse as few companies had trickled in; nonetheless, Wronksi's camp was at least three furlongs distant.

Jacek ruffled the horse's mane. "I am sorry, old girl, but it's hot and I am too tired to coax Heban, so you will have to suffer me with this short ride."

He guided her to the captain's camp, finding only a handful of men remained where he had last seen them. Dismounting, he gathered her leads. He was not about to let her out of his sight.

The men either partook in or watched a spirited round of dicing and barely acknowledged his presence when he walked up. Wronski was not among them, and he asked after the man's whereabouts.

A soldier who looked—and smelled—as though neither soap nor water had touched his body in months, glanced up. "The captain has gone to find his lieutenant. You might still catch him by the horses over yonder." The grimy man pointed to the east, where a row of tents blocked Jacek's view.

Leading Jarosława, he wove his way between the crowded canvas structures into an open field with a makeshift stable beyond. Here, he was caught up short by the sight of a sleek sable horse being saddled by a gray-haired man. He picketed his mare, wordlessly approached, and ran his hands over the beast's neck and forehead. On its flank was the remnant of a familiar brand, recently altered, and within its ebony forelock ran a subtle streak of chestnut.

"Where did this horse come from?" he asked the man.

The elder cinched a buckle, remaining as silent as Adam and Margaret when confronted about their mischief-making.

"I said—"

"He heard you." Wronski stepped out of a feed tent. Wiping his hands on a cloth, he smiled, though it did nothing to soften the hard glint in his eyes. "He chose not to answer you." Wronski directed his stony smirk at the old man.

With a grunt of acknowledgment, the man continued about his business.

Wronski swung his gaze back to Jacek, letting the smile slide from his face. "To what do I owe the pleasure of your return to my camp so soon, Pan Dąbrowski?" He held up his hand, palm out. "Don't tell me. You have come about young master Filip, yes?"

"That I have. I take exception to you luring him away from his brethren. But first, I wish to discuss this horse."

"Ah, why waste time with civility when directness gets one to the point quicker, I always say. Politeness merely bogs matters down, does it not?" Wronski's tone took on a frosty quality. "What about the horse?"

"This animal is a warhorse from a particular breeder in Halicz." Jacek pointed to the horse's flank. "The brand is still visible, although someone has made a clumsy attempt to disguise it. Furthermore, the animal itself not only boasts the same lines as the steed that was taken from me, but it has this very distinct marking." He fingered the horse's forelock. "I have only ever seen one other horse with such a variation in color—the same one you admired when we first met—and that horse belongs to Biaska. There could not be two."

Wronski plastered on the mock expression of geniality once more. "As I told you before, I bought the horse off—"

Jacek lowered an eyebrow. "I thought you took it from a band of pagans returning to Crimea?"

Wronski covered his heart with his hand. "Did I say that?"

"You did, at the same time you mentioned 'ill-gotten goods.' If you bought the animal, perhaps you can produce a bill of sale."

Wronski clung to his charming demeanor, making Jacek trust him even less. "Forgive me my poor choice of words. You see, I neither took it nor bought it, but I traded for it, which is akin to buying it, as I'm sure any adjudicator would concur. That means I came by the animal fairly, and it is therefore my property. Though I am still not convinced we are talking about the same horse. But enough talk of horses. Let us raise a jug in a far more pleasant setting, yes?"

"Where would that be?"

"There is a bordello where the drink is strong and the women pleasant. I plan to sample some of what is offered on both scores. Why not join me? We will talk business first and take our pleasure after."

Jacek raised an eyebrow. "I have a wife."

Wronski threw his head back and brayed out a hearty laugh. "As I well know. And I have one too, though I'm not as fortunate as you in having

279

enjoyed her company in Żółkiew. Circumstances have separated us for months, and ... Well, naturally, you understand." He winked.

Jacek did understand, and a married man seeking the company of a whore didn't surprise him. Soldiers far from home often set aside their moral compasses. Men believing they were about to be slaughtered yearned for an intimate touch to send them to their Maker. But he couldn't fully comprehend what they felt, for he was wed to a woman who rendered temptation a beast he never grappled with. A spark existed between them that could not be duplicated with another. Perhaps it would fade one day, but it only seemed to grow stronger as time went by. He compared every woman he encountered to the perfection that was Oliwia, and spending time in another's arms was not only a waste of his time but an affront to what he held most dear. That he was smitten was as obvious as the sun hanging in the sky, or so his companions often told him as they goaded him about it.

Wronski droned on, pulling Jacek from pleasant thoughts of the last time he lay with Oliwia. "Men such as us have our needs. Now that you are separated from your lovely wife, yours are no doubt in need of attention, yes? So here I offer you the perfect solution. And if you find this place lacking, there are other sporting houses nearby where the women are well versed in how to fulfill a man's every need—including those that might be considered, ah, somewhat debauched, even among less polite society."

Jacek checked his surprise. "Such as?"

"See? I knew I would stimulate your interest! You must come with me and find out for yourself." Wronski dropped his voice conspiratorially. "The proprietor at one establishment I frequent has promised to stock his stable with unspoiled girls. Tender, succulent things. Mm, mm, mmm." He clapped Jacek on the shoulder. "If your preference runs to boys, I am confident he can accommodate you, and if you desire exotic meat, I'm sure that could be arranged as well. Being close to the border has its advantages."

Jacek hid his disgust. Wronski spoke of humans as if they were haunches of venison to be savored at a feast. "This friend of yours—the proprietor— where does he get his ... stock from?"

Wronski eyed him. "Mostly here, from nearby villages."

"They come willingly, then?"

"Not always, no."

Never, I would venture. "And the ones that don't do so willingly? The 'tender, succulent things.' Where do they come from?"

Wronski twiddled one of the reins. "Raiders, I suppose," he snapped. "Tatars."

Jacek couldn't contain himself. "The same Tatars we battle?" He congratulated himself on the casualness in his voice. "And these *raiders* you mention—our own countrymen who steal innocents and those that buy them—are they not just as reprehensible as our enemy?"

"Of course not!" Wronski scoffed. "Those *tender things*—who are not all unspoiled babes, mind—are being saved from a life of despair in a sultan's harem far from home. Why, they are not even allowed to practice their Christendom! Better they be broken in by the likes of us than infidels!"

Wronski's twisted justification for his own depravities ignited a blaze of fury deep in Jacek's gut. His thoughts ran to his own sweet-smelling fledglings. Robbing a child of his or her innocence, enslaving them to be used for men such as Wronski's degenerate enjoyment, then casting them off like so much garbage when their youth was spent, caused his stomach to turn over. But now was not the time to unleash his emotions.

"I have been studying the great Roman leaders. Commodus had it right, you know."

Jacek blinked. Where the devil had *that* statement come from? Did Wronski harbor a bag full of slithering snakes in his mind? "Commodus. You mean the emperor who"—*was utterly mad and nearly destroyed Rome*—"uh, fought as a gladiator in the Colosseum?"

"The same. Oh, he may have been brutal, but there was much he had right."

The unhinged emperor had got nothing right, and while Wronski's claim piqued Jacek's curiosity, he refrained from encouraging the man by asking exactly what Commodus had achieved besides cruelty and ruin.

"His people loved him." Wronski jerked his head toward the sable. "As for the horse, I suggest a friendly game of cards if you'd like a chance at taking her from me."

281

"There is still the matter that you took her from *me*." Jacek jabbed a thumb against this chest.

"Your word against mine, Commander." Wronski raised his gaze to Jarosława. "She is a bit long in the tooth. You might need to add something else of value if you plan to wager her."

Jacek would never wager his prized warhorse; she was his family. Furthermore, he had no doubt Wronski would cheat to win her.

"Another time perhaps—for both offers. I am expected by Crown Field Hetman Koniecpolski, who may be interested in hearing my claim," Jacek lied. The crown field hetman had not summoned him.

Play fair with a viper and die.

He hoisted himself up into his saddle, and Jarosława let out a grunt. "In the meantime, I think it best if you dissuade my brother-in-law from lingering in your camp. If you wish to see him, you may do so when you and your men join us on the practice field. We start at seven sharp tomorrow." He gave Wronski a pointed look.

The man flashed that slime-filled smile. "You and I both know my men and I will never join you on the practice field, just as we know you do not have a meeting with Koniecpolski, so I see no need to continue the pretense." With that, he tapped his fingers to his temple in a partial salute and watched as Jacek turned to go.

Jacek rode back to camp, half expecting a dagger to embed itself in his back. Thoughts churned in his head like a frenzied eddy. The more he learned of Wronski, the more the man exposed himself for the unscrupulous blackguard he was. He brought to mind a snail oozing out of its shell, revealing itself as a globule of mucus. If only he was as harmless.

Lurking among Jacek's condemnations of the man was the lingering suspicion he had participated in Oliwia's assault. She had heard a similarity between her attacker's voice and Wronski's, and Jacek wholly trusted her recollection. Moreover, the dastardly nature of the act fit with Wronski's unscrupulous character.

If his banner was to be under Jacek's command, Jacek needed to bring him to heel. Though he wasn't enamored of leading Wronski's Elear rabble himself, the Commonwealth needed a united front—not only to defeat the

Ottomans, but for Żółkiewski's sake. And for that, Jacek would rein in his dislikes and fulfill his duty to Crown and country.

CHAPTER 29

And Now We Go to War

J acek took in the faces of the men shouting over one another around
him. A year ago—Christ, only weeks ago—he would have pinched his
own cheek to be sure he was among the vaunted magnate commanders
from among Poland's greatest families and their officers. But they seemed
to find any number of grievances to argue over, and war council meetings
devolved into shouting matches over which family did what to whom and
when. When arguments faded, they found new fodder to divide them
further.

As more magnates swelled their ranks, what would a meeting of the great
lords foment?

Koniecpolski occasionally joined them, and his expression reflected the
frustration brewing inside Jacek, though these leaders were typically better
behaved in the crown field hetman's presence than outside of it. As the
highest-ranking officer in camp, he had the luxury of excusing himself to
attend to "other urgent matters," leaving this lot to quarrel among
themselves. These same urgent matters often pulled Koniecpolski away
from Śledziówka, leaving his regulars and the rest to guess at his travels.
Some speculated he visited a secret lover, others believed he met with
Grazziani, and another group of agitators was sure he remained in camp,
hidden away, to spy on them all.

Unless the field hetman was gathering intelligence, Jacek didn't give a fig what he did away from camp. What they needed now, before more troops arrived, was to put aside their squabbles and knit together as one cohesive front.

Jacek had compelled Henryk and Lesław to accompany him to the meetings under the pretext that, as his lieutenants, they needed to hear the latest intelligence. While this was true, he also needed them there to keep him in check and make sure his temper—and mouth—did not run away from him.

Like now, for instance, in Koniecpolski's absence, as one commander interrupted another, shouting him down. "We were aware Osman has placed Iskender Pasha in charge of the Ottoman troops. This is old information."

Henryk leaned to his ear. "Here we go again."

Jacek grunted his agreement.

"I pray Żółkiewski arrives soon. I fear only he can bring order to this lot."

"Amen," Jacek whispered back.

"That is not what I said!" the disrupted man yelled back. "Were you not so enamored of your own voice, you would have listened instead of bellowing and know he was talking about there being no evidence Pasha is gathering troops at the moment. According to Grazziani's latest intelligence, he plans to invade *next* year."

Jacek let out a puffed-cheek breath.

"Hold your tongue," Henryk warned him.

Jacek ignored him and raised his own voice. "It is too early to criticize. Has this 'intelligence' been closely examined? Are we positive it's reliable, or might it be a spy's ruse?"

As if Jacek had merely spoken into the wind, a potentate's man barked, "So what are we doing *here* when we should be home, preparing for the harvest and protecting our lords' lands from marauding Tatars?"

Shouts of "Hear, hear!" rose up amid a volley of counter grumbles.

"Who here questions Żółkiewski's ability to lead a military campaign?" a magnate hollered. "He is an addled old man trying to relive his glory days!"

285

"After the debacle at Orynin, why does the king put any faith in him?"

"For good reason, the king made him crown grand hetman for life. I daresay Żółkiewski is far more capable than your man Potocki. Why, that fool couldn't lead his way out of the Sultan's ass!"

"Żółkiewski's incompetent! He cannot even control the Cossacks! I tell you now, my men and I will not follow the hetman's lead if we find it wanting."

"Nor will we!"

Shut up, you windbags!

"The damned Zaporozhians are to blame for this mess! They will not stop their pirating on the Black Sea despite the Peace of Busza," another commander chirped.

"And you think the sultan is any better at controlling the Tatars? Remember that in that treaty, Iskender Pasha also agreed to bring the Tatar dogs to heel, and yet they continue to raid our lands with impunity."

"Why should Pasha uphold it? Every time there is a conflict, the hetman signs another treaty and concedes more to the Turks. The Peace of Busza ceded Chocim and the Commonwealth's ability to intervene in Moldavia—"

"And Wallachia and Transylvania, yet we just fought and thumped Prince Bethlen, and here we are ready to step into Moldavia."

"All treaties are a waste of ink and paper," another grumbled.

The imbecile who had been interrupted in his complaints about Hetman Żółkiewski retook the floor. "The hetman is so submissive, he might as well bend over and let the pasha do literally what he allows him to do figuratively!"

"Perhaps he enjoys the buggering, and that's why he seeks to negotiate once more with Iskender Pasha!"

Jacek clenched his fists. How in hell could this goat turd know the hetman's intentions? Had he sprouted wings and flown to Żółkiew last night? Had the hetman then taken the idiot into his confidence and poured out all his thoughts? And to speak of the hetman with such disrespect! *Cast-off spawn of a leprous sow!*

"The hetman is the hero of Kłuszyn!" Kalinowski's captain thundered. "How dare you speak of him that way, swine!"

Yes! I knew I liked him! Jacek held back the roar of approval effervescing in his belly.

"Kłuszyn was ten years ago!" a mustachioed man cried.

"We are here to relieve the hospodar, not engage the Ottomans!"

"How the devil do you relieve the hospodar without engaging the Ottomans? The hospodar is one of them!"

"Piss on the hospodar! One moment he prostrates himself to the sultan, and the next he declares himself Poland's closest ally. Grazziani is an adventurer who cares for only one thing: Grazziani."

More shouts erupted, and Jacek found himself perched on the edge of his seat, coiled, ready to spring up and defend his hetman. *Fools! Idiots! The hetman has more wisdom and heart than all of you put together!* Henryk's hand on his arm stayed him.

"I need to leave these dolts before I do something I will regret," he growled.

"Better to stay, my friend, so we understand what we're dealing with."

"I *already* understand what we're dealing with, and I am beyond disheartened!" Jacek hissed. *An army of cowardly, self-righteous jackasses braying out their spurious eminence!*

Now men talked over each other of strategies for situations they could no more than guess at. The evening continued as countless others had, dragging on until the wodka was gone, the good wine long finished or hidden away. Mercifully, this night did not end in fisticuffs as others had.

By the time Jacek and his companions returned to their camp, he was spent … and the night was yet young. So young, in fact, that Henryk announced he, Dawid, and Marcin were headed to a nearby tavern.

"Come with us for some revelry," Henryk urged. "Several rounds of wodka between mugs of strong piwo will help you forget those clodpoles."

Jacek looked up at a swath of moonlight, then scoured the camp with his gaze. None but a handful of men smoking pipes around a fire were about. "Where is Filip?"

287

Lesław yawned. "I will see to him. Now go and see if you can't turn your foul mood into a more cheerful state of mind."

Jacek scowled. "Wodka will not help."

Henryk grabbed him by the nape. "Perhaps not, but being among gay folk will."

Lesław and Henryk had it partly right. The boisterous tavern patrons did distract Jacek, and while Henryk and Marcin flirted with the tavern maids, he found himself beside a subdued Dawid, taking in the other patrons. His attention was drawn to a pair of men across the room. Something about the larger of the two rang with familiarity in Jacek's mind. He took in the fellow's merchant garb, and a memory brightened.

He motioned to a serving girl, who nearly knocked over another girl to get to him. She smoothed her apron as she presented herself and a beaming smile. "At your service, m'lord. What can I get you?"

He returned the smile. "Bring me a jug—no, make that two jugs—of what they're drinking." Inclining his head toward the duo engrossed in conversation, he held up a coin he had plucked from his sash. Her eyes brightened, as he'd known they would. She snatched it, made a clumsy attempt at a curtsy, and ran off.

The serving maid did not make him wait long, and when she returned, he bestowed her with another coin.

"I'll be back," he mumbled in Henryk's general direction. When Dawid raised his eyebrows hopefully, he motioned for him to follow and carried his cup and the jugs toward the table where the two men sat, oblivious to everyone around them.

"If what you're saying is right," said the large man in a low voice, "whoever's in charge needs to know."

"I *am* right. I saw it with these eyes," a smaller, swarthy man said in a harsh whisper as he pointed to eyes as black and burnished as obsidian.

Jacek deposited cup and jugs on their rough-hewn tabletop. The conversation came to an abrupt halt as both men looked up at him.

To the large man, Jacek said, "Mantas Butkus, the grain trader from Halicz, yes?"

Confusion clouded his features, and his companion's mouth thinned into a mistrusting line.

"Jacek Dąbrowski of Biaska. You and I shared a drink in a tavern much like this one in—"

"Halicz! Of course I remember! It was in the spring, yes?"

"Exactly. May my companion and I join you?"

Mantas laughed heartily. "A man who brings drink to the table is welcome anytime. Sit, please! Allow me to introduce my old friend, Hovhannes Alen."

The name confirmed Jacek's guess about the man's Armenian origins. Alen dipped his head as Jacek and Dawid slid onto the bench. "Pan Dąbrowski, an honor. Please. Call me Hovik."

"As long as you call me Jacek. And this is Dawid Pawelski." He topped off all three cups and raised his own. "To old acquaintances and new ones. *Na zdrowie!*"

"*Na zdrowie!*" they chorused and threw back their drinks.

Mantas swiped his mouth with the back of his hand. "Hovik trades in cloth."

Jacek arched his eyebrows. "Have you any silk for sale? I am always on the hunt for a special gift for my wife."

"Alas, no. I sold it all across the border. Like you, the Ottomans indulge their women in silks too." Hovik winked before taking another gulp. "I do have a bolt of fine linen remaining, however."

"Perhaps I will take a look later. Where do you find is the best place to vend your wares?"

Hovik's eyes darted about, and Mantas answered for him. "Normally, he ventures to Kilia or Akkerman, but this time he went no farther than Tehinia. Isn't that right, Hovik?"

Jacek shook off his shudders at the mention of Akkerman, for it conjured nightmarish memories of Khadjibey, where he had first been chained to an oar on a slave galley. No doubt Dawid, who had been with him during that time of unspeakable horror, was suffering the same memories. Quickly, he stuffed the reminder of hell on earth back into its box and slammed the lid shut.

He ran a sweaty palm along his thigh. "Sounds like a very fortunate circumstance for you, in a number of ways. What, pray, made the difference this time?"

Hovik cleared his throat. "Well, you see, there was a large contingent of Ottoman soldiers this side of the fortress who had just been paid, and they were eager to buy up all I had." He let out a nervous laugh. "Soldiers with little to occupy them turn their attention elsewhere, yes?"

Mantas guffawed. "Which proved very profitable for you."

A gathering of Ottoman soldiers. Oh so slowly, Jacek raised his cup and took a sip as he marshaled his spiraling thoughts.

Before he could form his next query, Dawid took the lead. "We have heard rumors of a Turkish army gathering. It seems those rumors may hold some truth, yes?"

"It appears so," Mantas chortled. "For some reason I do not understand, my friend grows shy when there is talk of Ottoman forces." He elbowed Hovik. "Tell him what you saw."

Hovik sent Mantas a glare. "Because it is dangerous to speak of such matters openly. One never knows whose ears are cocked their way." He darted a glance or three over his shoulder.

"You are as jumpy as a rabbit, with no need to be, for you are among friends here." Mantas spread his hands wide.

"There are spies everywhere." Hovik shot Dawid a dubious look, then seemed to assess Jacek's Norse features.

Jacek poured more liquid into Hovik's cup. "Please go on. Our lives are far too dull these days. I think I speak for Dawid when I say we would enjoy a good tale of adventure."

Dawid nodded his agreement.

Hovik downed half the contents of his cup. "I would not call it an adventure."

Jacek gave him an encouraging grin. "I would argue otherwise, for you strike me as the adventuring sort." The frightened man most certainly did not, but God would forgive Jacek another lie.

"Well, I suppose it was, in a way." Hovik's shoulders seemed to relax, and a smile quirked a corner of his mouth. He went on to describe, in excruciating precision, his journey from his home across the Dniester before he finally arrived at the details that interested Jacek. "It was like this: several soldiers accosted me as I made for my favorite inn. Soon I was among them, in their camp, with my wagon, servants, and all."

Jacek injected nonchalance into his tone. "How large was their camp?"

Hovik shrugged. "Hard to tell because it went on for a while. There were some Tatars there, but they stayed away." He spat and mumbled, "Thank goodness for small favors."

Mantas grabbed a jug and filled his cup. "From the sound of it, more are coming. They told Hovik to hurry back with as many wagons as he could fill. Like I told you before, Pan—er, Jacek. Mark my words. War is brewing."

Hovik dropped his voice to a conspiratorial whisper. "The hospodar of Moldavia is about to have his wings clipped. No doubt the Ottomans' appearance has to do with yanking him off his throne. It is a show of force, yes? And to keep others from meddling in their business." He arched an eyebrow as if to punctuate his comment.

"I would not be surprised," Jacek said blandly.

"Moldavia has been a festering thorn for a long time now," Dawid added.

"A very long time," Mantas agreed.

Hovik nodded and returned to his drink.

"Have you gentlemen heard of the raids?" Mantas was as talkative as a *swata*—a matchmaker, and like the swata, he was a useful resource.

Jacek brushed a crumb from his żupan. "What raids?"

"At least two villages have been pillaged in the past few weeks. The people's possessions, their food, their stock, all taken. Their homes burned to the ground."

"What of the villagers?"

"Slaughtered—even children—and those that weren't were taken away. Disappeared. Horrible, horrible." Mantas shook his head.

Dawid slid Jacek a sidelong glance. "Sounds like Tatars."

Or the Lost Men.

They spent several more minutes discussing rumors of raids and warfare, and when Jacek reckoned neither Mantas nor Hovik had any new information to give up, talk turned to politics and family. Soon the jugs were empty.

Jacek glanced over his shoulder at Henryk, who seemed to have little idea Jacek and Dawid had left his side—his friend was far too intent on the maid sitting in his lap. Next to him sat Marcin, sipping his wodka as he ogled Henryk's companion with obvious envy.

Tapping Dawid's arm, Jacek rose from the table. "We must rejoin our companions. Thank you for sharing your table."

Mantas lifted an empty jug and winked. "And thank *you*, my lords, for sharing your drink. May we meet again soon. Godspeed."

"Godspeed."

The serving girl had been eyeing Jacek like a hawk searching for prey, and he gestured her to him while Dawid excused himself. Laying more coin into the palm of her hand, he bent to her ear. "Two more pitchers for my friends, yes? Make them very, very full."

Another smile broke out on her face. "Of course, m'lord." Another clumsy curtsy and she was off.

Jacek slapped his cup on the tabletop and slid in beside Henryk. The maid slipped off his lap and flounced away. They all craned their heads and watched her go. "I hope I wasn't the cause of your lap-warmer's departure."

"No, she had to attend to something. I'm not sure what, and it doesn't matter because I was growing weary of the company." Henryk clacked his cup against Jacek's. "Your appearance was well-timed, my friend."

Jacek barked a laugh. "You? Weary of a maid's company? What has come over you of late? Could it be the gray glimmering in your mustache?"

Henryk gave him a shove. "Oh, shut up! I have no gray. You only say that because you're jealous."

Mirth tugged another laugh from Jacek. "Of *what*, pray?"

"My superior sword skills, of course. While you have been growing fat and lazy in domestic bliss, I have kept up with my training."

"Who says I haven't?"

"Pah. You merely play at it. I wager that even without the one finger, I can beat you with my left hand."

Marcin rolled his eyes behind Henryk's back.

Dawid rejoined them, sitting on the opposite side, now empty of patrons. "What have I missed?"

Jacek took a swig of his drink. "It seems Henryk is challenging me to a clash of sabres," he said dryly.

Dawid shook his head. "Save it for the enemy." To Henryk, he said, "Where did your maid go?"

Henryk flipped a hand. "The back somewhere. If you're interested, she seems a willing enough wench."

"Not I. Perhaps Marcin."

"He already tried," Henryk offered. "She has no interest in Marcin." Henryk grabbed Marcin by the nape. "Worry not, friend. We will patronize someplace where you will have to fight the women off, yes?"

Dawid looked at Jacek and raised an eyebrow.

"He's *definitely* not interested," Henryk snorted.

Henryk was right. Jacek wasn't attracted to any willing wenches save one … and she was two hundred miles away in Żółkiew. Safe. He hoped.

Dawid raised a cup to Jacek. "I find the trait admirable, particularly under the circumstances."

Jacek put the peculiar statement—peculiar for Dawid, that was—at the back of his mind for closer examination later.

Henryk swilled his piwo and refilled their cups while Jacek told him what they had learned from Hovik and Mantas.

Dawid dropped his voice. "If memory serves, those raids took place at times when Wronski's camp was empty."

Jacek hadn't drawn the parallels. "Are you sure?"

"Not entirely, but I will look into it if you wish."

"I wish."

Henryk's eyes fixed on the grungy tabletop. "What do you make of the men arguing in the war council earlier and these two merchants you spoke to?"

"What do you mean?"

Henryk shifted on the bench. "Are you confident Żółkiewski knows what he is doing?"

Jacek's brows knotted together.

293

"What I mean is," Henryk rushed to add, "does he have full knowledge of what he's up against?"

"Of course he does!" scoffed Jacek, though the question reverberated inside his head, raising doubt about his own answer. Too many details were not summing up.

Marcin leaned in. "What is it you reckon the hetman's up against?"

Henryk shrugged, but Dawid murmured, "Perhaps an army larger than the one he's anticipating. Perhaps an army that would rather fight than negotiate."

Which means it will not only be the hetman up against such a force. It will be all of us at this table and many more besides. Jacek shook off the disquieting thought.

"But we will be at least ten thousand," Marcin argued, "and the Moldavian forces will add fifteen thousand more to our number. Surely that will be more than enough to crush the enemy."

Henryk raised his eyebrows. "But can we trust the hospodar to bring fifteen thousand?"

"It will likely never come to that," Jacek muttered. "The hetman has negotiated truces before—remember when we were here in 1612?—and he no doubt will again. This is Iskender Pasha we meet, and he has accommodated the hetman in the past. Why would he stop now?" Though he voiced his convictions stridently, a seed of doubt had been planted and was now sprouting in the back of Jacek's mind. Once again, Oliwia's words capered through his consciousness. *Old. Poor health.*

Henryk slapped his palm atop the table. "Well, enough warmongering for one night, I say. A soldier needs entertainments to take his mind off such unpleasant subjects." He jerked his head toward Marcin. "What say you, Marcin? Shall we continue our reveling with a visit to the lovely ladies who grace the brothel down the road?"

Marcin's eyes strayed to his cup. "As soon as I drain my drink."

Henryk turned to Dawid. "Are you foregoing again, Dawid?"

Dawid gave him a head bob.

A young girl appeared in the doorway that led to the kitchens, wide-eyed as she scanned the crowd. One of the tavern maids pushed a jug into her hand and motioned her toward a table. As she approached, one of the men took her in with wolfish eyes that had Jacek's hackles on end.

"Henryk, before you go, I have a question about the sporting houses. I wanted to know … do they offer young girls and boys?"

Marcin's mouth swung open. Henryk gave Jacek a censorious look down the bridge of his nose. "I don't know. As neither of those choices appeal to me, I've not asked."

"They don't appeal to me either. I heard some disturbing rumors, and I am trying to determine if they are true or not."

"It's not exactly the sort of thing one announces publicly among God-fearing folk, now is it? While I haven't much patronized the establishments here, I've heard no such rumblings." Marcin nodded in agreement beside him, and Henryk continued. "Give me a fully bloomed, experienced woman who enjoys her trade any night, and if she's older, all the better … as long as she isn't a crone. Taking a child is … Well, the thought makes my pecker shrivel and run for cover." He feigned a racking shiver.

Henryk clapped Marcin on the shoulder. "Ready? If we linger much longer, I'll fall asleep, and I would hate to disappoint the ladies."

Marcin grinned and stood first. "As would I."

Henryk followed, winking at Jacek. "We will see you dullards in the morning."

But it was well before morning when Henryk came crashing into Jacek's tent. Gripping his sabre out of habit, Jacek bolted upright. The space was dimly illuminated by a lantern Henryk held aloft, revealing a wriggling figure Henryk gripped by the collar. In the background stood a figure Jacek recognized as Marcin.

"What the hell is going on?" Jacek barked.

"I thought you should know," his second panted, "we encountered this one at the whorehouse." He shoved the figure, sending it sprawling beside Jacek's cot. Angry eyes filled with steely storm clouds fixed on Jacek.

"Filip? What the devil—"

Bending at the waist, Henryk placed his palms on his thighs. "We discovered him there with Wronski."

Jacek was on his feet in one beat of his heart. "Was he partaking or being used?"

Surprise flashed in Henryk's eyes. "Judging by the smile on his face before he saw me, I would venture the former." Giving Filip a pointed glare, he grumbled, "Which is a far more pleasant state than Marcin and I found ourselves in, thanks to you."

Jacek released a silent breath of relief just as Filip staggered to his feet. The lad swayed, and the smell of sour spirits engulfed Jacek. *By all the saints!*

Filip stabbed a finger toward Henryk and Marcin. "I was Commander Wronski's *guest*," he slurred, "and these … these fellows of shameful moral merit appointed themselves my jailers and—"

"Shameful moral merit?" Jacek arched a brow. "Should you be slinging mud while standing knee-deep in a pigsty?"

"By Christ and all the saints!" Filip nearly tangled his feet and toppled over. He brought to mind a sapling being buffeted by a spring wind.

Jacek looked between his lord-brothers. "How on earth did he manage …?"

Henryk returned a smirk. "Being sixteen could have some bearing."

"On the contrary, that might have hampered him further."

Filip bellowed. "I am standing. Right. Here! Do not speak of me as if I am not present! Christ, you are as disrespectful as my sister. She must have handed off the leash she has wrapped about my neck directly to you!"

"Filip," Henryk warned, "I would hold my tongue were I you."

"But you are not me! And why shouldn't I speak the truth? She is a tyrannical bitch!"

Jacek struck like lightning, cocking his fist back and slamming it into his brother-in-law's face. A sickening crunch of bone, and Filip flew backward with a howl.

"You hit me!" Blood dripped through his fingers as he covered his nose, muffling his protest. Tears coursed from his eyes, mingling with the mess.

"And good thing he did too," Henryk snarled, "or I would have done it myself, you churlish whelp."

Marcin stood over Filip and growled, "And if *he* hadn't, I *certainly* would have."

Filip staggered to his feet, his indignation fully cocked. "I need a cloth … something! I need help getting to my tent."

Jacek pulled in a lung-clearing breath to steady his quaking nerves. "You want us to believe you're a man. Well, one in your condition finds his own way back, *boy*."

"This is *not* over!" Filip stormed from the tent.

"I have no doubt," Jacek muttered to his back. He thanked Henryk and Marcin. "I'm sorry about your revelry, but it is not too late to return."

Marcin shook his head. "I am too tired."

"Me as well," chimed Henryk. "Jacek, what do you make of Filip spending time at a whorehouse with Wronski?"

"I'm not troubled by Wronski encouraging Filip to lie with a whore—it was only a matter of time, and Filip would have found his way there eventually. What does trouble me is the sense that Wronski is up to something. Everything he does seems calculated, and I cannot help but wonder what webs he is spinning."

What if Wronski *was* behind the raids … and he was drawing Filip into those dark waters?

CHAPTER 30

Sisters-in-Arms

Oliwia sat up when Eugenia entered the room. The Lady of Silnyród stopped, placed a hand on a hip, and frowned.

"I thought we agreed you were to remain flat on your back until the bleeding stops."

Oliwia lay back with a groan. "It *has* stopped." *Almost.*

"I don't believe you."

Oliwia clenched the bedcover in her fists. "I *forbid* you to examine me again. The only eyes I will allow to look between my legs belong to my husband and the midwife."

Bright blond curls poked through the door opening. "Is our little lady misbehaving again?" Magdalena tsked. "And what's this talk of your husband viewing parts that should be kept hidden away?"

Oliwia raised her head and mock-glared at Magdalena. "This coming from *you*, of all people!"

Magdalena feigned a gasp and placed a hand against her bare décolletage. "Well, I never!"

"Yes, you have," Oliwia tossed back.

"Yes, I have," Magdalena giggled.

Eugenia rolled her eyes. "Both of you are incorrigible." She made her way to Oliwia's bedside and carefully lowered herself onto the mattress. She pressed a cool hand against Oliwia's forehead.

Magdalena stood at the foot of the bed. "Fever?"

"No, thank the Virgin."

"Funny you should invoke the Virgin while our Oliwia bears the proof that she is far from one, don't you think, Lady Eugenia?"

One corner of Eugenia's mouth quirked with a smile.

"Stop, both of you!" Oliwia flailed a hand.

A knock came at the door, and Magdalena excused herself.

"Good. She's gone for a while." Eugenia's smile told Oliwia the lady harbored no ill will for Magda. "There is something I have been meaning to speak to you about. Do you remember when we rode here from Silnyród and I mentioned a possible solution to some of Biaska's financial woes?"

Oliwia perked up. "Yes."

"What if I were interested in purchasing the estate from you?"

"Are you serious?" Oliwia blurted.

Eugenia tilted her regal head. "I have some funds left me by my mother, and though it's not much, I do love the place. Would you be in accord if I wanted to proceed?"

"Yes. Most definitely, yes!" Oliwia berated herself for overplaying her eagerness. Besides her runaway mouth, Jacek also teased her for being a terrible card player, for she could no more keep her face blank than a child being handed a sweet.

"Good. Then that is—"

Magdalena burst back into the chamber. "Letter for Lady Oliwia," she sang and fanned herself with it, the curly headed she-devil.

"Please say it is not Tomasz relaying more bad tidings from Biaska." After the last few missives she'd received, she wasn't sure she could stand more depressing news. Biaska's finances sounded as if they were positively disintegrating, and Tomasz was trying without success to scrounge enough funds for the balance due to the Amsterdam merchant. They had reserved barge space for the estate's grain and the bill was due, though that yield was shrinking with each flooding storm. She tried to find the humor in the irony—a smaller yield meant a smaller shipping fee—but failed.

Oliwia extended her hand to accept the letter, but Magdalena darted away. "Ooh, such strong, masculine handwriting! Could it be from a lover you have not told us about?"

"It is from my husband." Oliwia feigned a growl. At least she *prayed* it was from Jacek. It had been weeks since she had last heard from him. "Now stop tormenting me and bring it here!"

While Eugenia fussed over Oliwia's pillows, Magdalena ambled back to the bedside, cooing, "You are awfully demanding for one who is at our mercy, Lady Oliwia."

Nadia rushed into the room. Her confused gaze bounced between Eugenia and Magdalena.

Oliwia waved, catching the maid's attention. "Nadia, would you kindly fetch a guard to wrangle these two beasts away?"

Nadia's eyes popped wide, and she rooted herself to the spot as if she had no idea which way to go.

"Being wrangled by a young, strong, handsome guard," Magdalena hummed. "What a lovely idea. Too bad they're in such short supply these days."

"Magda," Oliwia laughed. "Stop before my sides burst."

"We can't have that." Magdalena grinned and held the letter within Oliwia's reach. "Would you like me to read it to you?"

"No!" Oliwia snatched it from her fingers. Her heart jumped when her eyes lit on Jacek's familiar handwriting. While Oliwia carefully broke the seal and unfolded the snowy paper, Eugenia rose and took Magdalena by the arm. "Let us leave her in peace for a little while. You too, Nadia."

Oliwia barely heard Magdalena make another inappropriate comment about Żółkiew's depleted soldiers as she sank back into the pillows and began to read.

17 July, In the Year of our Lord 1620

My most beloved Liwi,

Torrential rains today force us to take cover in our tents, at last giving me the opportunity to pen this long overdue letter to you. First, I long to know how you are. How is the babe? I hope he (or she) is not bruising your ribs beyond what you can bear. By my estimation, this one will emerge in a little over three months, and I pray that I will be there to welcome him or her into our lives.

Our days pass in infinite boredom, but that is the way of encampments. We can only practice and prepare so much. I have been holding tournaments now and again as a way for the men to practice while hopefully enjoying the competition as they try to best one another. Nothing like Biaska, of course, and there are no purses to be won, but the men do earn the right to crow of their prowess.

For those of us in command, life is also filled with councils late into the evenings, which seem to be filled with much arguing and little resolving. I look forward to the arrival of the crown grand hetman and his contingent, as I believe it will quiet the squabbling and put all to rights. By my estimation, he will have left to join us by the time this letter reaches you. Meanwhile, the Biaska Chorągiew Husarka will stand ready for whatever comes. We will make you proud, my lady.

I do not know if Filip has written to you—I hope he has—but he is hale. We had a tussle several days ago that stemmed from the amount of time he has been spending in Captain Gabriel Wronski's camp. I have tried to dissuade him, but he is in command of his own mind, and his will is strong.

As for Wronski, the man vexes me. He seems to derive great pleasure by flaunting his insubordination. I must take command before the hetman arrives, or he will think his trust in me as Wronski's commander ill-placed. He will ask, as do I, how this soldier can be a colonel if he cannot get his lot to follow? Though the Lost Men are famous for following rules of their own making, that fact is no excuse for my lack of effectiveness.

I will continue in all earnestness searching out a solution where Filip is concerned. Meanwhile, please do not trouble yourself with worry for either of us, my sweet. You must instead turn all your attention on growing a healthy child in your womb.

I miss our children, and I miss you, sweet Liwi, in more ways than I can put into words. Your smile that greets and uplifts me, your sharp wit in such perfect balance with your kind heart, your small arms twining about me as you sleep, as if you are holding me safe in your embrace. My thoughts often turn to our last night together, and how sweet that was, as so many nights before it. I cannot wait to be reunited with you once more, and with God's grace, that will be very soon.

It does my heart good to know you are safe behind Żółkiew's fortifications and that you and the little one are in good hands, for it is one less worry for your devoted husband.

Take good care of yourself in my absence, dear wife, and know that I adore you always and forever.

Your loving husband and humble servant,

Jacek

Tears welling in her eyes, she pressed the letter to her breast as if doing so would hold him to her. Her thoughts traveled a worn path to that last night, much as his must have. "Liwi, I need you," he had whispered, and her knees had turned to the consistency of butter in a summer kitchen. His hands and mouth had been everywhere on her, and wanton that she was, she had fed off his desire, clawing at him to press skin to skin, to revel in his warmth, his power, and know he was alive. That they were both alive.

She reread the letter until she had memorized every phrase. For a man of so few words, he wrote the most eloquent letters, offering a glimpse of what lived deep in his heart and his soul. It was almost worth letting him go to receive such poetic prose from the valiant warrior she loved with her whole being. Almost.

Closing her eyes, she sent another fervent prayer to the Virgin Mother, imploring Her to keep Jacek safe.

"I could not bear to lose him," she whispered aloud.

How long she lay thusly, she did not know, but the sound of the latch gently turning and the swishing skirts that followed had her fluttering her eyes open.

Eugenia—of course all that gentleness was Eugenia—crept to the bedside. "Was it a lovely letter, my dear?"

"Yes, lovely and long, for a change." Its length was telling, though, and her mind churned with what he *hadn't* said. In previous letters, he had expressed confidence that a new treaty would be negotiated before any fighting erupted, but that sentiment was alarmingly absent this time. Despite summer's heat shimmering in the fields beyond her window, a chill rippled through her, raising gooseflesh on her arms.

Eugenia smiled. "Shall I help you sit up so you can write him back?"

Oh, how Oliwia wanted to confide her worries to her friend, but Eugenia had a husband she adored at the front as well, and though his missives were far more frequent than Jacek's, they were also shorter and devoid of much of consequence. Therefore, Eugenia had little idea of the growing tensions in the camp.

She returned Eugenia's smile. "Yes, I would like that very much, although I may wait a while."

"Trying to find the right words so he is not distressed about the babe?"

"Yes, that." How would she explain the bleeding that had begun days ago that kept her bedridden? While she had not yet lost the child, the peril lingered. The babe's fate was in God's hands. "There's also the matter that with the hetman gone, we no longer have our swift corridor of correspondence."

While the hetman had been in residence, he had been in constant contact with his commanders at the border, his scouts and spies, and the hospodar. Correspondence had been necessarily swift, and she and Eugenia had taken advantage. But with the hetman's departure, their relay had begun to lag, just as the buzzing throughout the estate had. Silence echoed in Żółkiew's halls, and the exodus of the hetman's army had left indelible sadness and disquiet in its wake.

Oliwia hugged the letter. "Waiting an hour or so will not matter."

"Of course it won't."

The door opened a little wider, and in darted Nadia, who nearly tripped when she stopped to curtsy. "Someone is in the sitting room who would like to see m'lady."

Oliwia raised her head and frowned. "Who is it?"

"Pani Regina Żółkiewska, m'lady."

"Oh! Have her come in, by all means." Oliwia tried to hoist herself up on her elbows, but Eugenia grabbed her arm and restrained her. "I must straighten myself," she hissed. "I'm a frightful—"

"Do not trouble yourself, Pani Oliwia." Lady Regina's cool voice drifted from the doorway. She swept into the room like the woman of breeding she was. Oliwia had been intimidated since first meeting her, but now, prostrate in bed and rumpled, she wanted to shrivel with embarrassment.

The lady drew closer to her side. "We mustn't sacrifice a babe's health for vanity's sake."

303

Oliwia opened and closed her mouth and opened it again. "No, of course not, Pani Żółkiewska."

With Nadia's help, Eugenia pulled over a chair. Lady Żółkiewska dipped her head. "Thank you. Now if you would kindly leave us …"

"Of course," they both chirped as they scurried from the room.

Once the door closed, the lady sank into the seat, her back as straight as a plank. Though a woman of some years, she took great pride in her appearance, and her age hadn't occurred much to Oliwia before. But her lines and creases had deepened since her husband's departure, making her appear haggard and frail.

"I apologize for neglecting you, Lady Oliwia," the woman began.

"Thank you, my lady, but you have not neglected—"

Lady Regina held up her hand. "I have indeed. I was despondent over my husband's and son's departure, and it made me forgetful. But that is no excuse to neglect a guest … especially one who is suffering difficulties."

Oliwia swallowed a knot in her throat. "Forgive me if I am impertinent, my lady, but I think of myself as a sister-in-arms rather than a guest. With our husbands off to fulfill their duties and we left behind to do our own duties, I believe we share a melancholic commonality that transcends hostess and guest, yes? And we must support one another, remain strong so we can lean on one another."

Lady Regina clasped her hands primly in her lap and regarded Oliwia with watery brown eyes, her lips a tight, firm line. Oliwia cringed inside. Once more, it seemed, she had overstepped and pushed this lady to the brink of losing her composure.

After tortuous moments, the lady at last spoke. "Very well put, my lady. Not only are you a great beauty, but you have a mind as well. No wonder your husband dotes on you." She cleared her throat. "How are you faring, child?" The creases around the woman's eyes softened.

"Better, I believe." *I hope.*

"You will allow the baba to look in on you, yes? She has been with our family since the dawn of time. In fact, she brought all my children into this world and …" She wrung her hands. "She was present at my daughter Katarzyna's bedside when she … when we lost …"

Oliwia's heart fractured. Katarzyna had only been married to Crown Field Hetman Koniecpolski a few years when she died in childbirth.

Lady Regina tossed her head back and shook it. "Listen to me, behaving like a maudlin old woman," she sniffled. Her glossy eyes fixed on Oliwia. "Did your husband ever tell you how enchanted my Kasia was by him during his stay here with us in 1612?"

Oliwia bit back the urge to bark out, *"Another one?"*

"No, of course he didn't. You must ask Magdalena about it sometime. Of course, she was rather enchanted herself, and I daresay she tried her best, but he would not capitulate. Apparently, he was quite smitten with a dark-haired, light-eyed woman from Biaska." The lady let out a little chuckle, and though Oliwia's innards twisted—some good, some bad—she was loath to blow her off course and therefore clamped her mouth shut. "I see I have shocked you, Lady Oliwia. Please don't be offended. You see, I understand what it's like to be the wife of a handsome soldier. My Stas was once quite the catch." She wiggled her eyebrows, and Oliwia glimpsed the girl she had once been.

"He still is, to me." Her voice came out in a hush, then rose in volume once more, taking on a dreamy quality. "We have always shared something special, and I see the same rare magic between you and your husband. He worships you, and you adore him." She clenched a fist and pressed it against her heart. "We must never forget how lucky we are. We must hold on to that magic and treasure it as long as we can, yes?"

"Oh yes," Oliwia whispered. She had an urge to reach for the woman's hand and hold it, but the lady's hands were firmly back under control and resting on her lap.

Lady Regina's eyes traveled somewhere distant. "I always pictured myself at this age sharing mulled wine with my husband as we sat before the fire, reviving our memories and delighting in tales of our children and grandchildren. Not sending him off to war with a kiss and a remembrance." She expelled a laborious breath and met Oliwia's gaze once more. "But that is not the way it goes for the wife of a man who's driven to protect his country, is it?"

Oliwa's throat clogged, and tears stung her eyes. "No, it's not."

"Well, I will relish my time with my Zofia. She is a great comfort to me, like you and Magda and Eugenia. And I know that in the end, all will be well, for it will be as God intended." Lady Regina's tone had taken on a determined quality, as if she was trying to convince herself.

As Oliwia waited for sleep to claim her that night, she digested her extraordinary conversation with Lady Regina. Soon her thoughts turned to Jacek and how the bed seemed to expand the longer he was away. She ran her hand over the cool, empty sheets, recalling having him beside her.

He was a large man, and he had a style of sleeping that filled the greater part of the bed—at least the part she happened to be occupying. When they first married, they slept little due to what typically transpired when their bodies came together. But as time went by, she noticed as they shifted throughout the night, he inevitably followed her, whether she filled some small space in the middle of the mattress or clung to the edge of the bed. He seemed to seek her out in his sleep, and when he found her, he folded himself about her as if she were a pillow, his long limbs twining and locking her in his grasp. And he was hot! Lord, sleeping with him brought to mind being too close to a brazier stacked with fresh wood. It was welcome in the winter, but in the summer, most nights she discarded their bedclothes and her clothing along with it. He never objected. At times, she wondered if it was his plan all along. And right now, she would have welcomed him and his heat.

With these visions gamboling through her head, she closed her eyes and let her body melt into the mattress.

The sounds of metal clashing, horses braying, and desperate voices crying out startled her from slumber. A scene painted red with blood played out before her. Hussars' lances splintered into useless pieces. Sabres arced downward into flesh and bone. An arrow pierced a man's heart, and the impact knocked him backward. The blow didn't unmount him, and he turned, still astride a gray horse, his sapphire-blue eyes skewering hers, pleading, begging. He reached out a bloody hand and parted his lips, but no words came.

Slowly—painfully so—he mouthed, "Liwi," as fear appeared in his orbs.

She lunged for him, but another arrow struck him, and life faded from his eyes as he crumpled and crashed to the blood-soaked ground beneath the horse's hooves. She came away empty, and her soul cried out across a yawning abyss.

She woke from the nightmare with a start, sweat beading her brow and heart slamming against her rib cage. When she turned her hands over, they were slick with sticky, warm blood against her nightgown as white as an egret's feather. A crimson stain spread, obliterating the white, and she screamed.

CHAPTER 31

Portents

Jacek urged Heban into a gallop, and the horse smoothly stretched out its stride. But when they came to the tight turn at the end of the track, the beast balked and vaulted outside the line, nearly spilling Jacek onto his backside. In the distance, Jarosława neighed, no doubt in disapproval. Where the devil had she come from? He chuckled despite his frustration with the gelding's skills, which were as raw as freshly churned cheese.

"She's right, you know. If you expect to honor your lineage by being in a cavalry charge, you will need to do much better than this." He puffed out a long-winded breath. "Come. Let's try it again."

Before he could settle Heban for another run, Marcin whistled at him. Jacek trotted over to the outer corral where Marcin—and an indignant Jarosława—stood.

"Last-minute council meeting, Pan Jacek."

Jacek rolled his eyes. "What for this time?"

"I expect it has something to do with Crown Grand Hetman Żółkiewski's arrival in camp tomorrow."

Since the hetman's forward guard had arrived yesterday with news of Żółkiewski's approach, the camp had buzzed. Action—and peace in and out of the camp—at last!

Jacek dismounted and handed the reins to a hovering pacholik. As he pulled off his gloves, he jerked his chin toward his mare. "How did she get in here?"

Marcin grinned. "She *insisted* by head-butting me, and who am I to deny a lady?"

"Especially when that lady is at least five times your size."

"Exactly," Marcin chuckled. "Shall I fetch your lieutenants?"

"No, I'll go alone this time. Hopefully, it will be brief."

The council tent was crowded when Jacek ducked into its interior, and he had little choice but to stand near Wronski. The man side-eyed him and smirked. Somehow Wronski had wormed his way into the council meetings despite not been invited to participate in the first place. The captain of the Forlorn Hope was now as ensconced as a tick on a horse's hindquarter and about as irritating.

Christ, but Jacek couldn't wait for the real Elear commander to arrive so he could rid himself of the foul, festering barb that was Wronski! He had given up trying to get the rogue to follow orders, concentrating instead on repairing his relationship with Filip—in vain—although directing more attention to his brother-in-law and less to Wronski had garnered one small victory: Filip spent his nights in Jacek's camp. This he knew because his brother now slept beside him in his own tent—without so much as a reference to a leash. Being a light sleeper, Jacek made sure the lad did not venture out—another black mark against Jacek where his brother-in-law was concerned, to match the now-faded black eyes Jacek had given him when he'd broken his nose. Where Filip spent his days was more of a mystery, though Jacek often glimpsed him sparring with Wronski's men.

"Why, Pan Dąbrowski, you are looking as miserable as you did yesterday. Really, sir, you should consider changing your diet from pickled cabbage to honey balls."

"The only thing that will alter my mood for the better is changing company."

Wronski chuckled mirthlessly. "I understand, for I share that sentiment. Though I am of good cheer, my disposition could be improved upon."

"I cannot help but wonder at that good cheer. Have you plundered a village? Taken a child by force?" More devastating raids in Moldavia had been carried out over the last month, but no one had yet been caught or accused of the crimes because potential witnesses were either dead or captured and whisked away to be sold. The few that survived could not identify their attackers for being knocked unconsciousness during the attack or suffering a tragic wound, like having their eyes put out. The marauders were nothing if not savagely thorough.

Wronski's mouth twisted in a bitter smile. "I believe you are once more confusing me with Tatar filth."

Jacek drew himself up to his full height and looked down his nose at the flea-infested devil's spawn. "Save religion, I understand they are one and the same."

Wronski opened his mouth to deliver an angry volley, but Koniecpolski swept into the tent. A hush fell over the assemblage.

"Thank you all for c-coming. I know you have m-much to do," the hetman stuttered, "so this will be brief. As you know, the crown grand hetman and his retinue arrive tomorrow. W-we will remain here for several d-days, and then we march to Gruszka, where we w-will be joined by other f-forces and divide up into our r-regiments."

A burble bloomed as attendees fired off questions about Grazziani, the mustering site, the Ottoman troops, and the Tatars.

Koniecpolski held up his hands. "Patience, my lords. We will know m-more when the hetman ar-rives on the morrow. Now go and p-prepare your camps for d-departure."

He lumbered from the tent, and the gathered group began funneling after him. Wronski squeezed against Jacek as they shuffled toward the flap. "And so it begins."

"And so it does."

Outside, the sun's rays beat down on Jacek's head, and he pulled off his kolpak. "When we move out, Filip will be coming with his own clan."

Wronski looked up at him and flashed a wicked grin. "Do not be so sure Filip considers you and your men his brethren. He prefers my banner to yours, as he's made abundantly clear by spending time among us whenever you let him off his tether. If you don't believe me, ask him."

"I did not say he would have a choice in the matter. If I have to leash him to bring him along, then so be it. Neither you nor he will get the best of me." Jacek pivoted to put as much distance between himself and Wronski.

Wronski called after him. "You have already been bested, Pan Dąbrowski. Thrice now."

Jacek had no patience for Wronski's daft utterings, so he lengthened his strides and made for his tent.

"Blast it!" came Marcin's voice as Jacek drew closer.

He stepped inside his tent, letting his eyes adjust to the dimmer interior. Marcin was bent over an open trunk where Jacek's battle regalia was usually stored. Said regalia lay in neat piles on the carpeted floor, and Marcin muttered and cursed while appearing to ransack the chest.

"What the devil are you doing, Marcin?"

Marcin stood, fisted a hand on a hip, and scratched the back of his neck with the other. He stared at the open trunk. "Searching for your wings."

"My wings?" Jacek stepped beside him and peered inside the mostly empty container.

"Yes. I wanted to replace a few of the more ragged feathers with those I just plucked from an egret." Marcin pointed to a side table that held a dozen or more snowy feathers. "Might you have moved them, my lord?"

"I? No. I haven't looked at them since we embarked on our journey. Have you checked the other trunks?"

"Those in here, yes. I will check the rest and the wagons too, though I don't know why they would be anywhere but here. I packed them myself." He continued staring at the trunk's interior as if doing so might conjure them.

"When did you last see them?"

"Right before we left Żółkiew." Marcin raised horrified eyes to his. "You don't think someone has stolen them? How can you ride into battle without them?"

"I don't think anyone has stolen them, and the chances of engaging in battle are scant. Besides, colonels do not don them."

Marcin nodded and meticulously placed the items back where they belonged. After he completed the task and left, Jacek rummaged through every container large enough to hold a pair of wings. He hadn't expected to find them—Marcin was too thorough—but searching kept him from acknowledging his burgeoning disquiet.

That the wings had seemingly flown away caused something to tilt inside of him. He might not need them for battle, but he did need them ... to keep a sense of foreboding at bay.

Filip guffawed at a story one of Wronski's guards had just finished, following the lead of the other men seated around a cook fire in the commander's camp under the night sky streaked with stars. He wasn't certain what the man had relayed due to his thick Ruthenian accent and odd way of stringing words together.

This lot was similar to the soldiers he was used to in their battle hardness, but they were unlike Biaska's troops in their level of shine. Here, the men were more tarnished, and the tales they told centered on their own selfish gains rather than what they had done for God and country.

The soldier beside Filip filled his cup with piwo before Filip could decline. He hadn't earned any prize or pay yet on behalf of the banner, and everything he consumed was added to a growing list of coin he owed Lord Wronski. Different from the way of Biaska, where he'd never paid for a meal in the great hall. Commander Wronski assured him one mission would cover the debt and put more money in his pocket besides—a sum much larger than his meager pay at Biaska, to spend however he pleased.

More than monetary reward, though, Filip craved recognition. Respect. He wanted to prove himself on the battlefield and let the accolades rain down on him after vanquishing the enemy. With Wronski, he would get that chance, so he continued to adjust, to fit in, to become one of them.

He quickly drained the cup, set it down, and stood before the soldier could fill it again.

"I bid you all good night," he announced. Their protests struck a warm chord inside him that he carried back to his own camp. That chord turned icy and brittle when he stood outside Jacek's tent, glowing with lantern light from inside. His brother-in-law was still awake. Dread rose up inside him. He prodded his tender nose, and it throbbed in response.

Anger had simmered below Filip's barely controlled surface of civility since the night Jacek had broken his nose, and it threatened to erupt every time he laid eyes on his brother-in-law or the brute spoke to him.

Pulling in a deep breath of conviction, he stepped into Jacek's tent.

His brother-in-law looked up from where he sat at his writing table. Spread over the table's surface were sheets of paper filled with writing and diagrams. The sight piqued Filip's curiosity, but he had no desire to engage, so he turned his back on Jacek and plopped onto his pallet to prepare himself for bed.

He could feel his brother's gaze boring into him as he spoke. "Did you spend an enjoyable evening in Wronski's camp?"

"*Commander* Wronski, and yes." From the corner of his eye, Filip detected Jacek rubbing his nape, a gesture he often made when he was vexed. *Good!*

"I would like to bridge this chasm between us. I would like for you to spend your evenings taking comfort here, among your brethren." Jacek's voice carried a dispirited tone that gave Filip a sense of satisfaction.

I don't give two figs what you would like. "I *am* spending my evenings among my brethren when I'm in Commander Wronski's camp."

Jacek pushed out a breath. "Then perhaps we can compromise. Might you consider—"

"Compromise ended the night you hit me." Filip's voice was tight as he removed his żupan, taking great care to avert his gaze from Jacek. "Other than having to spend my nights sleeping under the same canvas roof as you, I am spending my evenings exactly as I wish."

"Filip, I—"

"I'm tired." With that, he stretched out on the pallet and rolled to his side so he faced the tent wall.

A long while later, his brother expelled another sigh and extinguished the lantern. "So be it. Good night." His voice was subdued and laced with what Filip could only describe as regret.

Without answer, Filip shut his eyes. Anger twined with doubt and other emotions he couldn't identify. At last, his maelstrom of thoughts dissolved in his fatigue, and he drifted into a dreamless sleep.

Another meeting in Koniecpolski's tent turned out to be little more than a repeat of the previous one. This affair was smaller, however, restricted to the top corps of officers, and included logistics details for their upcoming move to Gruszka. Somehow Wronski had interjected himself once again. No one seemed perturbed by his presence—hell, they barely noticed—but Jacek found himself peeved with little idea what to do about his annoyance. Was Wronski fulfilling a duty in his true commander's absence so he could brief him? Was he injecting himself out of an inflated sense of self-importance? Or was he gathering intelligence for more nefarious reasons?

Wronski seemed to be weaving a web, using Filip as one of its silken threads or placing him in its dead center. Perhaps both. Jacek's dilemma revolved around how to separate every silken fiber without endangering Filip or further severing the link between his brother-in-law and himself.

Jacek returned to his tent and flung himself upon his cot. Though the sun still hung high, he was wrung out like the garments in a laundress's basket. He laced his fingers over his stomach and stared at the canvas ceiling.

Wronski was the devil incarnate, and Jacek fought to rein in the overwhelming urge to beat the beast bloody with his nadziak or choke him until the life drained from his cold eyes. Should he let those emotions break free, he might get sucked into Wronski's twisting whirlpool and drown. Intuition told him Wronski was plotting, though exactly what, he didn't know. Consequently, he needed a cool head so he could observe, so he could glean what lurked beneath Wronski's veneer.

That Filip seemed so at ease with Wronski and his men, joking and laughing and looking as though he *belonged* among them ... The slight stung. Jacek may have been guilty of treating his brother-in-law harshly, but he had only ever done so out of love for the boy—not to use him.

How he wished he could see Oliwia. Talk to her. Her presence alone would be enough to quiet his roiling thoughts.

How did she fare? Her belly surely resembled a watermelon by now—he dared not think otherwise, for it could invite the devil's mischief—and he pictured her small hands resting atop the mound.

A sudden pull to rush back to Żółkiew washed over him. Was it an omen? What if the Tatars broke through, as they had in 1618? What if they invaded Żółkiew and took her? She and the child would be killed or enslaved, pulled away from him, away from one another. He couldn't bear it.

Dear God, he needed to curtail his fears before they drove him mad. He *had* to corral them, to turn his attention in a different direction. But they held him hostage.

He had witnessed far too many horrors in his thirty-two years to pretend tragedy would not befall his own. Only nights before, Moldavian villagers had gone to bed, secure in their abodes, and in one blow, delivered in seconds, their lives had been shattered.

Oliwia and his children were not immune. Oh, she was capable and resourceful and steelier than any woman he had ever known, but she was nonetheless vulnerable. Protecting her and their children was *his* duty. So what was he doing here, hundreds of miles from home?

Hoisting himself onto an elbow, he slid out a packet of letters from beneath his pillow and carefully untied them. Most had come from Liwi in Żółkiew, but some were from Tamara and included drawings from Adam and Margaret that looked more like chicken scratchings than art. Would they sketch like their mother one day? One in particular drew his eye. It consisted of smiling stick figures in a line holding hands. A large figure on a horse held the hand of a smaller figure with long dark hair, who in turn held a succession of three smaller figures that diminished in size. A large

315

circle with lines arrayed around it filled a top corner—a child's rendering of the sun, he presumed.

A sunny family.

He dropped back, letters piled on his chest, and flopped an arm over his eyes. He hadn't written Oliwia or Tamara or his mother in days … weeks, even. He needed to pen messages, but mostly he needed to let Oliwia know they were moving farther south. Though the path was leading them closer to possible peril, he had to reassure her, but for now, his well was dry.

Fatigue stole over him and settled in his limbs. He imagined himself in bed, lifting Oliwia into his arms, soaking up her warmth and her soft, drowsy sighs while Piotr nestled on his other side. As he gave himself over to sleep, uncertainty followed him down and tormented him.

Every man fell out to greet Crown Grand Hetman Żółkiewski when he and his contingent rode into camp the following day. The shift his presence brought was palpable, sending spirits soaring.

Now that he had come, they would resolve this Moldavian mess and get back to their own lives.

That night, the great hetman, with his priest flanking him, gathered them all in a circle in a clearing beside his camp. Jacek stood close and could not help but notice the hetman's sunken eyes and gray complexion. He told himself it had been a long journey and that Żółkiewski's countenance simply reflected his fatigue after the trek.

When the hetman spoke, though, his voice resonated and held not a trace of weariness.

"I have delayed joining you here because I have been waiting for word from Warzawa, and I now have it." He shook a piece of paper in the air, its royal seal unmistakable. "The king and the Sejm are in accord that we should come to the aid of Hospodar Gaspar Grazziani, our ally and friend in Moldavia, who fears not only for his throne but his life." A cheer went up among the gathering, and he waited until it died down to shake the paper once more. "With this order, we will march into Jassy and restore the rightful ruler. The Ottomans will hear our steps as we come for them, and they will quake with fear because they are weak and they know they cannot defeat us." The assembly fairly drowned out the hetman as he added in a strident voice, "We will send the pagans back to where they came from and never let them darken the door of Christendom again! Victory will be swift and justice ours!" He shook his fist in the air.

The whoops and war cries and shouts were deafening. Jacek had added his own and could not hear himself for the noise. The hetman surveyed the crowd, a smile playing on his mouth. With a patting motion, he calmed the men down once more.

"Now that you know our mission, I ask every man here …" He pointed a crooked finger at the throng, pausing as he went, as if singling out every single soul assembled before him. Power surged in that moment. "Are you with me?"

"Yes!" they cried.

"Are you with me?" he repeated.

The soldiers roared in agreement.

"Are. You. With. Me?"

The thunder of the men's voices shook the air, sending chills dancing up and down Jacek's spine.

Żółkiewski lifted his hands in the air and looked toward the sky. "Lord, I have their approval! We are in your hands."

Men hugged, laughed, and cavorted as if they had just vanquished the dragon Typhon.

This was why Żółkiewski was beloved. *This* was why Jacek would follow the hetman wherever he ordered Jacek to go. Even so, a tiny voice in Jacek's head questioned whether that might lead him straight into calamity.

CHAPTER 32

The Command

Jacek sat in the mess tent with Henryk, Marcin, Dawid, and Lesław, Filip presumably being in Wronski's camp. The army had arrived in Gruszka the day before after a ten-mile march from Śledziówka. It was the second of September, and spirits were high, though their still-low numbers were a source of unease.

Beside Jacek sat Dawid, absently stirring his groats. "I thought the hetman would have gathered more than seven thousand troops."

"Pah!" Henryk, seated across the table, scoffed. "How many more do they need when they have us? Remember Kłuszyn and how our small husaria force decimated an army of forty thousand? Or was it sixty? In any case, David defeated Goliath."

Jacek backhanded Dawid's arm. "Have you no faith? More troops are on the way. Once Iskender Pasha realizes our might, he will surely negotiate."

Lesław nodded. "We are only just arrived. There are more magnates' armies that must catch up yet, along with Grazziani's Moldavians and more Lisowczycy under Commander Rogowski."

Dawid grunted. "From what I have seen of the Lost Men, I have my doubts we're better off with a full contingent of that unruly lot."

Marcin tore a hunk of bread and grinned. "There's a reason folk say they are the kind of cavalry God does not want and the devil is afraid of."

Lesław bobbed his head. "So it's good they are on our side, yes? They are fearsome."

"On our side as long as there is a common enemy to fight. Once that enemy is gone, they will turn on their own like rabid dogs," Dawid rejoined.

Lesław pursed his lips. "Then best mind your possessions so a Lost Man does not relieve you of them."

"Whether he's on your side or not," Henryk added. "So we are the cavalry God *does* want and the devil is afraid of. For the record, I am in accord with Dawid."

Jacek didn't disagree. "The Lost Men are a necessary evil." *I hope the hetman knows what he is doing by bringing them into the fight and that he can keep them in check.*

Henryk scoffed. "Necessary? I'm not so certain. Furthermore, no one in camp likes the damned marauders … except the damned marauders. They swarm the women as if they were their own private traveling brothel."

Jacek snorted. "It won't be a worry much longer. I'm fairly certain Hetman Żółkiewski will chase all females off."

Henryk feigned a frown. "Damn! Why do the hetmans always have to spoil our fun?"

Jacek lifted an eyebrow. "Could it be because they are more concerned with victory and saving their forces' hides than appeasing said forces' lusts?"

"Yes, but we won't be engaging in warfare, remember?" Henryk argued. "Although, should it come down to a fight, I am confident we will rout them quickly. I say two hours and we are done with the Ottoman curs."

His brothers-in-arms rumbled their agreement.

Jacek wanted to believe it was true, but a tendril of dread lurking in his gut rose up and flicked its tail, reminding him of its presence.

Before he could think on it, a guard stepped into the tent. "Is Colonel Dąbrowski here?" Jacek acknowledged him. "Crown Grand Hetman Żółkiewski would like to see you in his quarters, Colonel."

Masking his curiosity, Jacek rose and followed the guard to Żółkiewski's tent. Inside, the great hetman sat at a table, paper before him and quill in hand. His son, Jan, stood behind him. The hetman looked up at Jacek, his expression unreadable. His face held fewer lines, and a ruddy tinge to his cheekbones gave him a healthier air than the first day he had arrived at Śledziówka. A trim man, he appeared a little fuller and his shoulders straighter. *Thank Christ and all the saints!* His skin that day had been gray and his posture stooped; he had appeared downright decrepit.

Jacek took up his usual soldier's stance—feet apart and hands clasped behind his back—and waited.

The hetman set down his quill and tented his gnarled fingers. "Colonel Dąbrowski, I will come straight to the point."

Jacek pulled in a breath and girded himself.

"I am putting you in command of my regiment."

Unable to contain his surprise, Jacek's gaze shot to Jan and back to Żółkiewski. "Pardon? But ... but I thought I was the pułkownik of—"

Żółkiewski stayed his query with a wave of his hand. "So you are. And now you are also leading my pułk. You are my field commander."

"The entire regiment? Infantry, plus light and heavy cavalry?" Jacek blurted.

"That is what I said, Colonel. Unless you deem yourself unfit for the post." Żółkiewski narrowed his gaze.

"No, sir. I am perfectly fit, my Guard, er, Grand, um ..." Christ, he was stammering as badly as Liwi had! He cleared his throat. "I would be honored, Crown Grand Hetman. Thank you."

"Good. Jan, would you list the composition of the colonel's troops?"

Jan lifted a piece of paper. "You will be in command of close to six hundred husaria, another six in light cavalry, a haiduk banner of three hundred, and assorted infantry of roughly two hundred. You will be one of a total of five regiment leaders, not all of whom have arrived yet."

Żółkiewski thanked his son and turned his attention back to Jacek. "I suggest you become well acquainted with your deputy commanders, Colonel, so you can forge a cohesive force."

Jacek bowed, his excitement on full display. "I shall, sir."

Żółkiewski's mouth seemed to twitch on one side. "I expect you at every war council meeting, starting today. You will be briefed on our latest intelligence, the state of our numbers, and our plans moving forward."

"Of course." Jacek shifted his weight. "Do you still expect Iskender Pasha will be willing to negotiate?"

"I'm counting on it."

When Jacek didn't move, Żółkiewski picked up his quill and bent back to his missive. "You are dismissed, Colonel Dąbrowski."

Jan Żółkiewski followed this with a nod.

"Yes, sirs." Jacek spun on his heel and nearly overran Crown Field Hetman Koniecpolski, presently entering the tent. The man nodded, and Jacek sidestepped him and darted outside.

He paused to draw in a series of breaths outside the tent, where several guards eyed him curiously. He didn't care. His heart pounded with joy. The hetman believed in him enough to bestow him with the command of seventeen hundred men! The chance to prove himself at the head of the hetman's pułk was his.

The gathering of the war council later that day was small despite being well-attended, as numerous forces had yet to arrive. Jacek looked around at the grim faces, and three observations bubbled up. First, the magnates that were present seemed to cluster together in factions and regard Hetman Żółkiewski with hooded gazes. The second observation was that while not all the high lords had arrived, they already seemed to make up half of the gathered army. Lastly, but for Hetman Koniecpolski, Jacek was the youngest man present. The fact didn't intimidate but rather filled his chest with pride.

The meeting came to order with Żółkiewski seated behind the familiar table that served as his desk while Koniecpolski and Jan flanked him.

"Let me restate our mission," began Żółkiewski. "Our foremost objective is to protect Hospodar Gaspar Grazziani, who has recently broken ties with the Porte and put himself in grave danger. He has asked for—and been granted—the protection of the Crown and is in need of succor." The hetman continued, reviewing the events leading up to the expedition, all of which Jacek had heard before but listened to with keen interest nonetheless.

When Żółkiewski paused for questions, Walenty Kalinowski, the starosta of Kamieniec, spoke up. "Do we intend to put Grazziani back on the throne?"

"That will depend upon the pasha's move, but ideally, that would be the outcome."

"And the king? What requirements does he direct we abide by?"

"He, along with the Sejm, has granted me full authorization to do as I must to accomplish the mission."

"What of our supplies?" someone barked, cutting off the interaction between the hetman and the magnate from Kamieniec.

"W-we are adequately provisioned," Koniecpolski replied as Żółkiewski sagged back into his seat.

"Do we know the composition of the hospodar's army yet?" Żółkiewski's son-in-law, Jan Daniłowicz, asked.

"Not yet, but w-we will know soon enough."

"We are heavy on cavalry," another magnate commander declared. "Do we have enough infantry?"

Żółkiewski sat forward and glared, obviously annoyed by the question. He was known to favor cavalry over infantry, often eschewing the latter, and apparently didn't appreciate having his choices questioned. Jacek tucked the reaction away. "Yes, we have infantry, made up of Poles and Germans. We also have the king's haiduk banner—our own well-trained regulars personally overseen by Crown Field Hetman Koniecpolski—and a company of reiters. We are complete."

"That's not enough," someone behind Jacek mumbled.

"How many guns?" another called.

"Sixteen," came Koniecpolski's answer.

"Is that enough?"

"Guns, infantry, or the army itself?"

"All three."

Żółkiewski rose, bracing his weight on his fists as he leaned upon the table. The movement seemed to take great effort. "My lords, the enemy is weak, disorganized, and nowhere near. They have no idea of our movements. I know this because I have a number of spies who all bear the same information. But make no mistake. We will do everything we must to protect the Commonwealth's interests and safeguard the hospodar." In the silence that followed, his gaze skipped to every man present. "Tomorrow, we march to Jaruga and cross the Dniesper into Moldavia. There, we will be joined by more forces, and we will march on Jassy to rescue Hospodar Grazziani with the aid of his army."

He sank into his seat, and his face reflected a pallor that hadn't been there at the start of the meeting.

Koniecpolski took over the briefing. "Fording the river will be slow g-going, and there is no time to waste. Therefore, *only* the Grand Crown Hetman's w-wagons will be allowed to cross."

"Packhorses for the rest of us, then," someone grumbled.

Koniecpolski either didn't hear or ignored the comment. But Żółkiewski's hawk eyes shot straight to somewhere over Jacek's shoulder and fastened there.

Christ! How were Żółkiewski and Koniecpolski going keep these bickering, self-serving, counterfeit hetmans in check?

"We are relegated to packhorses," Jacek advised Marcin hours later, "but the distance is not so far."

They stood beside the makeshift corral next to Jacek's camp.

Marcin stroked Heban's nose, and the horse yanked his head away. "Stubborn, that one. Maybe you should make *him* carry the load."

"No, I will be riding him to the border. Maybe the trek will make the beast more pliable." Though Jacek wasn't counting on it.

"Jarosława, then?" Grinning, Marcin ducked before Jacek could clap him.

"Never Jarosława. She is far too dignified a lady to haul my camp."

Jarosława nudged Heban out of the way and nuzzled Jacek's crown. He returned the affection by stroking her cheek. "I thought you would agree, my girl."

"If we have to charge, which horse will you ride?"

"I would prefer to ride Heban. Jarosława is far more reliable, but she's getting too old for the strain my weight puts on her bones. When we return to Biaska, I intend to turn her out in a thick green pasture where she will while away her days." She thumped her chin on his head. "Hey!"

Marcin laughed. "I reckon she's none too fond of the idea."

"Christ, does she hear *everything* I say?" She was worse than Liwi, he thought with affection.

Jacek picked up a brush and whistled a tune as he began brushing her coat.

Marcin went to work on Heban. "So what did you learn of our plans during the meeting of the great magnates?"

Jacek recounted the highlights, and Marcin nodded along. When Jacek was done, Marcin looked at him over his horse's back.

"So we enter Moldavia, march on Jassy, where we reestablish Grazziani as ruler, then show off our might to the Ottomans to force them to the negotiating table, where they acquiesce to the hospodar's leadership?"

"Yes, 'much like Zamoyski did in 1595,' the hetman said."

"How does he plan to 'show off our might'?"

Jacek checked one of Jarosława's shoes. "Hmm. I may need the farrier. As for displaying our power, he intends to fortify the plain near Cecora, on the other side of the Prut, as Zamoyski did when he extracted the Treaty of Cecora from the Turks."

"So he has picked the same spot deliberately?"

"He didn't say so, but I doubt it's a coincidence. He was there with Zamoyski, after all. I believe it's a symbolic move."

Marcin frowned. "Zamoyski installed a leader back then who was a Commonwealth vassal, yes?"

"Yes."

"So history repeats."

Hopefully. What Jacek had omitted from the discussion with Marcin was the bit about the tension that hung between the magnates and hetmans like Damocles's sword. Why worry Marcin over the conflict? Besides, Jacek's growing concern was enough for the both of them.

Later that night, Jacek composed a long overdue letter to Oliwia. His reluctance to write did not merely arise from the fact that his days were full and fatigue claimed him early in the evenings, but from his relationship with Filip—or lack thereof. Besides telling her that her brother was hale, what else could he say? "I broke his nose. I fear he's in very bad company, but my attempts to reel him back in have failed. We don't speak. He dismisses what I say. I've lost control. I'm not sure how to resolve our differences." No, he had to keep these truths to himself.

Instead, he spoke of other truths: of how honored he was that the hetman had put him in charge of his regiment, what an opportunity it was, and that he now spent time in the war councils among the magnates.

Tomorrow, we cross into Moldavia and march on Jassy. The hetman has a free hand to manage the Moldavian situation, and the man radiates confidence. After successfully securing the throne for Grazziani and negotiating a truce with the Ottomans without trial, his critics will at last be silenced. And I can return to you.

Jacek sat back, twirling the quill between his fingers. He turned over the reasons Żółkiewski embraced this expedition. Perhaps the hetman simply believed in re-establishing the hospodar to his throne—Moldavia was a critical buffer between the infidels and the Commonwealth—or perhaps he strove to prove something to his most vocal opponents and regain his former reputation. Perhaps both motivated him. Whatever the man's reasons, Jacek's purpose was clear. He was there to help the hetman attain his goals.

None of this did he write to Oliwia. Instead, he filled the rest of his short missive with words of a more personal nature and prayers that she and the babe were well and that soon they would all be reunited.

Three days after the crossing, they were encamped near Łozowa when a breathless messenger burst into Jacek's camp.

"Colonel Dąbrowski, Crown Grand Hetman Żółkiewski orders your immediate presence at his pavilion."

Jacek untucked his kolpak from his sash and plopped it on his head as the courier was pivoting away. "Did he explain the purpose of the meeting?"

"No," the boy panted, "just that I am to alert the highest-ranking officers to come at once."

Jacek wasted no time weaving his way through clustered tents. He was one of a mere handful of commanders when he entered the tent. The hetman, seated in his usual place behind the table, stared with a blank gaze, as if his mind was some distance away. His mouth was a hard, grim line, and his shoulders appeared to fold inward, as if a great weight pressed on them.

Beside him, Koniecpolski rocked on the balls of his feet and seemed to snort like a perturbed bull preparing to charge. "All p-present and accounted f-for, Hetman Żółkiewski."

Jacek glanced around at the small crowd, dismayed when he spied Wronski among them. Once more, the reprobate had weaseled his way into a briefing intended for the higher command.

"My lords," Żółkiewski began after the last man in closed the tent flap behind him, "I am in possession of some rather disturbing news regarding Hospodar Grazziani."

Murmurs of "Are we too late?" and "Has he been assassinated?" ran through the assemblage.

Żółkiewski held up a hand and quieted the crowd. "The hospodar lives. However, the matter of putting him back on Moldavia's throne has grown more complicated." The hetman pulled in a wheezy breath. "Sultan Osman

II sent a delegation to Jassy, presumably to remove Grazziani from his throne.

"The hospodar feared they also planned to take his head, so rather than wait for our arrival, as planned, he took matters into his own hands and had the delegation imprisoned. And there is more. The citizens of Jassy took it upon themselves to slaughter every last Janissary. Consequently, the hospodar has fled."

Spirit of God! The Janissaries were the sultan's private property, elite troops that belonged to him and him alone. Killing them was akin to destroying his personal possessions. Putting Grazziani back on the throne had indeed grown more complicated.

"So he is on his way here with his army, yes?" a magnate posed. "When are they expected to arrive?"

The hetman was racked by a sudden coughing fit, and he quaffed a cup of wine his son Jan handed him. When he recovered himself and spoke, his voice was like a rasp scraping metal. "They are expected in a few days. I will ride out to meet him and escort him back to camp. That evening, we will hold a feast in his honor, and your presence is required."

Jacek directed himself to both hetmans. "How does the mission change now that we have little hope of restoring the hospodar to Moldavia's throne?" A burble had been growing louder, but it came to a halt with Jacek's question.

Koniecpolski looked to Żółkiewski, who gave Jacek a hawk-eyed look. "The mission remains the same. We will take Jassy, force the Ottomans to negotiate, and reinstall Grazziani."

Just like that? Bemused, Jacek blurted, "How are we to accomplish these ends?"

"The same way we intended to when we set out. With the help of Moldavian troops."

Skepticism prompted more questions to align themselves in Jacek's brain, but before he could voice them, Żółkiewski stopped him. "I said the situation was complicated, Colonel, not impossible. I am confident we will prevail. You should be too." He gave Jacek a tacit dismissal when he directed an unrelated remark to a different colonel.

Jacek's cheekbones heated with the rebuke.

Wronski caught his ear when he hissed to the man beside him, "Moldavians cannot be trusted. We should confiscate their provisions as punishment when they arrive."

Spoken like a thieving Lost Man. Jacek turned to look at him, dismissing the smirk that seemed ever present on Wronski's face. "I would not count on a fleeing army bringing much to confiscate." Likely, they would be looking to resupply at the expense of the Crown army.

Wronski chuffed and turned away.

As the question of the hetman's motivation circled back through Jacek's thoughts, the meeting came to a close. He took his time ambling after his fellows on their way out. *What did the hetman truly seek from this expedition?*

Outside, he skirted a canvas wall when a glove slid from his belt and hit the ground. He bent to pick it up, startled by Hetman Żółkiewski's harsh voice.

"The man is a fool!" Alarm shot through Jacek's veins. Was the hetman talking about *him*? He sharpened his hearing. "He panics, loses his senses, and in a few reckless hours of madness, he destroys years of work!" Not him, then.

Next came Koniecpolski's calmer tone. "W-why not t-tell them the truth?"

"What, that it was *Grazziani* who ordered those Janissaries murdered? That he then fled—not to our encampment, oh no—but to the Kingdom of Hungary so he could escape to the Holy Roman Empire and bypass our army entirely? No, I cannot. The truth would ravage morale. As it is, we are having a difficult time keeping this fragmented force moving in one direction. Imagine if they knew the nature of the man they are here to succor; they would flee themselves."

Jacek stood frozen. Stunned. He looked around and, confident no one lurked nearby, stepped closer to the canvas.

Another voice spoke up, and Jacek recognized the hetman's son, Jan. "He's an adventurer, and a spineless one at that, but never did I imagine he would run for the Empire!"

Koniecpolski now. "It is fortuitous that our s-soldiers in Chocim intercepted him and h-his officials." The crown field hetman must have been pacing, for his stuttering voice ebbed and flowed. Jacek caught bits about a Chocim contingent escorting Grazziani to Łozowa after Żółkiewski, upon learning of the hospodar's flight, had fired off several letters ordering Grazziani to return and report to the Polish camp. He also made out a disgusted huff and words that could have been "forces" and "disappointing."

Now came Żółkiewski's voice, defeated and thin. "And now all pretext of entering Moldavia legally and any hope of gaining military reinforcement from that country are shattered."

"Then praise God Grazziani is bringing his own force with him," said Jan. "But, Father, must you lavish a feast upon this poltroon?"

"I must. It is necessary to shore up the façade for our men and for Grazziani himself."

Koniecpolski snorted, but his voice grew muffled, and Jacek leaned toward the tent, outrage pulsing in his veins. What came next, however, was not about Moldavia's ruler, but shifted to an entirely different dilemma when Jan asked, "What of these escalating raids on Moldavian lands?"

"W-would that we could blame it on the Tatars, but our s-scouts have spied no raiding parties. Furthermore, the d-devils are light-skinned. Their victims c-call them Poles."

"Sounds like the work of the Lisowczycy," said Jan. Moments of silence stretched. "Could this mischief be at the hands of Captain Wronski?"

Żółkiewski began speaking once more, but approaching footsteps had Jacek striding quickly away.

Back in camp, he couldn't contain himself. His head fairly buzzed with all he had heard, so he sought out Henryk and Lesław for a tête-à-tête in his quarters. After he recounted the conversation he had overheard, both his friends' jaws hinged open.

"What?" Henryk barked. "This ... this rogue of a hospodar is the reason we are here! And he has the temerity to flee to the emperor? Despicable coward!"

Lesław shook his head. "That we left our families to come to the aid of this worm of a man ... it defies reason, Jacek."

Jacek grappled for answers, and apparently so did Lesław, for he continued while Henryk strode to and fro, leaving a track in Jacek's carpet. "Yet, while there may be better choices, he is likely the most expedient selection, yes? He is sympathetic to Poland—"

Henryk snorted. "Because Poland is willing to sacrifice its treasure to save his worthless hide."

"True," Lesław agreed, "but let us not forget he brings troops, and we will need them if we are to confront Iskender Pasha, yes?"

Jacek rubbed his nape. "Yes. But, spirit of God, this interminable war with the Ottoman Empire makes strange bedfellows of us all."

Jacek sat astride Heban the next day, sweat dripping from his brow as he tried to coax the gelding into a tight turn. The horse balked, and Jacek jerked the reins.

"Damn you! You're getting worse!" If that was even possible.

Henryk, mounted on his own steed, watched from twenty feet away. "Perhaps a different approach would garner the result you seek."

"I don't need your advice," Jacek growled.

"That is debatable. Consider, at the least, that you are as hardheaded as he."

Jacek nudged the horse's flanks with his knees. "What the devil does that mean?"

"Hardheaded? It means stubborn."

Jacek puffed out a breath and wiped his brow. "Have you nothing better to do than harass me?"

"Not really." Henryk made a show of yawning. "Sitting in camp is infernally boring, and we don't even have the women to distract ourselves with, as you predicted."

"I shall give you something to do, then. Go find Filip and bring him back."

"Ha! Simply because you are now *Colonel* Dąbrowski in charge of the crown grand hetman's regiment does not mean you can order me about."

Jacek snorted. "Whether I command the hetman's regiment or not is irrelevant. As you are *Captain* Kalinowski, I most certainly can order you about."

"I suppose you have a valid point." Henryk turned his horse's head but stopped short. "Do my eyes deceive me, or is that an army approaching?"

The crown grand hetman and his retinue had departed the encampment early, and the place had been thrumming with anticipation ever since. Jacek swiveled his head in the direction Henryk was looking. On the horizon, a wide string of horse and footmen advanced, outlined against the summer sky. In the fore flew Żółkiewski's banners. The great hetman and his guards appeared to be escorting the hospodar and his entourage toward the encampment. Jacek slipped his looking glass from its leather pouch and lifted it to his eye.

"What do you see?" Henryk's voice had taken on urgency.

"I expect this is what we've been waiting for. The hospodar and his army are at last arriving." He lowered the glass and grinned at his second. "We should have a proper army now."

"Do we? I reckon there are about six hundred. Where are the rest?"

Jacek raised the glass to his eye once more. The first rows of infantry and cavalry had crested a rise. Where Jacek expected wave upon wave of men to follow, there was naught but empty ground.

"There must be more coming," he declared, his voice betraying the hope threaded through it. "They have many wagons and are simply lagging behind."

An old proverb popped into his head: *Hope is the mother of the stupid.*

Wordlessly, he and Henryk waited. View after view through the glass did not change the number of approaching men. Jacek put away the glass, and he and Henryk rode toward the front of the camp, where Hetman Koniecpolski awaited the incoming force.

331

Jacek guided Heban to his side. "This must be the hospodar's vanguard, yes?" That explained the small number.

Koniecpolski's stoic gaze remained fixed on the approaching soldiers. "No. This is the f-full force the hospodar is b-bringing with him."

Jacek's heart, buoyed only moments earlier, plummeted to his knees.

CHAPTER 33

Prelude

Jacek marched through the encampment toward Żółkiewski's pavilion with Henryk and Lesław trotting in his wake.

Henryk increased his pace, catching him up. "Why the devil are we sprinting?"

"So that, unlike last night, we can get a good vantage point." The feast had been crowded with a plethora of dignitaries and courtiers who had accompanied Grazziani, consequently squeezing Jacek and the other Crown colonels to the outer fringes. The celebration had been nothing more than a grand display of pomp and courtesy for the benefit of the hospodar … and, Jacek reckoned, to present the pretext of a united front to the audience.

Today's war council would be the first attended by Grazziani, and Jacek wanted to witness every moment. Since the hospodar's arrival the day before, the talk of the camp had centered on naught but the diminished force he had brought with him. Christ! Diminished was far too feeble a word to describe going from an expectation of fifteen thousand fighting troops to six hundred! Better that the hospodar had arrived with more warriors than his skinny-necked politicians. As it was, among the six hundred, a large part were not of Moldavia: they were mercenary Serbs.

"You *always* have a good vantage point!" Henryk quipped. "You tower over everyone else."

As they neared the pavilion, so did Grazziani's entourage. In its center was the hospodar himself, a bearded man dressed in embroidered silks, wearing a high-cuffed kolpak adorned with colorful plumage that waved as he walked.

Cursing under his breath at having missed his opportunity to garner a close spot, Jacek halted his lord-brothers in deference to the dignitaries. He hadn't noticed Wronski standing off to one side until the Elear darted ahead of Jacek, clearly intent on arriving ahead of Grazziani and his retinue. Jacek snagged the Lost Man's belt and jerked, causing Wronksi to stumble into position beside Jacek.

"What the devil are you doing?" Wronski hissed.

Jacek hissed back. "Helping you appear respectful, Captain Wronski, like the rest of us. No doubt you did not notice the hospodar and his courtiers, or you would have stopped to let them pass, yes?"

Wronski 's face was as red as his crimson żupan and devoid of his usual oily smile. Jacek fought a smirk.

Grazziani caught Jacek's eye and gave him a subtle dip of his head. His troupe shuffled toward the tent, and as the back of the contingent drew even with Jacek and his men, a guard turned. His gaze shot to Wronski, and his eyes widened. His attention riveted on Grazziani, Wronski didn't notice the peculiar reaction. Meanwhile, the guard yanked at another man's sleeve, pulling him from the entourage and bringing them both to a halt. That man, whose luxuriant attire suggested he hailed from the Moldavian noble class, raised his eyes and fastened on Wronski as the guard spoke into his ear with urgency. Grazziani and his retinue, meanwhile, filed into the tent.

Wronski looked back, presumably to snarl at Jacek, and his gaze flew to the two men speaking in a hasty hush. Moving like a whip, he whirled and hurried away, vanishing between a series of tents. The nobleman fired off a command, and the guard summoned a companion. Hands on the hilts of their blades, they dashed in Wronski's wake.

Jacek wasted no time in presenting himself to the dignitary, whose gaze followed the guards. "Colonel Dąbrowski at your service. It seems you have lost your escort. May my men and I have the pleasure?"

The fellow jumped. Jacek gave him a reassuring smile, and he eased. "Yes, Colonel. Yes, thank you."

They walked side by side, Henryk and Lesław falling in behind. "Your men seem to be in pursuit of someone they know," Jacek nudged.

The dignitary's answer was cautious and couched. "Simply a man they may have recognized."

Jacek kept the smile in place. "Hopefully not because he committed a crime against them … or you."

The dignitary's eyes bolted to Jacek's, then quickly hooded. "A crime? Ah, but 'crime' is a relative term, is it not, Colonel?"

Before Jacek could carefully craft a question about what the devil he meant by his ambiguous remark, they were beckoned to the tent by one of the hetman's attendants. "The hetman bids you hurry. The council is about to begin."

Within the walls of the tent, the air stifled one's breath, choked as it was with heat and sweat and the press of men's bodies. Jacek propelled his charge forward, thereby carving a space for himself, Henryk, and Lesław close to the hetman's desk. The dignitary bowed his head in thanks and moved toward his own colleagues, leaving Jacek to ponder what had transpired with the fellow's guards and Wronski.

With a call to order, Jacek pushed the question and the oppressive atmosphere to the back of his mind, concentrating instead on the three men conducting the meeting. Pinned to a stand was a crudely drawn map that displayed Jassy, the village of Cecora on the western shore of the Prut River, and the expanse on the river's east bank.

Koniecpolski quickly described their plan to move the Crown troops to that expanse—the same ground where Zamoyski had encamped twenty-five years prior.

Henryk leaned to his ear. "Just as you surmised, Jacek."

When the audience posed questions about what they planned to do once they got there, the two hetmans seemed to dodge. Jan Żółkiewski remained in a quiet corner as a growing buzz passed through the crowd.

Żółkiewski held up his hand to quiet them all. "This location has many strategic advantages, such as giving us the ability to block the road to Jassy, thereby keeping Iskender Pasha and his Turks from reaching it."

"Is this meant to aid in restoring Hospodar Grazziani to the throne?" one confused colonel asked. "And if so, how long must we remain to ensure he is secure as the Moldavian leader?"

Żółkiewski ignored the question and proceeded to describe the terrain.

The colonel held up his forefinger. "But—"

"I am not finished," Żółkiewski snapped. "This position also delivers tactical advantages. Besides offering favorable conditions for a camp of our size, the bend of the river presents a natural fortification. Should it become necessary, we will have room to maneuver in the foreground. The flat ground is favorable for charges by our hussars."

Grazziani stepped forward and pointed to the map. "There is also a forest, Crown Grand Hetman, which will give the enemy cover. I would like to propose a different strategy."

Żółkiewski dismissed the comment with a wave of his hand. "The woods are not so thick as that. Remember, I have been there."

"A quarter of a century ago," Grazziani rejoined.

Żółkiewski ignored the remark. "Furthermore, we *want* them to see the strength of our army. This will force Iskender Pasha to the negotiating table."

"With all due respect, Hetman," Grazziani seemed to grind out his words through clenched teeth, "the most effective way to get Pasha to the negotiating table is to strike now, while he is weak, before he has a chance to add to his numbers." Grazziani stabbed his finger against the map. "We capture Tehinia and the Danube crossings, then on to Kilia and Akkerman."

"You mean to seize Bender?" a member of the audience cried. "With our present force?"

The man echoed Jacek's thoughts. Attempts had been made to capture Tehinia Fortress—renamed Bender by the Turks since they had taken possession nearly a hundred years before—but none had succeeded. Without the fifteen thousand Moldavians they had expected, how the devil were they supposed to take the fortress? Never mind pushing their way beyond to Akkerman and Kilia.

Jacek looked around at the gathered faces and saw as much doubt for the venture reflected there as what lurked inside of him. Another magnate army had followed after Grazziani's entrance yesterday, with four hundred Cossacks and two hundred infantry, but their arrival had been overshadowed by the hospodar's disappointing numbers.

More magnates would trickle in, along with Lisowczycy banners, but even so, this fractured group was more closely resembling a relief force, not a true army that could take a fortress and sweep through Moldavia to the Black Sea coast.

Jacek's mind rebelled against the plan for personal reasons too. Even if their force grew by five times, he had no desire to pursue Iskender Pasha deep into Moldavia, for it meant more time away. Consequently, he found himself praying Żółkiewski's gamble would bear fruit. A show of force that led to negotiations and no clashes would speed his return to Żółkiew and Oliwia, where he would be present when his child was born.

Murmurs grew to a din of voices, and the courtesy that had prevailed at the outset of the council dissolved, with men shouting at one another. Again.

Koniecpolski rapped his *bułava*—his mace—on the tabletop, and the burble died down.

Not for long, however, as Grazziani seized the opportunity to plead with Żółkiewski. "Crown Grand Hetman, you must strike before the Tatars join Iskender Pasha's force. He is at his most diminished now, and you can defeat him once and for all!"

Żółkiewski eyed the hospodar. "We have limited resources, and besieging the fortress will waste time and deplete those resources. Furthermore, the use of force in our present circumstances is unnecessary and will not come to pass."

While debate continued, neither side gave up his position. In the end, the supreme commander of the Crown forces prevailed, much to Jacek's relief.

Hours later, Jacek sat at his table, guilt tugging at him as he penned a long overdue letter to Oliwia. Filip had once more disappeared—presumably to be part of Wronski's camp—and Jacek admonished himself for not taking a more assertive stance with his brother-in-law. But with his new duties as pułkownik of Żółkiewski's regiment, the ever-growing demand on his time spent among the acrimonious magnates, and his responsibility to his own men, he had little vigor to apply to the problem.

In his missive, he kept the subject of her brother brief, instead pouring out some of his frustrations.

These magnate-colonels often seem more interested in their own ambitions than in rallying to the crown grand hetman's lead. They relish asserting who is right among themselves over the most insignificant details, and they feed off the enmity. Discussing strategy can be exhausting. I worry that when the time comes, factions will not proceed with accord.

Each private army making up Żółkiewski's force seemed to spin in its own orbit. The dynamic troubled Jacek. While skilled soldiers made up their ranks, their loyalties were divided between the magnate they served and the crown grand hetman. Consequently, the cohesiveness of past campaigns was nowhere to be found. Jacek's confidence that Żółkiewski held the power, the will to draw them to him, was wavering. The hetman appeared too weary—or was it weak?—to wield his authority. Had Liwi been right about the hetman's advanced age impacting his ability to lead? Had Jacek placed too much faith in the crown grand hetman's capabilities?

In truth, some of the blame for the lack of accord could have been laid at the hetmans' feet. At times, their endeavor reminded Jacek of a headless beast, and he found himself sympathizing with the magnates. They had estates to worry after and protect. While they were on what many whispered was a fool's errand, their lands lay vulnerable to Tatar raids, for their private armies were here, in Moldavia, to protect a hospodar without a country, whose sole concern was his own neck and prestige.

Jacek twiddled his quill, contemplating what more to say. What he would not mention was his growing concern over their limited victuals. They had been fortunate so far because the land was fertile and the weather warm, allowing them to forage. But if the campaign stretched into fall? Winter?

He told himself it would not come to pass, that the hetmans seemed unperturbed, and that he was wasting unnecessary worry. He would take their lead. Determination set, he bent back to the letter but fell asleep before he could finish.

The following day brought good news as they decamped Łozowa for Cecora: Stefan Chmielecki and his eight hundred soldiers marched in. Two days later, on the eleventh of September, before they set up camp on the left bank of the Prut, Walenty Rogowski rode in with twelve banners of Lisowczycy. Fifteen hundred horse! Between the two forces, they added twenty-three hundred men, and the army swelled to nine thousand.

Jacek reveled at Rogowski's arrival for more than the banners he brought. At last, Wronski was no longer Jacek's subordinate. Not that Wronski had ever *behaved* like a subordinate, but now he was officially someone else's festering backside thorn. The only exchanges Jacek planned to have with the miscreant in the future would revolve around Filip. The mystery of the dignitary's guards' pursuit of Wronski had not revealed itself, and while Jacek's curiosity remained piqued, he was satisfied to dust his hands and turn his back on this particular Lost Man.

Filip wiped his forearm over his brow once more as he drank watered wine from a skin … a skin he had borrowed from the Biaska camp. Fresh off an hours-long drill, he was spent, and he plopped down on a boulder in Captain Wronski's camp. The men around him either grumbled or held their tongues.

Since the arrival of the Lisowczycy's commander, Walenty Rogowski, Filip had noticed two changes: the captain and his men stayed in camp now—no more mysterious excursions, like before—though perhaps being tethered had more to do with *where* they were encamped. Filip could not be certain, and his questions went unanswered.

The second and more drastic change was the blackened mood in camp. Filip turned over whether this shift was a result of Wronski's own demeanor transforming into a simmering gale. No more easy smiles, no more quips. The man stomped about, dressing down his subordinates whether they merited a tongue-lashing or not.

Which was likely why, when one of Rogowski's messengers strolled into their midst looking for the captain, one of Wronski's men ordered Filip to fetch him.

"He's less likely to bite your head off," the man explained.

Filip puffed out a breath, stood, and dusted off his breeches before trotting to Wronski's tent. He bid the messenger follow. The flap was open, and Filip looked inside. Wronski was in his linen undershirt, his back to Filip, and he hunched over a table.

"Captain, someone—"

Wronski wheeled, his face contorted with fury. "How dare you step into my tent without warning!" His movement caused a golden object hanging about his neck to fly, and he swiftly tucked it under his shirt.

Filip recoiled, blurting, "I'm not in your tent!" His eyes snagged on a shiny object on the table, then skimmed over several more. They appeared to be bits of precious jewelry and objects made of silver plate.

Wronski stepped forward, obliterating Filip's view as he crowded him. "Why. Are. You. Bothering. Me?"

His cheeks burning with the rebuke, Filip lowered his gaze, and it landed on a gold chain about Wronski's neck, one he had never noticed before. "Commander Rogowski has sent a messenger who wishes to see you. He's right here."

Wronski filled his chest with an annoyed inhale and bumped Filip out of the way, dropping the tent flap behind him. "Next time," he ground out, "you come to me first before dragging a messenger with you. And you remain outside the tent, do you hear? I don't care if the flap's open! Now get out of my sight!"

340

Only too eager to oblige, Filip hastened away. Behind him, Wronski turned his ire on the messenger.

Perhaps it was time Filip headed back to Biaska's camp, where he had returned to sharing a tent with the squires. The drills were over for today, and being among Wronski's men did not offer the revelry it once had. As he approached the temporary corral, Wronski's dark horse lifted her head as if greeting him. He ducked inside the pen and strode to her.

"Such a beautiful girl." He stroked the horse, and as he did so, he took in the features of this magnificent combat horse. What a lovely addition she would be to Biaska's stock. His fingers paused on her brand, a mess of a thing that he wondered at. How could anyone identify whose property she was?

Curiosity pulled him to a different horse. That one held a distinctive brand that matched others he inspected.

A stable boy jerked his chin at him. "What might you be doing there, my lord?"

Filip shrugged, feigning casualness. "I hadn't noticed Captain Wronski's marks before. Someone has done a thorough job. Would that be you branding them?" He flashed the boy a grin.

The boy blushed. "I help, sir. But someday, I'll be doing it on my own."

Filip ambled back to the mare. "Yes, I expect you will." He pointed at her brand and chuckled. "But what happened here? It appears someone's hand slipped."

"I don't know, sir. I wasn't there when the captain acquired her."

"He came by her near the Black Trail in the early summer, yes?"

The boy shook his head. "No, sir. In Podolia, near Halicz, in early spring. I know because we were encamped nearby when he returned with her early one morning. Said he found her roaming about and reckoned she needed a home. She's a beaut, eh?" He patted the mare's flank.

If Wronski took her from Tatars, as he alleges, they were outside Halicz. Highly unlikely that time of year. So why lie? Filip's mind whirred as he smiled at the lad. "Yes, she certainly is."

CHAPTER 34

Interlude

The early morning air carried a crisp tinge of autumn as Jacek brought the looking glass to his eye. He scanned but could not pierce the thick forest across the Prut. They had finally established their camp near Cecora, on the left bank of the river, and the location was as the hetman said it would be. Except for the damned trees that seemed to move. Jacek couldn't shake the feeling of being watched, and it unnerved him. The hetman's scouts reported that the enemy was unaware of their movements and still at a distance away. Surprise would be on their side, but how reliable were those reports?

If they had planned to force the enemy to negotiate by overwhelming him with their numbers, Jacek feared they had failed. Four hundred more Moldavians had arrived, but no more forces were coming. Nine thousand was as large as their number would be for the duration of the campaign. He doubted even doubling that number would have infused him with confidence. Nevertheless, Żółkiewski maintained they had as many men as they needed and the pasha would negotiate. Soon they would end the mission and return.

Talk around the camp, however, indicated the men were less certain of the outcome. Restiveness fomented among the factions, with hints of defection. The magnates' fear of a Tatar invasion like the one at Orynin continued to grow despite intelligence to the contrary. Spies and scouts concurred: no large Tatar forces were on the move.

Jacek continued scanning the woods. The motion might have been a figment of his imagination, but what if it was real? Raiding had intensified; perhaps it was the mysterious marauders watching them, targeting them. There was only one way to find out. Jacek headed back to muster a squad to investigate.

Mounted on Heban, he stood in the midst of twenty men, about to impart his instructions when shouts erupted from the edges of the army's encampment.

"What the devil is going on?" Henryk yelled.

"Let's find out. You, Dawid, and Lesław with me." Jacek urged Heban toward the ruckus.

It led them toward the servants' camp. A retainer ran at them, flailing his arms. "The victuals! The feed! Our people! Gone!"

Jacek stopped beside the distraught man. "The servants fled with our supplies?"

"No! They took them!" The man babbled in Ruthenian, and Jacek couldn't follow what he said.

"Take us to them," he ordered, and the man scampered back in the direction from which he'd come.

They arrived in the servants' camp to find a knot of people weeping among a group of reiters. The soldiers were trying to calm them in vain.

Jacek dismounted and grasped a Polish servant's shoulder. "What happened?"

"They took them!" he cried.

"Took whom?"

"Our c-companions. The horse feed. The gunpowder. Our foodstuffs!"

"Who took them?"

"Tatars! The devils crept into camp and carried off our people and provisions! We only escaped because we were working elsewhere."

Jacek raised the looker, and his blood ran to ice. On the river's right bank, more than trees moved. The familiar shapes of Tatars clad in tan or blue-gray tunics and pointed caps moved in and out of the shadowed forest.

Some walked horses carrying sacks, others rode with small bundles, and another group sat astride their mounts holding ropes tethered to lines of bound captives. In the glass, he caught one pale face as it looked toward the safety of the right bank with heart-wrenching longing, misery, and terror.

The face was his.

The visage transformed into that of a young woman, and the emotions he had just witnessed were amplified in her expression. Tears coursed down her cheeks. She was jerked sideways by the rope secured around her neck, and she disappeared into the thick foliage.

She was gone. Forever.

The sight nearly brought Jacek to his knees. His breath caught in his chest, and when it came, it came so rapidly black spots danced before his eyes. His head was light, yet voices screamed inside it. Beside him, someone grasped his shoulder and pulled him away.

"Come." Henryk's familiar voice sounded in his head. "There is naught we can do now."

"We must go after them." Jacek heard himself pant, though it sounded so far away. "Do you understand what will happen to those people?"

Henryk's answer came swiftly, and it was heavy and grim. "Only too well. But we're not prepared, and if we give chase, we will do those people no good, for we will be slaughtered or captured ourselves."

Shame swamped Jacek as he let Henryk lead him away without protest. Jacek had always run to a fight, not away from it.

Only as he sat in the war council an hour later did he discover what Henryk meant, and his shame receded. He leaned forward as Żółkiewski blamed the scouts' reconnaissance.

"They got their information wrong," he admitted, his snowy-white head bowed. "And now we have lost a thousand servants."

Not only was Iskender Pasha's army close, but it was larger than originally thought. Added to his numbers were ten thousand Tatars led by Dewlet-Girej of Crimea and Kantymir Murza of the Nogai and the Budjak Horde—the same man who had devastated Podolia after the Battle of Orynin in 1618.

Henryk leaned to his ear. "Grazziani was right to warn us about the Tatars coming together with the Ottomans."

Jacek nodded. "I fear the best opportunity to overpower them has flown." Grazziani's war council plea had come nine days ago, and during that time Iskender Pasha had grown stronger. Yet Jacek couldn't disagree with Żółkiewski's decision to hold. Attacking Tehinia meant a siege. Even if by some miracle they had conquered the fortress quickly, they would have encountered the Tatar forces on their way to Akkerman and Kilia. Victory over the Turks would have proved nigh on impossible.

When asked about the supplies and how they were to replenish them and the servants, Żółkiewski evaded the question. Jacek, his arms crossed, dug his fingers into his biceps to contain his frustration. How could they solve the problem if he wasn't even willing to acknowledge it? Since when had the great hetman avoided the difficult questions?

Mounted on Heban the following day, his exasperation boiling over with the headstrong gelding, Jacek looked up and focused on one point across the river as he pushed three breaths through his lungs. Sweat ran in rivulets from his bare head. His armor hung heavy on his body, and he wanted nothing more than to pull everything off and plunge naked into the river. But Heban needed to get used to weight, so Jacek wiped his forehead and prepared for the next go.

"Is it possible I am breaking in a mule?" he huffed at the horse.

Dawid, astride his own mount as he practiced with a kopia, guffawed.

Heban's ear cocked back. Jacek gave the reins a playful tug. "You understand me, don't you, you stubborn beast?"

The blare of a trumpet had him whipping his head toward the center of the encampment, where the hetmans' quarters lay. Then his gaze swung back to Dawid, whose gaping mouth mirrored Jacek's.

Dawid gripped the lance. "That's a battle muster!" He turned his horse and headed for the call, and Jacek quickly fell in behind.

345

As they approached the trumpet, one of Koniecpolski's men-at-arms windmilled an arm and pointed toward the far side of the camp. "Rogowski's camp is under attack! Go!"

"Tatars! Over there!" another soldier cried as more funneled into the tight space. Now pacholiks appeared in various lines of sight, directing soldiers toward the Lost Men's camp.

Filip!

Jacek jumped Heban over a cluster of baskets as a wide-eyed servant looked on. A banner snapped high in the wind, and Koniecpolski signaled with his buzdygan. Jacek unsheathed his sabre and tore ahead. The dull popping of gunfire sounded. Smoke curled up his nose, followed by the stench of blood and fear.

"Right behind you!" someone called.

He glanced over his shoulder, and relief surged through him at the sight of his companions. Dawid, Henryk, Marcin, and Lesław flanked him on either side like a flight of geese in a V formation.

As they neared the two hetmans, the chaos of battle came into view. Dust and smoke hung heavy in the Lost Men's camp, making the defending Elears and the enemy appear as writhing daylight wraiths.

Filip was nowhere in sight.

Koniecpolski directed Jacek's band toward the far side, where Tatars clambered up the bank like a swarm of beetles. Cutting through the center of camp, where fighting was at its heaviest, would only slow him down.

"To me!" Raising his sabre, Jacek jumped Heban to the outer edge of the camp just as a Tatar and his horse crashed into a tent next to him. He circled the camp on the edges of the fray. The air cleared, exposing the invading Mongols, before thickening once more. Pulse pounding in his ears, he raced to confront them. The sound of men yelling, horses braying, and metal clashing was a muffled din in his head.

Heban reared as they smacked into a pair of horses, nearly unseating Jacek. The horse came down hard, and the momentum of Jacek's sabre swing accelerated. The blade sliced through fabric, muscle, and bone, and a shriek filled Jacek's ears. The Tatar pulled away.

Meanwhile, Heban came to a complete standstill. Jacek nudged with his knees, dug in his spurs, cursed loudly, and the horse swung his back end to the side so they sat broadside to a Tatar with his blade held high above Jacek's head. The perfect target.

Damned horse!

No time for the pistol.

Jacek lunged, chopping at the enemy horse's forehead, and the beast screamed and bucked to the side at the same moment Heban once again swung his backside. The Tatar's curved blade slashed air.

Something, or someone, thudded against Jacek's back. He looked up in time to catch the glint of a blade plunging toward him. A jerk to the side, and the weapon glanced off his shoulder. Jacek grabbed the man's arms and pulled them over his shoulders as though he donned a cloak, hauling him from his saddle. Power surged in his veins, and he slammed his foe to the ground. The man grunted and disappeared under hooves.

"They're fleeing!" Dawid yelled, and Jacek squinted into the dusty fog. The whoops of the Tatars pierced the air.

"Chase them!" another shouted.

Chest heaving, Jacek urged his horse, but Heban wouldn't move. Had he not been astride the blasted animal when the call came, he would have gladly traded him for Jarosława. Old as she was, she was far more reliable.

"Hold!" came a command.

A panting Henryk reined in his horse beside Jacek. "Koniecpolski says not to pursue lest it's a trap."

Hand cupping his mouth, Jacek relayed the command. "Stop! Let them go."

"It's a rout!" a soldier yelled, and cheers went up.

"Look for survivors," Jacek bellowed. He yanked on his reins, pulling Heban's head to the right. The horse's body followed. "Oh, by your leave, you damned horse!"

Jacek guided them toward the site where the heaviest fighting had taken place, Heban fighting his grip the entire way.

"No!" someone screamed behind them, and Jacek yanked the horse around—or tried to—but the beast wouldn't cooperate. So Jacek swiveled his head toward the commotion.

Lying on his back in the dirt, someone held up his arm to protect himself from a Tatar looming above him, poised to pierce his heart.

Recognition dawned in less time than it took to blink an eye.

"Filip!" Jacek roared and leaped from his saddle, but Heban sidestepped, and Jacek landed with a *whomp* that stole the air from his lungs.

Helplessly, Jacek watched as the blade came down.

CHAPTER 35

Victories and Losses

Time slowed. Sweat and blood and dust blurred Jacek's vision as he lay prone on his stomach. His body was numb and would not obey his brain's commands until at last he lifted a feeble hand toward his brother-in-law. Too far. A silent rasp escaped his lungs.

A whirl of motion darted into his peripheral vision. A grunt, a groan, and the fuzzy form of the enemy crumpled to the ground. Jacek hoisted himself onto his hands and knees only to slump to the ground once more. He couldn't breathe. *Push through it!*

Suddenly, a hand appeared, and he grasped it. It pulled, and he lumbered to his feet on wobbly legs.

"You will live," Henryk said dryly.

Jacek blinked until his vision cleared. Before him, Filip sat on his haunches, head down.

"Filip!" Jacek cried. Relief swamped him when the boy looked up.

He was disheveled, and tears tracked through the dirt on his face. He quickly dropped his head between his arms. Beside him lay a dead Tatar. At his feet stood Wronski, bloody blade at his side as he cocked his head at Filip. "You are unharmed, yes?"

Filip nodded weakly.

Wronski leaned down to wipe his blade on the dead man's tunic, then glanced over at Jacek.

Jacek staggered toward him and held out his hand. "I am in your debt."

Wronski clasped his hand and grinned. "It is always a pleasure to rid the world of one more infidel. Besides, we need as many soldiers as we can get." He jerked his head toward Filip, who continued to squat on the ground.

Releasing Wronski, Jacek crouched down beside Filip, an arm slung over his knee. He was suddenly aware his back throbbed. "Will you return to Biaska's camp with us?" he murmured.

A headshake and a sniffle were his only response.

"Filip," Wronski barked, and Filip's head snapped up. "Our camp is in complete disarray. Perhaps it is best if you went with your brother." Wronski extended his hand. Filip grasped it and let Wronski pull him to his feet. Jacek hauled himself up beside them.

His brother-in-law took angry swipes at his face and looked first at Wronski then at Jacek. Shame burned in his eyes. "It is my duty to help as I can here, where I am needed."

Jacek hung his head for a beat. The stab to his heart stung, like a wound doused with wodka. At last, he looked into Filip's gray eyes, nodded, and pivoted toward Henryk, who held Heban's reins.

"There is little use holding his reins. That blasted horse does not move when you want him to," Jacek groused. He paused and looked to his left, then to his right, alarm rising from his gut. "Where are the others? Are they all right?"

"We are right behind you, and we are fine," Marcin called as he came up beside them. Dawid and Lesław fell in.

Jacek sagged with gratitude.

Marcin elbowed him. "You, however, look as though a horse ran you over."

"A horse did," Henryk snorted.

Jacek mounted, and pain shot up his back, making him wince. "I must have hit the ground harder than I realized."

"I believe the horse's kick to your back after you fell is what caused the damage."

Jacek's mouth hinged open. "Heban did that?"

"That is the way it appeared, and on purpose too. I suspect he is none too fond of you, but then again, few are."

"Humph. The dislike is mutual."

In contrast to the evening before, when their people and provisions had been looted, spirits soared in the Commonwealth encampment. They had beaten back Iskender Pasha's army.

Emboldened by the victory, Crown Grand Hetman Żółkiewski hammered his fist into his palm as he called for swift, decisive action at the war council. The fiery speech inspired—and put a blush of vitality back in the man's cheeks.

"Tomorrow, we defend Poland. Tomorrow, we turn back the infidels who would put their yoke on us. Tomorrow, with God and justice on our side, we attack and fight the good fight. Victory will be ours. We will reclaim our folk and all that was taken from us."

Jacek nodded his agreement. Not only would they recover their people and their provisions, but they would capture the enemy's. If their folk had already been whisked away, they would use their captives for barter.

The gathering cheered. Hope floated on the air, so palpable one could reach out and touch it. Jacek could practically taste victory on his tongue, and its taste was sweet. His heart lifted.

Żółkiewski displayed a smile that reached his brown eyes, sparkling with determination—the first of its kind Jacek had seen since the hetman's arrival at Śledziówka. Here was the hetman Jacek had revered throughout his military career: resolute, confident, brilliant. He was back.

Jacek stood as straight and still as a tent stake while both hetmans unveiled tomorrow's plan.

"The Tatar cavalry will swarm, so we will employ two tabors, like the Hussite war wagons of old. These rolling stocks will be constructed tomorrow morning, they will act as mobile fortresses on each side to protect our flanks, and they will be manned by infantry and artillery. On the left, Wolmar Farensbach will lead. To the right, Teofil Szemberg."

Koniecpolski went on to explain that the central formation would act as the main striking force and would be made up of five columns of cavalry regiments.

Yes! Hussars front and center! "And who will flank the cavalry?"

The hetmans glanced at one another before Żółkiewski turned toward Jacek. "The tabors *are* the flanks."

A volley of questions came at once, and before Jacek could utter the next question, someone posed it for him. "With all due respect, won't that be too tight?"

Żółkiewski assured them they would have room to maneuver and went on to explain that the middle column was his regiment, to be commanded by Jacek. Jacek's hand twitched against his thigh at the sound of his name.

Added Koniecpolski, "Commander Rogowski's regiment and the Moldavians will bolster the right rolling stock's rear, with Stefan Chmielecki's force filling the same role on the left. Infantry not defending the mobile fortresses will align behind an embankment at the very back."

This caught Jacek off guard. How the devil could the infantry be effective if they were hindered by an embankment? As it was, they were light on infantry, and fifteen hundred of those men would be dedicated to the mobile fortresses. "Begging your pardon, Grand Hetman, but should they not be in *front* of the embankment? The obstacle could slow them down when they are most needed."

"That is what *I* said, but he won't listen," someone muttered behind Jacek.

"No, Colonel," Żółkiewski replied crisply. "It has been worked out, and this gives us our best chance for victory."

"See there?" the voice said. "Useless to argue."

Jacek, Henryk, and Lesław left the council on foot, and Lesław bubbled with excitement. "The hetman's plan is brilliant! With the husaria front and center, we will smash the enemy's front line." He pounded a fist into a palm. "We will overrun the sons of bitches and open the way for the rest of the army, just as we've done before. We are unstoppable."

352

Except the "rest of the army" will be stuck behind a rampart.

When Jacek did not respond, Lesław nudged his elbow. "What's troubling you?"

Jacek let out a sigh. "The plan is innovative and serves as a testament to Żółkiewski's military mind, but it is also inflexible. Its implementation is complicated and leaves little room for error. I'm not convinced this patchwork army can work together as one cohesive force, which is what we need if the plan is to succeed. The path to victory allows for no variation."

In short, it was an ambitious gamble with men's lives on the line.

"How is it inflexible?" asked Henryk.

"Everything depends upon the rolling fortresses remaining intact. Now picture these fortifications: each one contains four rows of wagons fifty-to-sixty long, loaded with cannon and hook guns and seven or eight hundred artillerymen, infantrymen, and bowmen. Each wagon is harnessed to a team of horses, with the heads of those horses almost touching the back of the wagon in front. Then the carts are chained together one after the other. Yes, they are formidable, nearly impenetrable, but they are also cumbersome, and everything must work in unison. One flaw, one opening, and the enemy can swarm in and cause havoc, yes? And if he does, imagine the difficulty of unchaining the carts and unharnessing the horses while under attack. Chaos.

"Between each of these moving fortresses are our five cavalry regiments. Expose the tabors and you expose the cavalry. If the fortresses veer, they might squeeze the regiments between them and hamper maneuverability even further."

So much could go wrong.

Henryk seemed to grind on what Jacek had said. "So every combatant, from the soldier manning the hook guns on the wagons to the reiter supporting the hussars at the rear, must fulfill his role with the utmost precision and operate with the rest of the army in perfect step."

Jacek pointed his finger at Henryk. "Exactly. What if there is confusion about those steps? The ability to maneuver, to adjust to changing circumstances, to regroup are all severely limited."

Lesław frowned. "One weakness puts the entire formation at risk."

353

Henryk scratched his stubbled chin. "Being confined between these tabors could hamper the calvary. The husaria will be at the front, and we are most effective when we spread out and gallop into the enemy's defenses at high speed with kopie raised. If we are compressed? Our line narrows. And when we ram a kopia through an enemy, will we have room to double back and grab up a fresh one? It could be a lot to overcome."

Was it possible Żółkiewski had omitted these scenarios when he had formulated the scheme? Was he still capable of considering every angle?

That stubborn weed of doubt continued to spread its roots, invading the cracks of Jacek's conviction.

Back in his tent, he turned over more questions. Could *he* devise a better plan in haste? Likely not, with the unknown variables in play.

He raised an inner shield to cushion the scenarios ricocheting through his brain and turned his attention to the critical task at hand. Seated on his cot, he polished one of the nadziaks that had been long stored and checked the inscription he had etched into the wood handle. Wrapping and tying it in a length of linen cloth, he made his way to the squires' tent, where he found his brother-in-law alone, seated outside on a stool, staring into an open campfire.

Filip looked up as he approached and tilted his head toward the side of the tent. "There's another stool there."

Jacek unfolded the seat, carefully laid his package on the ground, and focused on a twirling flame. "Where are your companions?"

Filip scrubbed the patchy scruff on his jaw. "I can't say."

"Can't or won't?"

"Yes."

Long moments passed in companionable silence. Jacek shifted his weight on the stool. "Why didn't you go with them?"

"I did not think I would be fit company."

"Probably for the best that you remained in camp rather than spending the evening as they are."

Filip canted his head toward him. "Would that be so bad?"

"While lying with a member of the fairer sex is undeniably diverting, we will all need our strength and our wits for the battle tomorrow. Women have a way of sapping both."

In Jacek's peripheral vision, Filip's Adam's apple bobbed. "I thought the squires were intended to stay behind the embankment with the infantry."

Jacek turned his head and squared his gaze on Filip. "They are, but the unexpected has a way of occurring on a battlefield, and when it does, it happens rather rapidly. Should the Ottomans overrun us, they will not stop at the rampart simply because it exists or spare a line of young men because they were not engaged in the fight at the outset. They will sweep through camp like locusts, take what they deem a prize, and that which they determine is of no value, they will destroy."

Filip glanced back at the fire. "Captain Wronski has invited me to take part, to stand with his banner tomorrow."

"The hetmans have ordered the squires and servants to remain back."

"What if I want to see the battle?" Filip's voice held a thoughtfulness, not a challenge.

"You will see plenty from your vantage point." Jacek lifted the bundle, laid it across his lap, and began untying it. "In the event you need to defend yourself or come to the aid of a companion, you might find this useful."

He lifted the nadziak, and Filip raised his hands to accept it. "What is this?"

"It is the weapon you wielded during the battle for Biaska, when you came to your sister's aid. It brought you good luck then, and it will do the same for you tomorrow."

Filip's eyes widened as he turned the war hammer over. "But it was broken."

"I had it repaired. See the metal bands around the shaft there? Better than new."

"You've kept it all this time?"

Jacek nodded. "I was waiting for the right time to give it to you."

Filip let out a soft chuckle. "I seem to remember being so small I nearly knocked myself out with it ... and that was the closest I came to stopping anyone."

"Your courage that day made up for your lack of size." Jacek brought his focus back to the fire.

More moments unfurled before Filip spoke again. "Do you think we will beat them back?"

"I don't know." It was as honest an answer as Jacek could give.

"Do you think the hetman knows what he's doing?"

Filip's gaze was fixed on the sky, now a deep blue vault, and Jacek faced him once more. "Why do you ask?"

"I heard some of the men talking about him being too old, too feeble. I also heard him arguing with Hetman Koniecpolski about infantry."

"What about infantry?"

"Hetman Koniecpolski says we don't have enough, that we are not using them to our advantage and that we can't rely merely on cavalry." Filip shrugged.

And that we shouldn't hold them behind the rampart.

That weed of doubt pushed its way ever upward, sprouting leaves and buds as it went. "We have over two thousand hussars. I would not wager against us."

"No, of course not." Filip cradled the nadziak in his lap.

Jacek picked up a pebble and flung it into the fire. "Filip, I ... I know you have thought me unfair of late and that I have not been as patient as I could with you, but I would like to put this quarrel behind us. At least for now."

"I would like that too," Filip murmured. "It is agreed."

"I'm glad of it. Will you stand with Wronski or with your companions behind the rampart?"

"I am not certain."

Nodding, Jacek bit back a reminder of the hetmans' orders. His brother-in-law would do what he was going to do, and Jacek would have no time to mind his actions once the fight began.

He rose. "I should go."

Filip shot up to face him, the nadziak clutched in one hand. A sheen glistened in his eyes. "I—" The lad seemed to choke.

Jacek pulled him into a fierce embrace and thumped his back thrice before releasing him. He cleared the quaver from his throat. "We will get through tomorrow, and then we will return to Biaska and renew the quarrel, yes?"

Filip burst out with a tearful laugh. "Agreed."

As Jacek left Filip behind, the coil of dread that had been sitting heavy in his gut continued to unwind and spread itself outward. It wasn't unusual for such uneasiness to rear its head on the eve of battle, and his was compounded by his concern for Filip.

He stepped into his dark tent, and a question he tried to parry burst forth.

What would happen to Oliwia if the battle went horribly wrong tomorrow and she lost them both?

Scoffing at himself, he sat on the edge of his cot. He had been too long away from battle, and his complacency showed. Come tomorrow, he had a duty to fulfill, and so he would.

Meanwhile, he would pen another letter to Oliwia, though he had only written her days before. He had things he needed to say, had a duty to say, in case …

He shook off thoughts of what could go wrong tomorrow as he put pen to paper.

September 18, In the Year of Our Lord 1620

My dearest wife, my most beloved Oliwia,

Tomorrow, we meet the enemy head on. The hetman has devised a plan that ensures victory, and soon you and I will be reunited.

The words he wrote were hollow, and he couldn't displace the sense that the Grim Reaper pointed a bony finger his way.

If for some unforeseen reason that does not come to pass, I would make a request of you. If you are so disposed, please call the babe Marek should he be a boy. If a girl, perhaps you would consider naming her after Ruta, my lost twin.

Though I might speak it every day for a thousand years, I could never express all that I feel for you deep in my heart. You have taken me out of the dark, into the light, and filled my world with color and music and joy I never thought possible outside of heaven. Know that I love you with all that I am and that you will always be forever in my heart.

"Death cannot part us," he murmured.

357

Minutes stretched before him as he tried to find more words with which to fill the page, but he was empty. He signed off, folded and tied the letter with twine, and placed it atop a small chest filled with his most precious belongings: a lock of Oliwia's hair tied in an emerald satin ribbon, locks from each of his children also bound with satin, and a wooden rosary.

He lay back and held his cross to his lips as he closed his eyes and sent prayer after prayer heavenward.

Jesus, Maria, Joseph, safeguard those I love. Protect me that I may return and safeguard them myself.

Unable to sleep, he was up before dawn lightened the horizon and made his way to the makeshift stable. Jarosława lifted her majestic gray head. Stroking her nose, he nuzzled her cheek. "You and I together once more, old girl." He was loath to take her into battle, but Heban would get them killed, and his other horses were not trained for war. If he was to live out the day, he needed a mount he could rely on. Only Jarosława would do.

Next he went in search of a priest to hear his confession and found himself in a line of soldiers with the same thought. He held in an ironic chuckle. Only before men were to take the battlefield against their enemies would one find a line of soldiers ready to confess their sins.

Later, he was among the same soldiers attending Mass in the open air. As the gathering broke up, he asked Henryk if he had been shriven. Henryk snorted. "No. It would take far too long and keep others from being absolved who deserve it far more than I."

At noon, the sky was bright and calm—preternaturally peaceful despite the drummers and trumpeters—as the troops began filing into formation. Watching his lord-brothers as they took their positions always swelled his chest with pride. Surely the Commonwealth's best stock were right before him, their backs straight and strong, their jaws set in determination, their grip on their kopie firm. Hussar wings rose from their armor backplates or their cantles, and they rustled ominously in the breeze.

The mystery of his own misplaced wings had not resolved, and he felt their loss upon his back, as though he were without armor and exposed.

He looked out over a sea of crimson and feathers and darkly glinting armor amid flags and banners of the Crown army. And he was part of their majesty as he stood behind them, ready to command.

He glanced behind him, seeking out Filip. When he didn't spy him behind the rampart and the line of infantry, he darted his eyes toward Rogowski's regiment on his right, where it was positioned at the rear of the rolling stock with the Moldavians. His gaze found Wronski, whose face held no smirk. It was pure ferocity, like a snarling panther waiting to be let out of its cage, and strangely, Jacek was comforted.

As he surveyed the rolling stocks, the regiments between, and the field beyond where the enemy forces lay in wait, Jacek was overwhelmed by an odd sensation: Here were the most powerful warriors on both sides, lining up to kill and be killed. A scene that would soon devolve into bloody chaos was eerily orderly at the midway point of this otherwise ordinary September day.

Why?

Was fighting for one's country and basking in the honor that came with it worth the heartache it cost in exchange?

A soldier's gasp of "Look at them all!" pulled him from his thoughts. He took stock of the spread of the enemy.

Spirit of God! So many!

Banners snapping in the wind announced not only Iskender Pasha's force but Kantymir Murza's Tatars, as well as others swelling their ranks.

Dear God, how will we defeat them?

No, he must not think it. How many times had he and his lord-brothers been thusly arrayed against a force far larger than their own, and how many times had they emerged victorious? Many times.

He had been younger then. Brasher. Fearless. Seduced by wearing the wings. Without the loves that now pinned his heart, he had been resolved to die for God and country, draped in glory. God had chosen to spare him, and Jacek prayed he would do so again.

359

Jarosława, bedecked in her silver and turquoise, shook her head and jangled.

We will prevail.

Jacek sought out the hetmans, gilded and proud, their bearded chins held high. Then came the signal: first a motion of Hetman Żółkiewski's buława, followed by a blare of the trumpet and a roll of the drum that matched the thundering in his chest.

Blood whooshing through his head, he raised his sabre and shouted, "Remember Kłuszyn!"

CHAPTER 36

Cecora

The hetman's plan was working! Despite Jacek's worry that the calvary would be too cramped, the center ranks rode forward as the rolling fortresses lumbered on either side, the formation like one enormous block driving through the heart of the enemy, decimating them. A bloody clash, but the Commonwealth held the upper hand. Their progress was effective … and relentless. Holes appeared in the enemy's front line, thanks to the hussars, exactly as Żółkiewski had drawn it out. At the front of the center column—Jacek's column—Henryk, Lesław, Dawid, and Marcin smashed into the fray, each landing a direct hit with the long lance.

Jacek cheered and surged in his saddle for a clearer view, imagining the impact of the kopia snapping as he drove it through a hated enemy.

One pass with the kopie from the front line, and now sabres rose and fell with practiced efficiency. Blood sprayed with each potent blow, and gaps in the enemy line widened. He itched to be among his Biaska brothers, lending his own blade, but duty kept him in the rear, assessing, yelling, directing his men, ever vigilant for signals from the crown grand hetman.

The campaign was going perfectly, and the enemy's defensive line wavered and fell back. Faith soared in his chest. *Yes!* They could win this!

He dared another look for Filip, but before he could swivel his head toward the rampart, motion to the right caught his eye. The rolling stock on that side seemed to slip ahead of the formation.

No, it was an illusion.

He squinted.

What the devil?

As realization dawned that the stock *had* slid, the hetman's voice pitched loud along with the alarmed cries of the commanders. The rolling stock swung, its rear now facing inward, squeezing the hussar regiments between it and the left stock, opening a gap.

"Push it back! Close the gap!" he heard himself bellow.

They were exposed! Jacek wasn't the only one to notice. A fresh wave of Tatar cavalry swept in, making for the rent, and chaos erupted in the formation.

Where he had marveled at the orderly, solid rectangle of troops progressing as one cohesive unit, now a mass of writhing horses and men, screaming in panic, overwhelmed his senses.

The defenders of the right tabor fired on the Tatars, but it didn't slow the vermin, and they continued to pour through the gap and wreak havoc, breaking up the formation.

Jacek looked toward Żółkiewski for his instructions, but the hetman was busy urging his troops to stay together, to stay in the fight. Jacek propelled himself forward, intent on keeping his regiment intact.

And then he saw him.

Filip, behind the tabor, amid the Forlorn Hope, like a calf caught in a herd of stampeding cows, trying to remain upright in his saddle, arcing his sword wildly. Jacek's heart plunged to his stomach.

Spurring Jarosława forward, he slid his primed wheel-lock from its holster. He fired into a Tatar's back before the man could connect his blade with a Crown soldier's neck. Jacek flew past as that man fell forward in his saddle. Together, Jacek and Jarosława plunged deeper into the melee, hazy with dust and smoke. A swarm of Elears emerged, abandoning their positions, preventing him from reaching the Tatars, who whooped as they cut down Teofil Szemberg's troops trapped beside the immobile fortress.

Filip had disappeared from sight.

"Stay and fight, you bastards!" he roared at the escaping Lost Men.

One of their number kicked out at him as he sped past. *"You* stay and fight!"

"Filip!" Jacek cried in vain. And now the Moldavians—that minuscule force Grazziani had brought in lieu of the promised fifteen thousand—who had been reinforcing the rolling stock with Rogowski's banners, suddenly turned and joined the Tatars in dispatching Szemberg's men.

"Defectors!" he raged. "Serpents, all!"

Two men turned toward him—a Tatar and a turncoat Moldavian—and he grabbed up his second wheel-lock in his left hand. They charged, and he fired. The Tatar's shoulder exploded, and he shrieked and flailed at the wound. The Moldavian circled to Jacek's left. Jacek lunged with the sabre in his right, catching nothing but air. As the Moldavian raised his blade, Jacek flipped the wheel-lock and brought the butt crashing against the man's sword hand. The blade flew to the ground.

"Jacek!"

Jacek snapped his head toward Henryk. His second was in the thick of the regiment, struggling to maintain order by thundering commands here and slashing at Tatars trying to rupture their formation there. Behind him, Dawid and Lesław beat the enemy back. Marcin was nowhere in sight.

Jamming the spent wheel-lock back in its holster, he used his knees to prod Jarosława toward his brothers-in-arms.

As she picked her way through the mayhem, he hoisted his nadziak. And then they were making for a horsed foe canted at an angle. Before the man could act, Jacek brought the hammer end of his nadziak down on the man's elbow. Another Tatar appeared from the side. Jacek backhanded his sabre and sliced the horse's shoulder. With a frightened snort, the animal lurched to the side, knocking its rider into another obstacle and spilling him from his saddle.

Jacek rammed his way to Henryk as a throng crested around them. Power coursed through Jacek's veins like lightning. He submerged into a shadow world where his vision sharpened. Within a methodical rhythm, he

363

wielded the sabre and nadziak. His mind was calm, empty of thought. The warrior was in control.

How long he fought thusly, he could not say, but just as he dispatched one enemy, two more seemed to spring up in his place, like the sprouting heads of the Hydra.

Sweat ran in rivulets from beneath his helmet into his eyes, blurring his sight. His chest heaved with great breaths. His arms and legs thudded heavily, as though lead bars were being strapped to them one by one. With a swipe at his eyes, he willed his limbs to keep working.

And then someone yelled, "Fall back!"

He looked toward the embankment—it was in total disarray—and spotted a *budzygan* signaling retreat. Above the din of battle, Commonwealth trumpets blared the same message.

"Retreat! Retreat!" he echoed.

Around him, chaos reigned. The enemy outnumbered the Commonwealth army two-to-one. Five-to-one. No, ten-to-one. They swarmed; they slaughtered.

A foe lunged for Henryk, who was crossing sabres with another. Jacek lifted his nadziak as high as he could—only to his shoulder now—and smashed it into the man's ribs. The man howled just as Henryk finished his combatant with a precisely placed chop.

"We need to go!" Jacek yelled. Together, they scanned for their companions. A space seemed to yawn open around them, and Jacek gulped in air. Relief waved through him when he spied Dawid and Marcin alive, fighting as though possessed. But where was Lesław? Jacek darted a glance toward the rampart, but a red blur of retreating hussars filled his vision.

"Where's Lesław?" Jacek yelled at Henryk.

"Headed for camp."

Thank God! Lesław was caught up in that sea of crimson.

"Have you seen Filip?"

Henryk shook his head. Jacek swiveled his head to and fro but saw only a wave of Tatars bearing down. He needed to get his men out!

"I've got Dawid and Marcin!" Jacek hollered. "Take the rest and get out of here now! That's an order."

Henryk turned his horse, and Jacek made for Dawid and Marcin on the fringes of the fray, where the line was quickly deteriorating. Marcin was closest, and Jacek joined him in fending off a Tatar.

"Go now!" he ordered after they'd wounded the man and left him incapable of fighting. Dawid joined them, and as Marcin peeled away, so did a large swath of men from the column.

The panic rising among the remaining regiment was palpable. They urged their mounts to go faster but collided with one another in their haste. Jacek quelled his own rising alarm as he brought up the rear. Jarosława was flagging.

"Come on, old girl. Get us behind the rampart. Then I promise you green grass that will make you fat and lazy the rest of your life."

He hunched his back, his muscles contracting, expecting the strike of an arrow or blade with every breath he hauled into his lungs.

At last, he was gaining the embankment. As his men sailed over it, his nerves eased a fraction and he took that moment to look around for stragglers.

There, to his right, Farensbach's men and Korecki's regiment clashed with Tatars beside the left stock. On the outer edge where Jacek nearly missed him, a grimacing Filip slashed frantically at a pair of Tatars.

Filip was too far away! Desperation seized Jacek, and he surged toward the trio. One of the foes flicked his wrist. The curved edge of a *kilij* flashed inches from Filip's exposed neck. Jacek belted out a war cry.

"Desperta ferro!"

Helpless to do aught else, he watched as the blade seemed to stutter. Filip pitched backward and disappeared from sight.

Spurring Jarosława between the Tatars, Jacek arced his nadziak and brought it down with a crushing blow. His target dodged at the last instant, and the strike skipped off his back.

No!

Motion snagged his eye. The other Tatar swung at him. Jacek was too late to parry the blow. He was doomed.

A blade swept past his ear, whizzing as it went. Something—or someone—

365

had deflected the hit!

Filip! Filip, upright again on his mount, had intercepted the strike meant for Jacek's head.

Warm blood sprayed across his neck. Was it his?

He had no time to think on it.

The second Tatar, the one he had missed with his nadziak, wheeled his kilij over his head. Jacek parried the blow. Beneath him, Jarosława jostled with the other horses, bringing Jacek closer to the Tatar's next strike.

Jacek's awkward position left him exposed, his sabre at a uselessly flat angle. With a twist, he smacked the blade against the man's thigh. The man jerked, and with his other hand, Jacek cocked the nadziak back and drove the claw into the man's skull, through his armored cap. The man screamed. His weapons flew from his grasp as he jerked in his death throes.

Turning, twisting, Jacek readied to dispatch Filip's foe, but the man was gone … and so was Filip.

"My horse!"

Jacek looked down. Filip clung to his horse's head as the beast sank to the ground. Beside him lay the body of the Tatar that had been at Jacek's back. His glazed eyes stared into emptiness far beyond the earthly world, and blood pooled around his head and his ruined forearm, soaking the ground.

A knot of Tatars broke away from Korecki's men and rode for them.

Jacek reached out his hand. "Let's go!"

Tears streaming down his cheeks, Filip froze.

"Now!" Jacek shouted.

Filip kissed his horse's nose, uttered a word, and turned away. He grasped Jacek's arm and hoisted himself up behind Jacek. The horse needed no coaxing, and she took off for the rampart like the filly she once was.

Jacek never looked back.

Together they jumped the rampart and didn't stop until Jacek spied Henryk and the rest of the Biaska banner, all horsed, as they stood beside the hetman's pavilion catching their collective breath.

Henryk's grim face was spattered with crusting blood. "Good to see you alive, my friend."

"Good to be alive." Jacek scanned the gathered men-at-arms. "Where is Lesław?"

A tear welled in Henryk's eye, and he swiped at it with the heel of his hand. "He was leading the men back to camp and—"

"No!" Jacek's heart compressed and sank like a stone in a pond. "Is he …?"

Dawid lifted his chin. "Taken, thanks to Wronksi, but still alive when I last saw him. When he learns the fate that awaits him, he may wish he was dead." He spat out the words as though they were bitter ash in his mouth.

Filip, still seated behind Jacek in the saddle, went rigid.

Jacek narrowed an eye. "What do you mean, he was taken 'thanks to Wronski'?"

Dawid seemed to notice Filip for the first time, and his gaze bounced between the lad and Jacek before resolve set his features. His mouth tightened into a grim line. "Wronski and his lieutenant had deserted Rogowski's regiment and were fleeing for camp, but a half-dozen Tatars were in pursuit. By a stroke of terrible luck, Lesław was stopped nearby, ushering men into camp when Wronski caught him up, begging for aid. This was Lesław, so naturally he let Wronski approach—they were brothers-in-arms, after all—and as he prepared to battle Wronski's pursuers, Wronski himself struck Lesław on the head and kicked him to the ground. Wronski and his man fled, leaving Lesław dazed and bleeding in the dirt as a sacrificial offering to the heathens. The Tatars likely recognized Lesław as szlachta and a high-ranking officer. He was a prize to be ransomed, and of course, there was his fine warhorse. They swarmed him like vultures and hauled him and the horse off."

Dawid paused and dragged a hand over his jaw, his composure visibly wobbling. He seemed to anchor himself. "Several of us tried to come to his aid, but a squad of Tatar calvary lined up. The hetman called us off and ordered us to get the rest of the regiment to safety."

Dawid hung his head.

Lesław! Anger and sorrow wedged in Jacek's throat, making him strain for air. Their valiant friend in exchange for Wronski? No!

An arrow might as well have pierced Jacek's chest. His vision went from scarlet to burgundy to black. When it cleared, he strafed the troops, his gaze hunting for Wronski.

As late afternoon shifted into twilight, the last of the Crown troops trickled in with Korecki. Only Teofil Szemberg and a fraction of his soldiers had broken through the enemy's force besieging the right tabor. The rest were lost.

Żółkiewski had called a war council, and as Jacek waited with the other colonels near the encampment's center, his mind worked furiously at how to rescue Lesław. Bits of accounts of the battle floated in and out of his consciousness.

He turned to the man beside him, who was none other than Walenty Kalinowski. "Why did the right fortress fail?"

Kalinowski huffed. "When the hetman drew up his *plan*, he and his intelligence gatherers had little understanding of the terrain. The right rolling fortress encountered a trench and had nowhere to go. By the time the men realized it, it was too late. They were unable to haul it back into position before the enemy saw the breach and poured in." Kalinowski paused to shake his head.

A blaze of anger ignited and spread from Jacek's gut, pounding its way through his body. Even if those manning the right tabor had seen the rut in time, what could they have done? The rest of the formation would have continued moving, producing the same result.

And therein lay one of the fatal flaws of the hetman's scheme. How could he have not foreseen it?

"The Tatars had been watching, waiting for their chance, and the jackals sprang as soon as they spotted the opening," Kalinowski added miserably.

Now Korecki, who had been blankly staring straight ahead, joined in. "They attacked the right flank while more swept around back and assaulted the formation's rear guard. They exploited our weakest points."

"The calvary panicked and ran," one commander said bitterly.

"Not the entire calvary," Jacek snapped.

"What became of Rogowski's troops?" asked Korecki. "And the Moldavians? They were to protect the rear."

Jacek harnessed his fury. "The Moldavians went over to the Ottoman side"—all eyes turned to him—"and the Lisowczycy abandoned their post. They rode past me as they fled the fight."

"There was no saving that side," a new man rumbled, and the group parted to reveal a battle-weary Walenty Rogowski, leader of said forlorn force, who pinned a glare on Jacek. "So I took my men to defend the left rolling stock."

A man spat on the ground. "They didn't all follow you, though, did they?"

"How could they?" Rogowski jeered. "The cavalry was too constricted, and they were caught by the enemy. My men fought hard, but many couldn't find their way through the ensuing chaos."

"Chaos caused in part by *your* mercenaries fleeing in complete disorder," one colonel snarled. "The crown grand hetman pleaded with them to return and fight, but they disobeyed. Cowards." He spat on the ground.

Rogowski's mouth tightened into a grim slash. "I saw many turn and run today, so watch where you throw your accusations. Were my men and I not present, your hides would be lying out there, rotting in the sun." He stabbed a finger toward the battlefield.

It occurred to Jacek that he hadn't spotted Wronski. "Commander Rogowski, have you seen Captain Wronski?" *So I can choke the conniving bastard to death.*

The man stared at him for several beats before shaking his head.

"We should gather our armies—what's left of them—and leave at dawn," someone muttered. Voices rose, some in agreement and some in protest, all with an opinion.

The hetman's appearance hushed every man there. As he stood flanked by his son, Koniecpolski, and Grazziani, his stooped posture gave the appearance that his frame had shrunk, bowed as it was by the weight resting on his thin shoulders. Every loss, every sorrow was carved in the man's ashen face, and sympathy vibrated in Jacek's chest.

"Today," the hetman began, "we lost many brave men. Commanders, *towarzysze*, retainers, reiters, infantrymen. I am chagrined by their loss, and I take full responsibility." Jacek tried to listen to the hetman's speech, but his mind was constantly tugged back to Lesław, and he choked back his emotion.

He did catch that they had lost nearly a third of their army on the bloody battlefield, whether captured or killed. The enemy, by contrast, had lost few. The day had been an utter disaster for the Commonwealth forces.

Jacek's knees buckled with the news. So many! How was that possible? Such a waste! How had the hetman miscalculated so thoroughly?

More grim tidings followed. From the prisoners they had captured, they gleaned that the attack against the Lost Men the day before had merely been a ruse, a reconnaissance mission for Iskender Pasha. He had sent Tatars in to assess their strength and resources, and the Commonwealth troops had been lulled into believing they had triumphed over the enemy. They had allowed their confidence to soar over a false defeat of the enemy. The army they had met today had been reinforced by two Tatar armies and Prince Gabriel Bethlen's Transylvanians. In total, their foes outnumbered the Commonwealth at least five times, and that overwhelming force was encamped a short distance away, to the southeast, waiting to strike. Salivating over dealing the final blow.

"We must retreat!" Kalinowski shouted.

"No." Żółkiewski's rasp cut like jagged steel. Soon he was drowned out as frantic men demanded this or that, shouting over one another to be heard. Neither Żółkiewski's nor Koniecpolski's attempts to calm the crowd had an effect. Grazziani stood to the side, keeping himself apart.

Jacek watched it all and seethed.

When the meeting finally broke up, he and Henryk threaded their way through the dark toward their camp. Lesław should have been with them, and his old friend's absence left a gaping hole in Jacek's soul.

"Don't blame yourself," Henryk mumbled as if he had read Jacek's thoughts.

"But it's my fault. I let him down, and now he's—"

"No, it's not. Your duty was to keep the regiment together, and that you did. Better than the other commanders, I would point out. Furthermore, by doing your duty, you saved countless lives. Had you strayed to save one of us, many more would have perished."

"Duty," Jacek snorted under his breath. The word was a yoke about his neck.

"Though you try to pass yourself off as God, you are not He. You cannot control everything." Henryk's voice carried the same weariness steeped in Jacek's bones. Hopelessness had settled there too, and he tried in vain to shake it off.

Jacek stopped midstride and looked around. He lowered his voice. "I tell you what my duty dictates. We must rescue him."

"Agreed."

"After the men turn in, you, Dawid, Marcin, and I will ride to the rampart. I have a plan."

"I will let the others know."

Back in camp, men ringed a lit lantern standing in for a cook fire. There had been naught to cook, so they chewed on groats in ponderous silence. Jacek perched on a rock and stared into the flame, devising ways to get Lesław back. He was anxious to get going, but these men needed his presence, so he rooted himself to the rock. His stomach should have grumbled over a lack of sustenance, but his appetite had gone missing for thinking on what his friend was enduring at this very moment.

Filip dropped beside him on his haunches, his voice subdued. "I do not believe I thanked you for saving my life today."

Jacek nodded. "You did the same for me."

"It ... it was not what I expected."

"Taking another man's life never is."

"Do you get used to it?"

"Used to it? No, nor should you. Life is sacred. Does it trouble you less? Yes, especially when you see the atrocities your enemies commit against your people. You come to see killing your enemy as a means of preserving life. One dead Tatar equals ten Christians he did not murder." He swiveled his head and studied Filip's angled profile reflected in the firelight. "Does that make sense?"

"I believe so." Filip turned and met his gaze. "They killed my horse," he whispered, and a tear welled in his eye.

"I know that animal was dear to you and his loss pains you, but better him than you."

The night hung heavy between them, like a rod draped in chain mail. Filip cleared his throat. "What did you cry out when you joined the fight? I've not heard it before."

Jacek let out a mirthless chuckle. "*Desperta ferro?* 'Tis an old war cry once used by Iberian soldiers, the Almogavars. They were Christians who fought the Muslims. It means 'Awaken iron!' and was used to terrify the enemy by reminding them of the iron that would soon cut them down. Before battle, the soldiers would perform a ritual where they struck their swords on stones to make them spark. I had no time to bring forth the sparks, but I reckoned the cry might prove a distraction."

"It worked."

Jacek picked up a pebble and chucked it at the lantern. The small pinging noise brought him a level of satisfaction. "What do you make of your friend Captain Wronski?"

Filip's eyebrows crumpled together. "Dawid must have been mistaken."

Jacek masked his surprise. "You've known Dawid far longer than you've known Wronski. Do you believe he is capable of such a miscalculation?"

"No."

"So if you believe him incapable of this error, do you then believe he fabricated the story? And what of the other witnesses who will attest to what he saw?"

Filip raised a stubborn chin. "Captain Wronski could not have run. He could not betray his own."

Was Filip trying to convince Jacek? Or himself?

"Search deep in your heart, Filip, and ask yourself where the truth lies. Trust what you find there and remember that a jackal is as cunning as he is ruthless." Filip stood abruptly and walked away. Jacek expelled a resigned sigh.

The last man turned in, leaving only Henryk, Dawid, Marcin, and him. He rose to his feet. Wordlessly, the others did the same and followed as he trudged to the camp stables. There, they mounted their outfitted horses and walked them, along with a spare, to the embankment. A half-moon hung in a sky that appeared as though it wanted to enfold the pale orb into its endless inkiness. Cold silver splashed over the battlefield's bleak shadows, highlighting the grotesque shapes of fallen horses and men and the hulking remains of the abandoned rolling stock now stripped of its guns and horses. Animals could be heard snuffling and growling as they moved among the corpses. A late summer breeze ruffled Commonwealth banners erected on the rampart, bringing with it shrill cries from the enemy camp several miles distant. Chills like devil's claws raked Jacek's spine.

Shaking off the sensation, he pointed at the menacing forest. "We will duck in there and, much like the Tatars did, use the woods for cover while we work our way to the enemy camp. Then—"

"You are proposing a suicide mission, Colonel." The voice startled them all, and they turned their heads in unison. A figure emerged from the dark, his head wreathed in smoke. The spectacle sent fresh chills cascading down Jacek's back.

The figure rode toward them, and as he drew closer, Jacek recognized embers glowing in a pipe the man smoked. "Do not let me alarm you, my lords. It is merely I, Samuel Korecki, trying to prevent the senseless loss of more good men."

Behind him, a palisade of guards appeared from the gloom, their faces obliterated by their helmets, lending them the semblance of wraiths.

What devilry was this? "I-I don't understand," Jacek stammered.

"Which is precisely why I am here. I suspect you intend to embark on some futile mission because you don't understand the consequences that mission might bring you and your men." He puffed on the pipe.

Jacek clenched his teeth. "With all due respect, you could have no idea of our intentions."

"Perhaps not an exact idea, but any dullard can see you and your warhorses are ready for battle. Since you are here under cover of night, and since you lost esteemed officers to the enemy today, I can only surmise you are preparing to recover their bodies or somehow sneak into the Ottoman camp and rescue them without getting yourselves killed."

Jacek stared at the obstacle that was Korecki while his brain ran calculations.

The prince let out a soft chuckle. "I can see you trying to work out how I know. I will save you the trouble and tell you. I too have men who were killed or taken today. I too am filled with rage and a need to find them. I too feel their losses eating a hole inside me. Unlike you, however, I understand how reckless giving in to that impulse would prove." He pointed his pipe toward the battlefield. "You see those forms moving over there? Tatars. They're in the woods too. Lying in wait, hoping you will do exactly what you're contemplating doing at this moment. They have already captured two other parties tonight who thought to retrieve their brothers' corpses." He lifted his chin toward Jacek's men. "Are you willing to lose more men tonight?"

Henryk shifted in his saddle. "We are here because we too wish to rescue our lord-brother. Not because we were ordered to do so."

Korecki nodded. "I understand that. And while it is commendable, it is foolhardy. You will forfeit your lives, and for what? As for you, Colonel, are you prepared to carry more of your men's deaths on your shoulders? For that is what you will do if you lead them out there tonight. Do you even know if your man is alive?"

Jacek narrowed his eyes. "Witnesses say he was when the heathens hauled him away."

"Wounded?"

Jacek nodded.

"Then there is an even chance he no longer lives. Even if he does, the Turks might decide they dislike the color of his hair or his lopsided nose and dispatch him before morning. So you see, you are proposing rushing into the clutches of the Tatars blindly to save someone who may already be in God's arms. It would be easier to simply put aside your weapons, cross the embankment, and present yourselves to the enemy. Your man, is he szlachta?" He sucked on his pipe, and the embers brightened.

Jacek bristled. "Yes. A hussar lieutenant."

Korecki exhaled blue-gray smoke. "Ah, then he will make good trade fodder. You may get him back yet, without having to give up your life and those of your men in the bargain." He gestured to the men behind him. "These soldiers have orders to guard the rampart and make sure no one gets in or leaves. They will use force if necessary. Therefore, I advise you to return to your camp and get as much rest as possible. You will need it come morning for whatever these devils have in store for us. We all will. Good night, my lords." He stood motionless, except for his incessant sucking and blowing. The man obviously would not leave until they did.

Dawid turned his horse's head toward camp. "Come, Jacek. Let's do as the man says."

"I'm with Dawid," Henryk muttered. "We will revisit the situation in the morning."

Silent despondency shrouded them as they plodded back to camp.

Alone in his tent, Jacek settled himself on his cot. He flung his arm over his eyes and let misery wash over him. Why was he lying here a free man when his brother-in-arms was a wounded captive?

"I vow I will come for you, Lesław. I will not forget you," Jacek choked out in the dark.

CHAPTER 37

Midnight and Malfeasance

A pall cloaked the encampment the following day. With Żółkiewski unable to will the commanders into rallying, the camp settled into idleness. Jacek couldn't decide if the respite was better or worse than charging into a battle that heavily favored the enemy. At least they would be doing *something* instead of lingering in inactivity where their thoughts were filled with their fates and those they had lost. Much as Korecki's words had angered him the night before, the prince had been right. Using a cooler commander's logic rather than the emotional frame of friend and lord-brother, Jacek acknowledged to himself and his brethren that the four of them would achieve nothing by venturing into territory controlled by Ottoman and Tatar soldiers.

"At best, we might become martyrs, but I have never known a dead martyr to free his friend." Saying it aloud, admitting defeat, left a vile taste in his mouth.

Jacek followed this up with a plea to Hetman Żółkiewski on Lesław's behalf.

Seated in his war tent, the hetman regarded him with hooded eyes. "Your lieutenant is one of thousands taken yesterday, Colonel. While I sympathize and understand your desire to free him, there is naught we can do at this time without endangering our depleted forces. His name has been added to a list of the missing, and rest assured that should hostage negotiations go forth, your lieutenant will be included among those we will trade for."

Hope lifted Jacek's heart an inch. "Has such an overture been made?"

"No, but it is not out of the question."

Heart sunken back to its low point, Jacek balled up his frustrations and rode to Wronski's camp, accompanied by Dawid—his witness—Henryk, and Marcin, who could not be dissuaded, and Filip, whom he had insisted come along.

A sentry greeted them, replying that he hadn't seen his commander since yesterday when Jacek asked after his whereabouts. Though Jacek surveyed the camp multiple times, he never caught sight of Wronski.

"Try Commander Rogowski's camp," the guard suggested, so they made for the leader's camp.

Rogowski ambled out of a tent and popped a handful of almonds in his mouth. The wiry leader of the Lost Men wore a belted blue tunic, dark trousers, and a pair of canary-yellow boots. His head was covered by a simple brown kolpak. His light eyes were keen, shifty, and protruding. Below a patrician nose rested a thick, graying mustache that reminded Jacek of a mink's tail.

He lifted his chin at Jacek. "Colonel Dąbrowski, what can I do for you?" The man's tone was neither welcoming nor hostile.

"I seek justice for one of my lieutenants, Lesław Nowakowski."

Rogowski spread his hands wide. "Here? How so?"

"My lieutenant"—he tilted his head toward Dawid—"witnessed your man, Gabriel Wronski, ambush him during the battle and turn him over to the enemy in order to save his own neck."

"Seems rather enterprising to me." Rogowski's lip curled in a smile or snarl, Jacek couldn't say. "Captain Wronski is one of my best. Are you sure your lieutenant is not mistaken? It was rather hazy and chaotic out there."

Dawid snorted. "There is no mistaking what I saw."

Ignoring the remark, Rogowski kept his gaze fixed on Jacek. "Tell me, Colonel. What price would *you* pay to save your neck?"

"I would not sacrifice my brother-in-arms."

Rogowski nodded. "Commendable. Consider this, however. Your missing lieutenant is *your* brother-in-arms, not ours."

"We are all brothers-in-arms against a hated enemy, would you not agree?"

"Yes, but some of us are more equal than others." Rogowski waved a dismissive hand. "I suggest you seek your justice *after* we have defeated the Ottomans. That is *if* you can produce more than one man's accounting as proof." With that, he turned his back and entered his pavilion.

Jacek stood in his stirrups, ready to protest, but a ring of Lost Men raised arquebuses.

Henryk stayed his arm. "This is not the time, my friend."

"The man's an arrogant ruffian."

Henryk held up his little finger. "One needs to make up for a thimble-sized prick somehow."

Marcin burst out with a laugh. Even Dawid's mouth twitched with a smile. Filip, however, was not amused and kept his chin in a stubborn set.

They picked their way through camp amid murmurs. Men who had their heads together dropped their voices and gave polite nods until Jacek and his group disappeared from view. Then the burble started right back up.

"Mutiny," Marcin stated when Jacek asked if he knew what was afoot. "Pot-stirrers saying the hetmans are preparing to flee and that they should too."

When Jacek took the disturbing rumors to Żółkiewski later that day, he found the old hetman surrounded by his innermost circle. They waved him off.

"W-we're aware of the state of the camp, Colonel," Koniecpolski said, "and are d-doing our utmost to keep the m-men calm. You can b-best help us by doing the same."

"Do we have a plan?"

Jan Żółkiewski met Jacek's gaze. "We are in the process of formulating one now based on new intelligence."

"Begging your pardon, my lords, but is this intelligence that can be trusted? The last bit of 'intelligence' lost us three thousand men."

Żółkiewski himself finally spoke. "I understand why you question the reports, Colonel. Once we have a final plan, you and the other commanders will be brought in."

Jacek pushed on. "Would you care for my help right now? With strategy or—"

"No, thank you, Colonel. We will call you if we need you."

With that, he was dismissed. Outrage simmering in his gut, he returned to camp with a throbbing head.

The end of the dismal day at last drew near, and Jacek's apprehension caused his underfed belly to roil. He had the sense of marching into a blizzard, stinging snow blinding them to the dangers engulfing them. But as he lingered with the men in camp, he let none of it show.

A group of squires drifted into camp. "Did you catch anything?" one of the soldiers yelled. A youth shook his head dejectedly.

Filip had gone hunting with them, and when he didn't appear, Jacek asked where he was. One of the lads pointed over his shoulder. "He spied a pair of squirrels and decided to stay behind to catch them."

A half hour passed, and then another quarter. Twilight was giving way to a heavy blanket of darkness rolling over the sky. Jacek grew more agitated, as if he sat on spikes, waiting, watching, and weary of both. He glanced over at Henryk playing dice with Dawid. "I'm going to search for Filip. You're in charge." Henryk nodded.

Jacek strode away from Biaska's camp, instinct driving him back toward Rogowski's. Going on foot offered better cover, even if it took longer, and he wanted to be sure Wronski and his ilk didn't know he was coming.

He trod through a section of the encampment unlit by torches, for this was the area that only yesterday housed Teofil Szemberg's men, lost along with the right rolling stock. Ghostly shadows seemed to waver, and where a life force had been thrumming through the rest of the camp, that buzz was muffled here, as if shrouds blanketed the deserted tents.

379

Whispers caught him up short. He stood and sharpened his hearing. Had he really heard voices, or had it been a haunting breeze on the battlefield?

"You will be well recompensed." He clearly heard the accented murmur, though he couldn't pinpoint its exact location. Something about the voice rang with familiarity. He swiveled his head side to side and remained stock-still.

A different voice mumbled words he couldn't make out. The first voice said, "Yes, half now, and half when the deed is done."

Another inaudible snippet of conversation, and Voice One huffed, "It is the only way."

The swishing of clothing moved away from him, leaving him cloaked in quiet. He stood for extended heartbeats and finally resumed his path, his steps lighter and softer now, his mind whirling as he went. He told himself to put the mystery aside for now; he had to find Filip.

Filip had told the other squires he had more hunting to do, but in truth, he had headed straight for Lord Wronski's camp. Jacek's tale of Lesław's capture had angered him; he had been convinced his brother-in-law invented the story to disparage the captain. But as his temper had settled, questions had begun to form. Jacek possessed many faults, but lying was not among them. So Filip had struck out, wanting to hear from the captain's own mouth that he had nothing to do with Lesław's horrible fate.

When Filip reached the camp, he found it deserted. Puzzled and more dejected than when he had started out, he headed for Biaska's camp. His route took him through a series of silent, dark tents that only this morning had held breathing, laughing towarzysze. Now those valiant warriors were captive or dead.

The day's tragedy held all of his attention until movement in the gloom had him melting into the shadows. Placing his hand on his sabre hilt, he evened his breathing. Ten feet away, the sides of a deserted tent seemed to ripple. A dim light winked on, as if someone had lit a candle.

Low voices could have been leaves swaying in the wind, but there was no wind. Filip crept forward and slowly unsheathed his sabre. He pulled in a breath, pushed it out, and peered through the tent flap.

On his knees, presenting his back, was Captain Gabriel Wronski rifling through the contents of a chest in a far corner. To one side, one of his lieutenants cackled with glee as he held up a lantern.

"We be getting a rich haul this time, eh, Captain? Them hussars love their baubles and whatnot, but they ain't needing them no more."

"Shut up, you imbecile, before someone hears you!" Wronski hissed. The light illuminated him as he extracted objects and tossed them onto a large square that resembled a cloak.

These miscreants were stealing dead men's possessions! Filip's heart plummeted to his knees as a pall of disappointment draped him. Jacek had been right. The trinkets Wronski continually seemed to acquire came slamming back, and Filip realized Wronski hadn't only stolen from the dead. Disgust and fury ignited and churned inside him. He had trusted Wronski. Admired him. And here he was, showing himself for the common thief he was. This could have been Lesław's tent, and Wronski's remorseless looting would have deprived Lady Eugenia and their children, leaving nothing of a husband and father. Filip's rage boiled over.

"Leave the lantern and go find the others," Wronski ordered the lieutenant.

Filip ducked to the side and waited as the man hustled away. Sabre to hand, he stepped inside the tent. "So this is how you treat those courageous men who sacrificed their lives today?"

Wronski whirled. He seemed to recognize Filip immediately because the same wide, easy smile broke out on his face. Filip saw it for the sham it was.

"Filip! You are just in time, lad. Come help me and claim treasures for your own."

Filip pointed the blade at him. "No. Rather, you place the booty back where it belongs and come with me."

Wronski rose to his full height and spread his arms wide. "Put that thing down before you hurt yourself." When Filip refused, Wronski's smile slid from his face. "What do you think you're going to do, lad?" His voice had taken on a brittle, menacing tone.

"I intend to turn you in to—"

Lightning quick, Wronski lunged and wrested the sabre from Filip's grasp. Filip flailed, and in the next instant, Wronski pounced. They grappled, upending the lantern, but Wronski was too powerful. In less than a beat, Filip found himself on his back, with Wronski straddling him, pressing the heels of his hands to his throat, crushing his windpipe. Filip couldn't draw air, and he clawed at Wronski's wrists, his hands, desperate to breathe.

Dear God, he was going to die!

A body stormed through the tent flap. The movement caught Wronski off guard, and he let up the pressure. Fire pumping through Filip's bloodstream gave him the strength to break the man's hold on his neck. Years of training took over, and he drove his forearm into Wronski's throat. He exploded beneath the Lost Man, flinging him to the side, where he thudded on the ground with a satisfying *oof!* The lantern winked out.

The intruder threw himself into the brawl. Filip would thank him later for saving his life, but right now, he wanted to finish Wronski himself. He warned the newcomer off in a raspy voice. "He's mine."

Then Filip was somehow straddling Wronski. He cocked his fist and aimed for Wronski's head, landing a punch on his shoulder instead. He began raining down blows, but Wronski caught his wrists and flipped him. Filip kicked out and caught a shin. Wronski's knuckles connected with Filip's ribs.

They wrestled, grunted, and groaned in the dark. Wronski wriggled from Filip's grasp.

The lantern came on, throwing light on the canvas walls, revealing Wronski midway through the opening.

Filip launched himself at the blackguard, wrapping his arms around the man's legs. He hauled Wronski down, but his limbs suddenly felt rubbery, numb, heavy. Wronski was wriggling from Filip's hold. He struggled to hang on, but Wronski broke free.

The intruder who had lit the lantern transformed with the light. Jacek sprang and landed with his knee on Wronski's back, driving him into the ground. Wind whooshed from Wronski's lungs, and his back made popping noises.

Jacek lifted the Elear and hurled him across the tent like a sack of grain. Wronski crumpled into a moaning heap.

Filip lay prone on his side. When he looked up, his brother-in-law was looking at him over his shoulder. "Are you all right?"

Coughing, grasping at his bruised throat, Filip hauled himself up and nodded.

Jacek took several steps and planted himself above the Elear, heaving in breath as he glared down at the miscreant. "What the devil were you doing in that chest?"

Wronski gulped air, swiped blood from beneath his nostril, and smirked. "Why, searching for a quill and paper to write a letter to my wife, of course. What did it look like?"

Furious words collided in Filip's mind, but he couldn't get them past his scratched throat. *He was stealing from a dead Polish soldier!*

"It looked like you were looting a dead Pole's belongings," Jacek snarled. "What kind of evil lives inside a man who thinks nothing of plundering his own? You truly are the Forlorn Hope." Jacek turned his head and spat.

A smile twitched Filip's lips. He couldn't recall being so glad to see his brother-in-law before. Not because he had come to Filip's aid, but because he had just restored Filip's faltering belief in good and honor.

Wronski continued in that caustic tone Filip had only recently recognized. "I am simply helping myself to what he no longer needs. Why let things go to waste, or worse, let them fall into the hands of barbarians?"

"He has a family," Jacek growled and pointed toward the cloak. *"They* need what little they have left of him, you despicable pile of sheep shit."

Wronski raised a puffy eyebrow. "Are you going to stop every single one of us tonight?"

"What do you mean?"

Filip finally got his mouth and tongue working again, and he croaked, "He means that his fellows are doing the very same thing we caught him

383

doing." Filip had discovered the truth from Wronski's men when he'd walked into their camp. They had practically danced with glee. *"Come with us. There are prizes enough for us all."*

Jacek swung blazing eyes to Filip. "Were you helping him?"

Filip's heart plummeted to his knees. "No! I was trying to stop him!"

"Really, Master Filip," Wronski tutted. "Did you not pay attention when I told you that lying is a grave sin?"

"I'm not lying!" Filip nearly shrieked. His heart cried out, and with his eyes, his entire body, he implored Jacek to believe him.

Jacek nodded. "I believe you."

Relief flooded Filip, and he struggled to keep himself from sagging onto his back.

"You will never make a good Lisowczyk," Wrosnki drawled. "Your conscience is far too limiting. What a disappointment."

Renewed rage brought Filip upright to his knees. "If you are an example of what being a Lisowczyk is like, I want nothing to do with your band. I admired you for what I believed was your courage and honor. Those traits only go so far as you need to get you what you want, no matter the price to others. I see now how mistaken I was."

Wronski snorted and looked up at Jacek. "So what do we do now? Are you going to arrest me? In case you haven't noticed, we are down a third of our force after yesterday's debacle. Is this truly the time to indulge your need to be sanctimonious?"

Filip vaulted to his feet. Fists clenched, he leaned over Wronski. "He is your superior. Show him respect!"

Jacek cocked his head at Filip as if asking if he was playacting … and Filip understood why. His behavior these last many months came crashing over him in a wave of shame.

Wronski leveled a glare at Filip. "Simply because he wears wings does not make him my superior. If he were, I wouldn't have bested him thrice."

Jacek's brows knotted together. "What does he mean, bested me thrice?"

Filip's mouth hinged open. "I have no idea."

Wronski held up a finger. "First, there is the matter of your brother groveling to be in my service. So much so, he brought me a prize of great magnitude in order to ingratiate himself."

The wings! Panic coursed through Filip. Though he'd tried, he hadn't managed to steal them back. If Jacek was to hear of Filip's transgression, it had to come from him, not Wronski. His limbs tautened, ready to spring at Wronski.

Jacek latched on to his arm. "He's not worth the energy pummeling him will sap from you."

To Filip's great relief, Wronski moved on, flipping out a second finger. "Second is the matter of the warhorse."

The purpose behind Filip visiting Wronski's camp in the first place slammed into him. "Jacek, that horse with the sable coloring and the botched brand is from the Halicz stock," he spewed excitedly. "I've looked her over, and I've talked to the stable boys. They can confirm it!"

"It seems this lying is an epidemic sweeping through my camp," Wronski remarked dryly. "I suppose it's time I took the strap to those lazy oafs again. I will let them know how you divulged their deceit. As for you, you miserable brat—"

"Perhaps trouncing him would sap my strength, but it would bring me great pleasure." Clenching his fists, Filip pinned Wronski with a dagger-laden glare.

Wronski held up the third finger. "As for the third—"

"You betrayed my lord-brother in order to save your own worthless hide."

"Ah. That would make four times, then. How I love to overachieve. The third—"

A great clamor of men and horses arose, drawing all their attention.

"Tatars!" Jacek and Wronski chorused.

Jacek fixed the Elear with a glower.

Wronski leaped to his feet. "You need me out there. I hate them far worse than I hate you."

Jacek emptied the contents of the cloak into the chest and slammed the lid. "Fine. We will settle our differences later."

They piled out of the tent. Wronski ran toward Rogowski's camp, while Jacek and Filip matched strides, sprinting in the direction of Biaska's.

Jacek glanced at him. "Ready to take up arms again?"

"Yes." *As long as I am fighting for Biaska this time.* A sense of belonging warmed Filip all over, even as they ran headlong into battle.

They arrived to men-at-arms springing into action and Henryk barking orders from atop his mount.

Jacek diverted to his tent, where Marcin awaited him. "Armor?" His erstwhile pacholik—who refused to cease being his pacholik—held Jacek's metal front and back plates.

"No time. Weapons and a helmet only." He lunged for his bow and quiver while Marcin picked up a wheel-lock and began priming it. "Should you not be preparing yourself rather than attending me? My wife released you from my service long ago."

"I *am* prepared. While you were busy gallivanting about the camp, *I* was busy getting ready." Marcin grinned as he checked the second wheel-lock. "Besides, Lady Oliwia was not in her right mind when she came to that decision."

Jacek slid his powder horn and bandolier with his cartridge box over his head and seated the straps on his shoulder. "Perhaps not, but she is the lady of the land, and her edict stands."

Marcin slipped each wheel-lock into its red leather holster, picked up the assemblage, and hoisted it over his shoulder. "I don't believe she understood the disservice she did you when she made it so. Admit it. You cannot function without me." Marcin handed him his helmet.

Jacek palmed it and plopped it on his head. "Are you saying I am incapable of preparing myself for battle?"

"Yes. Now I must see to the servants saddling your horse. Will you ride Jarosława or give Heban another chance to break your neck?"

386

Jacek paused to blow out a breath. "She is no doubt exhausted, but it must be Jarosława."

"Good. You too are exhausted, and controlling that imbecile Heban would be an even greater challenge for you than normal."

"You runneth over with compliments, Marcin," Jacek said dryly.

"My pleasure, my lord." With a mock bow, Marcin pivoted and exited the tent.

"By Christ, I am delighted you are with me," Jacek mumbled after Marcin departed.

"Why, thank you." Henryk's sudden appearance in the tent opening startled Jacek. "I am delighted to be with you as well."

"I was speaking to my sabre." Jacek kissed the cross-shaped langet.

"Of course you were."

"Filip is with us once more." Giddiness practically bubbled up inside of Jacek. Filip had finally opened his eyes and shaken off Wronski's spell.

Henryk's eyebrows crawled up his forehead. "You must be relieved."

"That I am."

The volume of men's yells outside Biaska's camp grew louder, along with the clashing of metal. Jacek detected a level of panic that hadn't been there moments before, and urgency tightened its grip on him.

He was adjusting his helmet when Dawid rode up. "Do we know how large a force we face?"

"That's what I've come to tell you," Dawid panted. "No one is attacking—yet. Rather, the magnates, their armies, and their servants are fleeing to the north."

Jacek's mouth hinged open. "And the tumult I hear is …?"

"The hetmans are trying to stop them."

"Dear God, then the rumors of mutiny were true!"

Henryk grabbed Jacek's nape. "Come. 'Tis time to battle our own countrymen."

CHAPTER 38

Crisis of Faith

Jacek sat astride Jarosława, surveying a nightmarish scene he struggled to comprehend. If only it *were* a nightmare, he could rub his eyes and wake up.

Hetmans Żółkiewski and Koniecpolski were in a frenzy, riding up and down the Prut's right bank, entreating men to return to camp, but their pleading was in vain. Lines of soldiers, servants, and magnates ignored them and continued along the river's right.

Jacek managed to catch Teofil Szemberg's attention and asked what was needed. "Grazziani means to escape, and the great hetman has charged me with persuading him to return to his quarters. Meanwhile, Stefan Chmielecki and the others are trying to turn this procession around. Find him. Bolster his squad. If you cannot locate him, do whatever you and your men can to stop these fools from leaving!" He stabbed a finger toward the crowd. "The enemy is lying in wait, and our countrymen are walking right into their hands."

"Where are they?"

"The right bank, the left bank!"

"Tatars are on both sides of the river?" *How the devil had they managed it? They are Tatars.*

Szemberg flailed his arm. "They are everywhere!" He galloped away.

Handheld torches and the silver cast of the half-moon illuminated untold numbers of men and horses moving along the right bank. Jacek recognized one of the younger magnates, and he rode for him while Henryk, Marcin, and Dawid rode into the fracas and shouted at the other groups to turn around.

Jacek reined in Jarosława beside him. "Why are you abandoning camp?" He refrained from calling him an idiot.

The man tugged his reins. "To reach home sooner and with my head attached to my shoulders! Besides, the hetmans are doing the same, so it's each man for himself."

"The hetmans aren't abandoning camp! They are by the ramparts, trying to convince people to return to safety."

The magnate shrugged. "Believe it if you must. I am taking my army home."

Jarosława danced a circle, as if urging Jacek to leave this imbecile behind. "Are you aware of the Tatars who await you and your men?"

"A rumor spread by those who would keep us here, nothing more." The potentate ordered his soldiers and servants forward, leaving Jacek behind.

How the devil am I to stop them?

Jacek fell back, searching out Chmielecki. When he found him, his heart thudded against his rib cage. The Tatar conqueror, along with his men and the field guard, plunged into the Prut and made for the left bank—where Tatars had just appeared! What the hell was the man doing? Others followed him into the roiling water, fighting to stay afloat.

Jacek watched in stunned horror as a half dozen of Chmielecki's men were swept downriver with their horses, getting sucked under, pale, panicked faces bobbing back up, going under again as the river sought to claim them for her own.

The man himself gained the left bank and clawed his way out of the water, only to be met by the glittering steel of enemy blades. From what Jacek could see, the Tatar force appeared small, and Chmielecki, the Tatar conqueror, lived up to his name. He, the field guard, and their troops fought their way past the enemy band and were swallowed up in the night.

Would they reach home?

Home.

A pang of longing dug into Jacek's chest, snatching his breath. How long had he been away? Visions streamed through his head, and he froze. Oliwia's alluring smile, Margaret's giggles, Adam's bravado, the smell of Piotr's hair. All that he held dear.

Marcin pulled up beside him, breathless. "This is utter madness! What must we do?"

I have no earthly idea. Jacek couldn't recall feeling so helpless as he looked every which way in search of the hetmans and guidance, but they were nowhere in his line of sight. "I know what we *don't* do. We don't follow them into the river, and we don't flee north up the right bank. One way leads to death by drowning, and the other leads into the hands of the Tatars."

"That's Hospodar Grazziani!" someone yelled.

A knot of men Jacek recognized as part of the hospodar's retinue pulled him from the river's grasp on the far bank. But then they appeared to restrain him and several others, and Moldavia's erstwhile ruler seemed to simultaneously plead and argue.

Jacek narrowed his gaze. Had he mistaken Tatars for Moldavians? No, they were clearly Grazziani's men, for Jacek recognized the one who had pursued Wronski that first day.

During an eerily silent beat, "recompensed" floated across the water to Jacek's ears. The rest of the hospodar's words were lost in the awful racket of men and horses as they drowned, fought the river, fought one another for purchase, fought Tatars on the right bank.

Piercing screams.

Chaos.

Terror.

Jacek scanned his surroundings. Too many horrifying scenes played out around him, and he wasn't sure if any action he took could reverse the tide of mayhem and death and devastation.

By the Holy Mother!

When he looked back to where Grazziani had gained the shore, he and his Moldavians had vanished.

"There goes Kalinowski! Stop him!"

Jacek's attention caught on Walenty Kalinowski, his camp benefactor and the starosta of Kamieniec, riding his mount through the river, aiming for the far bank. Midway across, a different horse and rider lost their footing and, caught in the current, collided with Kalinowski. Jacek leaned forward in his saddle, as if he could yank the starosta from a watery grave.

His heart sank like lead in his chest, and he watched impotently as the starosta thrashed and spluttered before disappearing beneath the dark waters.

Henryk pulled up beside him. "Spirit of God!"

Next came Dawid, who crossed himself. They all stared at the river's turbulent surface where Kalinowski had been only moments before.

Long past midnight, soldiers who had failed in their attempted crossing began returning to camp. Jacek watched as they trickled in one at a time at first, then in larger and larger numbers. He had done nothing to bring them back. Only the specter of death had accomplished that.

With Henryk, Dawid, and Marcin, Jacek made his way to the great hetman's tent. A crowd of noblemen were gathered outside, demanding that he and Koniecpolski appear.

"We want proof the hetmans did not escape," one yelled.

"Hear, hear!" a cry rose up.

Żółkiewski, flanked by his inner circle, stepped outside with the aid of his cane. He pulled himself upright. "We did not escape, nor did we ever intend to escape. What you heard were rumors concocted by sources as yet unknown to us, but we will track them down."

The men sent up a cheer. Jacek, Henryk, Dawid, and Marcin exchanged skeptical glances. Why hadn't these turncoats believed the hetmans at the outset of their flight? So many lives lost, and for what? And while these *valiant* soldiers had been in the midst of deserting their posts, leaving the ramparts and tents unguarded, servants and Lost Men and only the Lord knew who else had plundered the camp, including Żółkiewski's own tents! For now, Żółkiewski said nothing of these grievous thefts or punishments, leaving Jacek to ponder whether the hetman's entire backbone had dissolved. Rather than vow to mete out swift justice against the brigands, he basked in an oath the noblemen—who had only moments before demanded his appearance—shouted out.

"We are yours to command! We want to die with you!"

Jacek dragged himself back to camp as the sun crested the horizon, more dispirited than ever. How he longed for the peaceful rhythm of home!

Later that morning, the carnage strewn up and down the riverbanks and in the water grew visible. Wounded were hauled from the water's turmoil, but servants refused to retrieve corpses and gear for fear of succumbing to a hail of Tatar arrows. The macabre scene was left to bake in the sun.

Jacek and Henryk reported to the hetman's quarters for another hastily called war council as the sun cleared the horizon.

Żółkiewski, his face pale and gaunt, tapped a forefinger against the tabletop. "Last night's debacle—for it can only be called such—has resulted in the loss of two thousand more men." Jacek sucked in a silent gasp. Żółkiewski broke out in a series of coughs before recovering himself. "We are scattered, diminished, and more exposed than ever before. Our scouts have already ventured out this morning and are reporting countless of our escaped troops falling into the hands of the enemy."

Henryk whispered in his ear, "Do you suppose they regret their decision to flee last night?"

No doubt. Jacek anticipated what sort of justice the hetman would mete out for their transgressions.

A hand went up. "But we had heard—"

"What did you hear, Lord Korecki?" His voice sharp as glass, Żółkiewski pointed a shaky finger at Samuel Korecki. The prince had been among those who attempted the crossing without success, insisting he had not been on the run, but that he had been attempting to turn back the others.

The prince stared straight ahead, chin up, but that chin seemed to quiver. "There were rumors, my lord Żółkiewski, that the hetmans were planning to flee. Understandably, men panicked."

"And you didn't think to bring this matter to your hetmans' attention, when we might have stood a chance of quelling the men's fears?"

Jacek's memory flicked back to being dismissed only yesterday when he had approached these very hetmans with the unrest *he* had heard, and dismay stirred in his chest.

Before Korecki could answer, Koniecpolski boomed, "Where did these rumors c-come from?"

Whispers circled the room.

Szemberg stepped forward, helmet resting in the crook of his arm. "We believe they came from Hospodar Grazziani, Hetman." He dipped his head in a respectful bow. Żółkiewski merely blinked. "Not only did he spread the rumors, but he bribed Lord Walenty Kalinowski to accompany him."

"A lot of good that bribe did," someone snorted. "It's probably washed up downstream with Kalinwoski's corpse."

"Yes, but Grazziani managed to get away," someone else chimed.

Recompensed. The word replayed in Jacek's mind in an accented voice. Recognition flashed bright. *Dear God, I overheard Grazziani laying out the plot. I could have stopped this madness!*

Koniecpolski cleared his throat. "The h-hospodar did *not* manage to flee. We have learned that he was captured and beheaded by his own retinue shortly after his escape."

Voices rumbled through the assembly. Jacek turned to Henryk, whose slack-jawed countenance could have been a reflection of Jacek's.

"The hospodar … dead?" Henryk hissed. "Not that I miss him, but …"

"Agreed," Jacek whispered back. "This entire expedition, these staggering losses. And for what?"

Żółkiewski crumpled into his seat, seeming to have expended every ounce of energy he possessed. "Not only did our own troops attempt to desert, but others were caught looting the camp. Our *own* camp, including *my* tents. I am beyond outraged."

Pity those deserters and thieves, for a reckoning is about to be visited on them.

Jacek's mind flashed to Wronski's plundering, and he leaned to Henryk's ear. "Did you notice Rogowski or Wronski at any time during the ruckus at the river last night?"

Henryk shook his head.

The crown grand hetman rested his elbows on the arms of the chair and closed his eyes. "If Iskender Pasha decides to invade our camp right now, we are doomed."

One silent moment stretched into another. Just as Jacek believed Żółkiewski had fallen asleep, he appeared to rouse. "But handing out punishments at this moment will only hurt us further."

What?

The declaration stunned Jacek. If not now, when *did* the hetman plan to serve up justice? The looting had been carried out by servants, Zaporozhian Cossacks—whom Żółkiewski had vowed would never take part in the expedition in the first place—and the Lost Men. To not discipline the brigands sent the wrong message to the rest of the army from a hetman who was already looked upon as too weak to control his troops. *"Commit a crime, and there will be no consequence. Have a crime inflicted upon you, and you will receive no justice."* Could the hetman not see that his decision encouraged the very lawlessness that so "outraged" him?

A hussar from Walenty Kalinowski's regiment raised his hand. "With all due respect, Crown Grand Hetman, we would like to recover what was stolen from us. When can we expect action?"

Jan Żółkiewski stepped forward, his jaw clenching and unclenching. "As the crown grand hetman said, the time will not be now."

The hussar's next question echoed the one bouncing through Jacek's befuddled brain. "When *will* it be, then?"

"When we deem it appropriate. The matter is closed."

But it wasn't. It was merely covered up. A wound needed to be tended before it became infected, but the hetmans were choosing to ignore it and let it fester. While that might work for a time, the consequences, like the infection, would grow until they were too destructive to the body to ignore … and by then, it might be too late.

A tired grumble rose, with some men grousing about lost possessions, their companions admonishing them to be patient, others called for withdrawal, and still more advocated for negotiating with the enemy. None suggested confronting the Ottomans—the fight was amongst themselves. What a turn of sentiment from a few short days ago!

Jacek rubbed the pommel of his sabre with the pad of his thumb. How had everything gone so wrong so quickly?

It didn't go wrong quickly. It's been careening off a cliff since the very beginning.

Arguments among the men now grew heated, but Żółkiewski remained still, his gaze fixed on the tabletop. Here sat a corpse-in-waiting, a shell of a man Jacek had once respected beyond reason. A moment of clarity struck: the hetman was no longer the man to lead them out of this mess.

A collective cry rang out, followed by a shriek that pierced the earthly world and likely punched a hole in the heavenly one too.

Jacek leaped to his feet as murmurs of "What was *that*?" tore through the assemblage. He ran outside, Henryk on his heels. More screams filled the air, each more tortuous than the last. Jacek followed the sounds to the rampart, where a crowd that had gathered behind a wall of soldiers gawped toward the battlefield.

Steeling his spine, Jacek turned his head in the same direction. His heart stuttered in his chest.

Henryk caught him up, his breathing heavy. "What is it?"

Jacek pointed toward the source of the screams as he mustered control. "One of Grazziani's entourage," he choked out. On the edge of the battlefield, in full view of the embankment, the dignitary who had shown such keen interest in Wronski writhed in agony atop a tapered tree trunk staked into the ground.

Henryk sucked in air. "They've impaled him!"

Jacek looked to one of the soldiers guarding the embankment. The man appeared dazed, his jaw slack, as he stared at the horrific spectacle. "Have you a bow and arrow?" Jacek barked.

The shrieks grew louder, shriller.

Jacek held out his hand, urging the paralyzed guard. "Quickly, man!"

The soldier seemed to rouse from his stupor, fumbling with his bow and quiver. Jacek wrenched them from his grasp. Nocked an arrow. Pulled the bowstring. Let the shaft fly. A solid *thunk* and the screaming stopped. He sagged with relief, with sorrow, and let the bow clatter to the ground.

Korecki appeared beside Jacek, his eyes fixed on the dangling dead man. "Now you understand why I could not let you and your men pass." He crossed himself, turned, and walked away.

Hours later, they were back in a war council. A once proud, determined force had been reduced to a dejected, demoralized army one-half the size of the one that had been arrayed upon the battlefield two days ago.

Lost in his own despairing thoughts, Jacek heard little until a guard called from outside the tent. "Messenger from Iskender Pasha, my lords."

Żółkiewski's eyes flicked to his son. "Bring him in."

Jan Żółkiewski stepped to the tent's opening and held back a flap, giving a curt nod to the guard. A courier stepped inside. No older than Filip, he held his chin high as he entered the hetmans' domain, ringed by battle-hardened, dirty men with murder on their minds. His dark eyes glittered as he surveyed the assemblage.

Brave lad.

Żółkiewski crooked his fingers, and the messenger stepped forward and executed a crisp, reverent bow. From inside his tunic, he extracted a small roll of paper sealed at the seam and held it up. The priest held a rosary, and the lad's gaze moved to the cross dangling from it and held.

Koniecpolski reached out his hand, and the lad laid the scroll in his palm. The hetman cracked the seal and unfurled the missive. His eyes traveled over the contents.

"What does he say?" urged Żółkiewski. "Can you interpret it?"

"Yes. It is written in Latin. The pasha invites us to negotiate."

A breath Jacek didn't realize had been trapped in his throat released with relief. Perhaps there was a way out that wouldn't result in all of them losing their heads … or finding themselves impaled on a battlefield.

Jacek and Henryk plodded back to Biaska's camp after the war council meeting.

"Do you think we have a chance of reaching an agreement with the Ottomans?" Henryk's voice was subdued and grim.

Yes, the hetman had agreed to open negotiations, but that didn't ensure success. Something about Żółkiewski's posture as he dictated the message to his priest had unnerved Jacek, though he could not identify what. Perhaps he was merely tired from the events of the night and overwrought over the loss of so many—and the loss of Lesław—but that sprouting weed of doubt grew stronger and fuller as it pushed its way toward the light. Soon it would burst forth, and Jacek would have to face it.

"I don't know. Time will tell. At least it gives us a day of reprieve so we can rest." The irony that this campaign had been meant to get to this very point without bloodshed was not lost on Jacek. What a heavy price to pay, and for what? A conniving hospodar who not only fled but incited others to do so at their peril … and lost his head in the process.

Good riddance.

Henryk huffed. "It still doesn't refill the food stores that were stolen from us."

"No, but with some luck, we might catch a few squirrels or rabbits." Jacek's mind darted to Oliwia when he first met her and how she had boasted of her prowess at killing a pheasant with a well-aimed rock. How helpful that skill would be right now.

"Hardly enough to feed an army of three thousand."

"I wasn't speaking for the entire army. Just us." And now Jacek reminded himself of one of the magnates, looking out for his own at the expense of everyone else. When he had first started on campaign, all had been as clear as snow melt in the Carpathians. There had only ever been two sides. Everyone on their side of the conflict had been equally righteous, while those on the other side had been equally evil. The longer the mission went on, though, the more the lines blurred. Black and white, once so crisply distinguishable, were fading into gray hues, bleeding over into one another.

Back in camp, Jacek removed Jarosława's tack and began brushing her, focusing on the strokes and the spots on her hide he knew as well as his own hand. The exercise worked, and his mind emptied itself of carnage and war. He hummed a tune.

A throat clearing behind his back startled him, and he wheeled. Before him stood Filip, hands clasped behind his back in a stance that Oliwia claimed mimicked Jacek's own.

"I, uh, I'm sorry if I surprised you."

Jacek bent back to his brushing. "No need to be. What troubles you?"

Filip picked up a second brush and went to work on her other side. "How do you know I am troubled?"

"Once you have known someone ten years, you learn their silent signals. 'Tis not a bad thing."

"So you know my sister's 'tells'?"

Jacek chuckled. "No, and just when I think I do, she surprises me. Like all women, she's a mystery yet to be solved." *And I look forward to working that puzzle for the rest of my life.* The thought he might never get the chance again burst in his head. He shook off the omen and discreetly crossed himself. "I will say, however, that she knows every tell you and I have."

Filip grunted his agreement.

They worked in silence for several beats before Filip spoke once more. "I wonder what would have become of Liwi and I had you not rescued us in our village that day."

"I did not rescue you. Your sister did. She gave me little choice." *Because I could not have left her or you behind.*

"Liwi is like that. Protective." Filip paused his brushing. "In a way, it's … nice."

Jacek brought his head up from Jarosława's flank. "I thought you found her to be … What was it now? Stifling?"

Filip darted him a contrite look over the horse's back. "That is what I came to say."

"That your sister is stifling?" Jacek bent back down, a smile quirking his lips.

"That I have been, um, mistaken about many things, including her. But mostly I …" Filip's voice cracked. Jacek kept his head down; the boy was struggling enough without having to look him in the eye. "Jacek, I am sorry for … for putting my faith in someone like Captain Wronski. It was foolish. *I* was foolish." His voice dropped to a mumble. "I should have listened to you."

Jacek savored the moment. "Life is full of lessons, Filip. Some hard, some not. What's most important is that you were not physically harmed, and your honor prevailed in time. Now you learn from it and move on."

"I … I was not so honorable the entire time." Filip shifted from foot to foot. "The captain wanted me to prove my worth …"

Jacek cocked an eyebrow.

Words tumbled from Filip like a rain-swelled brook spilling over rocks. "He told me to bring him your hussar wings. He was fascinated by them, and I-I …"

Jacek scowled at his brother-in-law but held his dismay there. To do aught might destroy the fledgling truce between them. "So that's where they went. Well, you will fashion me a new pair."

"Yes. In fact, I have already begun the endeavor." Filip's squirming continued. "There was also … He took me to a, um, place—"

"Save it for confession. You need not tell me."

"Is it bad that I … I liked it?"

Jacek pressed his lips together to keep from bursting out with a laugh. "A priest will tell you it's bad. Some men—Henryk, for example—will tell you it's good."

"What do *you* say?"

"I say it's human nature." Jacek tossed his brush into a bucket and patted Jarosława's rump. "Come, or she'll expect to be spoiled like this *all* the time."

As Jacek lay upon his cot in the twilight, he basked in the modicum of joy that percolated inside him over the conversation with Filip. The easy mood between them had returned, as if they had never slung cross words at one another, and in a world turned on its head, Jacek grasped at that one thread of normality.

That one thread now pushed him to unreel less pleasant thoughts he had been holding in tight check behind a wall of detachment. He was ready to confront the doubts that had been welling—and he had been denying—inside him for weeks. The weed had burst through and reached for the light.

The crown grand hetman was old. Tired. Both in years and demeanor. He was a weary general trying desperately to calm disheartened men and instill a belief in them that this battle—that was never meant to be—was just and that it would claim no more, even though over half their troops were gone. Wiped out. In two passes around the sun.

The expedition had been poorly prepared from the outset, and the hetman had counted too many assumptions as reality. And perhaps the king had counted too much on the old hetman.

Żółkiewski had lost his troops' faith. He was commanding with a shaky hand. His control, once iron-tight, was slipping away like water through his fingers.

As Jacek had walked through the encampment earlier, it had crackled with tension. Men had been openly speaking of mutiny now, of following a new leader, and no one had bothered to stifle them.

The camp was dissolving into anarchy.

Even if one subscribed to mutiny—which he did not—who, besides himself, could be trusted to lead them safely home? Koniecpolski, though he was beholden to his once father-in-law. Walenty Kalinowski, an affable man, was now dead. What of Korecki or Chmielecki? Though they had returned, they had deserted. Rogowski sprang to mind, and Jacek laughed at himself.

The world was indeed on its head if he considered Rogowski a more capable commander than the crown grand hetman of the land, a man he had always admired, had always aspired to be. Sadly, he had placed too much belief in that one man.

For the first time in his life, Jacek saw Żółkiewski for what he was: a fallible human being, like the rest. Worse, he no longer believed the crown grand hetman's first order of business was best for the Commonwealth. Whether he was seeking redemption—a way to put a shine on his tarnished legacy before he died—or merely trying to defeat his old enemy Iskender Pasha, Jacek had lost faith that the man he once vowed to follow blindly could lead them out of the valley of death. A reckoning loomed.

CHAPTER 39

Riders of the Apocalypse

"The negotiations have failed," Żółkiewski announced in a war council six days later. The air within the tent grew thick, and disappointment carved a path like a finely honed dagger through tender flesh. The hetman stared at some far-off place and blinked lazily, as if unconcerned. Bored, even.

"What's to become of the captives?" Jacek called out. "Are the Ottomans willing to exchange?"

The hetman steepled his fingers. "There will be no hostage exchange. Their terms are unacceptable."

Jacek's shoulders slumped. *God of Mercy! Lesław!*

Ignoring the many eyes pinned on him, Jacek grasped at the finest of threads. "With all due respect, what are their demands?" There had to be a bridge to a compromise.

"You ask what their demands are, Colonel Dąbrowski? They are too costly, that's what they are. Pasha wants more gold than we can possibly gather." Żółkiewski's eyes grew hooded. "While I appreciate your concern, there is no more we can do. We have exhausted all avenues of agreement. Now we must turn all our attention toward making our preparations to retreat as quickly as possible."

Anger, toxic and raw, rose from Jacek's gut to his throat, constricting his airway. Whether it was directed at the crown grand hetman, both hetmans, or the injustice in God's world, he couldn't say.

Lesław's name had been among the hostages being offered for trade. His lieutenant was alive, but ... Jacek shuddered at the fate that awaited his friend and once more tumbled rescue schemes through his exhausted brain. The sight and sounds of Grazziani's impaled man exploded in his mind's eye while Korecki's words floated through his head, and those schemes receded.

Jacek had been on edge for the duration of the talks, as though he lay on a bed of prickers. So had the rest of the men in the Commonwealth encampment. They had filled restive days sharpening weapons, repairing wagons, reading verse, conserving depleting supplies, writing letters home they hoped would reach their loved ones, trying not to contemplate what would happen should the two sides not come to an accord.

So many questions had hung in the balance, and now Żółkiewski's proclamation fueled more. Commanders began voicing them at once.

Żółkiewski held up his hands, and the din died down. "There is naught for us to do but withdraw as soon as possible."

"Can we do so peacefully, or will the Ottomans attack?" asked a commander. Jacek turned toward the familiar voice and recognized Rogowski, who had been more visible of late. As for Wronski, Jacek hadn't seen him and was grateful for it.

"They are not of a mind to grant us safe passage."

"Then how will we—"

"Prince Korecki has proposed a viable solution." The hetman nodded toward the prince, giving him the floor.

Korecki stepped to the front of the assemblage with one of his lieutenants and turned to face them. He took a puff of his pipe as his officer unfurled a diagram he then held aloft.

The prince pointed at the drawing, which appeared to be a rectangle made up of many smaller rectangles. "We have already begun building a rolling stock similar to the ones used in the battle. Like those, this one will also be equipped with manned cannons and artillery, but it will be larger—

six wagons wide and a hundred long." He tapped the center of the sketch with the butt of his pipe. "The sick and wounded will be transported in carts within the rolling stock's perimeter." Now his pipe moved to the top of the rectangle and along each side. "In order to protect the rolling fortress from attack, infantry will march at the front, and three rows of hussars and Cossacks will march on each side. Each will carry loaded firearms." The pipe moved to the bottom. "Guarding the rear will be the Liscowczycy and German infantry."

Jacek studied the plan with keen interest. "What route are we to follow?"

Korecki pointed his pipe Jacek's way. "When the rolling stock is ready, servants will dig a passage in the northern section of the rampart. We will head north." He canted his head. "Colonel, you seem troubled. What is your question?"

"Excavating a passage large enough to accommodate the rolling stock and the rest of the army is a tremendous undertaking. After the Tatars captured so many, are there enough able-bodied servants to complete the endeavor in a timely manner? And if there are, how will we cross the river and reach the left bank with a wagon fort of this size?"

Korecki lifted a piece of paper. "I've received a count, and we have servants enough to dig an adequate opening in little over a day's time. As for the stock, it is quite flexible, really. We will break it down into a narrower, longer tabor, and we will cross at a point our scouts have identified where the water is low, almost like a ditch. The crossing will be slow going, but it will be manageable."

"We will move out tomorrow," added Żółkiewski, "so prepare your camps."

"What time?" Henryk asked.

"At vespers."

Two hours before dusk.

Tacit approval rumbled through the assemblage. What other choice was there?

Jacek and Henryk remained in conversation with Korecki and took their time ambling back from the council, lost in silent thought. As they passed beside one magnate's camp, two men spoke loudly enough to be overheard.

"You know why the negotiations went nowhere, yes?"

A grunt in response.

The first man continued. "Because Żółkiewski didn't want them to go anywhere."

"How do you know?" the second man said.

"I was there. He demanded that Kantymir present himself to the Polish camp to be taken hostage."

What? Jacek ducked behind a tent and yanked Henryk with him. He put a finger to his mouth to signal silence.

"Why?"

The first man scoffed. "As I first stated, the great hetman didn't want the talks to bear fruit."

The men moved off, their voices growing thinner until they were gone. Jacek swayed on his feet, fighting to keep his bearings amid the swell of anger swamping him anew.

Henryk cocked an eyebrow. "What does it mean?"

"Jesus!" Jacek rasped. "Żółkiewski proposed a humiliation he knew would be completely unacceptable. The *murza* must have refused the escort, exactly as Żółkiewski knew he would."

Henryk's brows drew together. "Why would the crown grand hetman make such a demand? It makes no sense."

Jacek pounded a fist into his palm. "It does make sense if your goal is to undermine the negotiations. This way he can tell his troops it was the other fellow who refused the terms, and he saves face."

"But why would he want to break them off in the first place? I thought this whole mission was about striking a new treaty."

"A new treaty *before* we were defeated, when we had more bargaining power. Now that we are crushed, the agreements the pasha would likely want to extract would add too much shame for the hetman to bear. An armed retreat of a diminished army is less humiliating than bowing to Iskender Pasha's demands. Remember, the great hetman was trying to reverse his reputation after the Orynin debacle. Cecora has magnified his foibles. Don't you see? His only hope to turn the tide here is to get us all back so he can say he saved us after the Ottoman Empire refused to treat. In that small feat, he will be declared a hero. Let the hostages rot until their families can ransom them."

"So he purposely leaves Lesław and the others behind because of ... pride?"

Jacek unsheathed his sabre partway and slammed back into place. "Yes. That is precisely what he has done."

Two days later, they abandoned the Polish encampment. Jacek, like the other colonels, had been assigned command of one quadrant of wagons to make sure they moved as smoothly as possible. Laden with his wheel-locks, bow, and quiver, he marched with his men beside a wagon in a line of a hundred. In front of him, Dawid was similarly outfitted, as was Henryk. Marcin carried an arquebus in place of wheel-locks, and Filip was armed with a bow and full quiver. Flanking them were two other queues of cavalrymen equipped with firearms, crossbows, and regular bows—all meant to repel the enemy attack that was coming.

Before setting out, they all swore to defend the rolling fort and each other. They also swore to kill anyone who tried to escape the formation on horseback. There would be no quarter.

Samuel Korecki directed the rolling fortress, where each cart was pulled by horses collected from the cavalrymen. Jacek's two draft horses, Heban, and his poor, proud Jarosława made up the team pulling the wagon next to him. As commander, he would take turns marching and riding. Being horsed gave him the advantage of height, making it easier to watch the other wagons under his supervision.

He glanced over his shoulder toward the enemy camp, and his thoughts once more locked on Lesław. In one last, desperate attempt to save his friend and lieutenant, he had proposed to the crown grand hetman that he exchange Wronski and his band for Lesław, arguing that he had caught the captain plundering a dead soldier's belongs. First, the hetman had regarded him as though he were daft, then Żółkiewski had scoffed and dismissed him with a reminder that he had temporarily forgiven the looters.

I should have suggested that Żółkiewski exchange himself *for Lesław.*

At this moment, guilt and fury permeated Jacek's bones. He had literally turned his back on his lieutenant and friend.

"Damnation, but I hate leaving him!" Henryk's frustrated words reverberated with Jacek's inner thoughts.

"Stay strong, old friend, until we come for you," Jacek muttered.

Throughout the day's march, he constantly scanned their surroundings, body braced and tensed, flinching at every movement, every sound—for naught. The attack never came.

After a sleepless night where the air seemed to vibrate with malice, they resumed their march toward the shallow river crossing the scouts had selected. They hadn't been long into their trek, but every nerve ending in Jacek's body fired off alerts, and sweat pasted his clothes to his skin. He didn't dare remove his armor, and he'd ordered his men to keep theirs on too. They were all walking targets.

This day, Filip trod behind him. "Perhaps they will not pursue us. They might be turning for home themselves." His voice brimmed with hope.

"We are dealing with Tatars and Turks," Dawid huffed from behind them. "They are nothing if not tenacious. Do not let your guard down."

Jacek glanced over his shoulder, his eyes landing on Henryk and Marcin farther back in the line. As he did so, his gaze skipped to the Lost Men bringing up the rear. Wronski was visible in the very front of their number, jaw taut, his eyes constantly shifting, searching, until they landed on Jacek. Wronski sneered. Jacek returned the sneer.

"Tatars!" someone cried, pulling Jacek's attention front and center.

"Where? *Where?*" Filip's head swiveled to and fro.

Though Jacek couldn't see them, he barked orders at his stirring regiment to ready their weapons and stay together.

"Guard the tabor! Stay close," he shouted.

Thunk!

An arrow embedded itself in the side of a wagon, and men scattered.

"Keep the formation!" Jacek bellowed a moment before a flurry sliced through the air and rained down on them. "Stay together! Stay strong! Stray from the formation, and you will be cut down."

His command was lost in the cacophony of chaos as projectiles found purchase in a wooden board or a horse's rump or a man's thigh. Here, a man threw up his shield, and a shaft glanced off the metal. There, an arrow drove itself into the dirt.

Jacek took in the men around him as he flexed his loaded bow. Dawid, Henryk, and Marcin were upright, whole, and ready. But Filip, who had been behind him a mere moment before, was gone. A burst of panic had him yelling.

"Fil—"

Dawid pointed at the wagon. While men threw themselves to the ground, beneath wagons, or rolled under horses' legs, Filip scrambled up and over the side of the cart. No sooner had he disappeared than he popped up, arrow nocked and his bow taut. He took aim, let fly, and had the next projectile ready before Jacek could utter either "Brave lad!" or "Watch yourself!"

The first enemy volley paused, but the respite did not last.

"Let's go!" Jacek yelled.

Down the line, the crown grand hetman gestured with his buława. "Get this blasted rolling stock through the river!"

Coming up behind the fortress was the Tatar cavalry in a gallop, blades high, arrows flying.

Ah, for a charge with a kopia right now!

The Elears at the back intercepted, and a brutal clash ensued between ground troops and the horsed Tatars. Infantrymen took aim. Arrows flew. Artillerymen fired hook guns from the wagons into the Tatar cavalry.

Meanwhile the wagon fortress lumbered. Crown troops were falling, but so were many Tatars.

Jacek's eye snagged on a known frame astride a Tatar horse, beating back a trio of foes with savage determination. Wronski fought like the devil himself, twisting and turning and punishing with each savage blow as he assaulted the enemy from the back of a horse he had apparently appropriated. And so did his brethren. They were fearless, bloodthirsty masters of killing.

Jacek blocked out the sounds of battle and narrowed his focus on one mission: getting the rolling fortress through the river ditch.

The thing shambled and lurched and creaked and groaned, coaxed by men cajoling horses to haul its girth across the river. At last, they dragged it through.

The Tatars kept coming.

Muttering under his breath, Jacek fired off a half-dozen arrows, striking several foes. He checked his pistols, but the enemy was too far to catch his bullets.

Henryk appeared beside him. "How are we faring?"

"Remarkably well, considering how many Tatars we battle. But we can't hold them off much longer."

"Żółkiewski does not want us to chase. He wants us all close to the fortress."

"What of the Lost Men?"

Henryk pointed across the field. "They are falling back."

"Where are Filip and Dawid?"

"There." Henryk jerked his chin toward the wagon Filip had scrambled into. Beside the wagon's wheel stood Dawid, bow arm firing in a steady rhythm.

Relieved, Jacek turned back to the melee at the back of the fortress. "Shall we help out our brethren and kill some Tatars?"

"Sounds strange, calling the Lost Men 'brethren.'"

"The enemy of my enemy is my friend."

They lined up beside a group of riflemen under Jacek's charge as a band of Rogowski-led Lost Men fell back. Some ran. Some, like Wronski, had taken a horse and rode.

"Spread out," Jacek ordered the artillery. "One row take a knee, the row behind stand. Take aim but wait for my signal! We want these sons of bitches close enough so we can blow them all to hell, but we can't fire until our men are behind the line. First signal, one volley from the front row. Second signal, back row fires. Then run back to the fortress as though the devil is on your tail … because he is!"

The men arranged themselves, firearms primed. As the Lost Men streaked toward them, Jacek's men took aim at the pursuing Tatars.

Closer, closer.

"Rea-dy! And now!" Jacek brought his sabre down.

A blast of smoke clouded the air, and the dull thud of balls hitting flesh reported back. Horses and men cried out. The haze cleared, and shapes emerged from the fog, closer now.

"And now!" Jacek roared.

The next volley went.

"And fall back!"

The Tatars kept coming toward the tabor … where cannon and hook guns awaited them.

Boom!

Boom!

Boom!

The enemy peeled away, heading back south from whence they came, and the men let out a subdued cheer.

Thank God and all the saints Tatars loathed firearms, or the Commonwealth might not have enjoyed the same advantage in reach.

Jacek took in the carnage on the makeshift battlefield. Bodies sprawled like discarded scarecrows, and horses lay in mangled poses amid dirt and blood and debris. The Elears joined the rear-guard infantry as they reassembled into formation behind the fortress.

A reprieve. Another hour, maybe two, before the Tatars finished them all.

409

"We march by night and camp by day."

A groan rose up at the crown grand hetman's announcement. After more attacks by bands of Tatars, after marching throughout the day in the heat, after losing more men and more hope, the troops were exhausted. Food was scarce, and foraging parties spent much time bringing little back to camp.

But Jacek couldn't find fault with the hetman's proposal—because he had suggested it. So they rested in a makeshift camp, keeping vigil in shifts lest the mischief-making Tatars should decide to harass them.

After another scant meal, they set out at sunset, heading north to Mohylów and the fortified camp a hundred miles distant. *So, so far.* And this time, they had fewer men to march alongside the tabor and more crowding the wagons of the wounded.

Filip called to Jacek as they walked near the front "What's that up ahead?" The sun had slipped over the horizon minutes before, and light streaked the sky. Ahead, the fields seemed to be … moving.

Jacek retrieved his looker from his belt.

"What do you see?" Henryk asked.

Jacek lowered the looking glass and raised it again. Hetman Żółkiewski had been watching with hawk-eyed interest and now rode up beside him.

"Have you something to report to the rest of us, Colonel?" came his tired rasp.

"I see smoke." Jacek passed the looker up to the hetman, who passed it on to his priest, who was walking beside him. "These old eyes can barely make out what's in front of me, much less what might be smoke miles away."

The priest squinted through the looker. "I-I'm not sure."

The looker then went to Koniecpolski, who joined them. "Smoke," they agreed, their faces grim.

Had the Tatars captured a village and burned it to the ground?

Jacek mounted Heban, harnessed to the team, for a better look. As they rolled toward the spot, the smoke thickened, choking throats and stinging eyes and noses. They tried to go around it, but a wall of fire seemed to follow, blocking their way.

What is this devilry?

Men coughed, and horses snorted, trying to pull away from the flames and the acrid smell.

And now here came Korecki. "The devils have set crops, fields, and villages in our path ablaze!"

All eyes turned to Żółkiewski. "We push through. They can't have burned the entire country. There"—he pointed—"see where it is already dying out. Keep the men marching." He plodded ahead.

Jacek pulled out a linen square, sprinkled water from his dwindling canteen over it, and offered it to the hetman. The hetman hesitated. With a subtle nod, he accepted the proffered cloth and covered his nose and mouth.

Jacek's eyes watered and his throat burned as they moved through the billowing black clouds, aggravated that he was helpless to aid his men or his horses.

He dismounted, muttering to himself. "No point in staying astride when I can't see anything."

Marcin caught him up and dropped his voice. "What if there is nothing for the horses to forage? They are already fighting the load of the tabor, and we have little feed left. How will they keep going?"

Jacek glanced at Heban, and bands of sympathy lashed his heart. The horse plodded with his head down but hadn't complained. He was probably too exhausted. Jacek's draft horses didn't look much better. Jarosława, proud steed that she was, barely flagged, though the lather on her flanks betrayed her laboring. "I don't know, Marcin."

And, dear God, how I wish I had a solution!

Morning came, and the extent of the Tatars' devastation became woefully clear. As far as the eye could see, blackened land surrounded them. Not a building or bush or blade of grass had been spared. Even where fires had died down for lack of fuel, fresh smoke billowed on the horizon.

They camped on the barren, burnt soil, desperate for rest. It never came. With no shelter, they endured the endless heat of the sun and the relentless Tatars, who swooped in and out the day long, harassing, probing, running at the rolling stock. The infantry staved them off, but how much longer would their powder and shot hold out?

After another night of marching, they stopped at a site as bleak as the day before. The Tatars had been busy firing everything in the Commonwealth troops' path, turning the landscape into hell on earth.

Jacek unharnessed his horses. Jarosława lay down, with Heban nearby, and Jacek rested his back against her as he stared out at the void, shading his eyes with his forearm. Where he once loved the sun's warmth on his face of an early autumn day, he now cursed it.

He had checked on every man before he took his rest, and the mood was uneasy. Even Henryk's normally cheerful demeanor flagged. "A hussar is not meant to walk, nor is his warhorse meant to be used as an ox," he had complained.

Jacek didn't answer, for he had no counter. He agreed with Henryk, but he also welcomed the hetman's will pushing them on. And right now, with morale hanging as low as ripe fruit on an apple tree, Jacek had no doubt that, given the chance, many would flee.

He closed his eyes and daydreamed of home, of spreading a blanket beneath the lacy shade of an oak tree on the green hills surrounding Biaska. Jarosława would graze nearby, gorging herself on thick, wet tufts of grass. He would lie back, staring up at a crisp autumn sky, and pull Oliwia beside him to steal kisses while the children gamboled around them. Their joyful laughter rang in his ears. A stream burbled nearby, and a soft spring breeze ruffled new leaves. No man needed anything but this.

"Tatars! And Turks!" a sentry yelled.

He snapped awake and lurched to his feet, sliding out his looker. Around him, weary men roused.

"Damnation!"

Henryk lifted himself onto an elbow. "How many?"

"I'm not sure. More than yesterday."

"Any Janissaries?" Janissaries meant artillery.

"Possibly. I see cannon."

"Double damnation!" Dawid pulled on his gear and readied his weapons. He sent Jacek a smirk. "I reckon they grew bored and are looking for another tussle."

"I reckon." Jacek retrieved his bow, tightened his sword belt, and nudged Jarosława with his boot. "I'm sorry, old girl, but I need you to get up for just a little bit longer." She hoisted herself partway up.

Jacek slid his cross from beneath his żupan and armor, kissed it, and tucked it back in, next to his heart. Infantrymen began readying cannons, hook guns, and muskets. He grabbed his wheel-locks and checked them again to be sure they were primed and ready.

Jarosława lay back down with a groan. Jacek crouched beside her and stroked her withers. "Too tired? Shall I let Heban take the lead instead?"

Surging to her hooves, she shook her mane and nickered at him.

He let out a chuckle. "Jealousy fires the blood, yes?"

She suddenly shifted, knocking him to the ground—seemingly intentionally. "Hey! What—"

A *thwap* reverberated, followed quickly by two more, then a *thunk*. His blood turned to ice. Jarosława screamed. Scrabbled. Dropped to the ground, creating a line of sight to Dawid, who cried out, his eyes wild and panicky as he reached for the shaft of an arrow buried in his hip.

While Jarosława thrashed on the ground, the whizz and thud of arrows sounded all around Jacek. Before him, Tatar and Ottoman cavalrymen raced toward the camp.

Jacek roared in anguish. A blood-red curtain dropped behind his eyes and quickly turned to black.

Oliwia sat in the ladies' salon, gazing out the window on this fine fourth day of October. Staring at the countryside, searching for the Biaska banner, had become an everyday pastime, though one she spent in vain, for there was no banner. Nor had they received word that the men were coming home.

How much longer? She rarely bothered to pick up her sewing anymore unless Lady Regina was present, and then only to make herself look productive in the lady's eyes. Today, only she, Eugenia, and Eugenia's maid occupied the bright space, so she had no pretenses to keep up.

"See anything?" Eugenia asked absently.

A large group of riders crested the horizon, and Oliwia squinted at the fluttering white banners. "Actually, I do. It appears to be a company of soldiers, but not our soldiers."

"Hmm ..."

The door softly opened, and Nadia scurried in. Did Nadia ever *not* scurry?

"A messenger brought this to your quarters, m'lady."

Oliwia's heart leaped. *A letter from Jacek!* But when Nadia handed her the missive, its familiar seal made her heart settle lower than it had been before. More bad news from Tomasz, no doubt. Worse than receiving yet *another* missive from Biaska, there had been no letters from Jacek in weeks. Not that he wrote daily or that his letters got to her on a regular schedule. But still, he had been in the habit of writing at least weekly, and she hadn't received word in far too long ... nor had Eugenia heard from Lesław, who was a much more faithful writer.

Eugenia looked up from her lacework and raised a questioning eyebrow.

Oliwia waved a dismissive hand. "From Biaska."

Eugenia bowed her head back to her work, and Oliwia broke the seal. Eugenia understood, for she had managed Matejko Manor for her father before taking on the oversight of Silnyród.

The letter was not from Tomasz, however, but from the priest, writing on behalf of Erwin Baran, the estate's horse trainer. Erwin was sorry to deliver the news that one of the new warhorses from this past spring had broken its leg after a fall. He went on to describe the details of the accident, along with the measures he had taken in trying to save the horse's life, though the words glanced off Oliwia's mind like a rock skipping over water.

These tidings—coupled with Tomasz's reports of sickness sweeping the village and grain left to rot because Biaska had endured heavy downpours and had not had enough hands to harvest—pressed on Oliwia's shoulders.

She needed to get home! But how could she leave when Jacek remained on campaign? He might be home any day.

Mary, Mother of God, she prayed her wish would come true, and soon.

Propping her elbow on the arm of the chair, she dropped her head in her palm.

"More bad news?" Eugenia prodded softly.

Oliwia let out a defeated sigh. "Yes. It seems that's all there is of late."

"It will get better," her friend promised.

Eugenia was simply being kind—she was always kind—but Oliwia's frustrations over these past few months came together in one misdirected eruption. "How can you say such things when you don't know? You're offering false hope. Only God knows!" She immediately regretted the words.

Eugenia's eyes and mouth went round, and her face crumpled. "Perhaps so I hear them and believe it's true. You are not the only one to suffer, Oliwia."

Oliwia sprang from her chair and knelt at Eugenia's feet. "I am so very sorry. I should not have lashed out at you. You have been the dearest friend to me, and I—"

Magdalena rushed into the room and pulled up when her eyes landed on them. "Is everything all right?"

"Yes," Eugenia sniffed as she patted Oliwia's hand.

Oliwia did not deserve the charitable gesture, and they both knew it. She stood, her cheeks blazing with embarrassment. "No. I was being beastly to Eugenia."

Magdalena smirked. "What, again? Really, Oliwia, your impatience will be the death of us all." Oliwia glared at her, but Magdalena ignored her and ran on. "Eugenia, dear, your father's men-at-arms are approaching."

Eugenia hopped up and ran to the window.

Oliwia followed, admonishing herself for blithely dismissing any flags but the red-and-yellow. "Is that his pennant? I saw it earlier but didn't recognize it." The company with the white banners was drawing closer to Żółkiew's walls.

Eugenia squealed, and her face brightened with joy. "Yes! Father is here!" She took Oliwia's and Magdalena's hands in hers and tugged them toward the door. "Come! Help me greet him!"

A half hour later, they stood in Lady Regina's morning room. Though the chamber was drenched in sunlight, a pall cast a shadow over every surface.

In the center of the room stood Lord Klemens Matejko, a robust man with a ruddy complexion. Today, though, his face held an ashy pallor that accented the deep creases around his eyes and mouth, and his once coal-black hair and mustache were streaked with thick strands of white.

Four ladies—Lady Regina, Magdalena, Eugenia, and Oliwia—sat before him, all eyes glued to him as he rotated his kolpak in his hands. Oliwia's own hands twisted in her lap.

"I'm afraid I have some distressing news to deliver, my ladies." He darted his eyes toward his daughter and gave her a weak smile.

"I was lately in Mohylów where I heard a rumor that on nineteen September, Hetman Żółkiewski's army clashed with the combined forces of Iskender Pasha, Kantymir Murza, Kalga Dewlet-Gireja, and Prince Gabriel Bethlen."

Eugenia's hand flew to her mouth but couldn't hold back her gasp.

Lady Regina took a step back. "A formidable force!"

Oliwia's wringing hands now fisted her skirts.

"Indeed. Witnesses say there were as many as fifty thousand."

At this, they *all* gasped. Oliwia braced herself, her heart thudding in her chest as Pan Klemens continued.

"It did not turn out well for the Polish troops."

Lady Regina's chin inched up, but the quiver in her voice betrayed the show of stoicism. "How many lost?"

"Three thousand on the day of the battle, and more the next night," he sighed. "They pulled back to their own camp, and the last this person knew, they were attempting to negotiate with the pasha."

"Who did you hear this from?"

Pan Klemens tightened his grip on his cap. "From Stefan Chmielecki. He and a number of his men escaped the night after the battle, urged on,

I'm afraid, by Lord Kalinowski, who in turn was encouraged"—he paused—"no, bribed by Hospodar Grazziani."

Magdalena's mouth dropped open. "The ruler they meant to rescue?"

"The same."

"And what became of Lord Kalinowski and his men?" Lady Regina asked.

Sadness flashed in Pan Klemens's dark eyes. "They perished or were captured by the enemy during their escape."

"And the hospodar?"

"Hopefully, he drowned too," grumbled Magdalena.

Pan Klemens shook his shaggy head. "He made it across, only to be killed by his own. Alexandru Iliaş now sits on the throne."

Eugenia's face was as milky as Oliwia's knuckles, and Oliwia grabbed her friend's hand and clung to it. Oliwia dared ask the question suspended like an executioner's blade. "And what of the others?"

"I do not know, my dears."

Helplessness engulfed her. Releasing her hold on Eugenia, she dropped her head in her hands and wept.

CHAPTER 40

Fields of Sorrow, Fields of Fire

"Jacek, get up! Now!" Henryk yelled as he and Marcin dragged Dawid toward the shelter of the wagon fortress.

Jacek ran his hands over Jarosława, carefully skipping over the arrows protruding from her neck and heaving chest. Her thrashing had stopped, and she seemed to search his face, bewilderment and fear evident in her soft brown eyes. Red froth oozed from her nose and mouth.

Bands of sorrow compressed his throat, his chest, and he couldn't breathe. His vision was blurred.

The thundering of enemy hooves seemed suspended in a fog, as did his comrades' pleas to run to safety.

He heard himself murmur calming words to his beloved combat horse. How she had been the best companion he or any hussar could ever have hoped for, how she was part of him, how she had helped him become who he was, how proud he was of her. He continued stroking her.

Turning his hands over, he realized they were wet, though not with blood. He touched his cheek, and it was wet too.

"There's no more time, old girl," he choked. "I must go, as must you." Slowly, he wrapped his hand around his nadziak.

"Jacek!" Now Filip was on one knee beside him, his hand gently shaking Jacek's shoulder. "You must take cover!" He looked down at Jarosława. "You need to leave her, Jacek."

"No. I cannot leave her to those jackals."

"Would you like me to do it?" Filip's soft voice quavered.

Jacek answered with a hard shake of his head. "No. It must be me."

"How can I help?"

"Get Heban to safety."

Filip scrambled to his feet. "Hurry, brother!"

Jarosława's breathing had grown labored. She snorted and let out a high-pitched noise, like a whimper. A wild look came into her eyes.

"It will be all right," Jacek soothed the horse. "Soon you will be grazing on the sweetest grass." Though his tone was soft, his innards were gutted. "I will miss you like my own limb, my dearest friend." The words caught in his throat.

He covered her eye with his hand, holding her head steady as he recited a prayer. She seemed to ease.

"We will see each other soon, yes?"

With gunfire and grim determination, the defenders thwarted the combined assault on the rolling stock, aided in part by Wronski and his squad. The infantry recaptured two of the Crown's own cannon lost during the initial battle weeks ago, which the Turks had thought to use against them.

The victory rang hollow, though, for the effort had come at more cost. More men killed, more horses dead, more corpses and carcasses left behind.

Żółkiewski lauded the effort with a rousing speech as he limped up and down the line of battered men, though his tone did little to lift spirits.

"Rest now. Tonight, we march on. Poland is near."

"He has lost his grip," one haiduk hissed behind Jacek. "What good is his speechmaking?"

The man's companion opened his mouth to reply when Jacek wheeled on them and spat out a retort.

"He's willing us all to reach Mohylów alive. And we're going to oblige him."

The men's eyes widened. "Yes, sir." The two shuffled away.

Jacek took several steps and dropped in the dirt beside Henryk. "How's Dawid?"

Henryk measured out gunpowder with great care. "Complaining like an old woman."

"Getting an arrow in your leg will do that to a man."

"Pah! This is his way of getting out of the march. Now he rides in the comfort of the wagons."

Filip smirked. "Doesn't appear comfortable."

Marcin arranged arrows in his quiver. "Tell you what, Henryk. If you think it's such an agreeable way to travel, I volunteer to injure you myself."

Henryk tossed back an insult that questioned Marcin's parentage.

Jacek's battered heart drew comfort from the men's banter, and he lay back and threw his forearm over his eyes, trying in vain to conjure visions of home.

Please, Lord God, let this be over soon.

They marched through the never-ending fires and smoke that night until they nearly dropped from exhaustion as the sun rose. The Tatars, who had been trailing them, stuck to their strategy of harassment and harangued them throughout the day, picking off a man here or a horse there. That only Kantymir's men seemed to pursue them now was of little comfort. They could not sleep. The food was gone. Water was drying up. Horses were falling, unable to rouse themselves, unable to go on.

Jacek had lost one of his draft horses. The other and Heban would surely be next. Occasionally, he glimpsed Wronski's sable—*his* sable—and he looked at it longingly, gladdened she still lived.

Within his chest beat a heart that physically hurt from the hole carved out by the death of Jarosława. Despite the pain, he staggered on, doing his utmost not to flag, trying to instill hope in the men he led.

By God's grace and Żółkiewski's sheer will, they lived through another night and drove toward the border at a relentless pace. After eight grueling days, the crown grand hetman was on the cusp of getting them all home.

The Tatars who pursued were a weaker force now, and though they watched and followed the rolling stock on its march to the border, they made no more attempts to stop it. Consequently, the men marched that day. Excitement burgeoned and rippled through the exhausted troops.

Tonight, Jacek would walk on Polish soil! He could practically taste her sweet air on his parched tongue.

Late afternoon, the entire procession stopped. Jacek craned his head to see what had brought them to a halt. Off to one side, the hetmans and a knot of commanders seemed to exchange heated words. Jacek strode toward them.

"But the men are exhausted, Hetman Żółkiewski," one commander protested. "We must rest for a little while. Then we can begin the march again this evening."

"Rest? When we are within sight of the border?" Jacek blurted. *Are you mad?*

Żółkiewski acknowledged Jacek with a nod. "Colonel Dąbrowski agrees with me. If we push on, we cross into Poland at midnight.

"We *must* push on," Jacek insisted.

The commander gave him a look of pure flint. "My men are exhausted. The enemy is done with us. We are no longer in danger—"

Jacek perched his fists on his hips. "I disagree, Commander. We are in danger of more men and horses dying from exhaustion or wounds. As long as the enemy is in sight, we are in danger of more attacks. Simply because they have held off does not mean they are done with us. And have you checked our powder supplies lately? They are nearly depleted! How the hell are we to repel another Tatar attack without firearms?"

The quarrel continued, with more commanders arguing for a rest than against it. As the debate raged, Żółkiewski's backbone seemed to dissolve.

421

"Enough, my lords. Do you have a destination in mind?"

"The village of Serwini."

Jacek's heart sank. "But, Hetman, if we stop—"

The hetman held up his hand. "Perhaps you weren't listening, Colonel. I said *enough!*"

And so it was that the crown grand hetman bowed to the loudest among his army, and they came to a stop in a patch of scorched earth six miles from Mohylów. No water, no feed. Nothing but the village the Tatars had just fired.

"And this is the haven the commanders sought instead of making for home?" Henryk grumbled.

"Poland is close. We will arrive soon," were the only words Jacek could muster.

He decided to check the wagons under his command and the horses afterward. His draft horse had been left behind when it was too exhausted to go on. He spared a moment to mourn it, and his heart lifted a fraction as he approached Heban. Though the warhorse was weak, he let out a sigh when Jacek scratched his ears and stroked his neck. "Almost there. One more night pulling the wagons. Then we will be done with this ordeal, and you will have all the water and feed you can stand, plus a story to tell your grandchildren."

As he passed Dawid resting on a pallet, he was surprised his lord-brother was alert and looking around. He hailed Jacek and winced from the slight movement. Gritting his teeth, he tried to mask his pain. His lips were cracked, his face gaunt and sweaty, his clothes bedraggled. His sorry state was mirrored in nearly every other face.

Jacek crouched down beside him. "I did not expect to see you awake."

"One can only sleep so much, especially when one's thoughts are filled with reaching home."

"The hetman has given the wounded and sick permission to ride out. Why not take advantage?"

Dawid scoffed. "And let those bloodthirsty Tatars pick me off like an unsuspecting vole? No, thank you. I have come this far, and I am not about to desert my brethren now."

Jacek pointed toward his leg. "I can see how much it troubles you, so I won't ask how it is. Instead, I'll ask how *you* are—besides anxious to reach Mohylów."

"Excellent, naturally. I can't remember a time when I've felt better." Dawid chuckled. "Actually, I can."

"Shall I guess? You were in the midst of wine and women."

Dawid shook his head. "Why is it when I go on campaign with you, I end up in dire circumstances? You are a detriment to my health."

"I am truly sorry, Dawid." Jacek's train of thought scampered away from him. He debated whether it was easier to die chained to a galley bench from being whipped to death or by drowning, by being beheaded on Moldavian soil … or dying of starvation and thirst within sight of one's country.

His companion's hoarse voice stirred him from his wretched musings. "If we are to die," Dawid began, "I would ask you to bestow me with one last favor."

"And I would grant it, if it were possible. What would you ask of me?"

"I would ask your blessing to wed your sister."

Jacek checked himself. Surely he was in the grip of delirium. Or he had finally dropped into a deep slumber and was having the most peculiar dream. "My … sister?"

"Yes, your sister. Tamara."

"You wish to marry my sister Tamara."

"Yes."

"May I ask why?" Jacek realized how daft he sounded.

"Why else? I'm in love with her, and I believe she cares for me as well." Jacek barked out a laugh. "Of all the ridiculous …"

Dawid's dark brows knotted together. "What's so ridiculous about asking her to be my wife? I know I haven't riches to speak of and—"

"'Tis not that." Jacek splayed his hand across his chest.

"Then what is it you find so amusing?"

"I thought she fancied Henryk."

"Henryk!" Dawid croaked.

"Yes. And I daresay, by comparison, you seem a far more respectable prospect."

423

"So you approve?"

"I did not say that." Then again, he had no say and little influence when it came to his sister's choices.

Dawid groaned. "Dear God, can you not grant a dying man his final wish?"

"You are not dying. Furthermore, I do not give you permission to die on me." Jacek wagged a finger at him.

"At this moment, I believe I have no choice. But indulge me. Why not?"

Jacek held up two fingers. "Two reasons. One, you will very likely break my sister's heart, and two, I want you alive so I can kill you for wooing her behind my back."

"I didn't woo her!"

"That's even worse." The first hint of a smile in days tugged at Jacek's mouth.

"Do you think we'll actually make it out?"

Jacek glanced to the north and let hope bloom in his chest. "I do."

"Then what I ask is even more important to me."

Jacek patted Dawid's shoulder. "You have my blessing." He glimpsed Dawid's mouth drop open as he spun away to look in on his regiment.

He was astonished by the renewed liveliness among his men, for they had been pushed to the outer edges of thirst, hunger, fear, and exhaustion for weeks. Their nearness to home had invigorated them, and he crossed himself in thanks.

The enemy must have sensed the shift, for they made another assault at the rear of the column. Jacek ascended a wagon for a better look. Once again, the infantry and the Lost Men were on them, driving them back.

Thank Christ and all the saints for those men and firearms! He could not help but question whether the enemy would have mounted an attack had the Commonwealth army not stopped to rest, however.

Nothing could be done for it now, and he shook off the thought. Instead, his mind turned to the Forlorn Hope. He couldn't deny the modicum of admiration he held for the mercenaries. The army would not have made it this far had it not been for their courage, their tenacity, and their willingness to defend the tabor's rear.

His mind shot to Wronski and how the blackguard had betrayed Lesław. A fresh pang clawed at Jacek's chest and ignited the fire in his belly. Before they reached Poland, he had to confront the scoundrel.

As he went in search of him, his eyes reported a startling sight: Wronski, walking beside the line of wagons, a pair of hussar wings fluttering on his back. *Jacek's* wings. Oh yes, it was most definitely time for a reckoning. Jacek marched straight for him.

He hadn't gone far when Szemberg headed him off, barking that the crown grand hetman had called an urgent war council meeting before the final push into Poland. Jacek blew out a frustrated breath and watched Wronski's retreating winged back before turning and summoning Henryk.

Henryk matched him stride for stride, their gait a practiced one over many years serving together. "How many more times do you reckon the Tatars will run at us?"

"No idea." But the sun was dipping closer to the horizon; never had Jacek welcomed dusk as much as he did now. "Only six more miles, and we are home." He would fall to his knees and kiss his home soil.

They ducked inside the hetman's makeshift command tent, where a crowd of towarzysze and commanders were deep in what appeared to be clandestine conversation. When the hetmans appeared, they snapped their mouths shut and turned eyes on Żółkiewski. The old hetman wobbled on his cane, more stooped than ever. A folding armchair had been set up for him, but instead of sitting, he leaned his hands on its back and straightened. The movement appeared to pain him. Flanking him were his son, Jan, and Koniecpolski, and behind them stood his priest.

Żółkiewski opened the meeting by asking the priest to bless the gathering. That done, the crown grand hetman began recounting the miles they had traveled since leaving Cecora behind. He commended the colonels, commanders, and officers for their service and discipline. Then he went on to describe what lay ahead: the ground they would cover in tonight's final journey, the nine hours he expected it would take, and ways in which they would organize and disperse once they arrived in Mohylów.

He scanned the assemblage. "Are there any questions?"

One of the hussars who had been thick in the discreet discussion cleared his throat. "One, Crown Grand Hetman. During the looting of the camp on the night of September 20, we lost many valuable possessions." He swept his hand, gesturing to the men surrounding him who had also taken part in the hushed conversation. "You withheld punishments after the incident, and we request that you allow a search among the servants, the Lisowczycy, and others we suspect of thieving. We request that search be conducted now, before we pick up camp and make our final march to the border."

Żółkiewski let out an exhausted sigh and seemed to shrivel. "My lords, I understand you are aggrieved—"

"We were robbed!" one of them cried. "And right now, those men are allowed to walk about with impunity!"

Żółkiewski held up a hand, looking as though he could barely hold his weight up with the other. "Yes, yes. But the timing—"

The hetman was right, and Jacek gave him an inner cheer. Stopping their progress now left them exposed to more of what was taking their lives: the Tatars, hunger, thirst, injuries. Then again, the search and punishments should have been carried out when the crimes were discovered … when they had idled for days in camp during the sham negotiations. Now the lesion had been allowed to fester, and the consequences of leaving it be were returning to roost. Lancing the infection would prove far more painful now than at the outset of the crimes; that lancing needed to be done with extreme care.

"This is the *only* time," the first hussar countered. "Once we cross the border, the miscreants will flee with our goods and without consequence for their actions."

"I assure you they will not," the hetman wheezed.

Voices rose in argument. He held up a hand, palm out, but the gesture—like his assurance—had no effect, and he dropped his head in defeat.

Jacek pushed his way to the front and wheeled on the soldiers. The motion alone brought them to a standstill. He gestured toward the hetman. "For God's sake, show your country's crown grand hetman respect and listen to what he is trying to say to you!" *Allow the hetman to set this right at last!*

426

Żółkiewski's eyes flew open, and he lifted his head. He offered Jacek a half smile. "Thank you, Colonel."

Jacek gave him a dip of his head and remained where he was.

Żółkiewski coughed, and his voice came out as a wheeze. "We are all of us anxious to reach home. Conducting searches will mean hours of delay, and I am unwilling to postpone our arrival any further."

Jacek breathed an inner sigh of relief. The hetman's strength was sparking once more.

"Instead, I vow that after we cross the border, we will detain the suspects and execute a strict search. Those who are responsible for robbing you of your possessions will be *severely* punished. That, my lords, is my solemn promise."

Jacek's heart plummeted to his knees, and he wrestled back the urge to cry out. While the officers who had demanded justice rejoiced in this decision, Jacek turned to the hetman. "Crown Grand Hetman, I do not think it wise to alert the thieves—"

Żółkiewski leveled him with a hard glare. "Colonel, while I appreciate your steadfastness, I am weary of your challenges. My decision is final, and I will brook no argument. Push me, and I will see you *and* your men court-martialed for your insubordination."

The rebuke tore a gash inside Jacek. Worse, the hetman had just unleashed the consequences of his previous inaction without a thought for what he had set into motion. Jacek's mind whirred with what loomed as the burble inside the tent rose and men milled about. Whether the officers were satisfied with Żółkiewski's solution hardly mattered, and Jacek grabbed Henryk's arm and propelled him outside the tent.

"Good God, what has he done?" Henryk hissed beside him.

"I fear he has inadvertently driven spikes into our path. And I helped him by shouting everyone down."

"It doesn't matter, Jacek. He would have said the same thing eventually anyway. Now that it's out, do you think we can keep the looters from finding out what awaits them?"

A servant who had attended the meeting dashed from the hetman's tent.

"No. It's too late. The best we can do is pray." Keeping the formation together and reaching Poland had turned into a challenge Jacek wasn't sure they could overcome. His vision of stepping onto home soil evaporated along with his hope, and he raged inside at the hetman's weakness and lack of vision. If Jacek never again cuddled his children or held his wife, he would lay the blame at Żółkiewski's feet. He had just given up his life because he had revered a man blindly for too long.

CHAPTER 41

Flight into Hell

Jacek's fears manifested themselves almost as swiftly as the news of Żółkiewski's intentions spread throughout the camp. Panic replaced the excitement that had thrummed through the rolling fort only a short while ago.

Suddenly, those who thought they would go unpunished for the crimes they had committed three weeks prior faced harsh repercussions when they crossed the border in nine hours.

Why hadn't Żółkiewski used his cunning and dodged, evaded, placated the officers without exposing his hand until the actual crossing?

The hetman had been hanging on to control of his demoralized force by the thinnest of threads, and Jacek saw no way of keeping it from snapping. If they had dismissed Żółkiewski on the battlefield when he'd pleaded with them to return to the fight, dismissed him the night after the battle when they'd fled or plundered the camp, dismissed him when he tried to speak, they would surely dismiss him now. No urging on his part would stop the unbridled urgency tearing through the Polish army.

Dread oozed through Jacek's bloodstream like stinking tar.

As they readied to march at dusk, the consequences of Żółkiewski's proclamation leaped from Jacek's imagination and took root in reality. Men began abandoning their positions, in stealth at first, but as desperation and opportunity collided, a trickle became a flood of soldiers and servants unharnessing horses, making to flee, urging others to do the same. Gaps opened up in the rolling fortress, and in the confusion, men could not plug the breaches.

Meanwhile, the Tatars lay in wait.

"Get back to your posts!" Jacek bellowed at a group of infantrymen. They ignored him, and his pleas became even less significant when they, horsed, and he, standing on the ground, added to their advantage. They raced away, and one had the temerity to gallop for him, knocking him on his backside.

He shouted at his men to stop them, and though they tried, none had the advantage of horses for the pursuit. Their mounts were still harnessed to wagons. Instead, he hollered at them to rush to their steeds and prevent anyone stealing them.

Scenes of escape flared along the rolling fortress, like a series of small fires. Soldiers rushed to one yawning gap created by deserters only for another to open farther down the line. The impenetrable fortress became a leaky sieve, punctuated by tussling and yelling, orders, then pleas to keep the formation, and cries to flee for home.

Commonwealth soldier fought Commonwealth soldier to pin him to his post.

"Hell has broken loose within sight of Mohylów," Jacek muttered.

Anarchy gained a foothold, and the tumult proved too much. A tidal wave seemed to crest and crash through the breadth and length of the war fortress.

The trailing enemy smelled opportunity like a heap of week-old carp.

If hell had indeed arrived on the plain, it opened its maw and spewed out devils to do its bidding, for here came the Tatars once again, swooping in more boldly than they had before, their triumphant whoops piercing the cacophony. Loosing arrows, they raced straight for the breaches in the rolling stock. With no artillery stopping them, they came in waves. A vision of a wooden ship with crabs scurrying about its hull etched itself in Jacek's brain.

Here came Koniecpolski astride his combat horse, wheeling his budzygan and bellowing for men to stay in order. "Compress the formation! Keep it intact! Defend the fortress and one another. Flee now, and you and the entire army perish! Staying together is our only hope to survive!"

His commands seemed to fly on the wind and out of men's earshot. With Tatars pouring in, full-fledged terror now held sway.

Someone yelled, "The border is only six miles away! Run for it!"

Jacek darted a look over to the hetman's tent, where Jan had just emerged. A Cossack spotted him and stumbled in the opposite direction. Jan lunged but missed his mark. Both men stopped in their tracks and stared the other down.

Jan's brows crashed together. "I order you—" The Cossack dashed away, and Jan's voice was swallowed up in the noise.

Jesus, God!

If he were going to help bring this mob back under control or engage the enemy—or both—Jacek needed a horse. His eyes strayed toward Heban, still harnessed to the wagon. The horse's eyes were wild, and he fought his leads. Jacek ran toward him and discovered an infantryman tearing at the trappings to separate the warhorse from the rest of the team.

"That's my horse!"

Snarling, the man brandished a pistol. "Not anymore."

Jacek tackled him but didn't bring him down. They grappled, and Jacek's boot caught the infantryman's wrist. The scoundrel's hand flew to the side, but he stubbornly held on to the firearm. Before the man could square up his aim, Jacek landed his fist on his jaw. The man crumpled to his knees, and Jacek relieved him of his pistol and the reins and quickly led Heban away. Miraculously, the horse didn't resist.

On the fringes, Tatars and Commonwealth troops clashed while the hetmans and colonels tried to ride the disintegrating line of wagons that made up the fortress. In the far distance, a handful of men ran on foot, swinging to the east and the Dniester, but were cut down by Tatars who chased after.

Jacek vaulted onto the horse's back and urged him toward two servants trying to pull more horses away. Heban bucked, nearly spilling Jacek to the

431

ground. Something thumped him in the back, and he turned awkwardly and slid to the side, vaguely registering a war hammer on the ground beside him. The horse twisted, facing at a right angle from where he'd been pointed moments before, and stopped, his chest heaving with fatigue.

Jacek yelled in frustration.

"Where the devil were *you* going?" Wronski, astride the sable, faced Jacek and stared him down. Behind him rose a familiar pair of hussar wings decorated in white eagle feathers.

"Was that *your* war hammer that hit me?"

"No, it was your brother-in-law's. What a pity your poor excuse for a warhorse decided to vault at that very moment. He thwarted my precise throw."

Jacek whipped his sabre from its scabbard. "You were trying to *kill me?*" He stabbed the blade into the air. "In the midst of this ... this hell?"

Wronski shrugged. "Not kill. Wound ... or maim, perhaps. Ah! And render you incapable of taking care of your wife in the bedchamber." His lips then twisted into a leer. "I never got the chance to tell you the final way I bested you."

"What in blazes are you talking about?" Spirit of God, but Jacek had no time for this lunatic's ramblings!

Wronski held up four fingers. "The ways in which I've shown myself superior. In case you've forgotten, the first was your brother-in-law's devotion"—with his free hand, he reached up and flicked a feather on a wing—"the second was the horse, the fourth was your lieutenant." He folded down the fingers, save one. "But the third ... the third was by far the sweetest of all and the one I cherish the most: your wife's modesty."

Jacek's brows crashed together in confusion.

Wronski covered his heart. "What a lovely sight she was, emerging from the river, water glistening *everywhere* on her exquisite skin. And the way she responded to my touch. Heaven! And oh! How she kissed—"

Jacek surged forward, catching Wronski across the face with the hilt of his sabre. The startled Elear cried out and grabbed at his split cheek where blood welled.

Fury pounding in his head, Jacek jerked on Heban's leads, and the headstrong horse danced a circle beside Wronski. So *Wronski* was the blackguard who had accosted Liwi. He pointed his sabre at the scofflaw's throat. "Where is the man who was with you that day?" *I will kill him too.*

Commotion from the disintegrating defenses reverberated all around them, but they were locked in a battle within a bubble.

Wronski let out a mirthless laugh. "Arek? Feeding the worms, I suppose. What a worthless piece of shit he was, approaching your wife in the cathedral. He nearly gave us *both* away!"

"So you killed him." *Brutally.* A picture of the real Wronski was beginning to emerge. "Give me one reason why I should not run you through. Think quickly now, for my patience is stretched to its breaking point."

As though a cloud passed over the sun and blotted it out, Wronski's expression became pure malice. "I don't need one, for it is *you* who will feel the bite of *my* blade! And I won't miss this time." Wronski swung his arm up, and the glint of his sabre caught Jacek's eye.

Jacek twisted in his saddle as Wronski arced his blade down. Jacek deflected, but the motion was clumsy, his parry incomplete, and his side was now exposed. Heban stood rooted to the spot. The Elear's blade flashed, and Jacek threw his body backward, avoiding the blow. Bringing himself upright, he lunged with his sabre. Wronski lurched to the side, evading the strike, returning with one of his own.

Jacek jerked Heban's reins as the blade came down. The horse skittered to the side, and the sabre made a swishing sound as it swept past Jacek's ear. But here came Wronski's sabre again before Jacek could recover. Wronski jerked and toppled from his saddle with a cry. Jacek looked down, stunned to see Filip on foot circling an empty-handed Wronski, his blade at the ready.

Filip kicked his ankle. "Get up!"

Wronski lay in the dirt, his mouth twisted in an evil grin. "Are you so ready to die this day, Master Filip?" The Lost Man lunged for his sabre, but Filip was quicker. He kicked it out of reach and held the point of his blade to Wronski's throat. Pride soared in Jacek's chest.

"Nicely done, Armstrong," Wronski chuckled. "I taught you well."

"You had nothing to do with it. Everything I learned came from my lord-brothers at Biaska. Now take off those wings so I can return them to their rightful owner."

Wronski never got the chance, for a pack of Tatars swooped in, and Jacek found himself clashing with a different enemy. A flash of black hair, scraggly mustache in a round face, and slitted eyes glittering with hate. The Tatar flew at him, no more than a horse's length away, a wicked kilij in hand. Heban took a step backward, two steps forward. Jacek spun clumsily in the saddle, sure the man would gut him. Blood whooshing in his ears, he wrenched the reins, forcing Heban into a quarter turn at the last instant. Reflex had him slashing his blade across his foe's body with such force that the man's arm was nearly severed above the elbow. As the enemy soldier shrieked and clutched his arm, he was pulled from his saddle.

In Jacek's peripheral vision, Filip vaulted onto Wronski's horse in time to ring metal against Tatar metal.

Who had pulled the Tatar with the ruined arm from his horse?

A shot rang out, and the Tatar Filip had grappled with thudded to the ground. Marcin reined in his horse beside Jacek, the butt of his arquebus braced against his thigh.

"Well done." Jacek swiveled his head, but the squad of Tatars was no longer a threat.

Filip maneuvered the sable over and grasped Marcin's arm. "Thank you, brother."

Marcin grinned. "My pleasure, brother."

Here came Henryk. "A touching moment to be sure, but I do believe we have more Tatars to kill."

Jacek looked toward the wagons holding the sick and wounded. The carts were in disarray, some on their sides, others upright with Tatars plunging blades into their depths. "Dawid!"

Henryk spun and fired off several arrows that knocked Tatars from the wagons' sides. Hooking his bow over his shoulder, he picked up his sabre. "I've got him."

Marcin veered toward an artillery wagon with an unmanned hook gun.

434

Filip reined in the sable beside him, gestured with his recovered nadziak, and shouted, "Jacek, look!"

Jacek whipped his head, and Heban shifted so they faced the sight Filip gawked at. Jacek blinked. Blinked again to clear his eyes of dust and smoke. The vision didn't waver.

What in blazes?

Gabriel Wronski, astride the Tatar's horse, which stood on its hind legs scrabbling at air, looked to the heavens. His arm straight, he pointed his sabre at the sky. The wings on his back shuddered.

"I am Gabriel, archangel of God," he roared, "and I am here to claim your pagan souls for Him!"

The horse's front hooves thudded to the ground, and Jacek braced himself for a Wronski onslaught. To his shock, Wronski turned the horse and rode away from him and Filip ... straight into a dozen oncoming Tatars.

Dumbfounded, Jacek stared after Wronski's suicidal ride.

Filip stood in his stirrups. "Do we go after him?"

Jacek's answer came without hesitation. "No, let the Tatars have him."

The Lost Man repeated his cry until it, like he, was swallowed up by the enemy closing in around him.

Jacek yanked his gaze away. "Come. We have other necks to save."

Night shrouded the sky as they made their way back toward the Biaska banner. They paused to thwart pockets of men making to escape, cursing and growling at them.

Filip raised his nadziak, Jacek his sabre, both crying at them, "Get back or die, you fools!"

All around them, guns continued firing on the enemy, horses screamed, and metal clashed with metal. Out of the fog of battle and dark appeared Jan Żółkiewski, streaked in blood. "Thank God I found you!" He pointed his sabre toward a far corner. "My father has retreated yonder and wants you to meet him there. Alone."

"But you're wounded—" Jacek objected.

"Now! That's a command from your grand hetman!"

"Filip, get back to the banner and help the men do what's needed to restore the formation." With a grim nod, Filip turned and sped away.

435

Jan beckoned and Jacek obeyed, questions circling his mind as he raced beside the hetman's son. They pulled up at a spot where the hetman, astride his warhorse, awaited with a small entourage. On seeing Jacek, he dismissed all but his priest and led Jacek a short distance away, where they remained outside of the clergyman's earshot.

"We haven't much time, and I have orders I need carried out by someone I trust."

"Of course, Hetman, but would not someone in your inner sanctum be better suited? Your son, perhaps?"

"No, for they will do what they think is best, not what I order them to do. Right now, what they believe best is to stand by my side no matter the consequences. I cannot dissuade them, and I am too tired to try. Outside of those men, you are the only commander I trust, for you have shown your courage and your love of country over and over again. I now call upon that loyalty and bravery to do my bidding."

Heart hammering in his chest, Jacek swallowed. "What can I do?"

Żółkiewski's hooded eyes strafed the scene playing out over Jacek's shoulder. A small lantern threw shadows on the hetman's face, highlighting the crags etched deep. His voice bottomed out. "We are lost. I see now what I couldn't—or wouldn't—see before. This mission was doomed from the beginning."

Long moments unfurled, and Jacek felt time cascading away.

The hetman's rasp, when it came, startled him. "I should have done more."

"Sir?"

"I should have taken greater care to bring the Cossacks under control as I vowed to do when I signed the treaty; then perhaps we would not have come to Cecora in the first place. As for the mission itself, I should have taken more time and gathered a larger force. I should not have relied so much upon the intelligence I was brought. I should not have been so confident in the outcome. I should have made sounder decisions or allowed those with sharper minds than mine to do so and kept the men's morale intact. My arrogance has cost the country I love too many of its finest men. And my son—" His eyes glossed over, and he shook his head.

"Crown Grand Hetman?"

Żółkiewski shifted in his saddle like a man arranging his bones with great care. He leveled a tired, teary gaze on Jacek. "I agreed to the mission because my king and country asked it of me, but I had already worked out how to proceed, which made me deaf to the suggestions of my command. The proposal to rescue the hospodar was a boon for me, and one hubris would not allow me to pass up. I have treated with Iskender Pasha before and counted on the same result this time. The reports from my scouts fed that illusion, and I never questioned the intelligence or waited to verify its accuracy. Consequently, I did not know how wrong they had got it until it was too late."

Jacek held his tongue and let the great hetman continue unburdening his soul; his mind strayed to whether Żółkiewski had told all this to his confessor.

"I never expected to encounter the size of force the pasha gathered, nor did I anticipate an actual clash. A better man than I, one with military acumen and the courage to employ it, could have predicted these developments. You no doubt did, for you tried to tell me. I admit you vexed me, Colonel, but when I contemplated your actions through a clear lens, I realized that you were fighting for your country, even if you had to bring that fight to me. You showed rare courage, and Poland needs more men like you.

"I truly hoped for a peaceful outcome for my country, but I confess a part of me saw the chance to redeem my last failure and restore pride to my name. I did not want to die with the blot of Orynin on my legacy for my family to bear in shame. Alas, it seems I will have another blunder compounding the first." He lifted his chin and regarded Jacek. "How do you suppose history will remember me?"

Jacek blurted out the truth written on his heart. "As the most distinguished hetman the Commonwealth has ever known."

Żółkiewski let out a mirthless chuckle, but a fire brightened in his brown eyes. "I believe you mean that, and I thank you for the sentiment. May I give you a bit of advice?" Jacek nodded. "Hetmans and kings are mortal men, and like all mankind, they are fallible. They see the world through their own lens, and that lens becomes occluded whether by their own motives or reality. Be ever vigilant. Follow those who do what they do for love of God and country, but do not do so blindly. Always question. Your instincts are superb, and you should trust them."

An extended, resigned exhale emanated from the hetman. "Ironic, is it not, that my entire life I have pursued Tatars, and it is they who will be ending it. Tatar chasing, I have found, is akin to chasing a fluttering butterfly."

"A butterfly is too beautiful a creature to compare to the likes of those jackals," Jacek grumbled. "Rather, I think of insects that multiply and race from their underground nests to constantly replenish their forces, no matter how many you kill."

The hetman offered a weak smile and nodded. "An apt comparison."

Heban snorted and shook his mane.

Żółkiewski seemed to pluck both horse's and man's thoughts from their minds. "You are anxious to get back and save your men, so I shall get on with the reason I asked you here." He slid two folded missives from his cloak. "You are to gather your men—and any others you deem worthy— and ride out of here as quickly as possible. The war wagon is doomed; do not waste precious time trying to save it."

The hetman held up one of the missives and handed it to Jacek. "You will return to Żółkiew, where you will deliver this letter to my wife. The other you will send by one of my messengers—whomever my wife selects— to be delivered into the hands of King Zygmunt with all haste." He thrust the second letter at Jacek.

Startled, Jacek took the letters and tucked them into his sash. "But if I ride out, Hetman—"

"You are not fleeing the fight. You are fulfilling this last and final duty to me. Remember, I have chosen *you* specifically for this mission. You must not fail me."

"What of you, Hetman?"

"I will fight till the end, so that after my death my dead body will stop foes from getting to my homeland." Jacek began to protest, but the hetman held up his hand. His eyes blazed with determination. "You have your orders, Colonel. It is your *duty* to carry them out. I do not want more souls on my conscience."

Duty.

The hetman grasped Jacek's forearm and gripped it like a vise. "It has been my privilege to know you, Colonel Dąbrowski. Go with God." The fire that had burned so brightly in his eyes moments before was replaced by sorrow beneath the telltale sheen.

Jacek forced a sob from his throat. "It has been my honor and privilege to serve you and the Crown."

"You will continue to serve the Crown. I thank you, Colonel, for allowing me to go in peace to meet my God and Savior." The hetman nudged his horse and turned toward the priest, who had been throwing anxious glances their way.

Jacek headed back to his men, his mind a jumble of honor and duty and what he must do. His chest hollowed out as he pondered never seeing his beloved hetman again.

When he returned to his squad, he seemed to ride into the eye of a storm. Gales whipped all about him, but here it was eerily calm. That calm would soon shatter, and he was relieved to see they had retrieved their mounts.

Marcin ran to greet him, and Jacek flipped him Heban's reins as he dismounted. "Where is Dawid?"

"Over here, Jacek." Henryk sat astride a strange steed, hauling Dawid up behind him with Filip's help. Dawid flopped into place and laid his cheek against Henryk's back. His poor condition twisted a knot in Jacek's gut. How the devil would he get them all to safety?

Jacek swallowed doubt rising in his throat. "Where did you get the horse?"

Henryk smirked. "This horse? A Tatar gifted it to me."

Filip dragged a sleeve across his brow. "We reckoned it was fresher and could handle two men for a little while."

"Good. We are riding out."

"When?"

"Now." When the men's eyes widened, Jacek plucked a letter and flapped it. "Hetman's orders. We have missives that must be delivered."

439

Desperate sounds of battle exploded all around him, and he snapped into action. He had one more duty to fulfill to the crown grand hetman of the land, and he would not let his commander down.

CHAPTER 42

Baubles and Bodies

Jacek awoke in a dark room on a hard cot. The buzzing of men's snores surrounded him. He lifted his head and winced when it rang with pain. Slowly, he lowered it back down and let out a groan.

"I'm delighted to see that you live, my friend. I was becoming worried." Henryk's grimy face grinned from the bed beside him. "In case you wondered, we are in Mohylów's barracks."

Jacek looked up at the wooden ceiling, trying to focus. "How long have we been here?"

"We crossed the bridge at dawn—"

"Since this morning, then."

"No, since yesterday morning."

Jacek covered his eyes as the journey from the rolling stock graveyard streaked across his brain. Visions of running through vast undisturbed fields, Tatars chasing them, running, stopping, turning to fight off a band, running, running … until Mohylów's fortified walls loomed. The Tatars had fled, pursued by a sortie of Commonwealth cavalry, and Jacek, his men, and their horses had staggered their way across the bridge until they'd reached safety behind the walls.

"Before you ask," Henryk continued, "Filip is eating in their mess hall."

A chuckle rumbled in Jacek's chest. "So he is hale."

"As is Marcin."

Jacek turned his head toward Henryk, letting his hand slide from his eyes. "And Dawid?"

Henryk sighed, and Jacek's heart began a wild thumping. "Dawid has found himself in the very capable hands of an enchanting healer who assures me he will recover."

A portly woman with a wart on her cheek and its twin on her nose approached.

Henryk dropped his voice to a whisper. "Ah, and here is our enchantress now. Good luck, my friend."

The woman glared down at Jacek and began firing questions at him. He pressed a hand to his hurting head.

"What's the matter with your head?" she demanded.

"It hurts from your badgering," he moaned.

"'Tis not my badgering but rather that your body needs sustenance. I will see the serving maids bring you food and piwo at once, if you think you can hold it down."

"I can hold it down." Jacek returned her glare.

She walked away, and Henryk jabbed his thumb after her. "If you think *she's* a beauty, wait until you see the serving maids!"

A man sauntered over and plopped down beside Henryk. "They save the ugliest ones for the barracks. Keeps men like this one from despoiling them." The fellow gave Henryk a playful nudge.

Jacek looked up into the face of Teofil Szemberg and nearly leaped for joy ... until his head reminded him it wanted nothing to do with leaping.

"I cannot tell you how delighted I am to see you, Commander." Jacek hoisted himself up and leaned against a pillow.

Szemberg's lips tipped up beneath his bushy mustache. "I assure you, Colonel Dąbrowski, the sentiment is mutual."

"When did you arrive?"

"Yesterday late. I envy you sleeping through all the racket." He waved a hand around him.

"Wh-what ..." Jacek tried in vain to swallow. "Did you see what happened?"

Szemberg's playful expression turned down. He hung his head and nodded. "After you and your men left"—Szemberg held up his hand—"and before you prostrate yourself with guilt, we knew what the hetman ordered you to do after you left. That you are here is commendable. The hetman would have been proud."

Jacek's eyebrows crashed together. "Would have been?"

Henryk glanced away, blinking, as though fighting a tear.

Szemberg let out a long-suffering sigh. "The hetman, I'm afraid, did not survive. I will recount what happened as best I can. Let me start by saying that those few of us who made it here did so only by God's grace. He has saved us for some purpose. Yours, Colonel, is clear. Mine, I believe, is to write down all that happened so history will have a record. I have already taken up paper and quill.

"Of our nine-thousand-strong army that left for Cecora, only two thousand made it safely across the border. Some did so by fleeing the night after the battle—Stefan Chmielecki and the Field Guard, for instance, account for eight or nine hundred of those survivors. Most of those who caused the great ruckus the night of October 6 either died or were captured. Their agitating not only sealed their own fate but that of many unfortunates who did not take part in their schemes. Some who died did so at the hands of the Tatars, but many perished in the Dniester as they tried to cross. And I expect I know what you are thinking because I was present at the final meeting where you tried to warn the crown grand hetman what would happen if the looters knew they would be punished when they crossed. Panic over the threat of prosecution, the fact that we were so close, and the low morale of the army all fed into the breakdown of the formation that had brought us so far. They thought they could escape; all they did was hasten their demises.

"The crown grand hetman and his inner circle fared no better. They rode for the border and were close when the hetman chose to make a stand. He wanted to show his courage, his resolve, , and set an example for his men. So he pierced his horse to make it clear he would not ride off, that he would stay and face the enemy.

"His inner circle begged him to mount a different horse, but he marched instead—a mile—until he surrendered to their pleas and mounted up on a horse taken from a hussar. There was much confusion, with Tatars scattering and capturing the horses. At this time, only a dozen or so remained with the hetman. I don't know what happened, but the hetman rode off alone, and no one saw him alive again.

"When the Turks discovered his body later that morning, it was obvious he'd put up a fight for his life. He'd suffered a deep gash to his temple, and his sword hand had been hacked off. I only hope he killed many infidels before it was taken."

Did he make his choice out of bravery? Because he was old and tired? Or because dying honorably might buy him a measure of redemption? The answer had died on the battlefield with the crown grand hetman, and Jacek—and the rest of the world—would never know.

Jacek crossed himself. "What did the Turks do with the body?"

"The devils severed his head and sent it to Iskender Pasha as a trophy."

"So his body remains? I must gather it and take it to his widow." Not only did Jacek have a letter, but now he would bear tragic news and a body. He sank back against the pillow. "What of the others, like Crown Field Hetman Koniecpolski?"

"Captured and taken to Akkerman or the Black Tower at Yedikule. Besides Hetman Koniecpolski, they took Jan Żółkiewski, Samuel Korecki, Mikołaj Struś, and Wolmar Farensbach."

Jacek shuddered involuntarily at the thought of being locked up in either place, but most especially the notorious Yedikule—the Fortress of the Seven Towers—in Constantinople. Could that be where Lesław was now?

He needed to find his friend, meet with envoys who could get him before the sultan, who knew how to barter for hostages. What price would they set? He would need money … but Biaska's finances were limited. He had to find a way, even if it meant offering himself up in the bargain.

First, though, he owed a duty to Lady Żółkiewska.

Within several days, they were recovered enough to begin the two-hundred-and-six-mile journey to Żółkiew. A detachment of Mohylów's soldiers had ridden out the day prior and retrieved numerous corpses, Żółkiewski's among them. The few Tatar stragglers observed but didn't try to impede the recovery. Most had turned back after stripping the countryside of any remaining treasure, whether that treasure was in the form of living beings from the disastrous expedition or items of value from the rolling stock graveyard. Jacek reckoned the enemy had little interest in engaging a squad of well-armed quartz troops with naught but paltry rewards at stake. And so the Battle of Cecora concluded.

It was time to go home.

On good horses, Jacek and his party could fly and reach the city in four days. But they would be encumbered with a wounded Dawid and a wagon containing the hetman's remains ... if Jacek could find a way to pay for the wagon and their supplies.

They had lost everything—except Heban, the sable, and some of the men's horses and tack—and Jacek could only think of one solution to their dilemma.

He ambled to the corral where Heban and the sable were regaining their strength and found Filip hanging on the fence, watching the two horses. A pair of saddlebags was draped over a rung.

Jacek stood beside him. "Looking at Heban right now, one would have no idea that he is in fact a mule and not a horse."

Filip chuckled.

"But I can't in good conscience sell him," Jacek continued.

Filip gawked at him. "Why would you sell him?"

"Because we need the funds. As a warhorse, he could fetch a high price, but I would be deceiving his buyer." He sighed. "So I've decided to sell the sable instead. I have someone coming to look at her now."

"You can't do that!" Filip spluttered.

Jacek cocked his head. "I don't wish to, but have you a different solution?"

"I ... No."

They stood in charged silence for a few moments, and Jacek thought to break it. He lifted his chin toward the saddlebags. "What have you there?"

"Wronski's saddlebags. They came with the sable. I thought you might wish to go through them."

"Probably naught but rubbish, but yes, I will go through them. Care to help me?"

Filip shook his head, his face broody.

Jacek unbuckled the straps on the first bag and reached in. The pocket held a number of pouches, and he lifted one out. It was heavy and made of fine velvet—not at all what one normally found in a saddlebag. He opened the pouch and spilled its contents into his palm.

His mouth hinged open. "What the devil?"

Filip glanced down from his perch. "That looks like Liwi's necklace!" He hopped down for a closer look. He stirred the gold links and the ruby-and-pearl cross attached to them. "That *is* her cross!"

Jacek frowned at the contents in his hand. It *could* have been Liwi's necklace—it matched hers exactly, and Wronski had admitted to being the blackguard at the river that day. "It appears to be. But what are these other objects?" Other trinkets winked at them from Jacek's palm.

"Rings!" Filip blurted. "Earrings! And Moldavian coins!"

A small audience was beginning to gather, and Jacek stuffed the items back in the pouch and tucked it into his pas. He closed the saddlebag and threw the pair over his shoulder. To Filip, he mumbled, "I think it would be wise to go through these in the barracks."

They did, and soon they stood before Mohylów's sheriff, numerous precious items arrayed on his table … save the necklace, which Jacek had pocketed.

The man scratched his chin. "Well, Colonel, I would say you have snagged yourself quite a bit of booty here."

"But these aren't mine."

The starosta raised an eyebrow. "No? You recovered a mare that a horse thief took from you. You are entitled to the horse and everything she came with. What was the fellow's name?"

446

"Gabriel Wronski." A thought struck Jacek like a bell. "Do you have a list of those who have been recovered from the wagon fortress graveyard? I would like to know if his name is on it."

The sheriff picked up a ledger and flipped it open. He ran his forefinger over lines of script. "Wronski, Wronski … no Wronskis. No Gabriels either." He snapped the book closed and looked up at Jacek. "Now, about these baubles. Take them. Please. What would I do with them anyway?"

Jacek stammered. "Return them to their rightful owners?"

"Just how would I do that? Much of the plunder appears to come from Moldavia"—he pointed at several piles of coins—"and we are not exactly on speaking terms with that country at the moment." He gave Jacek an indulgent smile, as though to say he thought Jacek was an utter dimwit.

Filip, grinning from ear to ear, elbowed him. "You can pay for the hetman's wagon now."

The sheriff's eyes flew wide. "Are you the hussar who is returning the crown grand hetman's body to his widow?"

Jacek frowned. "I am."

"Well, why didn't you say so? Good God, man, this town would be delighted to *give* you the wagon and the team of horses to pull it too! The hetman has served Poland long and well, and he will be sorely missed." The man paused to wipe an eye. "He must be returned to his home for a proper burial, and Mohylów would be honored to help however it can. In fact, let us celebrate you with a feast! One can be arranged in a week."

Panic bubbled inside Jacek. "Uh, while we are greatly honored by your generous offer, we must decline because we must make haste. You see, we have a … a brother who is … due at his wedding, uh …"

"Before she marries someone else," Filip threw in. His lips quirked with a smile.

Jacek arched his eyebrows at his brother-in-law. "Yes. Plus, there is the matter of a dead body."

The starosta's gaze bounced between Jacek and Filip. "You will return to Mohylów sometime, yes? So we can honor you properly?"

"Yes, of course." Jacek bobbed his head. In his peripheral vision, Filip did the same.

447

Back at the barracks, Jacek clapped Filip on the shoulder. "Our brother had to make haste to marry his lady love because she was on the verge of marrying someone else? Well done!"

Filip offered him a satisfied smile. "I had heard the story before."

Henryk looked up from buffing his dagger. "Hmm … that story sounds familiar to me too. In fact, I might have been part of a story just like that once. Now what are you two clodpoles up to?"

Jacek told him about the visit to the sheriff and the loot he now owned. "As commander of this sorry lot, I declare that we will divide the spoils among us, yes?"

Henryk, Marcin, Dawid, and Filip gave a rousing cheer. Szemberg and a few soldiers from his retinue ambled over to take in the revelry.

Filip nudged Jacek. "Now that you don't have to sell the sable, I have an idea."

"Another one?"

"You keep her."

"What? No. You're the one who wrangled her from Wronski. Besides, I have Heban."

Filip let out a wry laugh. "Who is a pain in your posterior. Tell you what, then. Let's trade. The sable for Heban."

Jacek narrowed his gaze. "Why in blazes do you want Heban?"

Filip shrugged. "He and I are of a like mind."

"Stubborn?" Jacek snorted.

"Perhaps. Besides, he is a formidable beast that I wish to train. I welcome the challenge."

"Then he is yours." Jacek grasped Filip's forearm and shook.

Filip tapped his chin. "One more thing. Might you consider a name I thought up for the sable back when we first got her from the breeder?"

Jacek did not hold back his surprise. "I didn't know you had named her. What is that name?"

"Cesarzowa."

"Empress. A fitting name." Jacek gave Filip a head bob. "Cesarzowa it is!"

Jacek emptied some of the pouches on his cot so the men could appreciate the bounty he would soon split among them.

Szemberg looked over their shoulders, clucking, "My, what a haul!" Suddenly, he reached down and plucked up a simple golden locket on a chain. "What's this?"

Filip craned his head. "It's a trinket I saw Wronski wear, though I don't know where it came from."

"We can be sure it was ill-gotten, though," Jacek offered. *Scoundrel.*

Szemberg opened the locket and read something engraved inside. He whipped his head to one of his men. "Do you recall the Moldavian noble, the one whose guard said he recognized one of the men in our camp as being a marauder?"

The soldier's eyebrows drew down. "Yes. He claimed to have seen the man fleeing the village after he defiled and beat a twelve-year-old girl. He tried to track him through the camp after he spied him, but he never found him."

Szemberg shook the locket. "Do you remember him saying the blackguard took—"

"The girl's locket!" The soldier snatched the object from Szemberg's fingers and examined it. "This is the same name the guard mentioned. This is the girl's dead mother's locket!"

Szemberg raised his gaze to Jacek. "Do you think this man Wronski could be one and the same?"

"I do. He tried to rape my wife."

Behind Szemberg, Filip's face crumpled. "I had no idea. Liwi … this girl …"

Jacek gave him a nod. "I know, or you would have run him through."

A hard glint came into Szemberg's eyes. "Let us hope the Tatars cut him to ribbons."

"If they did, they didn't leave the pieces by the rolling stock graveyard. I checked with the sheriff."

But maybe they carried him off to sell to a slaver. There would be a fitting end. One side of Jacek's mouth curled with a vicious smile.

449

Jacek's heart raced when he beheld Żółkiew, anticipation and fear colliding inside him. The weather had turned cold this late October day, and worry of a different nature replaced that which had been his constant companion during these past terrible months. The questions crowding his mind and weighing heavy in his heart on his journey to the crown grand hetman's hometown centered on Oliwia and the baby, on his children and Biaska. Some of those questions would soon be answered.

Fresh dread spread from his gut to his limbs as he glanced at the wagon he and Filip trailed. In front of the cart rode Henryk, Dawid, and Marcin, exchanging insults and laughs.

For not the first time, Jacek turned over how to lessen the blows he was about to deliver to a widow and a wife whose husband was in a hostile land far away.

He shook off the uneasy thoughts and gestured toward Filip's nadziak, strapped to his saddle. "Are you ready to re-enter a more tranquil, civilized world for a while, where you'll only need to use that as a walking stick?"

The state of being tranquil and civilized was a fragile one, for the Tatars had launched more destruction on Podolia and Ruthenia, which the magnates and Crown troops couldn't defend because they had been decimated after the Battle of Cecora. Yes, it was Orynin being visited upon them once more. Would Jacek be asked to join scattered forces and help defend?

God, don't ask me to choose between duty and family. Not now.

"I'm ready." Filip looked around. "But it's all so different now, yes?"

"What do you mean?"

Filip stared off in the distance. "'Tis hard to put into words, but I see the world differently now."

"Through a lens obscured by death," Jacek said absently.

Several beats of silence passed before Filip broke it. "Why did you aspire to become a colonel? For the glory? So you can one day die honorably, as the great hetman did?"

Jacek was struck by the sincerity shimmering in Filip's eyes. Why *did* he do it? Suddenly, he had no answer, but he replied truthfully.

"I have been asking myself that very question lately. I have no answer."

In his mind's eye, a vision bloomed of him taking his last breath. His hair was streaked with gray, the lines on his face deep crevices, and he lay with his head cradled in Oliwia's pillowy lap. How much better would it be to pass on to the otherworld thusly than to die alone, far from family, on cold, unforgiving ground soaked with blood from the broken bodies littering it?

Filip cleared his throat. "Between people and animals, I've seen much blood spilled, but it does not compare to the bloodletting on a battlefield. Is this what it means to be a man?"

"No. To be a man, you must have integrity. You are speaking of men and of warriors. They are two separate beings; not all men are warriors, nor should they be. And not all warriors are honorable, as you have witnessed for yourself. There is honor in how one conducts oneself, how one treats those around him, how one devotes his life to his family. These are equally important, and one need not go to war to prove oneself."

Filip let out a mirthless laugh. "I hope you are not referring to politicians like Hospodar Grazziani."

Jacek returned a chuckle. "No, I think the devil has a special place for men like Gaspar Grazziani. I am sure he has recently discovered it." Sudden sadness overcame him. So many lives lost, and for what? An unscrupulous, double-dealing ruler.

"The rolling fortress … We might have made it, yes?" Filip murmured.

Jacek sat back and rubbed a knuckle on his chin as he pondered. "We will never know, though without the tabor, we would not have come so close to the border. We would have all perished or been taken captive long before reaching the border."

Filip nodded. "The rolling fortress was brilliant, but it was only as strong as the men defending it. With one broken link, the entire chain collapsed. Its links were both its power and its weakness."

451

Jacek bit back his surprise. "Yes. A very wise observation."

Cesarzowa seemed to sense something important about to happen after they entered the town gates, and on their approach to the manor's courtyard, she cocked her ears and picked up her hooves as if to prance.

Jacek clucked. "You are beautiful, and my, how well you know it." The horse had proved a delight, eager to please, and she seemed to connect with him on an otherworldly plane. She would never replace Jarosława, but perhaps a piece of Jarosława's soul had found its way inside his empress.

Their bedraggled procession entered the manor's courtyard. None but the steward, Brajan, and a fleet of servants and stable hands hurried out to greet them; disappointment and worry surged inside Jacek.

He reminded himself their quarters were on the opposite side of the castle where Oliwia could not see their entrance, that no one had been expecting them, and therefore she would not be present to greet him.

Jacek dismounted and pulled off his gloves. "Where is—"

A waving white handkerchief caught his eye. Lady Magdalena stood in the entryway, dwarfed by the massive arched doors as she flagged him. He paced toward her, willing his boots not to run. She was not the one he would choose to run to anyway.

"At last, you have returned, my lord." Her eyes strayed to the wagon being led away. "What's this?"

"It's ... My wife, is she—"

"Yes, yes. Come with me now."

She hurried inside, and he followed after, increasing his strides to keep up with her. "She was not expecting you," she prattled.

"Not expecting me? Why not?"

"Come, come!" Her steps quickened as she wove her way to the guest quarters.

"I am coming! Damn it, woman, what the devil is going on?" His duties to Lady Żółkiewska and Lady Eugenia were lost in a maelstrom of concern.

Magdalena walked him into the beautiful gardens at the rear of the castle and steered him to the right. She pointed toward a private arbor shaded by thick, twining vines.

"You will find her back there. She comes here often to be at peace." Magdalena gave him a small curtsy and retreated.

Heart in his throat, he straightened his shoulders and mustered his courage. The child might not have survived, but at least his Liwi lived. He took one leaden step after another.

Oliwia yanked at an errant thread poking out of her velvet cloak. The air was brisk today, and she pulled the garment around her and lifted her head to smell the air. Rain, perhaps, or—

Her thoughts, like her breathing, stalled. A tall figure emerged noiselessly from the dark canopy of leaves still clinging to branches and vines.

There stood her husband, handsome, straight, and a bit thinner than he'd been when he'd left. He watched her with hooded sapphire eyes as if he wasn't sure whether to approach or not.

"Jacek! You are here!" She leaped to her feet and flew to him, and he caught her in his arms and crushed her to him. "Oh, my love, you are alive!"

"And so are you, thank God and all the saints. I could not bear to live without you, Liwi." He buried his nose in her hair. "Let me hold you and convince myself you are real. Let me fill my nose with the scent of you."

Not a man to display his emotions, his words caught her off guard, and she hugged him back fiercely, breathing all of herself into him. They remained in a tight embrace for long minutes. The world seemed to slow and circle around them.

He pulled back, and tears pooled in his eyes and spilled down his cheeks. "I thought I might never see you again," he rasped.

"Why?"

"Childbirth is always a dangerous undertaking."

A knot tightened in her throat, but she managed to choke out, "Nor I you. War is a dangerous undertaking too, is it not? What of Filip? Is … is he all right?"

"Yes. I think you will find him a more thoughtful man now. He wishes to see you."

She swallowed and cast her eyes down for an instant before leveling them with his. "And the rest of the banner? Henryk? Marcin? Dawid?"

"All well, except Dawid, who was injured. I do believe with the right care—that with a feminine touch—he will recover fully."

Oliwia sagged against him with relief, her cheek against his chest. "I am so happy you have come back to me."

"I love you so much, my sweet Liwi."

She could no longer hold back her tears, and they fell in earnest, trailing down her cheeks. "As I love you, my fierce warrior. Perhaps I *should* send you off to war more often if I am rewarded with this sort of greeting."

He shook his head and kissed the top of her head. "No. Never send me away. I will remain your fierce warrior alone, and I will leave your side only long enough to chase our three children." His voice hitched. "I am so very, very sorry I was not by your side when you lost the babe. I should have been here." His voice rumbled in his chest. "But you may order me about to your heart's delight from now on, though I will no doubt drive you mad."

Pulling away, she looked up at him, and her mouth dropped open.

"The thought is so terrible?"

"No. It's just that … Jacek, we have four children now. I thought you knew. Did you not get my letter?" No, of course not, because she had only sent it a week ago, not knowing where he was … or if he lived.

Surprise lit his eyes. "I … No, I did not know. I thought you had lost the babe." Fresh tears welled, and his voice broke with emotion. "Is it healthy? A girl? A boy? What have you and God gifted me with?"

She studied the face she loved so much and stroked his wet jaw. "A healthy boy, my love. He came early, and it is a good thing as he was born as large as a Christmas goose. As you asked, I named him Marek. But if you wish to change it, it is not too late. He has yet to be christened."

He blinked, looking dazed. "No, there is no need to change it. I am here in time for the baptism?"

"Yes," she laughed.

A smile spread over his handsome face. "So you are hale? And he is hale?"

"We are all of us hale. Adam, Margaret, Piotr, Marek, and I."

He scratched the back of his head. "Then you've heard from Tamara about the other children?"

She took his hand in hers. "Come. I will show you."

"You have letters, then?" He seemed to stumble behind her, and she stifled a laugh at his stupefied self.

"Better than letters. Why is it you thought the babe did not survive?"

"Magdalena seemed rather curt when she is usually so gay. I assumed something had gone terribly wrong."

"No. She was likely anxious on my behalf and wanted to see us reunited as quickly as possible. She is a bit of a romantic, that one."

He stopped and hauled her to him, his hands coming to rest on her waist. "Liwi, I have some terrible news I must deliver to … to … The hetman is dead." Oliwia gasped. "And Lesław—"

Her hand flew to her mouth. "No! He is not dead, is he?"

Jacek shook his head, and his eyes overflowed. "No, but he was captured. I don't know how he fares, Liwi." He blinked up at the sky. "Dear Lord, but it was horrible. So horrible. And I don't know how to tell these women, but I must before they hear of the wagon we accompanied back."

Oliwia swallowed, steadying the quaver in her voice. "I will be beside you when you do, if that would help you."

He brought his gaze back to hers. "Yes, it would. I have another I am mourning I must tell you about."

Her heart fractured for him as he went on to tell her he had lost his beloved Jarosława. Oliwia did not press him for details but instead brushed her thumb over his hand while he quietly grieved.

He pulled in a great breath, and she jumped into the quiet with a desire to soothe his frayed emotions. "Perhaps you will find a suitable replacement out of the herd you brought from Halicz this past spring. Erwin says several are showing great promise." She refrained from telling him about the animal who had broken its leg.

Jacek seemed to brighten. "I did recover one of the warhorses from Wronski. Rather, Filip did, and he named her Cesarzowa, though she is mine to ride. I also collected a fat purse, which should help Biaska's finances. But if you need to sell the warhorse, I understand."

Placing her hands on his forearms, she lost herself in his eyes. "I could never deprive you of your warhorse, no matter how dire the straits. What is the saying? A Pole without a horse is …"

"… a body without a soul." He suddenly dipped his fingers into his pas and wrestled out a velvet pouch, which he placed in her palm. "Oh, and there is this."

She stared at the bundle. "What is it?"

"Open it and find out." His mouth twitched with a smile.

She untied the lacing, opened the pouch, and carefully shook out its contents. Cool gold links and a cross. Rubies and pearls and tiny diamonds glittered. "My necklace!" she shrieked. "Wherever did you find another one like it?"

"I didn't find another one like it. It's *your* necklace. I recovered more than the warhorse from Wronski."

"You mean he …" Realization struck her dumb, and she gulped. "He was the one at the river's edge?" No wonder his presence had so disquieted her!

"Yes, but more on that later. Right now, there is a sight I've been yearning to see." He slipped the necklace from her palm and placed it around her neck. He touched the cross reverently. "It is back where it belongs."

She pressed her fingers to it and choked out a whisper. "Thank you. I never thought I would see it again." He brushed a knuckle against her cheek, and her eyes fluttered. She pushed up on tiptoe to kiss him when Magdalena's disembodied voice came from the foliage.

"Lady Oliwia? Lord Jacek? Lady Regina has requested your presence. She is anxious to hear news of her hetman … and Lady Eugenia is wondering why her lord did not return."

Jacek dropped his head back and blew out a breath.

Oliwia took his hand. "We are coming now, Magdalena."

CHAPTER 43

Duty Must Be Done

Jacek clutched Oliwia's hand in his like a lifeline. Dear God, he didn't want to bear this news. He didn't want to be responsible for crushing these women's hearts. All of him wanted to turn and flee.

Oliwia must have sensed his reluctance, for she stopped before the closed salon door. "Deep breath," she whispered and inhaled deeply.

"It will not help," he hissed. "This mission had no purpose! It was an abomination, an utter failure, and I must explain to these women why I stand before them and not their husbands."

Oliwia took his face in her hands, and her fiery crystal eyes bored into his. "Listen to me, Jacek Dąbrowski. Your mission did have a purpose. It was to instill hope in an old hetman who would have died with none—you have brought back his letters! You took away a burden so he could die in peace. You were meant to bring these tidings, horrible as they are, to these women. Imagine if they were to hear about these tragedies through gossip. Now they will hear it from someone who loves and admires these men, who will show their loved ones kindness and compassion. Your other mission was to return to me whole and to see your newborn son. You have fulfilled your mission admirably, my lord."

He blinked away the tears that wanted to spill anew and hauled in a deep breath. Holding Oliwia's eyes with his, he knocked on the door and unlatched it when a feminine voice called out.

As Oliwia closed the door behind him, he bowed first to Lady Regina, then wide-eyed Magdalena, and finally Eugenia, whose pinched face and twisting hands tugged at his innards.

Lady Regina offered him wine, which he accepted. The air was thick and seemed to stall, as if the room existed in a bog or a vat of molasses. His breathing grew labored. Beside him, Oliwia's warmth radiated out, soothing him as he took in three pairs of expectant eyes glued to him.

Spirit of God, where to start?

Lady Regina clasped her hands in front of her. "We have learned from Colonel Matejko that the battle did not go in the Commonwealth's favor. Beyond that, we know little. I can see by your demeanor, my lord, that while you bring us news, it is not good."

He swallowed around the fist wedged in his throat. "I'm afraid not, my lady."

She dipped her head and gestured toward Eugenia. "Then perhaps you should start with news of Lord Lesław. Lady Eugenia has been quite beside herself."

Jacek turned to Eugenia and cleared his sticky throat. "On the day of the battle, many fought bravely, and Lesław most of all. He—"

Eugenia's hand flew to her mouth, and she let out a choked cry.

"Tell her, Jacek," Oliwia hissed beside him. "Tell her he is not dead."

"Lady Eugenia, he was not killed in battle. He was taken captive instead," he blurted. Christ, but he was bungling this! Eugenia wrapped her arms about herself, and Magdalena steered her toward a chair. She sank down into it, her eyes closed, her body vibrating with tears she fought to hold in. Magdalena gave her a handkerchief and rubbed her shoulder, her back, and nodded at Jacek to continue.

"For five days, Hetman Żółkiewski negotiated in earnest with the pasha. They exchanged documents that listed hostages' names, and Lesław's was among them." He paused to marshal his words. "Unfortunately, the pasha did not negotiate in good faith, and the talks broke off. I can only presume

Lesław has been taken to Constantinople with the other captives. We will send envoys and find out the sultan's demands, and we will fulfill those demands and bring him home. I promise."

Eugenia turned her head and buried her face against Magdalena's hip. Sobs racked her frail frame. "Wh-what do I tell the children?"

Dear God, I have no idea! Jacek stood rooted to the floor, unsure what to say. Fortunately, Oliwia said it for him, her voice gentle. "You will tell them that their father is a brave soldier who is off fighting on campaign and vanquishing evil men."

Eugenia rose to her feet abruptly, her face streaked with tears. "I c-can't!" She flung herself at the door and flailed at the latch. Jacek reached out, pulled his hands back, reached out again.

"Magdalena, go with her," Lady Regina barked.

The moments it took Magdalena to escort Eugenia from the chamber were pure agony.

Clenching and unclenching his fists, Jacek squared himself up and faced Lady Regina. He covered his heart with his hand. "Forgive me, Lady Regina. I did that rather badly."

She lifted her chin. "There is no good way to deliver such news. Now. What do you have for me?"

He opened his mouth, closed it, opened it again.

She raised an imperious eyebrow. "So bad as that?"

Oliwia slipped her hand into his. He squeezed it and pulled in another deep breath. "The crown grand hetman fell in battle on the night of October 6 while courageously leading us to the border and safety. I have brought home his body and a letter he charged me with delivering to you, my lady." He extracted the letters and held them out.

Lady Regina stood stock-still, her eyes locked on his, not acknowledging the letters he tried to hand her. Had she heard him? He retracted his arm and held it awkwardly at his side.

She seemed to return to herself and gave a little shake of her head. "And my son?"

"The night your husband died, Jan was taken pris—"

Her eyes rolled back in her head, and she fell backward as Jacek lunged for her.

Oliwia let out a little squeak and was by his side, helping him lower the lady into a chair. Shaken, Jacek stepped back.

Oliwia crouched beside her and patted her hand. "Lady Regina, may I get you something to drink?"

The woman blinked and sat up. Her eyes found his again. "Was he injured?"

"I didn't see him injured, my lady."

She cast her eyes down. Long minutes passed before she finally looked up and held out her hand. "I will take those now. Thank you for bringing them … and for bringing my husband home. I know this can't have been easy for you." She took the letters and turned to Oliwia. "Thank you, my dear. Now take your husband from here and find some joy, yes?"

Oliwia asked if she needed anything, if she wanted her to stay, and other questions Jacek didn't comprehend for the heavy pounding in his chest. When Oliwia led him away from the chamber, he babbled, "I didn't tell her that they beheaded her husband."

"Shh. Come. Let's return to the garden."

He let her lead him outside into the crisp autumn air. Suddenly, words poured from him. She held his hand and listened.

Oliwia's heart squeezed as emotion overwhelmed her stoic husband. She was helpless to do more than hold his hand and listen as he told her how he had brought Lady Regina a headless corpse, how her son was covered in blood when he last saw him.

"I have no idea if he was injured. And the hostage negotiations were … I did not speak the truth to the hetman's widow. The pasha was willing to talk, but the hetman didn't want them to succeed, so he made the terms impossible. He played with Lesław's life, Liwi!"

When he was spent, he looked at her. "I want to meet my son."

460

"And he wants to meet you."

She tugged his hand and led him through a winding maze of hedges, his heavy footfalls crunching on gravel. She loved that sound. Loved hearing his voice, loved his warm hand in hers. How lucky she was to have her husband back.

A pang dug at her heart, and she glanced over her shoulder at him. He stopped in his tracks and pulled her close. "You know I must go and free him, yes?"

"Yes. But let's not speak of it now. Let's rejoice in being together again."

He leaned down and kissed her, and she kissed him back with fervor. When they pulled apart, he seemed more like himself again.

"Ahem. Would you kindly keep your pawing to the privacy of your bedchamber? There are children about."

They both snapped their heads toward the voice.

Jaceck's jaw swung open. "Tamara? What the devil are you doing here?"

Tamara rolled her eyes. "How lovely to see you too, brother."

"I am sorry. That was not a proper greeting." He took a few awkward steps toward her, clasped her hands in his, and leaned down to kiss her cheeks. "It's good to see you. But what are you doing here?"

Tamara laughed. "Oliwia missed the children, and you were so long away, so she wrote and asked us to come. And here we are." She flung out her hands, palms up. "Um, has Dawid returned with you? Is he all right?"

Oliwia held her breath. Jacek did not yet know about Tamara's feelings for the hussar. How would he react once he knew?

He took his sister's hands in his and lowered his gaze. The motion shot Oliwia's heart into her throat. *More bad news?*

"His leg was pierced by a Tatar arrow, but I believe he will recover. I told him, and I will tell you, I approve."

Tamara wrestled a hand away to cover her mouth. Her eyes brightened with tears, and so did Oliwia's. "Now go find him, sister. He will want to see you." She hurried away, and he called after her, "But I will suffer no kissing or other … demonstrations of affection."

Oliwia let loose a giggle. Mother Mary, but that felt good! Jacek turned to her with a raised eyebrow. A corner of his mouth twitched. "I will,

461

however, gladly suffer *your* shows of affection. Now. *Where* are my children?"

"Come. Let us visit your brood, my lord."

Oliwia's renewed exuberance lifted Jacek's spirits and soothed his soul. He needed this, needed her.

She paused before a closed wooden door. Even through its heft, he could make out tiny, shrill voices, and his heart began to gallop. He needed to get inside and wrap up his sons and daughter.

Oliwia opened the door a crack, and Jacek stuck his head through the gap.

Adam's brown eyes widened. "Papa!" he hollered, and then he was vaulting to his feet and hurtling his compact body toward Jacek. Jacek threw the door open and spied Margaret's bright blue eyes right before Adam flung himself at him. Jacek caught him and scooped him up. The boy's face was plastered with strawberry preserves.

Margaret squealed with joy, picked up her skirts, and latched on to Jacek's leg, her small arms wound round tight. She looked up at him with an enormous smile and an adoring gaze. "Papa! You have come!"

Jacek looked down at the little bundle firmly attached to his leg as if lashed there and ruffled her dark brown waves—soft curls like her mother's. Jacek began to walk straight-legged, dragging the leg with the passenger, as he headed for Anka holding a dozing Piotr in her arms. The children broke into squealing laughter and startled the baby awake.

Oh no!

Jacek braced himself for Piotr's piercing wails. Instead, Piotr blinked up at him—and broke out into a two-toothed, drooly grin.

"Welcome back, m'lord," Anka gushed. "Would you care to hold him?"

Still smiling, Piotr turned red, grunted, and let go a most unbabylike noise, followed by a stench that had Margaret pinching her nose. "Pee-yoo!"

Anka began admonishing the babe for doing what came naturally. In his peripheral vision, Oliwia covered her mouth with her fingers, holding back her mirth, but Jacek threw his head back and barked out a laugh. "Do not scold the boy on my account, Anka." *I am overjoyed that everything seems so … normal.*

She hurried off to change Piotr, clucking as she went.

Jacek began pulling Adam from his body. "Time for me to pick up your sister." Margaret jumped up and down on the toe of Jacek's boot.

"No! No! No!" Adam flailed his arms.

"For such a small person, you certainly make a lot of noise."

Adam grabbed Jacek's face and began to pat him vigorously with gummy hands. "Did you kill many tars and tomans, Papa?"

"Not so many." Jacek captured one tiny hand, and the boy wriggled while Jacek tried to snare the other. "Help me, wife. I am wrestling a sticky octopus."

She crossed her arms and leaned against a wall. "Oh no. I am enjoying this far too much." A smile threaded through her voice.

The boy worked his hand free, grabbed Jacek's face again, and planted a sloppy, gooey kiss on Jacek's mouth. "Love you, Papa," he exclaimed happily.

Overcome, Jacek hugged the boy to his shoulder—*sticky preserves be damned!*—stroking and kissing his silky hair as he whispered, "Papa loves you too, Adam."

He set the contented boy down, then unhooked his daughter from his leg and swung her into his arms. He stuffed his nose into her neck and nibbled at her tender skin, causing her to erupt in a series of little-girl giggles. "Papa! You're scratchy!"

He didn't realize Oliwia had disappeared until she emerged with a bundle in her arms. She presented him with a sleeping pink-faced baby, and he slid Margaret onto her feet to gather the baby in his arms.

"Meet your son Marek, my lord," Oliwia sang.

He stared in wonder at the flawlessly formed tiny human. "How old is he?"

"Eight days."

"He is perfect." Cradling Marek in one arm, he pinched Oliwia's chin between his thumb and finger and drew her in for a tender kiss. "Thank you."

She let out a lilting laugh. "You are welcome, but don't ask me to do that again. Not soon anyway."

"Let me see, Papa."

Jacek crouched and held a finger to his mouth. "Shhh."

Margaret nodded and mimicked him, a serious expression on her sweet face. "Shhh." Her warm little body leaning against Jacek, she reached over and stroked the baby's head. "You like him, Papa?"

"I do. Very much."

Margaret peered at him, her angelic little face screwed up with concern. She looked exactly like her mother. "Papa, are you sad?"

Overcome with emotion, he shook his head and laid a kiss on her head. "No, sweet."

Oliwia leaned down and lifted Marek from Jacek's arms. "Sometimes people who are very happy look sad, Margaret."

"But Papa is crying." Margaret's voice quavered as if she verged on tears herself.

"He merely has a cinder caught in his eye." Oliwia winked at him, and his heart nearly burst.

Adam raced over, and both children clambered on him as though he were a spruce tree. He stood and beamed at Oliwia as the little ones clung to him. "I believe I know what the hull of a barnacle-encrusted ship feels like."

"Welcome back, my lord. Perhaps you are not home, yet you are closer than before."

"I would argue that where you and the children are, so is home."

An appealing blush dusted Oliwia's cheekbones, and in that moment he wondered that he could ever tear himself away again.

Lady Regina arranged a small feast in honor of their return, though the occasion was anything but celebratory. The lady herself, who seemed to have aged a decade since he had delivered his news, carried herself with stoicism. Lady Eugenia, however, did not attend, though Magdalena was present and bolstered Lady Regina. Talk was subdued and centered on the benign: the harvest, new recipes, the merits of the priests' latest sermons. After months of warfare, Jacek found the banal conversation a balm.

As he looked around the assembled guests, he drew comfort from Magdalena chattering with Oliwia, Henryk winking at a serving girl, Dawid and Tamara exchanging telltale glances, and Filip arguing with Marcin about the merits of Polish horses over Arabians, with both agreeing Polish were best in the end.

Magdalena turned to speak with Lady Regina, and Jacek fumbled for Oliwia's hand under the table and drew her close, unable to get enough of what anchored him.

Lady Regina suddenly stood, and the screeching of chair legs filled the room as others did the same.

"I would like to thank you, all of you"—she shifted her gaze from face to face, lingering on each for a beat—"for what you have done on my husband's, my son's, and my behalf. This time would be far more difficult without your presence." She paused and pressed a linen square to her nose. "I would like to read to you a portion of what he wrote in his last … his last letter."

After a throat-clearing cough, she resumed while the gathering stood rod-still. "Do not disturb yourself, most beloved wife, for God watches over us, and if I should perish it will be because I am old and of no further use to the Commonwealth, and the Almighty will grant that our son may take up his father's sword"—she stumbled and choked but quickly recovered—"and temper it on the necks of pagans and, if it should come to pass as I said, avenge the blood of his father. What God wants to give by His grace, let it be done, and His Holy Will will be loving to us to the last of our lives. Signed, loving husband and father Stanisław Żółkiewski, Grand Hetman of the Crown." Lady Regina lowered her hand and her eyes with it, and the letter slid from her grasp. Jacek squeezed Oliwia's hand, and the table held a collective breath as Żółkiewski's widow composed herself.

At last, she looked up, her haunted gaze moving over each one yet again. "The body of my husband, who gave his entire life to and for the Commonwealth, was defiled by our enemy. My son rots in an infidel prison. I call on each and every one of you who served the great hetman of the crown to pledge to me that, when the time comes, you will bring Jan back so that he may carry on his father's work. Are you willing? If you are, vow that you will make it so."

And so they did. Jacek added a silent vow that he would never abandon Lesław as long as he drew breath.

Later, when they retired to their quarters, Oliwia wore a knowing smirk.

"What is that sly smile for, wife?"

"I received a letter that Maurycy is returning from Austria and will grace Biaska with his presence on his way to Wąskadroga. I, for one, do not plan to be there during his visit."

He cocked an eyebrow. "No? And where will you be?"

"Right by your side, whether you are in Constantinople rescuing Lesław or in Silnyród, standing in for him. Or perhaps at the court in Warszawa, trying to win over the king to your cause."

"Liwi, you are not going to Constantinople."

"Am I not?"

He gave her an exasperated look, all the while fighting a smile. "We will discuss it later." He pulled her close and kissed the blazes out of her.

She pulled away, laughing. "A very convincing argument, but you will need to try much harder, my lord."

He burst out with a laugh of his own, warming him from his crown to his toes. For now, he would indulge himself the sweetness of domestic pleasures in a loving wife and healthy children. Now was the time to let his soul heal from its wounds before taking on new ones.

THE HUSSAR'S DUTY

Biaska, three months later

Jacek looked up from the maps he studied upon the desk when Oliwia sailed into the solar. Today, she wore a blue gown that matched her eyes, and he sat back, enjoying the sight of her graceful form as she moved toward him.

"Is it time for your meeting with Tomasz?" He would need to roll up his maps and vacate.

Shaking her head, she held up a packet of letters. "No, I merely bring letters for the lord."

He grinned as he took them from her. "Ah. In truth you do not 'merely bring letters for the lord,' but you are here to discover what they say."

She sat on the arm of his chair and draped her hand on his shoulder. "Well, who can blame me when one of those letters holds the royal seal?" She pointed to the stack.

Jacek's eyebrows shot to his hairline. "It does?" Sure enough, and he broke the seal and held up the letter so she could read it with him.

She gasped. He reread it. Filip burst into the room holding a pair of nearly complete hussar wings. "These are mostly goose, but I thought you might like some eagle … Why the devil do you two look so shocked?"

Jacek tossed the letter onto the map. "Do you recall that when we arrived at Żółkiew, I carried *two* letters for Lady Regina?"

Filip nodded but broke into a frown when Oliwia leaped up and twirled in a circle. Jacek held back a chuckle. "The first letter was to her, from the great hetman. The second was for the king. That letter was a narrative of the Cecora expedition, but it apparently included a request that the king"—Jacek picked up the letter and began to read—"grant to 'one Jacek Krzysztof Dąbrowski, devoted knight and faithful servant of the Crown, lands adjacent to the holdings of his wife, one Oliwia Armstrong Dąbrowska.' Therefore, dear brother, you are addressing the new landholder of a swath of land beside Silnyród in Podolia *and* of a manor house, its demesnes, and a village on the western border, once belonging to Antonin Wąskaski of Wąskadroga—and by inheritance, his son, Maurycy. Ha! I now own part of the Wąskaski family's former holdings. I invite Maurycy to eat my dust."

Filip went carp-mouthed.

Oliwia stopped twirling. "What do you suppose Maurycy will have to say about that?"

"Does it matter? He ran back to Austria, and if he's smart, he will stay there. Come here, wife, and kiss your landed husband!" Jacek's chest puffed.

Oliwia obliged, while Filip responded with an eye-roll Jacek found greatly amusing.

"We must go see your new manor house, my lord, and soon," Oliwia gushed. Her eyes landed on the maps. "What are you studying?"

"Uh …"

She pointed an accusing finger. "Why, that looks like the southern border by Kamieniec and Chocim. And there's Silnyród!" Her crystal-blue eyes narrowed. "Jacek, what are you about with these?"

"Did you not hear, Liwi?" Filip practically bounced in place, and Jacek shot him a warning glare.

Oliwia cinched her arms over her chest. "Hear what?"

"The Sejm has voted to collect more taxes for a bigger army to finish what was not accomplished at Cecora last year. The campaign is to be led by Jan Karol Chodkiewicz, who defeated the Swedes at Chocim in 1605!"

Oliwia gave Jacek a glare.

He threw out his hands. "What? I did not say I would join the fight."

"Except the Commonwealth is short on commanders now, *Colonel* Dąbrowski, and the king is always looking for strong new leaders." She pointed at one of the other letters. "Is that from Lady Regina?"

Jacek picked it up and ripped it open. "Yes, it is."

Oliwia peered over his shoulder. "Oh! She has finally heard from the envoy about ransoming her son. And she wants *you* to handle the negotiations! Does she mention Lesław?"

"No, nothing." For months, they had received no replies to their inquiries. Nor had Klemens Matejko or Teofil Szemberg, who had also appealed to the sultan on their behalf. Then again, Lady Regina had not heard until now, and she had far more powerful connections. So there was hope yet for Lesław.

Jacek glanced up at Oliwia. "I did swear to Lady Regina that night that I would fulfill my duty if I was called upon."

Oliwia tapped her chin. "Hmm … I suppose we could go once Dawid and Tamara are wed. And while we are in Constantinople for Lady Regina's son, we will have more power to appeal for Lesław as well." She clapped her hands. "Yes, that's brilliant! Wait. What sort of clothing should I bring?"

She smiled sweetly, the imp, and Jacek narrowed his eyes. "While *we* are there? What clothing you should bring? There is no 'we' bargaining for Jan Żółkiewski's freedom, just as you will have no need of clothing because you are not going."

"Humph. I don't see where you have any choice, Colonel."

As he looked into his wife's eyes, duty battled desire. He should have rejoiced at the call to return, but when he searched his heart, he found a wavering commitment and more doubt than he had ever allowed in the past. Yet his conviction burned bright, and he would perform his duty with his entire being, as he always had, for he was at his core a warrior who loved his country much like he loved his wife and family. Unconditionally.

THE END

Go back to the beginning! If you haven't read *The Heart of a Hussar*, download it here.

He's determined to protect his country. But can he defend himself against the ultimate betrayal?

Muscovy, 1610. Jacek Dąbrowski yearns to be recognized for his valor. Hoping his recent promotion to lieutenant will help secure the lands he desires, the twenty-two-year-old Polish cavalry officer earns instead the enmity of his captain. And his out-of-character rescue of two innocents from slaughter sets in motion a chain of grave consequences.

Griffin Brady

Discovering the young woman and her brother are not Russian enemies and have no kin, Dąbrowski escorts them back to the castle in his homeland. But as the rivalry with his superior grows and the blossoming beauty sparks a fire in his heart, the brave horseman may find his dreams of glory lying in tatters.

Can the courageous warrior survive hidden schemes that could destroy all he holds dear?

Here's an excerpt:

A desperate struggle came into view and seized his attention. Through the thick smudge of smoke billowing from a burning cottage, he made out bodies crumpled across the front threshold. In the yard between Jacek and the cottage, a man wrestled with a small feminine form while a small boy tugged on his leg, keening pitifully. ˙

"Leave her alone!" the child cried.

The girl thrashed and kicked with an unbound desperation, making her a more difficult victim to subdue than her slight body insinuated. The man grunted his displeasure as he tried to overpower his quarry. He raised a wicked dagger, intent on crashing the hilt into the base of her skull.

"Stop!" Jacek bellowed. "Release her!"

The man's head jerked up, fury twisting his face.

"Why should I?" he snarled, wrenching his captive across his body. He lodged the honed point of the knife against her exposed slender white neck.

Sitting erect, unmoving and taut as a drawn bowstring, Jacek appraised the man. Obviously Polish, his garments and arms bespoke a lowly soldier's station.

"What company do you belong to?" Jacek demanded.

"Why does it matter?" the man growled, holding his weapon to the struggling girl. He yanked her dark plait hard, exposing a silver chain that encircled her neck and plunged in a long, narrow V under her bodice.

Eryk pulled alongside Jacek, and in a tight voice said, "Because he's deciding whether to kill you where you stand or spare your life this day."

The man laughed malevolently. "I am an officer in Aleksander Lisowski's regiment, and I'm entitled to my spoils. This girl is my reward," the soldier raged. "You can keep the brat and sell him to the Tatars." He kicked at the youngster, now folded over his knees, crying inconsolably in the dirt at the girl's scrabbling feet.

One of Lisowski's Lost Men? Brigands, the lot of them, good for naught but carrion. Dispatching this one would trouble Jacek's conscience not a whit.

From the corner of Jacek's eye, Eryk leaned forward and relaxed his reins as he rested his hands on his saddlebow. Jacek transferred his sabre to his left hand and slid his broadsword from its sheath beneath his left thigh.

"I am Lord Commander Eryk Krezowski of Biaska," Eryk drawled. "Be you truly an officer, legitimate or not, I am your superior. Therefore, *I* choose my spoils first. If any remain, you pick from what is left. That girl is part of *my* booty."

Jacek's gaze remained fixed on the assailant, and he detected a flash of recognition in the man's eyes upon hearing Eryk's name.

One second, then two more ticked by. Eryk stood in his stirrups with a roar.

"Do you understand?"

Jacek and Eryk positioned their blades with deadly speed, leveling them at the soldier. Eryk continued in a cold, calm voice. "If you choose to die, say whatever prayers you wish to say now before you meet the devil, and we'll be done with it. But if you choose to live, you will drop your weapon and free her. I don't give a damn either way. If she dies along with you, I'll be disappointed, but it will matter little. She'll be one more dead Muscovite." He shrugged.

Jacek stepped his horse closer and aligned the tip of his broadsword with the man's neck. *Try it, filth. Go on!* Jacek checked the wicked grin quirking a corner of his mouth.

Eryk scrutinized the soldier, who had grown still save his darting rat's eyes. Flames licked their way through the thatch and wood of the cottage, crackling and popping as they cast off fiery showers of embers. The man lowered his dagger and released the girl, shoving her to the dirt.

She grasped her throat and coughed in raspy breaths while the boy smothered her back with his small body.

"I will have your name, soldier," Eryk growled.

The man's chest heaved, his nostrils flaring. "I am Romek Mazur," he spat. "I serve Lisowski."

"Truly a Lost Man, then." Eryk straightened in his saddle. "Romek Mazur, hear me. As one of Lisowski's band, you are a marked man in Poland. I could kill you now and be lauded by the Crown for saving them the trouble. Be grateful I am feeling generous and deign to spare your life today. If I hear of you preying on innocents again, be assured I will finish what I began here today."

Romek's eyes blazed with hatred. "No Muscovite is an innocent."

"She is a girl undeserving of what you had in store for her. Now go before I change my mind."

Romek scurried away like the vermin he was and jumped atop his steed, spurring a quick path out of the village.

Eryk jerked his head at Jacek. "Let's go."

As Jacek reseated his blades, he glanced at the boy and girl. Whether it was the light or some other trick of the eye, he couldn't say, but for a moment he saw his sister in the bend of the girl's head and the delicate curve of her shoulder.

He tilted his chin at the children. "What of them, Commander?"

"We cannot bring them with us," countered Eryk.

Jacek looked around the leveled settlement. "There is nothing left here." He had no idea why it mattered; they were the enemy, after all.

"You understand I did not actually intend taking her as plunder." Eryk darted his gaze to the girl on her knees in the dirt.

"I do, yes," Jacek replied evenly.

Eryk sighed and walked his horse toward them. The girl, who had grown silent, wrapped her arms around the boy.

"Please!" she implored in Polish. "I will go with you, but please do not hurt him!"

Eryk leaned over his horse's neck and murmured, "Where is your family, girl?"

She glanced over her shoulder at the bodies in the doorway.

"All dead, then?"

She nodded as she looked back up at him, meeting him squarely with dry eyes.

He straightened, backed up, and nodded at Jacek. "Get the girl." He swung toward Henryk. "Bring the boy."

Henryk deftly dismounted, seized the youngster, tucking him under his arm, remounted, and secured the child before him. The snuffling boy twisted, but his efforts were for naught.

The girl lifted her face as Jacek approached. He was struck by fear-filled light eyes in featureless, dirt-smeared skin; flashes of porcelain peeked from the stripes of filth. He was also struck by the fact that she pulled herself up, clenched her fists at her sides, firmed her trembling chin, and glared at him. Her fright now masked by audacity, he realized she was not a girl, after all—not yet a fully bloomed woman, but she soon would be. If she lived that long.

Her bravado crumbled as the boy renewed his weak struggles.

"We will not harm either of you, but you cannot stay here." Jacek extended his hand. "Vyatov is in ruins, and your people have either fled or been killed. Come."

Wondering what happens next? Get *The Heart of a Hussar* and find out! And while you're at it, check out the trailer by either scanning the QR code below or by going to YouTube: https://youtu.be/vgvcR3g0D7U

Griffin Brady

GLOSSARY

Buzdygan *'Booze-de-gun'* – mace, usually wielded by a higher-ranking officer

Chorągiew *'Ho-rongev'* – company, banner, usually between 100-200 men

Chorągiew Husarka – a hussar banner or company

Chorągiew Rodowa – a clan banner or company

Commonwealth – short for Polish-Lithuanian Commonwealth; a term that refers to the united Kingdom of Poland and Duchy of Lithuania

Crown – the Kingdom of Poland

Elear – a member of a regiment that rode for the adventurer Aleksander Lisowski; also known as "Lisowczycy," meaning lost men, forlorn hope

Ferezeya *'Fair-ah-zay-ah'* – a nobleman's overcoat, worn over a żupan or kontucz; sleeveless and often fur-lined

Haiduk or Hajduk – foot soldier of Hungarian or Turco-Balkan background used by the Polish infantry from the 1570s to the 1630s

Heavy lancers – see husaria

Hetman – general

Husaria *'Hoo-sah-reeah'* – Polish term for heavy cavalry; Polish winged hussars

Husarski *'Hoo-sahr-ski'* – another word for husaria

Hussar – another word for husaria

Kilij *'Kee-lee'* – a Turkish saber

Kołacz *'Ko-watch'* – traditional Polish wedding cake or wedding bread

Kolpak – aka 'calpac'; a man's fur hat

Koncerz *'Kone-sesh'* – a tuck; a thin four-foot blade with a triangular or square cross-section used like a short lance to punch through armor

475

Kopia – long, hollow lance wielded by a hussar, from 13-20 feet-long, often with a 3-6-foot company pennant attached to it

Kumis – fermented mare's milk (also known as airag)

Mazurka – aka mazurek; an up-tempo Polish folk dance

Muscovites – Russians

Muscovy – Russia

Nadziak *'Nahd-jack'* – war hammer with a hammer head on one side and a claw on the other

Pacholik *'Pahk-ho-leek'* – a retainer or squire; a poor nobleman aspiring to be a towarzysz; serves a towarzysz

Pan – lord, sir; title for a nobleman

Pani – lady; title for a noblewoman

Pas – sash

Piwo *'Pee-voh'* – beer, ale

Porte – the central government of the Ottoman Empire (also known as the Sublime Porte, High Porte, Ottoman Porte)

Porucznik *'Poh-rootz-neek'* – a commander's second, the lieutenant

Postpolite ruszenie *'Pos-politah roh-shanya'* – noble host, or levy of knights

Pułk *'Pull'* – regiment

Pułkownik *'Pull-kov-neek'* – colonel

Rotmistrz *'Rot-meetsrch'* – aka 'rotameister'; commander of a company of towarzysze

Starosta – mayor, official in charge of security

Szabla Husaria *'Shah-blah hoo-sah-reeah'* – a hussar's sabre; highly valued and prized; next to the kopia, the favored weapon of a hussar

Szlachcic *'Shlahth-cheets'* – Polish nobleman

Szlachta *'Shlahth-dah'* – Polish nobility

Szlachcianka *'Shlahth-chiankah'* – noblewoman

Szlachcianki *'Shlahth-chiankey'* – noblewomen

Tabor – a series of wagons linked together into a fortification and mounted with guns, artillery, bowmen, and the like. Especially useful to combat enemy forces on flat, open ground. Also referred to as mobile fortress, rolling fortress, rolling stock, wagon fortress, wagon fort, war wagon

Towarzysz *'Toe-vah-jez'* – literally a "companion" in Polish; a hussar; a nobleman of wealth with his own armor, horses and retinue; knight class
Towarzysze – plural of towarzysz (same pronunciation)
Wodka – vodka
Żupan *'Jzo-pahn'* – a man's outer garment; resembles a long coat with a high collar; buttons down the front; normally worn over trousers and a linen shirt

Name/Place Pronunciation Guide

Benas *'Bennis'*
Biaska *'Bee-aska'* – fictional estate and village
Chełmno *'Helm-no'*
Chmielecki *'Mee-ah-leski'*
Chocim *'Hah-cheem'*
Dąbrowski *'Dom-broff-ski'*
Dawid *'Dah-veed'*
Eryk *'Eric'*
Filip *'Fee-leep'*
Gruszka *'Groosh-ka'*
Halicz *'Hah-leech'*
Heban *'Hey-bon'* – ebony
Hospadar *'Ha-spa-dar'* – lord, master
Jacek *'Yaht-sek'*
Jacuś *'Yaht-sosh'* – diminutive of Jacek, used for a boy
Jarosława *'Yah-ro-swah-vah'* – combination of "powerful" and "glory"
Katarzyna *'Ka-tar-zayna'*
Koniecpolski, Stanisław *'Koh-nietz-polski, Stan-ee-swahf'*
Kłuszyn *'Coo-shin'*
Lesław *'Less-wahf'*
Lisowczycy *'Lee-soff-choot-seh'* – Commonwealth mercenaries also referred to as the lost men, the forlorn hope, or chorągiew elearska (company of elears)
Lisowczyk *'Lee-soff-chook'* – singular of Lisowczycy

Lisowski, Aleksander Józef *'Lee-soff-ski, Alexahnder Yo-zeff'*

Liwi *'Lee-vee'* – diminutive of Oliwia

Łozowa *'Wo-zo-va'*

Marcin *'Mahr-cheen'*

Matejko *'Mah-tayee-ko'*

Maurycy *'Mow-rit-se'*

Mohylów *'Mo-hi-loof'*

Oliwia *'Oh-lee-vee-ah'*

Piotr *'Pee-oh-tr'* – Polonized version of Peter

Mikołaj Potocki *'Mee-ko-why Po-tot-ski'*

Śledziówka *'Schlay-doov-ka'*

Silnyród *'Cheel-nay-root'*

Stanisław *'Stan-ee-swahf'*

Statyw *'Sta-tiff'* – tripod

Teofil Szemberg *'Tay-offeel Shem-bairg'*

Tamara *'Tah-mah-rah'*

Wąskadroga *'Vohn-ska-drogah'* – fictional castle belonging to Antonin Wąskaski; means "narrow road"

Wąskaski *'Vohn-ska-skee'*

Yedikule Fortress *'Yeh-dee-koo-lay'* (Turkish) or *'Yeh-dee-koo-la'* (Polish) – fortress in Istanbul that housed an infamous royal dungeon; also known as the Fortress of the Seven Towers

Wronski *'Vron-ski'*

Zaporozhian *'Zah-poh-roe-see-ahn'*

Żółkiew *'Jeull-kiev'*

Żółkiewski, Stanisław *'Jeull-kevski, Stah-nee-swahf'*

Griffin Brady

AUTHOR'S NOTES

1. In Chapter 2 ("Rodzina"), the fictional character Oliwia and her steward, Tomasz, fret over the bad harvests resulting from colder temperatures. In 1620, they might have been experiencing the effects of the Little Ice Age, which involved parts of Europe and North America from 1300 to 1850. The cooling happened gradually when it began sometime around 1300 and dropped to even colder temperatures in the mid-16ᵗʰ century, lasting until the mid-19ᵗʰ century. Average global temperatures dropped as much as 3.6°F, wreaking havoc on crops. Also affected were waterways that experienced freezing, like portions of the Baltic Sea and rivers in Great Britain and the Netherlands.

2. The Moldavian Magnate Wars were a series of conflicts spanning from the late sixteenth century into the early seventeenth century. Amid ongoing cross-border raids instigated by Cossacks into the Ottoman Empire's territory on one side and Tatar raids into the Commonwealth on the other, a semi-permanent war zone developed. In this festering hotbed, magnates from the Commonwealth began interfering in Moldavia's affairs in order to extend the Commonwealth's influence, which upset the Ottoman Empire. Wallachia, Transylvania, Hungary, and the Habsburgs were also part of the mix, with all parties vying for control. The conflict would continue with the Battle of Cecora in 1620, where the Grand Hetman of the Crown Stanisław Żółkiewski lost his life, and would only conclude after the Battle of Chocim in 1621 and the Treaty of Chocim that followed.

3. Stanisław Żółkiewski preferred diplomacy over warfare and was often criticized for giving up too much in treaties. For instance, in 1617 when he treated with the Turks and ceded the Danube hospodarities to them in the

Peace of Busza (see note 19). He also favored cavalry over infantry, and consequently his armies were heavy on cavalry, which did not always work to his advantage. Most of his cavalries were made up of *towarzysze* (hussars or companions) and "Cossacks," which was a general term applied to the Lisowczycy and other light cavalry, such as German reiters.

He had lost the confidence of the Ukrainian magnates after losing the Battle of Orynin on September 28, 1618. Polish forces under Hetmans Stanisław Zolkiewski and Stanisław Koniecpolski faced Crimean Tatars from Budjak, commanded by Khan Temir. The battle took place near Orynin in Podolia: after one day of battle, the Tatars bypassed the Poles, taking advantage of internal divisions within the Polish camp, and headed northward, ransacking the southeastern corner of the Polish–Lithuanian Commonwealth. As a result of their raid, a number of towns and villages in the voivodeships of Podole, Ruthenian, Braclaw, and Volhynia were burned to the ground and their residents taken into slavery.

4. Slovita (Slavuta, Sławuta) is the village the fictional character Gabriel Wronski ransacks in order to finance his campaign. It's a real town with a population of 35,000, located about 24.7 miles from Lviv. It was founded in 1633, after this story takes place, but it was likely a collection of people and commerce before it was officially founded.

5. In much of the dialogue that involves the Polish king Zygmunt III Vasa, the characters simply refer to him as King Zygmunt.

6. The term "hadjuk," from the late 16th century through the mid-19th century, was used to describe a variety of people: infantrymen, freedom fighters, rebels, irregular troops, guerilla fighters, or outlaws and highwayman, depending upon the location, time period, and who was using the term. For instance, in European territories controlled by the Ottomans in the 17th century, they were brigands and bandits. But in Poland and Central Europe, they were deemed outlaws who protected Christians from Ottomans and were held in a favorable light. They preyed mostly on

Ottomans—especially rich Turks—as a means of revenge or a way to punish the Ottoman oppressors. In some folkloric tradition, they were the equivalent of England's legendary Robin Hood, stealing from the rich and giving to the peasantry in the name of rebelling against injustice and authority.

7. Noblemen displayed coats of arms, though coats of arms worked a little differently in the Commonwealth. Noble families adopted those belonging to others, fitting themselves under an "umbrella," if you will. While there were over forty thousand noble families, there existed approximately seven thousand coats of arms (and variations). Thus it wasn't uncommon for two noble families to share the same coat of arms, such as Żółkiewski and Koniecpolski, with some differentiations.

8. The Black Trail refers to one of three main trails the Crimean Tatars used to transport slaves they captured from territory located in the southeastern region of the Polish–Lithuanian Commonwealth. Historians aren't certain how the trail got its name. They theorize it was named either for black traces the Tatars left on *chernozem*, a fertile, humus-rich black soil, or after the Black Forest, where Tatars often gathered forces before a raid.

9. The Feast of the Assumption of Mary, also known as the Feast of the Assumption of the Blessed Virgin Mary, falls on August 15 and is celebrated as a day for gathering herbs, flowers, and plants from fields and gardens.

10. The description of Regina Żółkiewska is purely in the mind of the author. Placing her daughter Zofia Daniłowiczówna, who is the grandmother of King Jan Sobieski and was married to Jan Daniłowicz (present at the Battle of Cecora), at Żółkiew Castle in June of 1620 was also conjecture. Zofia's husband was the voivode of Lwów, and she had younger children. Consequently, she likely would not have been visiting her parents. Another daughter, Katarzyna, married the Crown Field Hetman Koniecpolski but died the following year giving birth to Koniecpolski's son.

11. Żółkiewski did walk with a limp after sustaining a bullet to the knee in his younger years. Depicting him walking with a cane in this story is the author's invention.

12. The main character, Jacek Dąbrowski, serves as a colonel (*pułkownik*) under Żółkiewski. He is also the *rotmistrz* (commander of a company of towarzysze), and his second, Henryk Kalinowski, holds the rank of captain or lieutenant (*porucznik*). In actual fact, hussars did not use ranks that translate to those we are accustomed to. Since they were all equals, they were all designated as "junior officers" under their commander (rotamaster or rotmistrz). For the sake of facility, the designations of colonel, captain, and lieutenant have been applied to this story. A hetman is a general, and there were two types of generals in Poland and Lithuania: the crown grand hetman, and the crown field hetman. Both were offices assigned by the king for life. The crown grand hetman was the highest ranking of the two and second only to the king.

13. The actual rotmistrz who commanded Crown Grand Hetman Stanisław Żółkiewski's regiment during the battle is referred to in chronicles by his last name only, which is Makowiecki. He was the starosta of Halicz. Research turned up little; consequently, Jacek's actions are the author's invention.

14. During a conversation between Jacek and the crown grand hetman (Chapter 40, "Flight Into Hell"), Żółkiewski says, "Tatar chasing, I have found, is akin to chasing a fluttering butterfly." He actually spoke the words, "Tatar chasing, as if also a butterfly in the air chased" during the Sejm of 1619, when he was called forward to explain why he wasn't doing a better job of containing the Tatars, whose raids continued to escalate. It was during this time that the Sejm voted to invade Crimea; they abandoned the plan, however, when they realized the treasury had no funds with which to mount the campaign.

15. Oliwia invokes "Neminem captivabimus," which was first introduced by King Władysław III in the Acts of Jedlnia and Kraków (1425, 1430, and 1433). It was an edict that protected a member of the *szlachta from being punished or imprisoned by the king without a* proper warrant issued by a court of justice*, and it served to release a nobleman who had been unlawfully arrested. It was one of the* szlachta's privileges and granted them the right of personal safety. *Neminem captivabimus* related only to following due process and had nothing to do with a prisoner's guilt.

16. Cecora is in present-day Romania and is called Țuțora. Jassy is also in Romania and is modern-day Iași. Śledziówka is the modern-day Ukrainian village of Śledy/Ślady/Slidy. Gruszka, the mustering site where the army was divided into regiments, is modern-day Hruzhka/Hrushka, Ukraine. The fortified town of Mohylów is present-day Mohyliv-Podilskyi in Ukraine. The exact location of Łozowa is uncertain and is therefore an approximation based on writings. Over time, the names of cities and towns have changed, as has the topography. In addition, those names might have been called one thing in one country and something different in another country. Sometimes those names get confused with other present-day towns, and pinpointing their exact locations becomes a challenge. In some cases, they have disappeared altogether. Where possible, the Polish names have been used. (And even the Poles had different names for the same place!)

17. The term "Cossack" was used as a catchall for any cavalry besides the hussars (the heavy cavalry) and does not necessarily refer to the Zaporozhian Cossacks who ravaged Ottoman settlements on the Black Sea. Despite Żółkiewski declaring that no Zaporozhian Cossacks would take part in the events at Cecora, a number were in fact present.

18. The terms "pagan," "heathen," and "infidel" were often used to describe the Ottomans and the Tatars by the Poles in historical letters and narratives, which is why the author chose to use them in this story.

19. The Peace of Busza (Busha, Bose) was also known as the Treaty of Jaruga and was negotiated by Stanisław Żółkiewski and Iskender Pasha in Busza, near the Jaruga and Dniester rivers on September 23, 1617. While the Polish and Ottoman armies did meet, they chose to negotiate rather than clash. This no doubt influenced Żółkiewski's belief that the meeting between the two armies in Cecora would produce the same result. He did not believe the conflict would ever develop into an armed one.

The Peace of Busza dictated terms whereby the Commonwealth ceded the Khotyn to the Ottomans and agreed to stop meddling with the Ottoman vassals in Transylvania, Moldavia, and Wallachia. In fact, the Ottoman Empire was granted the right to select the rulers in those regions. In addition, the Commonwealth once more agreed to rein in the Cossacks and stop them from raiding the Black Sea and into the Ottoman Empire. In exchange for these promises by the Commonwealth, the Ottoman Empire vowed to stop the Tatar raids.

The Cossacks and Tatars would continue to raid the borderlands, violating the provisions of the treaty. Though the Battle of Cecora would be the result of these violations, the Peace of Busza would be confirmed by the Treaty of Chocim, signed after the Battle of Chocim in 1621.

20. According to a variety of sources, the opponents, Iskender Pasha, Khan Temir, and Gabor Bethlen had anywhere from 20,000 to 60,000 troops between them that they brought to the fight.

21. The rolling fortress the Commonwealth army used during their retreat did in fact cross the river, but that crossing was different than how it's portrayed in the book. They were not under attack when they made the crossing. Also, they reconfigured the rolling stock so that it was three wagons across (instead of six) and two hundred long (instead of one hundred). Therefore, a longer, thinner version crossed the river before being reassembled into its wider, shorter version once more.

485

22. Crown Grand Hetman Stanisław Żółkiewski is said to have declared, "I will fight till the end, and even after my death my dead body will stop foes from getting to my homeland," right before his death.

23. Stanisław Żółkiewski's letter to his wife was written from his camp in Moldavia the night of Oct. 6, 1620, right before his death. There are a number of interpretations, but the author chose to use the following version with one small revision. In the letter, Żółkiewski said: "Do not disturb yourself, most beloved wife, for God watches over us, and if I should perish it will be because I am old and of no further use to the Commonwealth, and the Almighty will grant that our son may take up his father's sword, temper it on the necks of pagans and, if it should come to pass as I said, avenge the blood of his father." Whether the son had been captured yet—and whether the hetman knew it—is unclear.

Historical Figures

Bethlen, Gabriel

Installed by the Ottoman Empire as the Prince of Transylvania from 1613 until his death in 1629. He was an opponent of the anti-Protestant Habsburgs and the Holy Roman Empire. In 1619, Bethlen invaded Hungary but was driven out in November after King Zygmunt II of Poland sent in the mercenary Lisowczycy, who defeated Bethlen and his forces at the Battle of Humenné.

Chmielecki, Stefan

A Polish nobleman who served as commander to several magnates during his lifetime. At Cecora, he tried to turn back the Commonwealth troops attempting to flee the camp the night of September 20-21. Instead of turning them back, however, he and his unit ended up fleeing themselves and, unlike many deserters that night, reached Poland safely. He would go on to fight the Tatars on a number of fronts until his death in 1630.

Grazziani, Gaspar

The ruler of Moldavia, Gaspar Grazziani (also known as Gaspar Graziani and Kasper Gratiani, among other spellings) was originally a vassal of the Ottomans. He started talks with King Zygmunt III after deciding he would be better off under Polish rule. As part of his appeal to the king, he promised to send between 15,000-25,000 (depending on the source one reads) men to aid in the conflict that was brewing between the Ottoman

Empire and the Polish-Lithuanian Commonwealth over Moldavia. In the end, he showed up with only 600.

Iskender Pasha

Admiral of the sultan's fleet until he took over command of the Ottoman army.

Kalinowski, Walenty Aleksander

Powerful magnate of Podolia and colonel at the Battle of Cecora. Among his titles, he was the starosata of Kamieniec.

Kantymir-Murza

Also known as Khan Temir and "The Bloody Sword." Kantymir was a powerful war lord and the leader of the Budjak and Dobruja Hordes. He also formed the Nogai Khanate and acted as a vassal for the Ottoman Empire, though the Empire had trouble controlling him. He spent much of his career raiding the Polish-Lithuanian Commonwealth and fighting against Commonwealth armies, clashing with Stanisław Żółkiewski several times on the battlefield. In 1637, the sultan had him murdered.

Koniecpolski, Stanisław

A Polish magnate descended from a powerful family, Koniecpolski chose a military career while still in his teens. He came under the command of Stanisław Żółkiewski, who had a powerful impact on his career. He married Żółkiewski's daughter, Katarzyna, though she died giving birth to his first child. He later remarried. In 1618, he earned the title of crown field hetman and eventually the crown grand hetman in 1632. Along with a number of other magnates, he was captured at the Battle of Cecora and sent to Yedikule Fortress, where he was held until a negotiated release in 1623. Revered as one of Poland's most brilliant military commanders, Koniecpolski spent most of his years in warfare. He died in his fifties (year of birth not exact) in 1646.

Korecki, Stefan

A Commonwealth magnate and colonel, Korecki spent most of his life in warfare. He fought under Stanisław Żółkiewski at Kłuszyn and led his private armies against Tatars and Moldavians, sometimes without the king's approval. An enemy of the Porte, Korecki was captured in 1616 and sent to Yedikule Fortress, from which he escaped. He was subsequently captured at the Battle of Cecora in 1620 and sent to Yedikule once more. Unlike other captives taken during that battle, the sultan refused to negotiate his release, and he was eventually strangled in his cell in 1622.

Lisowski, Aleksander Józef

A Lithuanian nobleman and soldier who led a *konferacja* (a semi-legal rebellion practiced in the Commonwealth) for unpaid wages. He also took part with the rebels against the royalists in the "Zebrzydowski Rokosz" (Zebrzydowski Rebellion) in 1607-1609. Lisowski eventually became the leader of a band of mercenaries that fought on behalf of the Commonwealth. They took their pay in the form of pillage. Lisowski and his men were opportunistic, often preying on their own countrymen. Because they were skilled, fearsome fighters, the Crown looked the other way. Lisowski's men adopted the name "Lisowczycy," which means lost men, forlorn hope, or *chorągiew elearska* (company of elears), after his death in 1616. They were eventually hunted down and executed and later officially disbanded by the Sejm (the lower house of Polish Parliament).

Osman II, Sultan

At the age of fourteen, Osman came to power after the overthrow of the Ottoman ruler, who was also Osman's uncle. Osman was ambitious and eager to prove himself, personally leading campaigns against the Commonwealth in the Moldavian Magnate Wars (though he did not personally take part in the Battle of Cecora). After the Ottomans' defeat at Chocim in 1621 by the Commonwealth army, Osman was forced to sign a humiliating peace treaty. He returned to Constantinople in shame, blaming the defeat on the cowardice of the Janissaries. Meanwhile, his uncle's supporters continued to conspire against him. When Osman decided to counteract the Janissaries' power, they staged a palace uprising, and Osman was imprisoned in Yedikule Fortress. He was strangled in 1622 at the age of seventeen.

Otwinowski, Samuel Hieronim

Poland's first Iranianist (linguist who specializes in Iranian languages), Otwinowski was in Turkey for ten years and served as a translator with hetman Stanisław Żółkiewski and the Crown Chancellery. He was well regarded by the Ottomans, which was why his cold reception in 1619 set off so many red flags in the Commonwealth.

Potocki Family

Powerful, influential Polish magnate family. Stefan Potocki was part of the Moldavian Magnate Wars and was defeated with his army July 1612. He later died in Ottoman captivity. Hetman Stanisław Żółkiewski wrote in his memoirs that Jakub Potocki (Castellan of Kamieniec) was ordered by the king to prepare ladders for the assault on Smoleńsk and became one of the first men up on the great fortress's wall before it was breached and taken by the Poles on June 11, 1611.

Rogowski, Walenty

Elected commander in 1617 of the Lisowczycy (lost men, forlorn hope), a mercenary band of feared and reviled Polish soldiers who were compensated not by Crown wages, but through plunder. Rogowski took part in the defeat of Prince Gabriel Bethlen's Transylvanian troops at the Battle of Humenné in November 1619. He also led Lisowczycy banners at the Battle of Cecora, which made up a third of that force.

Szemberg, Teofil

A Polish soldier and diplomat who took part in the Battle of Cecora. He survived and would go on to write an account of the expedition through his own personal experience. In 1621, he would return and take part in the Battle of Chocim, which would become the final chapter in the Moldavia Magnate Wars. Szemberg died in 1638.

Vasa, Zygmunt III

King of Poland, elected in 1587 and reigned until his death in 1632. Zygmunt was born in Sweden to King John III and his wife, Katarzyna Jagiellonka of Poland, while his parents were held captive. He was raised Catholic and remained so throughout his life. He held the title of King of Sweden until 1599 when he was deposed by his uncle, King Charles IX Vasa, though he would not give up his claim to the Swedish throne. In fact, he went to war with Sweden to reclaim his crown. The Polish-Swedish War would continue intermittently until 1629 (the term "Polish-Swedish Wars" is a broad term that includes a series of wars between the two countries from the sixteenth century until the eighteenth century). Zygmunt III was criticized for his Swedish ambitions at Poland's expense. He was also criticized for warring with Muscovy (the Polish-Muscovite War, also known as the "Dymitriads") during his reign.

King Zygmunt attempted to institute a number of reforms which the Polish nobility (the *szlachta*) viewed as a threat to their power and their "Golden Freedom." Conflict between the king and nobility led to the Zebrzydowski Rokosz (Zebrzydowski Rebellion).

Żółkiewski, Jan

Son of Stanisław Żółkiewski and Regina Żółkiewska. Captured at the Battle of Cecora and imprisoned in Yedikule Fortress. He was eventually ransomed and brought home in 1623, where he died of his wounds.

Żółkiewski, Łukasz

Nephew of Stanisław Żółkiewski, captured at the Battle of Cecora.

Griffin Brady

Żółkiewski, Stanisław

A Polish magnate and diplomat who was lauded as one of Poland's most brilliant generals, best known for victories such as the Battle of Kłuszyn. He served as crown field hetman, and in 1613, the king appointed him grand hetman of the crown, Poland's highest military ranking and a lifetime position. Żółkiewski had an uneasy relationship with the king (many thought he should have been awarded grand hetman of the crown far sooner than 1613 and that the king withheld it from him purposely). Żółkiewski had negotiated an agreement with the Muscovite boyars and entered Moscow in 1611 prepared for King Zygmunt III's son, Prince Władysław IV, to take the throne. The king thwarted this plan, which ultimately lost Poland the opportunity to gain Muscovy's throne. Żółkiewski would continue his military career engaged in numerous campaigns on the Commonwealth's southern and eastern borders.

In his later years, Żółkiewski favored diplomacy over military action, which earned him criticism from the Commonwealth's magnates, who felt he gave up too much to the Porte. Their criticism grew especially harsh after his defeat at the Battle of Orynin in 1618, when Tatars ravaged Podolia and Volhynia.

He was in his seventies when he eventually lost his life at the Battle of Cecora in 1620 after a number of questionable calculations. His substantial wealth would eventually pass to his great-grandson, Jan Sobieski, who would become King of Poland and lead one of the great hussar victories at the Battle of Vienna in 1683.

Żółkiewski founded the town of Żółkiew, which is modern-day Zhovkva in Ukraine.

ACKNOWLEDGMENTS

Michał Paradowski of kadrinazi.blogspot.com, for your incredible knowledge of a time and place too few have heard about, for answering my DM, for alerting me to Majewski's invaluable chronicle, and for generously and timely fielding my many, many (many!) questions. I learned so much, and I am immensely grateful for your help and your patience. Dziękuję!

Jenny Q. for your tremendous juggling skills, your unflagging patience, your honest feedback, your collaboration, and your attention to detail. The Biaska gang thanks you.

Judith at Word Servings for your sharp wit that always makes me laugh, for being persnickety, for being such a lovely person to work with.

Cathy at Avalon Graphics for fitting me in even though you were on a personal sabbatical, for your patient revisions, and for smiling through them all. You rock!

Stephanie, for all you do to keep my website and social media up to date and looking awesome, for your marketing acumen, for your eye-popping graphics, and for your kindness the whole time you are fielding my ramblings.

Andrea and Chris, and my other beta and ARC readers, whose willingness to read and provide their honest feedback is more valuable than you will ever know.

To my husband Tim, who is always ready to be my sounding board and help me move past the sticky plot points and uncooperative characters. I couldn't do this without your support, and I am beyond grateful. I love you!

A NOTE FROM THE AUTHOR

Thank you so much for reading *The Hussar's Duty*! I had a ball traveling back to the 17th century and visiting with Jacek and Oliwia once more, and I hope you did too.

If you enjoyed the story, I would love it if you would leave a review on Amazon, Goodreads, or BookBub to help readers like you find the story. And if you do leave a review, I would love to read it! Email me the link: gkbrady@griffin-brady.com.

Stay up to date on historical tidbits, upcoming releases, cover reveals, giveaways, and discount deals by joining my newsletter. Simply go to: https://www.griffin-brady.com/contact/. I look forward to connecting with you!

Griffin Brady

ALSO BY THIS AUTHOR

The Heart of a Hussar (Book 1 of 2)
A Hussar's Promise (Book 2 of 2)

The Playmakers Series®
(writing as G.K. Brady, award-winning contemporary romance author)

ABOUT THE AUTHOR

Griffin Brady is an award-winning historical fiction author with a keen interest in the Polish Winged Hussars of the 16th and 17th centuries. She is a member of the Historical Novel Society and Rocky Mountain Fiction Writers. Her debut novel, *The Heart of a Hussar*, was a finalist for the 2021 Chaucer Early Historical Fiction Award and a 2021 Discovered Diamond.

The proud mother of three grown sons, she lives in Colorado with her husband. She is also an award-winning bestselling romance author who writes under the pen name G.K. Brady.

Made in the USA
Columbia, SC
14 March 2024

32771819R00276